THE BEST SHORT STORIES OF

Theodore Dreiser

Novels by Theodore Dreiser

THE BEST
SHORT STORIES OF
Theodore Dreiser

WITH AN INTRODUCTION

BY James T. Farrell

THE WORLD PUBLISHING COMPANY

CLEVELAND AND NEW YORK

Published by THE WORLD PUBLISHING COMPANY

2231 West 110th Street, Cleveland 2, Ohio

By arrangement with the estate of Theodore Dreiser

Contents

Contents

Introduction

THEODORE DREISER was a good storyteller and this collection contains some of his best stories. Due to the fact that his novels are so powerful and caused so much controversy, his stories have been neglected by critics. But among them are some of the finest and most moving short stories written by an American in this century.

In these tales there is variety of scene and range and depth of emotion. The emotions of mismated married people; the crazed feelings of a simple Midwestern old farmer who has lost his Phoebe, the partner of his life; the greed for gold of an illiterate farmer and his equally illiterate family; the despair of an Arabian beggar who approaches his end, poor, ragged, and despised; the feelings of Dreiser himself for Paul Dresser, his song-writing brother; the words and personality of a New Englander who lives by the Word of the Bible; the superstitious feelings of an Irish immigrant who works as a sandhog under the Hudson River—here is range and variety. Dreiser paints and re-creates a broad human scene and, in each instance, he reveals his probing, searching mind, his ability to assimilate and make use of many details, and a compassion for humanity, its dreams and tragic sufferings, which is linked up with a sure insight into the nature of people.

During his entire literary life, Theodore Dreiser sought for a theory of existence. His mind seems constantly to have been filled with "whys." Why was life? Why was there this human spectacle of grandeur and misery, of the powerful and the weak, the gifted and the mediocre? Why did men drive and struggle for the prizes of this world—sometimes with little more than a jungle morality? And his fiction was a revelation of what he saw and how he felt about these questions. He found no answers, and most certainly he avoided cheap answers as he did the cheap tricks of commercial and plot short story writers. He was a deeply serious and brooding man, and in his writing he treated his characters with seriousness. They became intensely human in their dreaming, aspiring, and struggling as well as in their unhappiness, bewilderment, and moments of tragedy.

Dreiser saw a struggle between instinct and convention, and this was a major motif in both his novels and his stories. He saw how convention and conformity frustrates men and women. Here in this volume, there are several stories which deal with this subject matter. "Free," the story of a gifted architect with definite artistic ability and of his dying wife dramatizes the frustrating role of convention in the life of a man with singular gifts. All of his life, Rufus Haymarket has been loyal and faithful to his wife in deed and action. She has controlled and dominated their social life. He has sacrificed his own impulses and many of his tastes in order that she will be happy. And when she lies dying, he dreams of freedom. He gazes out of the window of their apartment on Central Park West in New York City, thinks over their common life together and of his many frustrations. With her he has not found happiness or fulfillment. But she will die and then, for a brief span of years, he will be free. He is troubled by such thoughts. He does not want to have to think in this manner. But he has missed so much, a love that would be deeply satisfying, a life less bound by conventional tastes and values, and his need for freedom is rooted within him. And then his wife dies. Then he is free. But he realizes the meaning of his freedom. "Free! . . . Yes—free . . . to die!" This is a story of futility, but it is told with such sympathy and compassion that it acquires emotional force. Its simple tragedy becomes awesome, almost mysterious in the way that tragedy in real life is sometimes awesome and full of mystery. There are other stories of unhappy marriages,

"Convention," "Marriage for One," and "The Shadow." These, again, are marked by a sympathy and understanding on a parallel with these same qualities that endow "Free" with such depth of feeling.

Along with "Free," there are two other Dreiser stories in this volume that have already become acknowledged classics, "The Lost Phoebe" and "Nigger Jeff." Henry and Phoebe lived together on their farm for forty-eight years. Their love had changed into a condition of habit and mutual need. Then, Phoebe died. Henry lived alone, and in time his mind became deranged. Day after day, he tramped the countryside searching for his lost wife. He could not accept the fact that she was dead—she had merely gone away. He would find her. The memory of Phoebe when young returns to him vividly. His search is not for the old woman who died, but for the young girl who had been his bride: his search is for dreams long since faded. He dies in deranged happiness, seeking the beautiful young Phoebe he knew years ago. In this story, it is as though life itself were speaking to us through the author. And it is a tale not only of the sad end which comes to us in old age; also, it is a tale of a lost dream, a dream that once endowed life with a beauty that was akin to poetry. Time, the enemy of all men, has eaten away beauty and rendered dreams obsolete. And yet the dreams remain. Dreiser's handling of this theme is truly poetic.

"Nigger Jeff" is a sympathetic and vivid account of a lynching. The main character is a reporter from a big city newspaper (undoubtedly a St. Louis journal) who is sent into a country district to cover a story where there might be a lynching. The description of the lynching, and the account of its impact on the young reporter, is presented so vividly and movingly that we feel that we are on the scene ourselves. And the "cruel sorrow" of the colored mother whose son has been hanged by a mob can only bring a choke in our throats. The young reporter says, in the last line of the story, "I'll get it all in!" Dreiser did get it all in and this means the human feelings, the terribleness of human sorrow that is caused by such a lynching.

Totally different is "My Brother Paul," Dreiser's account of his older brother. The feeling he had of brotherly affection is finely and sensitively revealed. Also, the story is quite genuinely nostalgic. It creates the Broadway atmosphere at the turn of the century so well that I found myself longing to have lived in that era and in Paul Dresser's world. Often, Dreiser has depicted emotions of greed, and he has described how human beings can destroy one another. Here, he writes of generosity of feeling, of manly affection, of kindness and helpfulness.

But every story in this book bears the mark of genuineness and caliber. In every story, there is respect—deep respect for human beings. Great art reveals the importance of human feelings and emotions. This is what Dreiser achieved. He cut beneath the surfaces of conventional attitude and sought, painstakingly, carefully, and sensitively to see human beings as they are and to render and re-create them truly but with sympathy.

We all must come to terms with time and death. Growth and maturity are evidenced in the way we make our terms with these. Dreiser's lifelong quest for a theory of existence was bound up with his own answers to time and death, his own willingness to face them in a spirit of moral bravery. This is one of the sources of his pessimism. It is a healthy pessimism, and when we encounter it we can gain a deepened sense of and respect for life. And these fifteen stories are but some of the works which Dreiser left us in his own quest and journey through the world. They tell us of men and women dreaming, struggling, and becoming caught in tragic bewilderment; they create a sense of wonder about those feelings which are the common clay, the common ground, the common elements of our humanity. Often they are somber, but their somberness breaks out in a revelation of that wonder and mystery of life which Dreiser felt so deeply.

Theodore Dreiser was a great writer of our century, and these tales of his fully bear the mark of his greatness, his sincerity, and his genius. Written years ago, they remain vital today. They belong to our literary tradition and they should long stand among the major short stories written in twentieth-century America.

JAMES T. FARRELL

October 5, 1955
New York City

THE BEST SHORT STORIES OF
Theodore Dreiser

Khat

"O, thou blessed that contains no demon, but a fairy! When I follow thee thou takest me into regions overlooking Paradise. My sorrows are as nothing. My rags are become as robes of silk. My feet are shod, not worn and bleeding. I lift up my head—O Flower of Paradise! O Flower of Paradise!" OLD ARABIAN SONG.

"When the European is weary he calls for alcohol to revive him; when he is joyful he thinks of wine that he may have more joy. In like manner the Chinese woos his 'white lady,' the poppy flower. The Indian chews bhang, and the West African seeks surcease in kola. To the Yemen Arab, khat, the poor man's happiness, his 'flower of paradise,' is more than any of these to its devotees. It is no narcotic compelling sleep, but a stimulant like alcohol, a green shrub that grows upon the hills in moist places. On the roads leading to the few cities of Arabia, and in the cities themselves, it may be seen being borne on the backs of camels to the market-place or the wedding feast —the wet and dripping leaves of the shrub. The poor and the well-to-do at once crave and adore it. They speak of it as 'the strength of the weak,' 'the inspiration of the depressed,' 'the dispeller of sorrow and too deep care.' All who may, buy and chew it, the poor by the anna's worth, the rich by the rupee. The beggar when he can beg or steal it—even he is happy too." AMERICAN CONSULAR REPORT.

THE dawn had long since broken over the heat-weary cup and slopes of the Mugga Valley, in which lies Hodeidah. In the centre of the city, like a mass of up-turned yellow cups and boxes surrounded by a ring of green and faced by the sea, were the houses, with their streets and among and in them the shopkeepers of streets or ways busy about the labors of the day. Al Hajjaj, the cook, whose place was near the mosque in the centre of the public square, had already set his pots and pans over the fire and washed his saucers and wiped his scales and swept his shop and sprinkled it. And indeed his fats and oils were clear and his spices fragrant, and he himself was standing behind his cooking pots ready to serve customers. Likewise those who dealt in bread, ornaments, dress goods, had put forth such wares as they had to offer. In the mosque a few of the faithful had entered to pray. Over the dust of the ill-swept street, not yet cleared of the rubbish of the day before, the tikka gharries of the better-to-do dragged their way along the road about various errands. The same was speckled with natives in bright or dull attire, some alive with the interest of business, others dull because of a life that offered little.

In his own miserable wattle-covered shed or hut, no more than an abandoned donkey's stall at the edge of the city, behold Ibn Abdullah. Beggar, ne'er-do-well, implorer of charity before the mosque, ex-water-carrier and tobacco seller in Mecca and Medina, from whence he had been driven years before by his extortions and adulterations, he now turned wearily, by no means anxious to rise although it was late. For why rise when you are old and weary and ragged, and life offers at best only a little food and sleep—or not so much food as (best and most loved of all earthly blessings) khat, the poor man's friend? For that, more than food or drink, he craved. Yet how to come by it was a mystery. There was about him not a single anna wherewith to sate his needs—not so much as a pice!

Indeed, as Ibn Abdullah now viewed his state, he had about reached the end of his earthly tether. His career was and had been a failure. Born in the mountain district back of Hodeidah, in the little village of Sabar, source of the finest khat, where formerly his father had been a khat farmer, his mother a farmer's helper, he had wandered far, here and there over Arabia and elsewhere, making a living as best he might: usually by trickery. Once for a little while he had been a herdsman with a Bedouin band, and had married a daughter of the tribe, but, restlessness and a lust of novelty overcoming him, he had, in time, deserted his wife and wandered hence. Thence to Jiddah, the port of debarkation for pilgrims from Egypt and Central Africa approaching Mecca and Medina, the birthplace and the burialplace of the Prophet. Selling trinkets and sacred relics, water and tobacco and fruit and food, and betimes indulging in trickery and robbery, he had finally been taken in the toils of the Cadis of both Mecca and Medina, by whose henchmen he had been sadly drubbed on his back and feet and ordered away, never to return. Venturing once more into the barren desert, a trailer of caravans, he had visited Taif, Taraba and Makhwa, but finding life tedious in these smaller places he had finally drifted southward along the coast of the Red Sea to the good city of Hodeidah, where, during as many as a dozen years now, he had been eking out a wretched existence, story-telling, selling tobacco (when he could get it) or occasionally false relics to the faithful. Having grown old in this labor, his tales commonplace, his dishonesty and lack of worth and truth well known, he was now weary and helpless, truly one near an unhonored end.

Time was, in his better days and greater strength, as he now bethought him on this particular morning, when he had had his full share of khat, and food too. Ay-ee! There had been some excellent days in the past, to be sure! Not even old Raschid, the khat drunkard, or Al Hajjaj, the cook, who might be seen of a late afternoon before his shop, his pillow and carpets and water chatties about him, his narghili lit, a bunch of khat by his side, his wife and daughter at the window above listening to him and his friends as they smoked or chewed and discoursed, had more of khat and food than had he. By Allah, things were different then! He had had his girls, too, his familiar places in the best of the mabrazes, where were lights and delightful strains of song, and dancing betimes. He had sung and applauded and recounted magnificent adventures with the best of them. Ay-ee!

But of late he had not done well—not nearly as well as in times past. He was very, very old now, that was the reason; his bones ached and even creaked. An undue reputation for evil things done in the past—Inshallah! no worse than those of a million others—pursued him wherever he went. It was remembered of him, unfortunately, here in Hodeidah, as in Mecca and Medina (due no doubt to the lying, blasting tongue —may it wither in his mouth!—of Tahrbulu, the carrier, whom he had known in Mecca)—that he had been bastinadoed there for adulterating the tobacco he sold—a little dried goats' and camels' dung, windblown and clean; and as for Taif, to which place he had gone after Mecca, Firaz, the ex-caravan guard who had known him in that place—the dog!—might his bones wither in the sun!—had recalled to various and sundry that at Mecca he had been imprisoned for selling water from a rain-pit as at that of the sacred well of Jezer! Be it so; he was hard pressed at the time; there was no place to turn; business was poor—and great had been his yearning for khat.

But since then he had aged and wearied and all his efforts at an honest livelihood had served him ill. Betimes his craving for khat had grown, the while his ability to earn it—aye, even to beg it with any success!—had decreased. Here in Hodeidah he was too well known (alas, much too well known!), and yet where else was he to go? By sea it was all of three hundred miles to Aden, a great and generous place, so it was said, but how was he to get there at his time of life? No captain would carry him. He would be tossed into the sea like a rat. Had he not begged and been roundly cursed? And to Jiddah, whereby thousands came to Mecca, a full five hundred miles north, he dare not return. Were he there, no doubt he would do better: the faithful were generous. . . . But were he caught in the realm of the Grand Sherif— No; Hodeidah had its advantages.

He arose after a time, and, without ablutions, prostrating himself weakly in the direction of Mecca, adjusted his ragged loin- and shoulder-cloths and prepared to emerge for the day. Although hungry and weak, it was not food but khat that he desired, a few leaves of the green, succulent, life-giving plant that so restored his mood and strength and faculties generally. By Allah, if he had but a little, a handful, his thoughts concerning life would be so much more endurable. He might even, though cracked and wretched was his voice, tell a tale or two to idlers and so earn an honest anna. Or he would have more courage to beg, to lie, to mourn before the faithful. Yea, had he not done so often? With it he was as good as any man, as young, as hopeful; without it—well, he was as he was: feeble and worn.

As he went forth finally along the hot, dusty road which

led into the city and the public market and mosque, lined on either side by low one-story mud houses of the poor, window-less, and with the roadway in front as yet unswept, his thoughts turned in eager seeking to that khat market, hard by the public square and beyond the mosque, whose pineapple-shaped dome he could even now see rising in the distance over the low roofs before him. Here it was that at about eleven o'clock in the morning the khat camels bearing their succulent loads would come winding along the isthmus road from the interior. He could see them now, hear their bells, the long striding camels, their shouting drivers, the green herb, wet and sweet, piled in refreshing masses upon their backs! How well he knew the process of its arrival—the great rock beyond the Jiddah gate casting a grateful shade, the two little black policemen ready to take custom toll of each load and give a receipt, the huge brutes halting before the door of the low kutcha-thatched inn, there to pick at some wisps of grass while their masters went inside to have a restful pull at a hubbuk (water-pipe) and a drink of kishr, or maybe a bowl of curds. Meanwhile, a flock of shrewd youngsters, bribelings of the merchants of the bazaars within the city, would flit about the loaded animals, seeking to steal a leaf or to thrust an appraising glance into the closely wrapped bundles, in order that they might report as to the sweetness and freshness of their respective loads.

"What, O *kowasji*, is the quality of your khat to-day? Which beast carries the best, and has thy driver stinted no water on the journey to keep it fresh?"

To find the true answers to these questions had these urchins taken their bribe-money in the bazaars. But the barefoot police-man would chase them away, the refreshed drivers would come out again, fiercely breathing calumnies against the grand-mothers of such brats, and the little caravan would pick its way upward and downward again into the market.

But to-day, too weary to travel so far, even though by sighs and groans and many prayers for their well-being he might obtain so little as a leaf or two from the comfortable drivers, he betook himself slowly toward the market itself. En route, and especially as he neared a better portion of the city, where tikka gharries might be seen, he was not spareful of "Alms, in the name of Allah! Allah! Alms!" or "May thy hours in paradise be endless!" But none threw him so much as a pice. Instead, those who recognized his familiar figure, the sad antithesis of all industry and well-being, turned away or called: "Out of the way, thou laggard! To one side, dog!"

When he reached the market, however, not without having cast a wishful eye at the shining pots and saucers of Al Hajjaj en route, the adjoining bazaar had heard of the coming of the green-laden caravan, and from the dark shops, so silent until now, cheerful cries were beginning to break forth. Indeed the streets were filled with singing and a stream of lean figures all headed one way. Like himself they were going to the khat market, only so much better equipped for the occasion—rupees and anna in plenty for so necessary and delectable an herb. Tikka gharries rattled madly past him, whips were waved and turbans pushed awry; there were flashes of color from rich men's gowns, as they hurried to select the choicest morsels, the clack of oryx-hide sandals, and the blunt beating of tom-toms. As the camels arrived in the near distance, the market was filled with a restless, yelling mob. Bedlam had broken loose, but a merry, good-natured bedlam at that. For khat, once obtained, would ease whatever ill feeling or mourning unrest or weariness one might feel.

Although without a pice wherewith to purchase so much as a stalk, still Ibn could not resist the temptation of entering here. What, were none of the faithful merciful? By Allah, impossible! Perchance—who knows?—there might be a stranger, a foreigner, who in answer to his appealing glance, his outstretched hands, an expression of abject despair which long since he had mastered, would cast him an anna, or even a rupee (it had happened!), or some one, seeing him going away empty-handed or standing at the gate outside, forlorn and cast down, and asking always alms, alms, would cast him a delicious leaf or spray of the surpassing delight.

But no; this day, as on the day previous, and the one before that, he had absolutely no success. What was it—the hand of fate itself? Had Allah truly forsaken him at last? In a happy babel, and before his very eyes, the delicious paradisiacal stimulant was weighed on government scales and taxed again—the Emir must live! And then, divided into delicious bundles the thickness of a man's forearm, it was offered for sale. Ah, the beauty of those bundles—the delight therein contained—the surcease even now! The proud sellers, in turban and shirt, were mounting the small tables or stands about the place and beginning to auction it off, each bundle bringing its own price. "Min kam! Min kam!" Hadji, the son of Dodow, was now crying—Hadji, whom Ibn had observed this many a day as a seller here. He was waving a bunch above the outstretched hands of the crowd. "How much? How much will you give for this flower of paradise, this bringer of happiness, this dispeller of all weakness? 'Tis as a maiden's eyes. 'Tis like bees' breath for fragrance. 'Tis—"

"That I might buy!" sighed Ibn heavily. "That I might buy! Who will give me so much as a spray?"

"One anna" (two cents), yelled a mirthful and contemptuous voice, knowing full well the sacrilege of the offer.

"Thou scum! O thou miserable little tick on the back of a sick camel!" replied the seller irritably. "May my nose grow a beard if it is not worth two rupees at the very least!"

"Bismillah! There is not two rupees' worth in all thy filthy godown, budmash!"

"Thou dog! Thou detractor! But why should one pay attention to one who has not so much as an anna wherewith to ease himself? To those who have worth and many rupees—look, behold, how green, how fresh!"

And Al Hajjaj, the cook, and Ahmed, the carpet-weaver, stepped forward and took each a bundle for a rupee, the while Ibn Abdullah, hanging upon the skirt of the throng and pushed contemptuously here and there, eyed it all sadly. Other bundles in the hands of other sellers were held up and quickly disposed of—to Chudi, the baker, Azad Bakht, the barber, Izz-al-Din, the seller of piece goods, and so on, until within the hour all was exhausted and the place deserted. On the floor was now left only the litter and débris of stems and deadened leaves, to be haggled over by the harjis (vendors of firewood), the sweepers, scavengers and beggars generally, of whom he was one; only for the want of a few pice, an anna at the most, he would not even now be allowed to carry away so much as a stem of this, so ill had been his fortunes these many, many days. In this pell-mell scene, where so many knew him and realized the craving wherewith he was beset, not one paused to offer him a sprig. He was as wretched as before, only hungrier and thirstier.

And then, once the place was finally deserted, not a leaf or a stem upon the ground, he betook himself slowly and wearily to his accustomed place in the shadow of one of the six columns which graced the entryway of the mosque (the place of beggars), there to lie and beseech of all who entered or left that they should not forget the adjuration of the Prophet "and give thy kinsman his due and the poor and the son of the road." At noon he entered with others and prayed, for there at least he was welcome, but alas, his thoughts were little on the five prescribed daily prayers and the morning and evening ablutions—no, not even upon food, but rather upon khat. How to obtain it—a leaf —a stem!

Almost perforce his thoughts now turned to the days of his youth, when as a boy living on the steep terraced slope of the mountains between Taiz and Yerim, he was wont literally to dwell among the small and prosperous plantations of the khat farmers who flourished there in great numbers. Indeed, before his time, his father had been one such, and Sabar and Hirwa, two little villages in the Taiz district, separated only by a small hill, and in the former of which he was born, were famous all over Arabia for the khat that was raised there. Next to that which came from Bokhari, the khat of Sabar, his home town, was and remained the finest in all Yemen. Beside it even that of Hirwa was coarse, thin and astringent, and more than once he had heard his mother, who was a khat-picker, say that one might set out Sabari plants in Hirwa and that they quickly became coarse, but remove Hirwa plants to Sabar, and they grew sweet and delicate.

And there as a child he—who could not now obtain even so much as a leaf of life-giving khat!—had aided his mother in picking or cutting the leaves and twigs of khat that constituted the crops of this region—great camel-loads of it! In memory now he could see the tasks of the cooler months, where, when new fields were being planted, they were started from cuttings buried in shallow holes four to six inches apart with space enough between the rows for pickers to pass; how the Yemen cow and the sad-eyed camel, whose maw was never full, had to be guarded against, since they had a nice taste in cuttings, and thorn twigs and spiny cactus leaves had to be laid over the young shoots to discourage the marauders.

At the end of a year the young shrubs, now two feet high, had a spread of thick green foliage eighteen inches in diameter. Behold now the farmer going out into the dawn of each morning to gaze at his field and the sky, in the hope of seeing the portents of harvest time. On a given morning the air would be thick with bulbuls, sparrows, weaver birds, shrilly clamoring; they would rise and fall above the plants, picking at the tenderest leaves. "Allah be praised!" would cry the farmer in delight. "The leaves are sweet and ripe for the market!" And now he would call his women and the wives of his neighbors to the crop-picking. Under a bower of jasmine vines, with plumes of the sweet smelling *rehan*, the farmer and his cronies would gather to drink from tiny cups and smoke the hubbuk, while the womenfolk brought them armfuls of the freshly cut khat leaves. What a joyous time it was for all the village, for always the farmer distributed the whole of his first crop among his neighbors, in the name of Allah, that Allah's blessings might thus be secured on all the succeeding ones. Would that he were in Sabar or Hirwa once more!

But all this availed him nothing. He was sick and weary, with little strength and no money wherewith to return; besides, if he did, the fame of his evil deeds would have preceded him perhaps. Again, here in Hodeidah, as elsewhere in Arabia, the cities and villages especially, khat-chewing was not only an appetite but a habit, and even a social custom or function, with the many, and required many rupees the year to satisfy. Indeed one of the painful things in connection with all this was that, not unlike eating in other countries, or tea at least, it had come to involve a paraphernalia and a ritual all its own, one might say. At this very noon hour here in Hodeidah, when, because of his luck, he was here before the temple begging instead of having a comfortable home of his own, hundreds—aye, thousands—who an hour earlier might have been seen wending their way happily homeward from the market, their eyes full of a delicious content, their jaws working, a bundle of the precious leaves under their arms, might now be found in their private or public mabraz making themselves comfortable, chewing and digesting this same, and not until the second hour of the afternoon would they again be seen. They all had this, their delight, to attend to!

Aye, go to the house of any successful merchant, (only the accursed Jews and the outlanders did not use khat) between these hours and say that you had urgent news for him or that you had come to buy a lakh of rupees' worth of skins. . . . His servant would meet you on the verandah (accursed dogs! How well he knew them and their airs!) and offer the profoundest apologies . . . the master would be unutterably sick (here he would begin to weep), or his sister's husband's aunt's mother had died this very morning and full of unutterable woe as he was he would be doing no business; or certainly he had gone to Tawahi but assuredly would return by three. Would the caller wait? And at that very moment the rich dog would be in his mabraz at the top of his house smoking his hubbuk and chewing his leaves—he who only this morning had refused Ibn so much as a leaf. Bismillah! Let him rot like a dead jackal!

Or was it one who was less rich? Behold the public mabraz, such as he—Ibn—dared not even look into save as a wandering teller of tales, or could only behold from afar. For here these prosperous swine could take their ease in the heat of the day, cool behind trellised windows of these same, or at night could dream where were soft lights and faint strains of song, where sombre shadow-steeped figures swayed as though dizzy with the sound of their own voices, chanting benedictions out of the Koran or the Prophets. Had he not told tales for them in his time, the uncharitable dogs? Even now, at this noon hour, one might see them, the habitués of these same well-ventilated and well-furnished public rooms, making off in state for their favorite diversion, their khat tied up in a bright shawl and conspicuously displayed—for whom except himself, so poor or so low that he could not afford a little?—and all most anxious that all the world should know that they went thus to enjoy themselves. In the mabraz, each one his rug and pillow arranged for him, he would recline, occupying the space assigned him and no more. By his side would be the tall narghili or hubbuk, the two water-pots or chatties on copper stands, and a bowl of sweets. Bismillah, he was no beggar! When the mabraz was comfortably filled with customers a servant would come and light the pipes, some one would produce a Koran or commence a story—not he any more, for they would not have him, such was his state—and the afternoon's pleasure would begin. Occasionally the taraba (a kind of three-stringed viol) would be played, or, as it might happen, a favorite singer be present. Then the happy cries of *"Taieeb!"* or *"Marhabba! Marhabba!"* (Good!), or the more approbative "O friend, excellent indeed!" would be heard. How well he remembered his own share in all this in former years, and how little the knowledge of it all profited him now—how little! Ah, what a sadness to be old and a beggar in the face of so much joy!

But as he mused in the shade, uttering an occasional "Alms, alms, in the name of Allah!" as one or another of the faithful entered or left the mosque, there came from the direction of the Jiddah gate, the regular khat-bearing camel route, shrill cries and yells. Looking up now, he saw a crowd of boys racing toward the town, shouting as they ran: "Al khat aja!" (the khat has come), a thing which of itself boded something unusual— a marriage or special feast of some kind, for at this late hour for what other reason would khat be brought? The market was closed; the chewers of khat already in their mabrazes. From somewhere also, possibly in the house of a bridegroom, came the faint tunk-a-lunk of a tom-tom, which now seemed to take up the glad tidings and beat out its summons to the wedding guests.

"Bismallah! What means this?" commented the old beggar to himself, his eyes straining in the direction of the crowd; then folding his rags about him he proceeded to limp in the direction of the noise. At the turn of a narrow street leading into the square his eye was gladdened truly enough by the sight of a khat-bearing camel, encompassed by what in all likelihood, and as he well knew was the custom on such occasions, a cloud of "witnesses" (seekers of entertainment or food at any feast) to the probable approaching marriage. Swathed round the belly of the camel as it came and over its load of dripping green herbs, was laid a glorious silken cloth, blazing with gold and hung with jasmine sprays; and though tom-toms thumped and fifes squealed a furious music all about him, the solemn beast bore his burden as if it were some majesty of state.

"By Allah," observed the old beggar wearily yet eyeing the fresh green khat with zest, "that so much joy should be and I have not a pice, let alone an anna! Would that I might take a spray—that one might fall!"

"Friend," he ventured after a moment, turning to a water-carrier who was standing by, one almost as poor as himself if more industrious, "what means this? Has not Ramazan passed and is not Mohorrum yet to come?"

"Dost thou address me, thou bag of bones?" returned the carrier, irritated by this familiarity on the part of one less than himself.

"Sahib," returned the beggar respectfully, using a term which he knew would flatter the carrier, no more entitled to a "Sir" than himself, "use me not ill. I am in sore straits and weak. Is it for a marriage or a dance, perhaps?"

"Thou hast said," replied the carrier irritably, "—of Zeila, daughter of old Bhori, the tin-seller in the bazaar, to Abdul, whose father is jemidar of chaprassies at the burra bungalow."

At the mere mention of marriage there came into the mind of Ibn the full formula for any such in Hodeidah—for had he not attended them in his time, not so magnificent as this perhaps but marriages of sorts? From noon on all the relatives and friends invited would begin to appear in twos and threes in the makhdara, where all preparations for the entertainment of the guests had no doubt been made. Here for them to sit on in so rich a case as this (or so he had heard in the rumored affairs of the rich), would be long benches of stone or teak, and upon them beautiful carpets and pillows. (In all the marriages he had been permitted to attend these were borrowed for the occasion from relatives or friends.) Madayeh, or water-bubbles, would be ready, although those well enough placed in the affairs of this world would prefer to bring their own, carried by a servant. A lot of little chatties for the pipes would be on hand, as well as a number of fire-pots, these latter outside the makhdara with a dozen boys, fan in hand, ready to refill for each guest his pipe with tobacco and fire on the first call of "Ya yi-yall!" How well he remembered his services as a pipe-filler on occasions of this kind in his youth, how well his pleasure as guest or friend, relative even on one occasion, in his earlier and more prosperous years and before he had become an outcast, when his own pipe had been filled. Oh, the music! the bowls of sweets! the hot kishr, the armful of delicious khat, and before and after those little cakes of wheat with butter and curds! When the makhdara was full and all the guests had been solemnly greeted by the father of the bride, as well as by the prospective husband, khat would be distributed, and the pleasure of chewing it begin. Ah! Yes, weddings were wonderful and very well in their way indeed, provided one came by anything through them.

Alas, here, as in the case of the market sales, his opportunities for attending the same with any profit to himself, the privilege of sharing in the delights and comforts of the same, were over. He had no money, no repute, not even respect. Indeed the presence of a beggar such as he on an occasion of this kind, and especially here in Hodeidah where were many rich, would be resented, taken almost as an evil omen. Not only the guests within but those poorer admirers without, such as these who but now followed the camel, would look upon his even so much as distant approach as a vile intrusion, lawless, worthless dog that he was, come to peek and pry and cast a shadow upon what would otherwise be a happy occasion.

Yet he could not resist the desire to follow a portion of the way, anyhow. The escorted khat looked too enticing. Bismillah! There must be some one who would throw him a leaf on so festal an occasion, surely! By a slow and halting process therefore he came finally before the gate of the residence, into which already the camel had disappeared. Before it was the usual throng of those not so vastly better than himself who had come to rejoice for a purpose, and within, the sound of the tom-tom and voices singing. Over the gate and out of the windows were hung silken carpets and jasmine sprays, for old Bhori was by no means poor in this world's goods.

While recognizing a number who might have been tolerant of him, Ibn Abdullah also realized rather painfully that of the number of these who were most friendly, having known him too long as a public beggar, there were few.

"What! Ne'er-do-well!" cried one who recognized him as having been publicly bastinadoed on one occasion here years before, when he had been younger and healthy enough to be a vendor of tobacco, for adulterating his tobacco. "Do you come here, too?" Then turning to another he called: "Look who comes here —Ibn, the rich man! A friend of the good Bhori, no doubt, mayhap a relative, or at least one of his invited guests!"

"Ay-ee, a friend of the groom at least!" cried another.

"Or a brother or cousin of the bride!" chaffed still a third.

"A rich and disappointed seeker after her hand!" declared a fourth titteringly.

"He brings rich presents, as one can see!" proclaimed a fifth.

"But look now at his hands!" A chortle followed, joined in by many.

"And would he be content with so little as a spray of khat in return?" queried a sixth.

"By Allah, an honest tobacco-merchant! Bismillah! One whom the Cadi loves!" cried a seventh.

For answer Ibn turned a solemn and craving eye upon them, thinking only of khat. "Inshallah! Peace be with thee, good citizens!" he returned. "Abuse not one who is very low in his state. Alms! Alms! A little khat, of all that will soon generously be bestowed upon thee! Alms!"

"Away, old robber!" cried one of them. "If you had ever been honest you would not now be poor."

"What, old jackal, dost thou come here to beg? What brings thee from the steps of the mosque? Are the praying faithful so ungenerous? By Allah! Likely they know thee—not?"

"Peace! Peace! And mayst thou never know want and distress such as mine! Food I have not had for three days. My bones yearn for so much as a leaf of khat. Be thou generous and of all that is within, when a portion is given thee give me but a leaf!"

"The Cadi take thee!"

"Dog!"

"Beggar!"

"Come not too near, thou bag of decay!"

So they threatened him and he came no closer, removing rather to a safe distance and eyeing as might a lorn jackal a feast partaken of by lions.

Yet having disposed of this objectionable intruder in this fashion, no khat was as yet forthcoming, the reason being that it was not yet time. Inside, the wedding ceremony and feast, a matter of slow and ordered procedure, was going forward with great care. Kishr was no doubt now being drunk, and there were many felicitations to be extended and received. But, once it was all over and the throng without invited to partake of what was left, Ibn was not one of those included. Rather, he was driven off with curses by a servant, and being thus entirely shut out could only wait patiently in the distance until those who had entered should be satisfied and eventually come forth wiping their lips and chewing khat—in better humor, perchance—or go his way. Then, if he chose to stay, and they were kind—

But, having eaten and drunk, they were in no better mood in regard to him. As they came forth, singly or in pairs, an hour or more later, they saw in him only a pest, one who would take from them a little of that which they themselves had earned with difficulty. Therefore they passed him by unheeding or with jests.

And by now it was that time in the afternoon when the effect on the happy possessor of khat throughout all Arabia was only too plainly to be seen. The Arab servant who in the morning had been surly and taciturn under the blazing sun was now, with a wad of the vivifying leaves in his cheek, doing his various errands and duties with a smile and a light foot. The bale which the ordinary coolie of the waterfront could not lift in the morning was now but a featherweight on his back. The coffee merchant who in the morning was acrid in manner and sharp at a bargain, now received your orders gratefully and with a pleasantry, and even a bid for conversation in his eye. Abdullah, the silk merchant, dealing with his customers in sight of the mosque, bestowed compliments and presents. By Allah, he would buy your horse for the price of an elephant and find no favor too great to do for you. Yussuf, the sambuk-carrier, a three-hundred-weight goatskin on his back, and passing Ibn near the mosque once more, assured Ali, his familiar of the same world and of equal load, as they trudged along together, "Cut off my strong hand, and I will become Hadji, the sweeper" (a despised caste), "but take away my khat, and let me die!" Everywhere the evasive, apathetic atmosphere of the morning had given way to the valor of sentient life. Chewing the life-giving weed, all were sure that they could perform prodigies of energy and strength, that life was a delicious thing, the days and years of their troubles as nothing.

But viewing this and having none, and trudging moodily along toward his waiting-place in front of the mosque, Ibn was truly depressed and out of sorts. The world was not right. Age and poverty should command more respect. To be sure, in his youth perhaps he had not been all that he might have been, but still, for that matter, had many others so been? Were not all men weak, after their kind, or greedy or uncharitable? By Allah, they were, and as he had reason to know! Waidi, the water-seller? A thief really, no whit better than himself, if the world but knew. Hussein, the peddler of firewood; Haifa, the tobacco tramp—a wretched and swindling pack, all, not a decent loin- or shoulder-cloth among them, possessed of no better places of abode than his own really, yet all, even as the richest of men, had their khat, could go to their coffee places this night and enjoy it for a few anna. Even they! And he!

In Hodeidah there was still another class, the strictly business or merchant class, who, unlike men of wealth or the keepers of the very small shops, wound up their affairs at four in the afternoon and returning to their homes made a kind of public show of their ease and pleasure in khat from then on until the evening prayers. Charpoys, water-pipes and sweetmeats were brought forth into the shade before the street door. The men of the household and their male friends sprawled sociably on the charpoys, the ingredients for the promotion of goodly fellowship ready to their hands. A graybeard or two might sit among them expounding from the sacred book, or conversation lively in character but subdued in tone entertained the company. Then the aged, the palsied, even the dying of the family, their nearest of kin, were brought down on their beds from the top of the house to partake of this feast of reason and flow of wit. Inside the latticed windows the women sat, munching the second-best leaves and listening to the scraps of wisdom that floated up to them from the company below.

It was from this hour on that Ibn found it most difficult to endure life. To see the world thus gay while he was hungry was all but too much. After noting some of this he wandered wearily down the winding market street which led from the mosque to the waterfront, and where in view of the sea were a few of the lowest coffee-houses, frequented by coolies, bhisties and hadjis. Here in some one of them, though without a single pice in his hand, he proposed to make a final effort before night should fall, so that thereafter in some one of them, the very lowest of course, he himself might sit over the little khat he would (if fortunate) be permitted to purchase, and a little kishr. Perhaps in one of these he would receive largess from one of these lowest of mabraz masters or his patrons, or be permitted to tell an old and hoarse and quavering tale. His voice was indeed wretched.

On his way thence, however, via the Street of the Seven Blessings, he came once more before the door of Al Hajjaj, the cook, busy among his pots and pans, and paused rather disconsolately in the sight of the latter, who recognized him but made no sign.

"Alms, O Hajjaj, in the name of the Prophet, and mayst thou never look about thy shop but that it shall be full of customers and thy profit large!" he voiced humbly.

"Be off! Hast thou no other door than mine before which to pause and moan?"

"Ever generous Hajjaj," he continued, " 'tis true thou hast been kind often, and I deserve nothing more of thee. Yet wilt thou believe me that for days I have had neither food nor drink—nor a leaf of khat—nay, not so much as an wheaten cake, a bowl of curds or even a small cup of kishr. My state is low. That I shall not endure another day I know."

"And well enough, dog, since thou hast not made more of thy life than thou hast. Other men have affairs and children, but thou nothing. What of all thy years? Hast thou aught to show? Thou knowest by what steps thou hast come so. There are those as poor as thyself who can sing in a coffee-house or tell a tale. But thou— Come, canst thou think of nothing better than begging? Does not Hussein, the beggar, sing? And Ay-eeb tell tales? Come!"

"Do thou but look upon me! Have I the strength? Or a voice? Or a heart for singing? It is true; I have sung in my time, but now my tales are known, and I have not the strength to gather new ones. Yet who would listen?"

The restaurant-keeper eyed him askance. "Must I therefore provide for thee daily? By Allah, I will not! Here is a pice for thee. Be off, and come not soon again! I do not want thee before my door. My customers will not come here if thou dost!"

With slow and halting steps Ibn now took himself off, but little the better for the small gift made him. There was scarcely any place where for a pice, the smallest of coins, he could obtain anything. What, after all, was to be had for it—a cup of kishr? No. A small bowl of curds? No. A sprig of khat? No. And so great was his need, his distress of mind and body, that little less than a good armful of khat, or at least a dozen or more green succulent sprays, to be slowly munched and the juice allowed to sharpen his brain and nerves, would have served to strengthen and rest him. But how to come by so much now? How?

The character of the places frequented by the coolies, bhisties (water-carriers), hadjis and even beggars like Ibn, while without any of the so-called luxuries of these others, and to the frequenters of which the frequenters of these were less than the dust under their feet, were still, to these latter, excellent enough. Yea, despised as they were, they contained charpoys on which each could sit with his little water-chatty beside him, and in the centre of the circle one such as even the lowly Ibn, a beggar, singing his loudest or reciting some tale—for such as they. It was in such places as these, before his voice had wholly deserted him, that Ibn had told his tales. Here, then, for the price of a few anna, they could munch the leavings of the khat market, drink kishr and discuss the state of the world and their respective fortunes. Compared to Ibn in his present state, they were indeed as lords, even princes.

But, by Allah, although having been a carrier and a vendor himself in his day, and although born above them, yet having now no voice nor any tales worth the telling, he was not even now looked upon as one who could stand up and tell of the wonders of the Jinn and demons and the great kings and queens who had reigned of old. Indeed, so low had he fallen that he could not even interest this despised caste. His only gift now was listening, or to make a pathetic picture, or recite the ills that were his.

Nevertheless necessity, a stern master, compelled him to think better of his quondam tale-telling art. Only, being, as he knew, wholly unsuited to recite any tale now, he also knew that the best he could do would be to make the effort, a pretense, in the hope that those present, realizing his age and unfitness, would spare him the spectacle he would make of himself and give him a few anna wherewith to ease himself then and there. Accordingly, the hour having come when the proffered services of a singer or story-teller would be welcomed in any mabraz, he made his way to this region of many of them and where beggars were so common. Only, glancing through the door of the first one, he discovered that there were far too few patrons for his mood. They would be in nowise gay, hence neither kind nor generous as yet, and the keeper would be cold. In a second, a little farther on, a tom-tom was beginning, but the guests were only seven in number and but newly settled in their pleasure. In a third, when the diaphanous sky without was beginning to pale to a deep steel and the evening star was hanging like a solitaire from the pure breast of the western firmament, he pushed aside the veiling cords of beads of one and entered, for here was a large company resting upon their pillows and char-poys, their chatties and hubbuks beside them, but no singer or beater of a tom-tom or teller of tales as yet before them.

"O friends," he began with some diffidence and imaginings, for well he knew how harsh were the moods and cynical the judgments of some of these lowest of life's offerings, "be gener-ous and hearken to the tale of one whose life has been long and full of many unfortunate adventures, one who although he is known to you—"

"What!" called Hussein, the peddler of firewood, reclining at his ease in his corner, a spray of all but wilted khat in his hand. "Is it not even Ibn Abdullah? And has he turned tale-teller once more? By Allah, a great teller of tales—one of rare voice! The camels and jackals will be singing in Hodeidah next!"

"An my eyes deceive me not," cried Waidi, the water-carrier, at his ease also, a cup of kishr in his hands, "this is not Ibn Abdullah, but Sindbad, fresh from a voyage!"

"Or Ali Baba himself," cried Yussuf, the carrier, hoarsely. "Thou hast a bag of jewels somewhere about thee? Now indeed we shall hear things!"

"And in what a voice!" added Haifa the tobacco-tramp, noting the husky, wheezy tones with which Ibn opened his plea. "This is to be a treat, truly. And now we may rest and have wonders upon wonders. Ibn of Mecca and Jiddah, and even of marvelous Hodeidah itself, will now tell us much. A cup of kishr, ho! This must be listened to!"

But now Bab-al Oman, the keeper, a stout and cumbrous soul, coming forth from his storeroom, gazed upon Ibn with mingled astonishment and no little disfavor, for it was not customary to permit any of his customers of the past to beg in here, and as for a singer or story-teller he had never thought of Ibn in that light these many years. He was too old, without the slightest power to do aught but begin in a wheezy voice.

"Hearken," he called, coming over and laying a hand on him, the while the audience gazed and grinned, "hast thou either anna or rupee wherewith to fulfill thy account in case thou hast either khat or kishr?" The rags and the mummy-like pallor of the old man offended him.

"Do but let him speak," insisted Hussein the peddler gaily, "or sing," for he was already feeling the effects of his ease and the restorative power of the plant. "This will be wonderful. By the voices of eleven hundred elephants!"

"Yea, a story," called Waidi, "or perhaps that of the good Cadi of Taiz and the sacred waters of Jezer!"

"Or of the Cadi of Mecca and the tobacco that was too pure!"

Ibn heard full well and knew the spectacle he was making of himself. The references were all too plain. Only age and want and a depressing feebleness, which had been growing for days, caused him to forget, or prevented, rather, his generating a natural rage and replying in kind. These wretched enemies of his, dogs lower than himself, had never forgiven him that he had been born out of their caste, or, having been so, that he had permitted himself to sink to labor and beg with them. But now his age and weakness were too great. He was too weary to contend.

"O most generous Oman, best of keepers of a mabraz—and thou, O comfortable and honorable guests," he insisted wheezily,

"I have here but one pice, the reward of all my seekings this day. It is true that I am a beggar and that my coverings are rags, yet do but consider that I am old and feeble. This day and the day before and the day before that—"

"Come, come!" said Oman restlessly and feeling that the custom and trade of his mabraz were being injured, "out! Thou canst not sing and thou canst not tell a tale, as thou well knowest. Why come here when thou hast but a single pice wherewith to pay thy way? Beg more, but not here! Bring but so much as half a rupee, and thou shalt have service in plenty!"

"But the pice I have here—may not I—O good sons of the Prophet, a spray of khat, a cup of kishr—suffer me not thus be cast forth! '—and the poor and the son of the road!' Alms—alms—in the name of Allah!"

"Out, out!" insisted Oman gently but firmly. "So much as ten anna, and thou mayst rest here; not otherwise."

He turned him forth into the night.

And now, weak and fumbling, Ibn stood there for a time, wondering where else to turn. He was so weak that at last even the zest for search or to satisfy himself was departing. For a moment, a part of his old rage and courage returning, he threw away the pice that had been given him, then turned back, but not along the street of the bazaars. He was too distrait and disconsolate. Rather, by a path which he well knew, he circled now to the south of the town, passing via the Bet-el-Fakin gate to the desert beyond the walls, where, ever since his days as a pack servant with the Bedouins, he had thought to come in such an hour. Overhead were the stars in that glorious æther, lit with a light which never shines on other soils or seas. The evening star had disappeared, but the moon was now in the west, a thin feather, yet transfiguring and transforming as by magic the homely and bare features of the sands. Out here was something of that beauty which as a herdsman among the Bedouins he had known, the scent of camels and of goats' milk, the memory of low black woolen tents, dotting the lion-tawny sands and gazelle-brown gravels with a warm and human note, and the camp-fire that, like a glowworm, had denoted the village centre. Now, as in a dream, the wild weird songs of the boys and girls of the desert came back, the bleating of their sheep and goats in the gloaming. And the measured chant of the spearsmen, gravely stalking behind their charges, the camels, their song mingling with the bellowing of their humpy herds.

"It is finished," he said, once he was free of the city and far into the desert itself. "I have no more either the skill nor the strength wherewith to endure or make my way. And without khat one cannot endure. What will be will be, and I am too old. Let them find me so. I shall not move. It is better than the other."

Then upon the dry, warm sands he laid himself, his head toward Mecca, while overhead the reremouse circled and cried, its tiny shriek acknowledging its zest for life; and the rave of a jackal, resounding through the illuminated shade beyond, bespoke its desire to live also. Most musical of all music, the palm trees now answered the whispers of the night breeze with the softest tones of falling water.

"It is done," sighed Ibn Abdullah, as he lay and wearily rested. "Worthless I came, O Allah, and worthless I return. It is well."

Free

The large and rather comfortable apartment of Rufus Haymaker, architect, in Central Park West, was very silent. It was scarcely dawn yet, and at the edge of the park, over the way, looking out from the front windows which graced this abode and gave it its charm, a stately line of poplars was still shrouded in a gray morning mist. From his bedroom at one end of the hall, where, also, a glimpse of the park was to be had, came Mr. Haymaker at this early hour to sit by one of these broader windows and contemplate these trees and a small lake beyond. He was very fond of Nature in its manifold art forms—quite poetic, in fact.

He was a tall and spare man of about sixty, not ungraceful, though slightly stoop-shouldered, with heavy overhanging eyebrows and hair, and a short, professionally cut gray mustache and beard, which gave him a severe and yet agreeable presence. For the present he was clad in a light-blue dressing gown with silver cords, which enveloped him completely. He had thin, pale, long-fingered hands, wrinkled at the back and slightly knotted at the joints, which bespoke the artist, in mood at least, and his eyes had a weary and yet restless look in them.

For only yesterday Doctor Storm, the family physician, who was in attendance on his wife, ill now for these three weeks past with a combination of heart lesion, kidney poisoning and neuritis, had taken him aside and said very softly and affectionately, as

37

though he were trying to spare his feelings: "To-morrow, Mr. Haymaker, if your wife is no better I will call in my friend, Doctor Grainger, whom you know, for a consultation. He is more of an expert in these matters of the heart"—the heart, Mr. Haymaker had time to note ironically—"than I am. Together we will make a thorough examination, and then I hope we will be better able to say what the possibilities of her recovery really are. It's been a very trying case, a very stubborn one, I might say. Still, she has a great deal of vitality and is doing as well as could be expected, all things considered. At the same time, though I don't wish to alarm you unnecessarily—and there is no occasion for great alarm yet—still I feel it my duty to warn you that her condition is very serious indeed. Not that I wish you to feel that she is certain to die. I don't think she is. Not at all. Just the contrary. She may get well, and probably will, and live all of twenty years more." (Mentally Mr. Haymaker sighed a purely spiritual sigh.) "She has fine recuperative powers, so far as I can judge, but she has a bad heart, and this kidney trouble has not helped it any. Just now, when her heart should have the least strain, it has the most.

"She is just at that point where, as I may say, things are in the balance. A day or two, or three or four at the most, ought to show which way things will go. But, as I have said before, I do not wish to alarm you unnecessarily. We are not nearly at the end of our tether. We haven't tried blood transfusion yet, and there are several arrows to that bow. Besides, at any moment she may respond more vigorously to medication than she has heretofore—especially in connection with her kidneys. In that case the situation would be greatly relieved at once.

"However, as I say, I feel it my duty to speak to you in this way in order that you may be mentally prepared for any event, because in such an odd combination as this the worst may happen at any time. We never can tell. As an old friend of yours and Mrs. Haymaker's, and knowing how much you two mean to each other"—Mr. Haymaker merely stared at him vacantly— "I feel it my duty to prepare you in this way. We all of us have to face these things. Only last year I lost my dear Matilda, my youngest child, as you know. Just the same, as I say, I have the feeling that Mrs. Haymaker is not really likely to die soon, and that we—Doctor Grainger and myself—will still be able to pull her through. I really do."

Doctor Storm looked at Mr. Haymaker as though he were very sorry for him—an old man long accustomed to his wife's ways and likely to be made very unhappy by her untimely end; whereas Mr. Haymaker, though staring in an almost sculptural way, was really thinking what a farce it all was, what a dull mixture of error and illusion on the part of all. Here he was, sixty years of age, weary of all this, of life really—a man who had never been really happy in all the time that he had been married; and yet here was his wife, who from conventional reasons believed that he was or should be, and who on account of this was serenely happy herself, or nearly so. And this doctor, who imagined that he was old and weak and therefore in need of this loving woman's care and sympathy and understanding! Unconsciously he raised a deprecating hand.

Also his children, who thought him dependent on her and happy with her; his servants and her and his friends thinking the same thing, and yet he really was not. It was all a lie. He was unhappy. Always he had been unhappy, it seemed, ever since he had been married—for over thirty-one years now. Never in all that time, for even so much as a single day, had he ever done anything but long, long, long, in a pale, constrained way—for what, he scarcely dared think—not to be married any more—to be free—to be as he was before ever he saw Mrs. Haymaker.

And yet being conventional in mood and training and utterly domesticated by time and conditions over which he seemed not to have much control—nature, custom, public opinion, and the like, coming into play as forces—he had drifted, had not taken any drastic action. No, he had merely drifted, wondering if time, accident or something might not interfere and straighten out his life for him, but it never had. Now weary, old, or rapidly becoming so, he condemned himself for his inaction. Why hadn't he done something about it years before? Why hadn't he broken it up before it was too late, and saved his own soul, his longing for life, color? But no, he had not. Why complain so bitterly now?

All the time the doctor had talked this day before he had wanted to smile a wry, dry, cynical smile, for in reality he did not want Mrs. Haymaker to live—or at least at the moment he thought so. He was too miserably tired of it all. And so now, after nearly twenty-four hours of the same unhappy thought, sitting by this window looking at a not distant building which shone faintly in the haze, he ran his fingers through his hair as he gazed, and sighed.

How often in these weary months, and even years, past—ever since he and his wife had been living here, and before—had he come to these or similar windows while she was still asleep, to sit and dream! For some years now they had not even roomed together, so indifferent had the whole state become; though she did not seem to consider that significant, either. Life had become more or less of a practical problem to her, one of position, place, prestige. And yet how often, viewing his life in retrospect, had he wished that his life had been as sweet as his dreams—that his dreams had come true.

After a time on this early morning, for it was still gray, with the faintest touch of pink in the east, he shook his head solemnly and sadly, then rose and returned along the hall to his wife's bedroom, at the door of which he paused to look where she lay seriously ill, and beside her in an armchair, fast asleep, a trained nurse who was supposedly keeping the night vigil ordered by the doctor, but who no doubt was now very weary. His wife was sleeping also—very pale, very thin now, and very weak. He felt sorry for her at times, in spite of his own weariness; now, for instance. Why need he have made so great a mistake so long ago? Perhaps it was his own fault for not having been wiser in his youth. Then he went quietly on to his own room, to lie down and think.

Always these days, now that she was so very ill and the problem of her living was so very acute, the creeping dawn thus roused him—to think. It seemed as though he could not really sleep soundly any more, so stirred and distrait was he. He was not so much tired or physically worn as mentally bored or disappointed. Life had treated him so badly, he kept thinking to himself over and over. He had never had the woman he really wanted, though he had been married so long, had been faithful, respectable and loved by her, in her way. "In her way," he half quoted to himself as he lay there.

Presently he would get up, dress and go down to his office as usual if his wife were not worse. But—but, he asked himself —would she be? Would that slim and yet so durable organism of hers—quite as old as his own, or nearly so—break under the strain of this really severe illness? That would set him free again, and nicely, without blame or comment on him. He could then go where he chose once more, do as he pleased—think of that— without let or hindrance. For she was ill at last, so very ill, the first and really great illness she had endured since their marriage. For weeks now she had been lying so, hovering, as it were, between life and death, one day better, the next day worse, and yet not dying, and with no certainty that she would, and yet not getting better either. Doctor Storm insisted that it was a leak in her heart which had suddenly manifested itself which was causing all the real trouble. He was apparently greatly troubled as to how to control it.

During all this period Mr. Haymaker had been, as usual, most sympathetic. His manner toward her was always soft, kindly, apparently tender. He had never really begrudged her anything—nothing certainly that he could afford. He was always glad to see her and the children humanly happy—though they, too, largely on account of her, he thought, had proved a disappointment to him—because he had always sympathized with her somewhat unhappy youth, narrow and stinted; and yet he had never been happy himself, either, never in all the time that he had been married. If she had endured much, he kept telling himself when he was most unhappy, so had he, only it was harder perhaps for women to endure things than men—he was always willing to admit that—only also she had had his love, or thought she had, an actual spiritual peace, which he had never had. She knew she had a faithful husband. He felt that he had never really had a wife at all, not one that he could love as he knew a wife should be loved. His dreams as to that!

Going to his office later this same day—it was in one of those tall buildings that face Madison Square—he had looked first, in passing, at the trees that line Central Park West, and then at the bright wall of apartment houses facing it, and meditated sadly, heavily. Here the sidewalks were crowded with nurse-maids and children at play, and in between them, of course, the occasional citizen loitering or going about his errands. The day was so fine, so youthful, as spring days will seem at times. As he looked, especially at the children, and the young men bustling office-ward, mostly in new spring suits, he sighed and wished that he were young once more. Think how brisk and hopeful they were! Everything was before them. They could still pick and choose—no age or established conditions to stay them. Were any of them, he asked himself for the thousandth time, it seemed to him, as wearily connected as he had been at their age? Did they each have a charming young wife to love—one of whom they were passionately fond—such a one as he had never had; or did they not?

Wondering, he reached his office on one of the topmost floors of one of those highest buildings commanding a wide view of the city, and surveyed it wearily. Here were visible the two great rivers of the city, its towers and spires and far-flung walls. From these sometimes, even yet, he seemed to gain a patience to live, to hope. How in his youth all this had inspired him—or that other city that was then. Even now he was always at peace here, so much more so than in his own home, pleasant as it was. Here he could look out over this great scene and dream or he could lose the memory in his work that his love-life had been a failure. The great city, the buildings he could plan or supervise, the efficient help that always surrounded him—his help, not hers— aided to take his mind off himself and that deep-seated inner ache or loss.

The care of Mr. Haymaker's apartment during his wife's illness and his present absence throughout the day, devolved upon a middle-aged woman of great seriousness, Mrs. Elfridge by name, whom Mrs. Haymaker had employed years before; and under her a maid of all work, Hester, who waited on table, opened the door, and the like; and also at present two trained nurses, one for night and one for day service, who were in charge of Mrs. Haymaker. The nurses were both bright, healthy, blue-eyed girls, who attracted Mr. Haymaker and suggested all the youth he had never had—without really disturbing his poise. It would seem as though that could never be any more.

In addition, of course, there was the loving interest of his son Wesley and his daughter Ethelberta—whom his wife had

named so in spite of him—both of whom had long since married
and had children of their own and were living in different parts
of the great city. In this crisis both of them came daily to learn
how things were, and occasionally to stay for the entire afternoon or evening, or both. Ethelberta had wanted to come and
take charge of the apartment entirely during her mother's
illness, only Mrs. Haymaker, who was still able to direct, and
fond of doing so, would not hear of it. She was not so ill but
that she could still speak, and in this way could inquire and direct.
Besides, Mrs. Elfridge was as good as Mrs. Haymaker in all
things that related to Mr. Haymaker's physical comfort, or so
she thought.

If the truth will come out—as it will in so many pathetic
cases—it was never his physical so much as his spiritual or affectional comfort that Mr. Haymaker craved. As said before, he
had never loved Mrs. Haymaker, or certainly not since that now
long-distant period back in Muskegon, Michigan, where both
had been born and where they had lived and met at the ages, she
of fifteen, he of seventeen. It had been, strange as it might seem
now, a love match at first sight with them. She had seemed so
sweet, a girl of his own age or a little younger, the daughter of
a local chemist. Later, when he had been forced by poverty to
go out into the world to make his own way, he had written her
much, and imagined her to be all that she had seemed at fifteen,
and more—a dream among fair women. But Fortune, slow in
coming to his aid and fickle in fulfilling his dreams, had brought
it about that for several years more he had been compelled to
stay away nearly all of the time, unable to marry her; during
which period, unknown to himself really, his own point of view
had altered. How it had happened he could never tell really,
but so it was. The great city, larger experiences—while she was
still enduring the smaller ones—other faces, dreams of larger
things, had all combined to destroy it or her, only he had not
quite realized it then. He was always so slow in realizing the
full import of the immediate thing, he thought.

That was the time, as he had afterward told himself—how
often!—that he should have discovered his mistake and stopped.
Later it always seemed to become more and more impossible.
Then, in spite of some heartache to her and some distress to

himself, no doubt, all would be well for him now. But no; he had been too inexperienced, too ignorant, too bound by all the conventions and punctilio of his simple Western world. He thought an engagement, however unsatisfactory it might come to seem afterward, was an engagement, and binding. An honorable man would not break one—or so his country moralists argued.

Yes, at that time he might have written her, he might have told her, then. But he had been too sensitive and kindly to speak of it. Afterward it was too late. He feared to wound her, to undo her, to undo her life. But now—now—look at his! He had gone back on several occasions before marriage, and might have seen and done and been free if he had had but courage and wisdom—but no; duty, order, the beliefs of the region in which he had been reared, and of America—what it expected and what she expected and was entitled to—had done for him completely. He had not spoken. Instead, he had gone on and married her without speaking of the change in himself, without letting her know how worse than ashes it had all become. God, what a fool he had been! how often since he had told himself over and over.

Well, having made a mistake it was his duty perhaps, at least according to current beliefs, to stick by it and make the best of it; —a bargain was a bargain in marriage, if nowhere else—but still that had never prevented him from being unhappy. He could not prevent that himself. During all these long years, therefore, owing to these same conventions—what people would think and say—he had been compelled to live with her, to cherish her, to pretend to be happy with her—"another perfect union," as he sometimes said to himself. In reality he had been unhappy, horribly so. Even her face wearied him at times, and her presence, her mannerisms. Only this other morning Doctor Storm, by his manner indicating that he thought him lonely, in danger of being left all alone and desperately sad and neglected in case she died had irritated him greatly. Who would take care of him? his eyes had seemed to say—and yet he himself wanted nothing so much as to be alone for a time, at least, in this life, to think for himself, to do for himself, to forget this long, dreary period in which he had pretended to be something that he was not.

Was he never to be rid of the dull round of it, he asked himself now, never before he himself died? And yet shortly afterward he would reproach himself for these very thoughts, as being wrong, hard, unkind—thoughts that would certainly condemn him in the eyes of the general public, that public which made reputations and one's general standing before the world.

During all this time he had never even let her know—no, not once—of the tremendous and soul-crushing sacrifice he had made. Like the Spartan boy, he had concealed the fox gnawing at his vitals. He had not complained. He had been, indeed, the model husband, as such things go in conventional walks. If you doubted it look at his position, or that of his children; or his wife—her mental and physical comfort, even in her illness, her unfailing belief that he was all he should be! Never once apparently, during all these years, had she doubted his love or felt him to be unduly unhappy—or, if not that exactly, if not fully accepting his love as something that was still at a fever heat, the thing it once was—still believing that he found pleasure and happiness in being with her, a part of the home which together they had built up, these children they had reared, comfort in knowing that it would endure to the end! To the end! During all these years she had gone on molding his and her lives—as much as that was possible in his case—and those of their children, to suit herself; and thinking all the time that she was doing what he wanted or at least what was best for him and them.

How she adored convention! What did she not think she knew in regard to how things ought to be—mainly what her old home surroundings had taught her, the American idea of this, that and the other. Her theories in regard to friends, education of the children, and so on, had in the main prevailed, even when he did not quite agree with her; her desires for certain types of pleasure and amusement, of companionship, and so on, were conventional types always and had also prevailed. There had been little quarrels, of course, always had been—what happy home is free of them?—but still he had always given in, or nearly always, and had acted as though he were satisfied in so doing.

But why, therefore, should he complain now, or she ever imagine, or ever have imagined, that he was unhappy? She did not, had not. Like all their relatives and friends of the region from which they sprang, and here also—and she had been most careful to regulate that, courting whom she pleased and ignoring all others—she still believed most firmly, more so than ever, that she knew what was best for him, what he really thought and wanted. It made him smile most wearily at times.

For in her eyes—in regard to him, at least, not always so with others, he had found—marriage was a sacrament, sacrosanct, never to be dissolved. One life, one love. Once a man had accepted the yoke or even asked a girl to marry him it was his duty to abide by it. To break an engagement, to be unfaithful to a wife, even unkind to her—what a crime, in her eyes! Such people ought to be drummed out of the world. They were really not fit to live—dogs, brutes!

And yet, look at himself—what of him? What of one who had made a mistake in regard to all this? Where was his compensation to come from, his peace and happiness? Here on earth or only in some mythical heaven—that odd, angelic heaven that she still believed in? What a farce! And all her friends and his would think he would be so miserable now if she died, or at least ought to be. So far had asinine convention and belief in custom carried the world. Think of it!

But even that was not the worst. No; that was not the worst, either. It had been the gradual realization coming along through the years that he had married an essentially small, narrow woman who could never really grasp his point of view—or, rather, the significance of his dreams or emotions—and yet with whom, nevertheless, because of this original promise or mistake, he was compelled to live. Grant her every quality of goodness, energy, industry, intent—as he did freely—still there was this; and it could never be adjusted, never. Essentially, as he had long since discovered, she was narrow, ultraconventional, whereas he was an artist by nature, brooding and dreaming strange dreams and thinking of far-off things which she did not or could not understand or did not sympathize with, save in a general and very remote way. The nuances of his craft, the wonders and subtleties of forms and angles—had she ever realized how significant these were to him, let alone to herself? No, never. She had not the least true appreciation of them—never had had. Architecture? Art? What could they really mean to her, desire as she might to appreciate them? And he could not now go else-where to discover that sympathy. No. He had never really wanted to, since the public and she would object, and he thinking it half evil himself.

Still, how was it, he often asked himself, that Nature could thus allow one conditioned or equipped with emotions and seek-ings such as his, not of an utterly conventional order, to seek out and pursue one like Ernestine, who was not fitted to under-stand him or to care what his personal moods might be? Was love truly blind, as the old saw insisted, or did Nature really plan, and cleverly, to torture the artist mind—as it did the pearl-bearing oyster with a grain of sand—with something seemingly inimical, in order that it might produce beauty? Sometimes he thought so. Perhaps the many interesting and beautiful build-ings he had planned—the world called them so, at least—had been due to the loving care he lavished on them, being shut out from love and beauty elsewhere. Cruel Nature, that cared so little for the dreams of man—the individual man or woman!

At the time he had married Ernestine he was really too young to know exactly what it was he wanted to do or how it was he was going to feel in the years to come; and yet there was no one to guide him, to stop him. The custom of the time was all in favor of this dread disaster. Nature herself seemed to desire it—mere children being the be-all and the end-all of everything everywhere. Think of that as a theory! Later, when it became so clear to him what he had done, and in spite of all the con-ventional thoughts and conditions that seemed to bind him to this fixed condition, he had grown restless and weary, but never really irritable. No, he had never become that.

Instead he had concealed it all from her, persistently, in all kindness; only this hankering after beauty of mind and body in ways not represented by her had hurt so—grown finally almost too painful to bear. He had dreamed and dreamed of something different until it had become almost an obsession. Was it never to be, that something different, never, anywhere, in all time? What a tragedy! Soon he would be dead and then it would never be anywhere—anymore! Ernestine was charming, he would admit, or had been at first, though time had proved that she was not charming to him either mentally or physically in any compelling way; but how did that help him now? How could it? He had actually found himself bored by her for more than twenty-seven years now, and this other dream growing, growing, growing—until——

But now he was old, and she was dying, or might be, and it could not make so much difference what happened to him or to her; only it could, too, because he wanted to be free for a little while, just for a little while, before he died.

To be free! free!

One of the things that had always irritated him about Mrs. Haymaker was this, that in spite of his determination never to offend the social code in any way—he had felt for so many reasons, emotional as well as practical, that he could not afford so to do—and also in spite of the fact that he had been tortured by this show of beauty in the eyes and bodies of others, his wife, fearing perhaps in some strange psychic way that he might change, had always tried to make him feel or believe—premeditatedly and of a purpose, he thought—that he was not the kind of man who would be attractive to women; that he lacked some physical fitness, some charm that other men had, which would cause all young and really charming women to turn away from him. Think of it! He to whom so many women had turned with questioning eyes!

Also that she had married him largely because she had felt sorry for him! He chose to let her believe that, because he was sorry for her. Because other women had seemed to draw near to him at times in some appealing or seductive way she had insisted he was not even a cavalier, let alone a Lothario; that he was ungainly, slow, uninteresting—to all women but her!

Persistently, he thought, and without any real need, she had harped on this, fighting chimeras, a chance danger in the future; though he had never given her any real reason, and had never even planned to sin against her in any way—never. She had thus tried to poison his own mind in regard to himself and his art—and yet—and yet—— Ah, those eyes of other women, their haunting beauty, the flitting something they said to him of infinite, inexpressible delight. Why had his life been so very hard?

One of the disturbing things about all this was the iron truth which it had driven home, namely, that Nature, unless it were expressed or represented by some fierce determination within, which drove one to do, be, cared no whit for him or any other man or woman. Unless one acted for oneself, upon some stern conclusion nurtured within, one might rot and die spiritually. Nature did not care. "Blessed be the meek"—yes. Blessed be the strong, rather, for they made their own happiness. All these years in which he had dwelt and worked in this knowledge, hoping for something but not acting, nothing had happened, except to him, and that in an unsatisfactory way. All along he had seen what was happening to him; and yet held by convention he had refused to act always, because somehow he was not hard enough to act. He was not strong enough, that was the real truth—had not been. Almost like a bird in a cage, an animal peeping out from behind bars, he had viewed the world of free thought and freer action. In many a drawing-room, on the street, or in his own home even, had he not looked into an eye, the face of someone who seemed to offer understanding, to know, to sympathize, though she might not have, of course; and yet religiously and moralistically, like an anchorite, because of duty and current belief and what people would say and think, Ernestine's position and faith in him, her comfort, his career and that of the children—he had put them all aside, out of his mind, forgotten them almost, as best he might. It had been hard at times, and sad, but so it had been.

And look at him now, old, not exactly feeble yet—no, not that yet, not quite!—but life weary and almost indifferent. All these years he had wanted, wanted—wanted—an understanding mind, a tender heart, the some one woman—she must exist somewhere—who would have sympathized with all the delicate shades and meanings of his own character, his art, his spiritual as well as his material dreams—— And yet look at him! Mrs. Haymaker had always been with him, present in the flesh or the spirit, and—so——

Though he could not ever say that she was disagreeable to him in a material way—he could not say that she had ever been that exactly—still she did not correspond to his idea of what he needed, and so—— Form had meant so much to him, color; the glorious perfectness of a glorious woman's body, for instance, the color of her thought, moods—exquisite they must be, like his own at times; but no, he had never had the opportunity to know one intimately. No, not one, though he had dreamed of her so long. He had never even dared whisper this to any one, scarcely to himself. It was not wise, not socially fit. Thoughts like this would tend to social ostracism in his circle, or rather hers—for had she not made the circle?

And here was the rub with Mr. Haymaker, at least, that he could not make up his mind whether in his restlessness and private mental complaints he were not even now guilty of a great moral crime in so thinking. Was it not true that men and women should be faithful in marriage whether they were happy or not? Was there not some psychic law governing this matter of union—one life, one love—which made the thoughts and the pains and the subsequent sufferings and hardships of the individual, whatever they might be, seem unimportant? The churches said so. Public opinion and the law seemed to accept this. There were so many problems, so much order to be disrupted, so much pain caused, many insoluble problems where children were concerned—if people did not stick. Was it not best, more blessed—socially, morally, and in every other way important—for him to stand by a bad bargain rather than to cause so much disorder and pain, even though he lost his own soul emotionally? He had thought so—or at least he had acted as though he thought so—and yet—— How often had he wondered over this!

Take, now, some other phases. Granting first that Mrs. Haymaker had, according to the current code, measured up to the requirements of a wife, good and true, and that at first after marriage there had been just enough of physical and social charm about her to keep his state from becoming intolerable, still there was this old ache; and then newer things which came with the birth of the several children: First Elwell—named after a cousin of hers, not his—who had died only two years after he was born; and then Wesley; and then Ethelberta. How he had always disliked that name!—largely because he had hoped to call her Ottilie, a favorite name of his; or Janet, after his mother.

Curiously the arrival of these children and the death of poor little Elwell at two had somehow, in spite of his unrest, bound him to this matrimonial state and filled him with a sense of duty, and pleasure even—almost entirely apart from her, he was sorry to say—in these young lives; though if there had not been children, as he sometimes told himself, he surely would have broken away from her; he could not have stood it. They were so odd in their infancy, those little ones, so troublesome and yet so amusing—little Elwell, for instance, whose nose used to crinkle with delight when he would pretend to bite his neck, and whose gurgle of pleasure was so sweet and heart-filling that it positively thrilled and lured him. In spite of his thoughts concerning Ernestine—and always in those days they were rigidly put down as unmoral and even evil, a certain unsocial streak in him perhaps which was against law and order and social well-being—he came to have a deep and abiding feeling for Elwell. The latter, in some chemic, almost unconscious way, seemed to have arrived as a balm to his misery, a bandage for his growing wound—sent by whom, by what, how? Elwell had seized upon his imagination, and so his heartstrings—had come, indeed, to make him feel understanding and sympathy in that little child; to supply, or seem to at least, what he lacked in the way of love and affection from one whom he could truly love. Elwell was never so happy apparently as when snuggling in his arms, not Ernestine's, or lying against his neck. And when he went for a walk or elsewhere there was Elwell always ready, arms up, to cling to his neck. He seemed, strangely enough, inordinately fond of his father, rather than his mother, and never happy without him. On his part, Haymaker came to be wildly fond of him —that queer little lump of a face, suggesting a little of himself and of his own mother, not so much of Ernestine, or so he thought, though he would not have objected to that. Not at all. He was not so small as that. Toward the end of the second year, when Elwell was just beginning to be able to utter a word or two, he had taught him that silly old rhyme which ran "There were three kittens," and when it came to "and they shall have no——" he would stop and say to Elwell, "What now?" and the latter would gurgle "puh!"—meaning, of course, pie.

Ah, those happy days with little Elwell, those walks with him over his shoulder or on his arm, those hours in which of an evening he would rock him to sleep in his arms! Always Ernestine was there, and happy in the thought of his love for little

Elwell and her, her more than anything else perhaps; but it was
an illusion—that latter part. He did not care for her even then
as she thought he did. All his fondness was for Elwell, only
she took it as evidence of his growing or enduring affection for
her—another evidence of the peculiar working of her mind.
Women were like that, he supposed—some women.

And then came that dreadful fever, due to some invading
microbe which the doctors could not diagnose or isolate, infan-
tile paralysis perhaps; and little Elwell had finally ceased to be
as flesh and was eventually carried forth to the lorn, disagreeable
graveyard near Woodlawn. How he had groaned internally,
indulged in sad, despondent thoughts concerning the futility of
all things human, when this had happened! It seemed for the
time being as if all color and beauty had really gone out of his
life for good.

"Man born of woman is of few days and full of troubles," the
preacher whom Mrs. Haymaker had insisted upon having into
the house at the time of the funeral had read. "He fleeth also
as a shadow and continueth not."

Yes; so little Elwell had fled, as a shadow, and in his own
deep sorrow at the time he had come to feel the first and only
sad, deep sympathy for Ernestine that he had ever felt since
marriage; and that because she had suffered so much—had lain
in his arms after the funeral and cried so bitterly. It was terrible,
her sorrow. Terrible—a mother grieving for her first-born!
Why was it, he had thought at the time, that he had never been
able to think or make her all she ought to be to him? Ernestine
at this time had seemed better, softer, kinder, wiser, sweeter than
she had ever seemed; more worthy, more interesting than ever
he had thought her before. She had slaved so during the child's
illness, stayed awake night after night, watched over him with
such loving care—done everything, in short, that a loving human
heart could do to rescue her young from the depths; and yet
even then he had not really been able to love her. No, sad and
unkind as it might seem, he had not. He had just pitied her and
thought her better, worthier! What cursed stars disordered the
minds and moods of people so? Why was it that these virtues of
people, their good qualities, did not make you love them, did
not really bind them to you, as against the things you could not

like? Why? He had resolved to do better in his thought, but somehow, in spite of himself, he had never been able to do so.

Nevertheless, at that time he seemed to realize more keenly than ever her order, industry, frugality, a sense of beauty within limits, a certain laudable ambition to do something and be somebody—only, only he could not sympathize with her ambitions, could not see that she had anything but a hopelessly commonplace and always unimportant point of view. There was never any flare to her, never any true distinction of mind or soul. She seemed always, in spite of anything he might say or do, hopelessly to identify doing and being with money and current opinion—neighborhood public opinion, almost—and local social position, whereas he knew that distinguished doing might as well be connected with poverty and shame and disgrace as with these other things—wealth and station, for instance; a thing which she could never quite understand apparently, though he often tried to tell her, much against her mood always.

Look at the cases of the great artists! Some of the greatest architects right here in the city, or in history, were of peculiar, almost disagreeable, history. But no, Mrs. Haymaker could not understand anything like that, anything connected with history, indeed—she hardly believed in history, its dark, sad pages, and would never read it, or at least did not care to. And as for art and artists—she would never have believed that wisdom and art understanding and true distinction might take their rise out of things necessarily low and evil—never.

Take now, the case of young Zingara. Zingara was an architect like himself, whom he had met more than thirty years before, here in New York, when he had first arrived, a young man struggling to become an architect of significance, only he was very poor and rather unkempt and disreputable-looking. Haymaker had found him several years before his marriage to Ernestine in the dark offices of Pyne & Starboard, Architects, and had been drawn to him definitely; but because he smoked all the time and was shabby as to his clothes and had no money—why, Mrs. Haymaker, after he had married her, and though he had known Zingara nearly four years, would have none of him. To her he was low, and a failure, one who would never succeed. Once she had seen him in some cheap restaurant that she chanced to be passing, in company with a drabby-looking maid, and that was the end.

"I wish you wouldn't bring him here any more, dear," she had insisted; and to have peace he had complied—only, now look. Zingara had since become a great architect, but now of course, owing to Mrs. Haymaker, he was definitely alienated. He was the man who had since designed the Æsculapian Club; and Symphony Hall with its delicate façade; as well as the tower of the Wells Building, sending its sweet lines so high, like a poetic thought or dream. But Zingara was now a dreamy recluse like himself, very exclusive, as Haymaker had long since come to know, and indifferent as to what people thought or said.

But perhaps it was not just obtuseness to certain of the finer shades and meanings of life, but an irritating aggressiveness at times, backed only by her limited understanding, which caused her to seek and wish to be here, there, and the other place; wherever, in her mind, the truly successful—which meant nearly always the materially successful of a second or third rate character—were, which irritated him most of all. How often had he tried to point out the difference between true and shoddy distinction—the former rarely connected with great wealth.

But no. So often she seemed to imagine such queer people to be truly successful, when they were really not—usually people with just money, or a very little more.

And in the matter of rearing and educating and marrying their two children, Wesley and Ethelberta, who had come after Elwell —what peculiar pains and feelings had not been involved in all this for him. In infancy both of these had seemed sweet enough, and so close to him, though never quite so wonderful as Elwell. But, as they grew, it seemed somehow as though Ernestine had come between him and them. First, it was the way she had raised them, the very stiff and formal manner in which they were supposed to move and be, copied from the few new-rich whom she had chanced to meet through him—and admired in spite of his warnings. That was the irony of architecture as a profession— it was always bringing such queer people close to one, and for the sake of one's profession, sometimes, particularly in the case of the young architect, one had to be nice to them. Later, it was

the kind of school they should attend. He had half imagined
at first that it would be the public school, because they both had
begun as simple people; but no, since they were prospering it had
to be a private school for each, and not one of his selection, either
—or hers, really—but one to which the Barlows and the Wes-
tervelts, two families of means with whom Ernestine had
become intimate, sent their children and therefore thought
excellent!

The Barlows! Wealthy, but, to him, gross and mediocre
people who had made a great deal of money in the manufacture
of patent medicines out West, and who had then come to New
York to splurge, and had been attracted to Ernestine—not him
particularly, he imagined—because Haymaker had built a town
house for them, and also because he was gaining a fine reputation.
They were dreadful really, so *gauche*, so truly dull; and yet
somehow they seemed to suit Ernestine's sense of fitness and
worth at the time, because, as she said, they were good and kind
—like her Western home folks; only they were not really. She
just imagined so. They were worthy enough people in their way,
though with no taste. Young Fred Barlow had been sent to the
expensive Gaillard School for Boys, near Morristown, where
they were taught manners and airs, and little else, as Haymaker
always thought, though Ernestine insisted that they were given
a religious training as well. And so Wesley had to go there—for
a time, anyhow. It was the best school.

And similarly, because Mercedes Westervelt, senseless, vain
little thing, was sent to Briarcliff School, near White Plains,
Ethelberta had to go there. Think of it! It was all so silly, so
pushing. How well he remembered the long, delicate campaign
which preceded this, the logic and tactics employed, the importance of it socially to Ethelberta, the tears and cajolery. Mrs.
Haymaker could always cry so easily, or seem to be on the verge
of it, when she wanted anything; and somehow, in spite of the
fact that he knew her tears were unimportant, or timed and for
a purpose, he could never stand out against them, and she knew
it. Always he felt moved or weakened in spite of himself. He
had no weapon wherewith to fight them, though he resented
them as a part of the argument. Positively Mrs. Haymaker
could be as sly and as ruthless as Machiavelli himself at times,

and yet believe all the while that she was tender, loving, self-sacrificing, generous, moral and a dozen other things, all of which led to the final achievement of her own aims. Perhaps this was admirable from one point of view, but it irritated him always. But if one were unable to see him- or herself, their actual disturbing inconsistencies, what were you to do?

And again, he had by then been married so long that it was almost impossible to think of throwing her over, or so it seemed at the time. They had reached the place then where they had supposedly achieved position together, though in reality it was all his—and not such position as he was entitled to, at that. Ernestine—and he was thinking this in all kindness—could never attract the ideal sort. And anyhow, the mere breath of a scandal between them, separation or unfaithfulness, which he never really contemplated, would have led to endless bickering and social and commercial injury, or so he thought. All her strong friends—and his, in a way—those who had originally been his clients, would have deserted him. Their wives, their own social fears, would have compelled them to ostracize him! He would have been a scandal-marked architect, a brute for objecting to so kind and faithful and loving a wife. And perhaps he would have been, at that. He could never quite tell, it was all so mixed and tangled.

Take, again, the marriage of his son Wesley into the De Gaud family—George de Gaud *père* being nothing more than a retired real-estate speculator and promoter who had money, but nothing more; and Irma de Gaud, the daughter, being a gross, coarse, sensuous girl, physically attractive no doubt, and financially reasonably secure, or so she had seemed; but what else? Nothing, literally nothing; and his son had seemed to have at least some spiritual ideas at first. Ernestine had taken up with Mrs. George de Gaud—a miserable, narrow creature, so Haymaker thought —largely for Wesley's sake, he presumed. Anyhow, everything had been done to encourage Wesley in his suit and Irma in her toleration, and now look at them! De Gaud *père* had since failed and left his daughter practically nothing. Irma had been interested in anything but Wesley's career, had followed what she considered the smart among the new-rich—a smarter, wilder, newer new-rich than ever Ernestine had fancied, or could. To-day she was without a thought for anything besides teas and country clubs and theaters—and what else?

And long since Wesley had begun to realize it himself. He was an engineer now, in the employ of one of the great construction companies, a moderately successful man. But even Ernestine, who had engineered the match and thought it wonderful, was now down on her. She had begun to see through her some years ago, when Irma had begun to ignore her; only before it was always the De Gauds here, and the De Gauds there. Good gracious, what more could any one want than the De Gauds— Irma de Gaud, for instance? Then came the concealed dissension between Irma and Wesley, and now Mrs. Haymaker insisted that Irma had held, and was holding Wesley back. She was not the right woman for him. Almost—against all her prejudices— she was willing that he should leave her. Only, if Haymaker had broached anything like that in connection with himself!

And yet Mrs. Haymaker had been determined, because of what she considered the position of the De Gauds at that time, that Wesley should marry Irma. Wesley now had to slave at mediocre tasks in order to have enough to allow Irma to run in so-called fast society of a second or third rate. And even at that she was not faithful to him—or so Haymaker believed. There were so many strange evidences. And yet Haymaker felt that he did not care to interfere now. How could he? Irma was tired of Wesley, and that was all there was to it. She was looking elsewhere, he was sure.

Take but one more case, that of Ethelberta. What a name! In spite of all Ernestine's determination to make her so successful and thereby reflect some credit on her had she really succeeded in so doing? To be sure, Ethelberta's marriage was somewhat more successful financially than Wesley's had proved to be, but was she any better placed in other ways? John Kelso—"Jack," as she always called him—with his light ways and lighter mind, was he really any one!—anything more than a waster? His parents stood by him no doubt, but that was all; and so much the worse for him. According to Mrs. Haymaker at the time, he, too, was an ideal boy, admirable, just the man for Ethelberta, because the Kelsos, *père* and *mère*, had money. Horner Kelso had made a kind of fortune in Chicago in the banknote business, and had settled in New York, about the time that Ethelberta was fifteen, to spend it. Ethelberta had met Grace Kelso at school.

And now see! She was not unattractive, and had some pleasant, albeit highly affected, social ways; she had money, and a comfortable apartment in Park Avenue; but what had it all come to? John Kelso had never done anything really, nothing. His parents' money and indulgence and his early training for a better social state had ruined him if he had ever had a mind that amounted to anything. He was idle, pleasure-loving, mentally indolent, like Irma de Gaud. Those two should have met and married, only they could never have endured each other. But how Mrs. Haymaker had courted the Kelsos in her eager and yet diplomatic way, giving teas and receptions and theater parties; and yet he had never been able to exchange ten significant words with either of them, or the younger Kelsos either. Think of it!

And somehow in the process Ethelberta, for all his early affection and tenderness and his still kindly feeling for her, had been weaned away from him and had proved a limited and conventional girl, somewhat like her mother, and more inclined to listen to her than to him—though he had not minded that really. It had been the same with Wesley before her. Perhaps, however, a child was entitled to its likes and dislikes, regardless.

But why had he stood for it all, he now kept asking himself. Why? What grand results, if any, had been achieved? Were their children so wonderful?—their lives? Would he not have been better off without her—his children better, even, by a different woman?—hers by a different man? Wouldn't it have been better if he had destroyed it all, broken away? There would have been pain, of course, terrible consequences, but even so he would have been free to go, to do, to reorganize his life on another basis. Zingara had avoided marriage entirely—wise man. But no, no; always convention, that long list of reasons and terrors he was always reciting to himself. He had allowed himself to be pulled round by the nose, God only knows why, and that was all there was to it. Weakness, if you will, perhaps; fear of convention; fear of what people would think and say.

Always now he found himself brooding over the dire results

to him of all this respect on his part for convention, moral order, the duty of keeping society on an even keel, of not bringing disgrace to his children and himself and her, and yet ruining his own life emotionally by so doing. To be respectable had been so important that it had resulted in spiritual failure for him. But now all that was over with him, and Mrs. Haymaker was ill, near to death, and he was expected to wish her to get well, and be happy with her a long time yet! Be happy! In spite of anything he might wish or think he ought to do, he couldn't. He couldn't even wish her to get well.

It was too much to ask. There was actually a haunting satisfaction in the thought that she might die now. It wouldn't be much, but it would be something—a few years of freedom. That was something. He was not utterly old yet, and he might have a few years of peace and comfort to himself still—and—and—— That dream—that dream—though it might never come true now—it couldn't really—still—still—— He wanted to be free to go his own way once more, to do as he pleased, to walk, to think, to brood over what he had not had—to brood over what he had not had! Only, only, whenever he looked into her pale sick face and felt her damp limp hands he could not quite wish that, either; not quite, not even now. It seemed too hard, too brutal —only—only—— So he wavered.

No; in spite of her long-past struggle over foolish things and in spite of himself and all he had endured or thought he had, he was still willing that she should live; only he couldn't wish it exactly. Yes, let her live if she could. What matter to him now whether she lived or died? Whenever he looked at her he could not help thinking how helpless she would be without him, what a failure at her age, and so on. And all along, as he wryly repeated to himself, she had been thinking and feeling that she was doing the very best for him and her and the children!—that she was really the ideal wife for him, making every dollar go as far as it would, every enjoyment yield the last drop for them all, every move seeming to have been made to their general advantage! Yes, that was true. There was a pathos about it, wasn't there? But as for the actual results——!

The next morning, the second after his talk with Doctor Storm, found him sitting once more beside his front window in the early dawn, and so much of all this, and much more, was coming back to him, as before. For the thousandth or the ten-thousandth time, as it seemed to him, in all the years that had gone, he was concluding again that his life was a failure. If only he were free for a little while just to be alone and think, per-haps to discover what life might bring him yet; only on this occasion his thoughts were colored by a new turn in the situation. Yesterday afternoon, because Mrs. Haymaker's condition had grown worse, the consultation between Grainger and Storm was held, and to-day sometime transfusion was to be tried, that last grim stand taken by physicians in distress over a case; blood taken from a strong ex-cavalryman out of a position, in this case, and the best to be hoped for, but not assured. In this instance his thoughts were as before wavering. Now supposing she really died, in spite of this? What would he think of himself then? He went back after a time and looked in on her where she was still sleeping. Now she was not so strong as before, or so she seemed; her pulse was not so good, the nurse said. And now as before his mood changed in her favor, but only for a little while. For later, waking, she seemed to look and feel better.

Later he came up to the dining room, where the nurse was taking her breakfast, and seating himself beside her, as was his custom these days, asked: "How do you think she is to-day?"

He and the night nurse had thus had their breakfasts together for days. This nurse, Miss Filson, was such a smooth, pink, graceful creature, with light hair and blue eyes, the kind of eyes and color that of late, and in earlier years, had suggested to him the love time or youth that he had missed.

The latter looked grave, as though she really feared the worst but was concealing it.

"No worse, I think, and possibly a little better," she replied, eyeing him sympathetically. He could see that she too felt that he was old and in danger of being neglected. "Her pulse is a little stronger, nearly normal now, and she is resting easily. Doctor Storm and Doctor Grainger are coming, though, at ten. Then they'll decide what's to be done. I think if she's worse that they are going to try transfusion. The man has been engaged. Doctor Storm said that when she woke to-day she was to be given strong beef tea. Mrs. Elfridge is making it now. The fact that she is not much worse, though, is a good sign in itself, I think."

Haymaker merely stared at her from under his heavy gray eyebrows. He was so tired and gloomy, not only because he had not slept much of late himself but because of this sawing to and fro between his varying moods. Was he never to be able to decide for himself what he really wished? Was he never to be done with this interminable moral or spiritual problem? Why could he not make up his mind on the side of moral order, sympathy, and be at peace? Miss Filson pattered on about other heart cases, how so many people lived years and years after they were supposed to die of heart lesion; and he meditated as to the grayness and strangeness of it all, the worthlessness of his own life, the variability of his own moods. Why was he so? How queer—how almost evil, sinister—he had become at times; how weak at others. Last night as he had looked at Ernestine lying in bed, and this morning before he had seen her, he had thought if she only would die—if he were only really free once more, even at this late date. But then when he had seen her again this morning and now when Miss Filson spoke of transfusion, he felt sorry again. What good would it do him now? Why should he want to kill her? Could such evil ideas go unpunished either in this world or the next? Supposing his children could guess! Supposing she did die now—and he wished it so fervently only this morning—how would he feel? After all, Ernestine had not been so bad. She had tried, hadn't she?— only she had not been able to make a success of things, as he saw it, and he had not been able to love her, that was all. He reproached himself once more now with the hardness and the cruelty of his thoughts.

The opinion of the two physicians was that Mrs. Haymaker was not much better and that this first form of blood transfusion must be resorted to—injected straight via a pump—which would restore her greatly provided her heart did not bleed it out too freely. Before doing so, however, both men once more spoke to Haymaker, who in an excess of self-condemnation insisted that no expense must be spared. If her life was in danger, save it by any means—all. It was precious to her, to him and to her children. So he spoke. Thus he felt that he was lending every force which could be expected of him, aside from fervently wishing for her recovery, which even now, in spite of himself, he could not do. He was too weary of it all, the conventional round of duties and obligations. But if she recovered, as her physicians seemed to think she might if transfusion were tried, if she gained even, it would mean that he would have to take her away for the summer to some quiet mountain resort—to be with her hourly during the long period in which she would be recovering. Well, he would not complain now. That was all right. He would do it. He would be bored of course, as usual, but it would be too bad to have her die when she could be saved. Yes, that was true. And yet——

He went down to his office again and in the meantime this first form of transfusion was tried, and proved a great success, apparently. She was much better, so the day nurse phoned at three; very much better. At five-thirty Mr. Haymaker returned, no unsatisfactory word having come in the interim, and there she was, resting on a raised pillow, if you please, and looking so cheerful, more like her old self than he had seen her in some time.

At once then his mood changed again. They were amazing, these variations in his own thoughts, almost chemic, not volitional, decidedly peculiar for a man who was supposed to know his own mind—only did one, ever? Now she would not die. Now the whole thing would go on as before. He was sure of it. Well, he might as well resign himself to the old sense of failure. He would never be free now. Everything would go on as before, the next and the next day the same. Terrible! Though he seemed glad—really grateful, in a way, seeing her cheerful and hopeful once more—still the obsession of failure and being once more bound forever returned now. In his own bed at midnight he said to himself: "Now she will really get well. All will be as before. I will never be free. I will never have a day—a day! Never!"

But the next morning, to his surprise and fear or comfort, as his moods varied, she was worse again; and then once more he reproached himself for his black thoughts. Was he not really killing her by what he thought? he asked himself—these constant changes in his mood? Did not his dark wishes have power? Was he not as good as a murderer in his way? Think, if he had always to feel from now on that he had killed her by wishing so! Would not that be dreadful—an awful thing really? Why was he this way? Could he not be human, kind?

When Doctor Storm came at nine-thirty, after a telephone call from the nurse, and looked grave and spoke of horses' blood as being better, thicker than human blood—not so easily bled out of the heart when injected as a serum—Haymaker was beside himself with self-reproaches and sad, disturbing fear. His dark, evil thoughts of last night and all these days had done this, he was sure. Was he really a murderer at heart, a dark criminal, plotting her death?—and for what? Why had he wished last night that she would die? Her case must be very desperate.

"You must do your best," he now said to Doctor Storm. "Whatever is needful—she must not die if you can help it."

"No, Mr. Haymaker," returned the latter sympathetically. "All that can be done will be done. You need not fear. I have an idea that we didn't inject enough yesterday, and anyhow human blood is not thick enough in this case. She responded, but not enough. We will see what we can do to-day."

Haymaker, pressed with duties, went away, subdued and sad. Now once more he decided that he must not tolerate these dark ideas any more, must rid himself of these black wishes, whatever he might feel. It was evil. They would eventually come back to him in some dark way, he might be sure. They might be influencing her. She must be allowed to recover if she could without any opposition on his part. He must now make a further sacrifice of his own life, whatever it cost. It was only decent, only human. Why should he complain now, anyhow, after all these years! What difference would a few years make? He returned at evening, consoled by his own good thoughts and a telephone message at three to the effect that his wife was much better. This second injection had proved much more effective. Horses' blood was plainly better for her. She was stronger, and sitting up again. He entered at five, and found her lying there pale and weak, but still with a better light in her eye, a touch of color in her cheeks—or so he thought—more force, and a very faint smile for him, so marked had been the change. How great and kind Doctor Storm really was! How resourceful! If she would only get well now! If this dread siege would only abate! Doctor Storm was coming again at eight.

"Well, how are you, dear?" she asked, looking at him sweetly and lovingly, and taking his hand in hers.

He bent and kissed her forehead—a Judas kiss, he had thought up to now, but not so to-night. To-night he was kind, generous—anxious, even for her to live.

"All right, dearest; very good indeed. And how are you? It's such a fine evening out. You ought to get well soon so as to enjoy these spring days."

"I'm going to," she replied softly. "I feel so much better. And how have you been? Has your work gone all right?"

He nodded and smiled and told her bits of news. Ethelberta had phoned that she was coming, bringing violets. Wesley had said he would be here at six, with Irma! Such-and-such people had asked after her. How could he have been so evil, he now asked himself, as to wish her to die? She was not so bad—really quite charming in her way, an ideal wife for some one, if not him. She was as much entitled to live and enjoy her life as he was to enjoy his; and after all she was the mother of his children, had been with him all these years. Besides, the day had been so fine—it was now—a wondrous May evening. The air and sky were simply delicious. A lavender haze was in the air. The telephone bell now ringing brought still another of a long series of inquiries as to her condition. There had been so many of these during the last few days, the maid said, and especially to-day—and she gave Mr. Haymaker a list of names. See, he thought, she had even more friends than he, being so good, faithful, worthy. Why should he wish her ill?

He sat down to dinner with Ethelberta and Wesley when they arrived and chatted quite gayly—more hopefully than he had in weeks. His own varying thoughts no longer depressing him, for the moment he was happy. How were they? What were the children all doing? At eight-thirty Doctor Storm came again, and announced that he thought Mrs. Haymaker was doing very well indeed, all things considered.

"Her condition is fairly promising, I must say," he said. "If she gets through another night or two comfortably without falling back I think she'll do very well from now on. Her strength seems to be increasing a fraction. However, we must not be too optimistic. Cases of this kind are very treacherous. To-morrow we'll see how she feels, whether she needs any more blood."

He went away, and at ten Ethelberta and Wesley left for the night, asking to be called if she grew worse, thus leaving him alone once more. He sat and meditated. At eleven, after a few moments at his wife's bedside—absolute quiet had been the doctor's instructions these many days—he himself went to bed. He was very tired. His varying thoughts had afflicted him so much that he was always tired, it seemed—his evil conscience, he called it—but to-night he was sure he would sleep. He felt better about himself, about life. He had done better, to-day. He should never have tolerated such dark thoughts. And yet—and yet—and yet——

He lay on his bed near a window which commanded a view of a small angle of the park, and looked out. There were the spring trees, as usual, silvered now by the light, a bit of lake showing at one end. Here in the city a bit of sylvan scenery such as this was so rare and so expensive. In his youth he had been so fond of water, any small lake or stream or pond. In his youth, also, he had loved the moon, and to walk in the dark. It had all, always, been so suggestive of love and happiness, and he had so craved love and happiness and never had it. Once he had designed a yacht club, the base of which suggested waves. Once, years ago, he had thought of designing a lovely cottage or country house for himself and some new love—that wonderful one—if ever she came and he were free. How wonderful it would all have been. Now—now—the thought at such an hour and especially when it was too late, seemed sacrilegious, hard, cold, unmoral, evil. He turned his face away from the moonlight and sighed, deciding to sleep and shut out these older and darker and sweeter thoughts if he could, and did.

Presently he dreamed, and it was as if some lovely spirit of beauty—that wondrous thing he had always been seeking—came and took him by the hand and led him out, out by dimpling streams and clear rippling lakes and a great, noble highway where were temples and towers and figures in white marble. And it seemed as he walked as if something had been, or were, promised him—a lovely fruition to something which he craved —only the world toward which he walked was still dark or shadowy, with something sad and repressing about it, a haunting sense of a still darker distance. He was going toward beauty apparently, but he was still seeking, seeking, and it was dark there when——

"Mr. Haymaker! Mr. Haymaker!" came a voice—soft, almost mystical at first, and then clearer and more disturbing, as a hand was laid on him. "Will you come at once? It's Mrs. Haymaker!"

On the instant he was on his feet seizing the blue silk dressing gown hanging at his bed's head, and adjusting it as he hurried. Mrs. Elfridge and the nurse were behind him, very pale and distrait, wringing their hands. He could tell by that that the worst was at hand. When he reached the bedroom—her bedroom —there she lay as in life—still, peaceful, already limp, as though she were sleeping. Her thin, and as he sometimes thought, cold, lips were now parted in a faint, gracious smile, or trace of one. He had seen her look that way, too, at times; a really gracious smile, and wise, wiser than she was. The long, thin, graceful hands were open, the fingers spread slightly apart as though she were tired, very tired. The eyelids, too, rested wearily on tired eyes. Her form, spare as always, was outlined clearly under the thin coverlets. Miss Filson, the night nurse, was saying something about having fallen asleep for a moment, and waking only to find her so. She was terribly depressed and disturbed, possibly because of Doctor Storm.

Haymaker paused, greatly shocked and moved by the sight —more so than by anything since the death of little Elwell. After all, she had tried, according to her light. But now she was dead—and they had been together so long! He came forward, tears of sympathy springing to his eyes, then sank down beside the bed on his knees so as not to disturb her right hand where it lay.

"Ernie, dear," he said gently, "Ernie—are you really gone?" His voice was full of sorrow; but to himself it sounded false, traitorous.

He lifted the hand and put it to his lips sadly, then leaned his head against her, thinking of his long, mixed thoughts these many days, while both Mrs. Elfridge and the nurse began wiping their eyes. They were so sorry for him, he was so old now!

After a while he got up—they came forward to persuade him at last—looking tremendously sad and distrait, and asked Mrs. Elfridge and the nurse not to disturb his children. They could not aid her now. Let them rest until morning. Then he went back to his own room and sat down on the bed for a moment, gazing out on the same silvery scene that had attracted him before. It was dreadful. So then his dark wishing had come true at last? Possibly his black thoughts had killed her after all. Was that possible? Had his voiceless prayers been answered in this grim way? And did she know now what he had really thought? Dark thought. Where was she now? What was she thinking now if she knew? Would she hate him—haunt him? It was not dawn yet, only two or three in the morning, and the moon was still bright. And in the next room she was lying, pale and cool, gone forever now out of his life.

He got up after a time and went forward into that pleasant front room where he had so often loved to sit, then back into her room to view the body again. Now that she was gone, here more than elsewhere, in her dead presence, he seemed better able to collect his scattered thoughts. She might see or she might not—might know or not. It was all over now. Only he could not help but feel a little evil. She had been so faithful, if nothing more, so earnest in behalf of him and of his children. He might have spared her these last dark thoughts of these last few days. His feelings were so jumbled that he could not place them half the time. But at the same time the ethics of the past, of his own irritated feelings and moods in regard to her, had to be adjusted somehow before he could have peace. They must be adjusted, only how—how? He and Mrs. Elfridge had agreed not to disturb Doctor Storm any more to-night. They were all agreed to get what rest they could against the morning.

After a time he came forward once more to the front room to sit and gaze at the park. Here, perhaps, he could solve these mysteries for himself, think them out, find out what he did feel. He was evil for having wished all he had, that he knew and felt. And yet there was his own story, too—his life. The dawn was breaking by now; a faint grayness shaded the east and dimly lightened this room. A tall pier mirror between two windows now revealed him to himself—spare, angular, disheveled, his beard and hair astray and his eyes weary. The figure he made here as against his dreams of a happier life, once he were free, now struck him forcibly. What a farce! What a failure! Why should he, of all people, think of further happiness in love, even if he were free? Look at his reflection here in this mirror. What a picture—old, grizzled, done for! Had he not known that for so long? Was it not too ridiculous? Why should he have tolerated such vain thoughts? What could he of all people hope for now? No thing of beauty would have him now. Of course not. That glorious dream of his youth was gone forever. It was a mirage, an ignis fatuus. His wife might just as well have lived as died, for all the difference it would or could make to him. Only, he was really free just the same, almost as it were in spite of his varying moods. But he was old, weary, done for, a recluse and ungainly.

Now the innate cruelty of life, its blazing ironic indifference to him and so many grew rapidly upon him. What had he had? What all had he not missed? Dismally he stared first at his dark wrinkled skin; the crow's-feet at the sides of his eyes; the wrinkles across his forehead and between the eyes; his long, dark, wrinkled hands—handsome hands they once were, he thought; his angular, stiff body. Once he had been very much of a personage, he thought, striking, forceful, dynamic—but now! He turned and looked out over the park where the young trees were, and the lake, to the pinking dawn—just a trace now—a significant thing in itself at this hour surely—the new dawn, so wondrously new for younger people—then back at himself. What could he wish for now—what hope for?

As he did so his dream came back to him—that strange dream of seeking and being led and promised and yet always being led forward into a dimmer, darker land. What did that mean? Had it any real significance? Was it all to be dimmer, darker still? Was it typical of his life? He pondered.

"Free!" he said after a time. "Free! I know now how that is. I am free now, at last! Free! ... Free! ... Yes—free ... to die!"

So he stood there ruminating and smoothing his hair and his beard.

St. Columba and the River

The first morning that McGlathery saw the great river stretching westward from the point where the initial shaft had been sunk he was not impressed by it—or, rather, he was, but not favorably. It looked too gray and sullen, seeing that he was viewing it through a driving, sleety rain. There were many ferry boats and craft of all kinds, large and small, streaming across its choppy bosom, giant steamers, and long projecting piers, great and mysterious, and clouds of gulls, and the shriek of whistles, and the clang of fog-bells, . . . but he did not like water. It took him back to eleven wretched seasick days in which he had crossed on the steamer from Ireland. But then, glory be, once freed from the mysteries of Ellis Island, he had marched out on dry land at the Battery, cloth bags in hand, and exclaimed, "Thanks be, I'm shut av it!"

And he thought he was, for he was mortally afraid of water. But fate, alas! had not decreed it as a permanent thing. As a matter of fact, water in one form or another had persistently seemed to pursue him since. In Ireland, County Clare, from whence he hailed, he had been a ditcher—something remotely connected with water. Here in America, and once safely settled in Brooklyn, he had no sooner sought work than the best he could seemingly get was a job in connection with a marsh which was being drained, a very boggy and pool-y one—water again, you see. Then there was a conduit being dug, a great open sewer which once when he and other members of the construction gang were working on it, was flooded by a cloudburst, a tremendous afternoon rain-storm which drove them from it with a volume of water which threatened to drown them all. Still later, he and thirty others were engaged in cleaning out a two-compartment reservoir, old and stone-rotten, when, one-half being empty and the other full, the old dividing wall broke, and once more he barely escaped with his life by scrambling up a steep bank. It was then that the thought first took root in his mind that water—any kind of water, sea or fresh—was not favorable to him. Yet here he was, facing this great river on a gray rainy November morning, and with the avowed object of going to work in the tunnel which was about to be dug under it.

Think of it! In spite of his prejudices and fears, here he was, and all due to one Thomas Cavanaugh, a fellow churchman and his foreman these last three years, who had happened to take a fancy to him and had told him that if he came to work in the tunnel and prosecuted his new work thoroughly, and showed himself sufficiently industrious and courageous, it might lead to higher things—viz, bricklaying, or plastering, in the guise of cement moulding, down in this very tunnel, or timbering, or better yet, the steel-plate-joining trade, which was a branch of the ironworkers' guild and was rewarded by no less a compensation than twelve dollars a day. Think of it—twelve dollars a day! Men of this class and skill were scarce in tunnel work and in great demand in America. This same Cavanaugh was to be one of the foremen in this tunnel, his foreman, and would look after him. Of course it required time and patience. One had to begin at the bottom—the same being seventy-five feet under the Hudson River, where some very careful preliminary digging had to be done. McGlathery had surveyed his superior and benefactor at the time with uncertain and yet ambitious eyes.

"Is it as ye tell me now?" he commented at one place.

"Yis. Av course. What d'ye think I'm taalkin' to ye about?"

"Ye say, do ye?"

"Certainly."

"Well! Well! Belike it's a fine job. I dunno. Five dollars a day, ye say, to begin with?"

"Yis, five a day."

"Well, a man in my line could git no more than that, eh? It wouldn't hurt me fer once, fer a little while anyway, hey?"

"It would be the makin' av ye."

"Well, I'll be with ye. Yis, I'll be with ye. It's not five I can git everywhere. When is it ye'll be wantin' me?"

The foreman, a Gargantuan figure in yellow jeans and high rubber boots smeared to the buttocks with mud, eyed him genially and amiably, the while McGlathery surveyed his superior with a kind of reverence and awe, a reverence which he scarcely felt for any other man, unless perchance it might be his parish priest, for he was a good Catholic, or the political backer of his district, through whom he had secured his job. What great men they all were, to be sure, leading figures in his life.

So here he was on this particular morning shortly after the work had been begun, and here was the river, and down below in this new shaft, somewhere, was Thomas Cavanaugh, to whom he had to report before he could go to work.

"Sure, it's no colleen's job," he observed to a fellow worker who had arrived at the mouth of the shaft about the same time as himself, and was beginning to let himself down the ladder which sank darkly to an intermediate platform, below which again was another ladder and platform, and below that a yellow light. "Ye say Mr. Cavanaugh is below there?"

"He is," replied the stranger without looking up. "Ye'll find him inside the second lock. Arr ye workin' here?"

"Yis."

"Come along, then."

With a bundle which consisted of his rubber boots, a worn suit of overalls, and with his pick and shovel over his shoulder, he followed. He reached the bottom of the pit, boarded as to the sides with huge oak planks sustained by cross beams, and there, with several others who were waiting until the air pressure should be adjusted, entered the lock. The comparatively small and yet massive chamber, with its heavy iron door at either end, responding so slowly to pressure, impressed him. There was only a flickering light made by a gasoline torch here. There was a whistling sound from somewhere.

"Ever work under air pressure before, Paddy?" inquired a great hulking ironworker, surveying him with a genial leer.

"Air what?" asked McGlathery without the slightest comprehension of what was meant, but not to be outdone by mere words. "No, I never did."

"Well, ye're under it now, two thousand pounds to the square inch. Don't ye feel it?"

Dennis, who had been feeling an odd sensation about his eardrums and throat, but had no knowledge that it was related to this, acknowledged that he did. " 'Tis air, is it?" he inquired. " 'Tis a quare feeling I have." The hissing ceased.

"Yuh want to look out fer that, new man," volunteered another, a skimpy, slithery, genial American. "Don't let 'em rush that stuff on yuh too fast. Yuh may git the 'bends.' "

Dennis, ignorant as to the meaning of "bends," made no reply.

"D'yuh know what the 'bends' is, new man?" persisted the other provocatively.

"Naw," replied Dennis awkwardly after a time, feeling himself the centre of a fire of curious observation and solicitation.

"Well, yuh will if yuh ever git 'em—haw! haw!" this from a waggish lout, a bricklayer who had previously not spoken. The group in the lock was large. "It comes from them lettin' the pressure be put on or took off too fast. It twists yer muscles all up, an' does sumpin' to yer nerves. Yuh'll know it if yuh ever git it."

"Member Eddie Slawder?" called another gaily. "He died of it over here in Bellevue, after they started the Fourteenth Street end. Gee, yuh oughta heerd him holler! I went over to see him."

Good news, indeed! So this was his introduction to the tunnel, and here was a danger not commented on by Cavanaugh. In his dull way McGlathery was moved by it. Well, he was here now, and they were forcing open the door at the opposite side of the lock, and the air pressure had not hurt him, and he was not killed yet; and then, after traversing a rather neatly walled section of tunnel, albeit badly littered with beams and plates and bags of cement and piles of brick, and entering another lock like the first and coming out on the other side—there, amid an intricate network of beams and braces and a flare of a half dozen great gasoline lamps which whistled noisily, and an overhanging mass of blackness which was nothing less than earth under the great river above, was Cavanaugh, clad in a short red sweater and great rubber boots, an old yellowish-brown felt hat pulled jauntily over one ear. He was conversing with two other foremen and an individual in good clothes, one of those mighties— an engineer, no doubt.

Ah, how remote to McGlathery were the gentlemen in smooth fitting suits! He viewed them as you might creatures from another realm.

Beyond this lock also was a group of night workers left over from the night before and under a strange foreman (ditchers, joiners, earth carriers, and steel-plate riveters), all engaged in the rough and yet delicate risk of forcing and safeguarding a passage under the river, and only now leaving. The place was full. It was stuffy from the heat of the lamps, and dirty from the smear of the black muck which was over everything. Cavanaugh spied Dennis as he made his way forward over the widely separated beams.

"So here ye arr! These men are just after comin' out," and he waved a hand toward the forward end of the tunnel. "Git in there, Dennis, and dig out that corner beyond the post there. Jerry here'll help ye. Git the mud up on this platform so we can git these j'ists in here."

McGlathery obeyed. Under the earthy roof whose surface he could see but dimly at the extreme forward end of the tunnel beyond that wooden framework, he took his position. With a sturdy arm and a sturdy back and a sturdy foot and leg, he pushed his spade into the thick mud, or loosened it with his pick when necessary, and threw it up on the crude platform, where other men shoveled it into a small car which was then trundled back over the rough boards to the lock, and so on out. It was slow, dirty, but not difficult work, so long as one did not think of the heavy river overhead with its ships and its choppy waves in the rain, and the gulls and the bells. Somehow, Dennis was fearfully disturbed as to the weight of this heavy volume of earth and water overhead. It really terrified him. Perhaps he had been overpersuaded by the lure of gold? Suppose it should break through, suppose the earth over his head should suddenly drop and bury him—that dim black earth overhead, as heavy and thick as this he was cutting with his shovel now.

"Come, Dennis, don't be standin' there lookin' at the roof.

The roof's not goin' to hurt ye. Ye're not down here to be lookin' after the roof. I'll be doin' that. Just ye 'tend to yer shovelin'."

It was the voice of Cavanaugh near at hand. Unconsciously McGlathery had stopped and was staring upward. A small piece of earth had fallen and struck him on the back. Suppose! Suppose!

Know, O reader, that the business of tunneling is one of the most hazardous and dramatic, albeit interesting, of all known fields of labor. It consists, in these latter days at least, in so far as under-water tunneling is concerned, of sinking huge shafts at either end or side of a river, lake or channel (one hundred feet, perhaps, within the shore line) to a depth of, say, thirty feet below the water level, and from these two points tunneling outward under the bottom of the river until the two ends meet somewhere near the middle. The exact contact and precise joining of these outer ends is considered one of the true tests of skilful engineering. McGlathery personally understood all this but dimly. And even so it could not cheer him any.

And it should be said here that the safety of the men who did the work, and the possibility of it, depended first on the introduction at either end, just at the base of the shafts and then at about every hundred or so feet, as the tunnel progressed outward, of huge cylindrical chambers, or locks, of heavy iron— air locks, no less—fifteen feet in diameter, and closed at each end by massive doors swinging inward toward the shore line, so that the amazing and powerful pressure of air constantly forced outward from the shore by huge engines could not force them open. It was only by the same delicate system which causes water locks to open and close that they could be opened at all. That is, workingmen coming down into the shaft and desiring to pass into the head of the tunnel beyond the lock, would have to first enter one of these locks, which would then gradually be filled with air compressed up to the same pressure as that maintained in the main portion of the tunnel farther in. When this pressure had been reached they could easily open the inward swinging door and pass into the tunnel proper. Here, provided that so much had been completed, they might walk, say, so much as a hundred or more feet, when they would encounter another lock.

The pressure in the lock, according to who had last used it, would be either that of the section of the tunnel toward the shore, or of the section beyond, toward the centre of the river. At first, bell cords, later telephones, and then electric signals controlled this—that is, the lowering or raising of the pressure of air in the locks so that one door or the other might be opened. If the pressure in the lock was different from that in your section, and you could not open the door (which you could not), you pulled the cord or pushed the button so many times, according to your position, and the air in the lock was adjusted to the section of the tunnel in which you stood. Then you could open the door. Once in, as in a water lock, the air was raised or lowered, according to your signal, and you could enter the next section outward or inward. All these things had been adjusted to a nicety even in those days, which was years ago.

II

The digging of this particular tunnel seemed safe enough —for McGlathery at least, once he began working here. It moved at the rate of two and even three feet a day, when things were going well, only there were days and days when, owing to the need of shoring and timbering and plate setting, to say nothing of the accidental encountering of rock in front which had to be drilled away, the men with picks and shovels had to be given a rest, or better yet, set to helping the joiners in erecting those cross beams and supports which made the walls safe. It was so that Dennis learned much about joining and even drilling.

Nevertheless, in spite of the increased pay, this matter of working under the river was a constant source of fear to him. The earth in which he worked was so uncertain. One day it would be hard black mud, another soft, another silt, another sand, according as the tunnel sloped further and further under the bed. In addition, at times great masses of it fell, not enough to make a hole in the roof above, but enough, had it chanced to fall on one of the workers, to break his back or half bury him in mud. Usually it was broken by the beams overhead. Only one day, some seven months after he had begun and when he was becoming fairly accustomed to the idea of working here, and when his skill had increased to such an extent that he was considered one of the most competent workers in his limited field, the unexpected happened.

He had come down one morning at eight with the rest of his gang and was working about the base of two new supports which had just been put in place, when he noticed, or thought he did, that the earth seemed wetter than usual, sticky, watery, and hard to manage. It could not have been much worse had a subterranean spring been encountered. Besides, one of the gasoline lamps having been brought forward and hung close by, he noticed by its light that the ceiling seemed to look silvery gray and beady. He spoke of it to Cavanaugh, who stood by.

"Yis," said his foreman dubiously, staring upward, " 'tis wet. Maybe the air pumps is not workin' right. I'll just make sure," and he sent word to the engineer.

The shaft superintendent himself appeared.

"Everything's all right up above," he said. "Two thousand pounds to the square inch. I'll just put on a little more, if you say so."

"Ye'd better," replied Cavanaugh. "The roof's not actin' right. And if ye see Mr. Henderson, send him down. I'd like to talk to him."

"All right," and off he went.

McGlathery and the others, at first nervous, but now slightly reassured, worked on. But the ground under their feet became sloppy, and some of the silvery frosting on the roof began to drop and even trickle as water. Then a mass of sloppy mud fell.

"Back, men!"

It was the voice of Cavanaugh, but not quicker than the scampering of the men who, always keenly alive to the danger of a situation, had taken note of the dripping water and the first flop of earth. At the same time, an ominous creak from one of the beams overhead gave warning of the imminence of a catastrophe. A pell-mell rush for the lock some sixty feet away ensued. Tools were dropped, precedence disregarded. They fell and stumbled over the beams and between, pushing each other out of the way into the water and mud as they ran, McGlathery a fair second to none.

"Open the door! Open the door!" was the cry as they reached the lock, for some one had just entered from the other side—the engineer. "For Christ's sake, open the door!" But that could not be done so quickly. A few moments at least had to elapse.

"It's breakin' in!" cried some one in a panicky voice, an iron-worker.

"Great God, it's coming down!" this from one of the masons, as three lamps in the distance were put out by the mud.

McGlathery was almost dying of fear. He was sweating a cold sweat. Five dollars a day indeed! He should stay away from water, once and for all. Didn't he know that? It was always bad luck to him.

"What's the trouble? What's the trouble?" called the amazed engineer as, unconscious of what was happening outside, he pushed open the door.

"Git out of the way!"

"Fer God's sake, let us in!"

"Shut the door!" this from a half dozen who had already reached safety assuming that the door could be instantly closed.

"Wait! Cavanaugh's outside!" This from some one—not McGlathery, you may be sure, who was cowering in a corner. He was so fearful that he was entirely unconscious of his superior's fate.

"To hell with Cavanaugh! Shut the door!" screamed another, a great ironworker, savage with fear.

"Let Cavanaugh in, I say!" this from the engineer.

At this point McGlathery, for the first time on this or any other job, awoke to a sense of duty, but not much at that. He was too fearful. This was what he got for coming down here at all. He knew Cavanaugh—Cavanaugh was his friend, indeed. Had he not secured him this and other jobs? Surely. But then Cavanaugh had persuaded him to come down here, which was wrong. He ought not to have done it. Still, even in his fear he had manhood enough to feel that it was not quite right to shut Cavanaugh out. Still, what could he do—he was but one. But even as he thought, and others were springing forward to shut Cavanaugh out, so eager were they to save themselves, they faced a gleaming revolver in the steady hand of the big fore-man.

"I'll shoot down the first damned man that tries to shut the door before me and Kelly are in," the big foreman was calling, the while he was pulling this same Kelly from the mud and slime outside. Then fairly throwing him into the lock, and leaping after him, he turned and quietly helped close the door.

McGlathery was amazed at this show of courage. To stop and help another man like that in the face of so much danger! Cavanaugh was even a better and kinder man than he had thought—really a great man—no coward like himself. But why had Cavanaugh persuaded him to come down here when he knew that he was afraid of water! And now this had happened. Inside as they cowered—all but Cavanaugh—they could hear the sound of crushing timber and grinding brick outside, which made it quite plain that where a few moments before had been beams and steel and a prospective passageway for men, was now darkness and water and the might of the river, as it had been since the beginning.

McGlathery, seeing this, awoke to the conviction that in the first place he was a great coward, and in the second that the tunnel digging was no job for him. He was by no means fitted for it, he told himself. " 'Tis the last," he commented, as he climbed safely out with the others after a distressing wait of ten minutes at the inward lock. "Begob, I thought we was all lost. 'Twas a close shave. But I'll go no more below. I've had enough." He was thinking of a small bank account—six hundred dollars in all—which he had saved, and of a girl in Brooklyn who was about to marry him. "No more!"

III

But, at that, as it stood, there was no immediate danger of work being offered. The cave-in had cost the contractors thousands and in addition had taught them that mere air pressure and bracing as heretofore followed were not sufficient for successful tunneling. Some new system would have to be devised. Work on both halves of the tunnel was suspended for over a year and a half, during which time McGlathery married, a baby was born to him, and his six hundred had long since diminished to nothing. The difference between two and five dollars a day is considerable. Incidentally, he had not gone near his old foreman in all this time, being somehow ashamed of himself, and in consequence he had not fared so well. Previously Cavanaugh had kept him almost constantly employed, finding him faithful and hard-working, but now owing to stranger associates there were weeks when he had no work at all and others when he had to work for as little as one-fifty a day. It was not so pleasant. Besides, he had a sneaking feeling that if he had behaved a little more courageously at that time, gone and talked to his old foreman afterwards or at the time, he might now be working for good pay. Alas, he had not done so, and if he went now Cavanaugh would be sure to want to know why he had disappeared so utterly. Then, in spite of his marital happiness, poverty began to press him so. A second and a third child were born—only they were twins.

In the meantime, Henderson, the engineer whom Cavanaugh had wanted to consult with at the time, had devised a new system of tunneling, namely, what subsequently came to be known as the pilot tunnel. This was an iron tube ten feet in length and fifteen feet in diameter—the width of the tunnel, which was carried forward on a line with the axis of the tunnel into the ground ahead. When it was driven in far enough to be completely concealed by the earth about, then the earth within was removed. The space so cleared was then used exactly as a hub is used on a wagon wheel. Beams like spokes were radiated from its sides to its centre, and the surrounding earth sustained by heavy iron plates. On this plan the old company had decided to undertake the work again.

One evening, sitting in his doorway thumbing his way through an evening paper which he could barely read, Mc-Glathery had made all this out. Mr. Henderson was to be in charge as before. Incidentally it was stated that Thomas Cavanaugh was going to return as one of the two chief foremen. Work was to be started at once. In spite of himself, McGlathery was impressed. If Cavanaugh would only take him back! To be sure, he had come very near losing his life, as he thought, but then he had not. No one had, not a soul. Why should *he* be so fearful if Cavanaugh could take such chances as he had? Where else could he make five dollars a day? Still, there was this haunting sensation that the sea and all of its arms and branches, wherever situated, were inimical to him and that one day one of them would surely do him a great injury—kill him, perhaps. He had a recurring sensation of being drawn up into water or down, he could not tell which, and of being submerged in ooze and choking slowly. It was horrible.

But five dollars a day as against one-fifty or two or none at all (seven, once he became very proficient) and an assured future as a tunnel worker, a "sand-hog," as he had now learned such men as himself were called, was a luring as well as a disturbing thought. After all, he had no trade other than this he had begun to learn under Cavanaugh. Worse he was not a union man, and the money he had once saved was gone, and he had a wife and three children. With the former he had various and sundry talks. To be sure, tunneling was dangerous, but still! She agreed with him that he had better not, but—after all, the difference that five, maybe seven, instead of two a day would make in their living expenses was in both their minds. McGlathery saw it. He decided after a long period of hesitation that perhaps he had best return. After all, nothing had happened to him that other time, and might it ever again, really? He meditated.

As has been indicated, a prominent element in McGlathery's nature was superstition. While he believed in the inimical nature of water to him, he also believed in the power of various saints, male and female, to help or hinder. In the Catholic Church of St. Columba of South Brooklyn, at which McGlathery and his young wife were faithful attendants, there was a plaster statue of a saint of this same name, a co-worker with St. Patrick in Ireland, it appears, who in McGlathery's native town of Kilrush, County of Clare, on the water's edge of Shannon, had been worshipped for centuries past, or at least highly esteemed, as having some merit in protecting people at sea, or in adventures connected with water. This was due, perhaps, to the fact that Kilrush was directly on the water and had to have a saint of that kind. At any rate, among other things, he had occasionally been implored for protection in that realm when McGlathery was a boy. On his setting out for America, for instance, some few years before at the suggestion of his mother, he had made a novena before this very saint, craving of him a safe conduct in crossing the sea, as well as prosperity once he had arrived in America. Well, he had crossed in safety, and prospered well enough, he thought. At least he had not been killed in any tunnel. In consequence, on bended knees, two blessed candles burning before him in the rack, a half dollar deposited in the box labeled "St. Columba's Orphans," he finally asked of this saint whether, in case he returned to this underground tunnel work, seeing that necessity was driving him, would he be so kind as to protect him? He felt sure that Cavanaugh, once he applied to him, and seeing that he had been a favorite worker, would not begrudge him a place if he had one. In fact he knew that Cavanaugh had always favored him as a good useful helper.

After seven "Our Fathers" and seven "Hail Marys," said on his knees, and a litany of the Blessed Virgin for good measure, he crossed himself and arose greatly refreshed. There was a pleasant conviction in his mind now, newly come there before this image, that he would never come to real harm by any power of water. It was a revelation—a direct communication, perhaps. At any rate, something told him to go and see Cavanaugh at once, before the work was well under way, and not be afraid, as no harm would come to him, and besides, he might not get anything even though he desired it so much if he delayed. He bustled out of the church and over to the waterfront where the deserted shaft was still standing, and sure enough, there was Cavanaugh, conversing with Mr. Henderson.

"Yis—an' what arr ye here fer?" he now demanded to know of McGlathery rather amusedly, for he had sensed the cause of his desertion.

"I was readin' that ye was about to start work on the tunnel again."

"An' so we arr. What av it?"

"I was thinkin' maybe ye'd have a place fer me. I'm married now an' have three children."

"An' ye're thinkin' that's a reason fer givin' ye something, is it?" demanded the big foreman rather cynically, with a trace of amusement. "I thought ye said ye was shut av the sea—that ye was through now, once an' fer all?"

"So I did, but I've changed me mind. It's needin' the work I am."

"Very well, then," said Cavanaugh. "We're beginnin' in the mornin'. See that ye're here at seven sharp. An' mind ye, no worryin' or lookin' around. We've a safe way now. It's different. There's no danger."

McGlathery gratefully eyed his old superior, then departed, only to return the next morning a little dubious but willing. St. Columba had certainly indicated that all would be well with him—but still—— A man is entitled to a few doubts even when under the protection of the best of saints. He went down with the rest of the men and began cleaning out that nearest section of the tunnel where first water and then earth had finally oozed and caked. That done he helped install the new pilot tunnel which was obviously a great improvement over the old system. It seemed decidedly safe. McGlathery attempted to explain its merits to his wife, who was greatly concerned for him, and incidentally each morning and evening on his way to and from his task he dropped in at St. Columba's to offer up a short silent prayer. In spite of his novena and understanding with the saint he was still suspicious of this dread river above him, and of what might happen to him in spite of St. Columba. The good saint, due to some error on the part of McGlathery, might change his mind.

Nothing happened, of course, for days and weeks and months. Under Cavanaugh's direction the work progressed swiftly, and McGlathery and he, in due time, became once more good friends, and the former an expert bracer or timberer, one of the best, and worth seven a day really, which he did not get. Incidentally, they were all shifted from day to night work, which somehow was considered more important. There were long conversations now and again between Cavanaugh and Henderson, and Cavanaugh and other officials of the company who came down to see, which enlightened McGlathery considerably as to the nature and danger of the work. Just the same, overhead was still the heavy river—he could feel it pushing at him at times, pushing at the thick layer of mud and silt above him and below which with the aid of this new pilot shield they were burrowing.

Yet nothing happened for months and months. They cleared a thousand feet without a hitch. McGlathery began to feel rather comfortable about it all. It certainly seemed reasonably safe under the new system. Every night he went down and every morning came up, as hale and healthy as ever, and every second week, on a Tuesday, a pay envelope containing the handsome sum of seventy-two dollars was handed him. Think of it! Seventy-two dollars! Naturally, as a token of gratitude to St. Columba, he contributed liberally to his Orphan's Home, a dollar a month, say, lit a fresh candle before his shrine every Sunday morning after high mass, and bought two lots out on the Goose Creek waterfront—on time—on which some day, God willing, he proposed to build a model summer and winter cottage. And then—! Well, perhaps, as he thought afterward, it might have been due to the fact that his prosperity had made him a little more lax than he should have been, or proud, or not quite as thoughtful of the saint as was his due. At any rate, one night, in spite of St. Columba—or could it have been with his aid and consent in order to show McGlathery his power?—the wretched sneaky river did him another bad turn, a terrible turn, really.

It was this way. While they were working at midnight under the new form of bracing, based on the pilot tunnel, and with an air pressure of two thousand pounds to the square inch which had so far sufficed to support the iron roof plates which were being put in place behind the pilot tunnel day after day, as fast as space permitted, and with the concrete men following to put in a form of arch which no river weight could break, the very worst happened. For it was just at this point where the iron roof and the mud of the river bottom came in contact behind the pilot tunnel that there was a danger spot ever since the new work began. Cavanaugh had always been hovering about that, watching it, urging others to be careful—"taking no chances with it," as he said.

"Don't be long, men!" was his constant urge. "Up with it now! Up with it! In with the bolts! Quick, now, with yer riveter —quick! quick!"

And the men! How they worked there under the river whenever there was sufficient space to allow a new steel band to be segmentally set! For at that point it was, of course, that the river might break through. How they tugged, sweated, grunted, cursed, in this dark muddy hole, lit by a few glittering electric arcs—the latest thing in tunnel work! Stripped to the waist, in mud-soaked trousers and boots, their arms and backs and breasts mud-smeared and wet, their hair tousled, their eyes bleary—an artist's dream of bedlam, a heavenly inferno of toil—so they labored. And overhead was the great river, Atlantic liners resting upon it, thirty or fifteen or ten feet of soil only, sometimes, between them and this thin strip of mud sustained, supposedly, by two thousand pounds of air pressure to the square inch—all they had to keep the river from bleeding water down on them and drowning them like rats!

"Up with it! Up with it! Up with it! Now the bolts! Now the riveter! That's it! In with it, Johnny! Once more now!"

Cavanaugh's voice urging them so was like music to them, their gift of energy, their labor song, their power to do, their Ei Uchnam.

But there were times also, hours really, when the slow forward movement of the pilot tunnel, encountering difficult earth before it, left this small danger section unduly exposed to the rotary action of the water overhead which was constantly operating in the bed of the river. Leaks had been discovered from time to time, small tricklings and droppings of earth, which brought Cavanaugh and Henderson to the spot and caused the greatest tension until they had been done away with. The air had a tendency to bore holes upward through the mud. But these were invariably stanched with clay, or, if growing serious, bags of shavings or waste, the air pressure blowing outward from below being sufficient to hold these in place, provided the breach was not too wide. Even when "all hands" were working directly under a segment wide enough for a ring of plates, one man was told off to "kape an eye on it."

On the evening in question, however, after twenty-eight men, including Cavanaugh and McGlathery, had entered at six and worked until midnight, pushing the work as vigorously as usual, seven of the men (they were told off in lots of seven to do this) were allowed to go up to the mouth of the tunnel to a nearby all-night saloon for a drink and a bite of food. A half hour to each lot was allowed, when another group would depart. There was always a disturbing transition period every half hour between twelve and two, during which one group was going and another coming, which resulted at times in a dangerous indifference which Cavanaugh had come to expect at just about this time and in consequence he was usually watching for it.

On the other hand, John Dowd, ditcher, told off to keep an eye on the breach at this time, was replaced on this particular night by Patrick Murtha, fresh from the corner saloon, a glass of beer and the free lunch counter still in his mind. He was supposed to watch closely, but having had four glasses in rapid succession and meditating on their excellence as well as that of the hot frankfurters, the while he was jesting with the men who were making ready to leave, he forgot about it. What now—was a man always to keep his eye on the blanked thing! What was going to happen anyway? What could happen? Nothing, of course. What had ever happened in the last eight months?

"Sssst!"

What was that? A sound like the blowing off of steam. All at once Cavanaugh, who was just outside the pilot tunnel indicating to McGlathery and another just where certain braces were to be put, in order that the pilot tunnel might be pushed forward a few inches for the purpose of inserting a new ring of plates, heard it. At a bound he was back through the pilot hub, his face aflame with fear and rage. Who had neglected the narrow breach?

"Come now! What the hell is this?" he was about to exclaim, but seeing a wide breach suddenly open and water pour down in a swift volume, his spirit sank and fear overcame him.

"Back men! Stop the leak!"

It was the cry of a frightened and yet courageous man at bay. There was not only fear, but disappointment, in it. He had certainly hoped to obviate anything like this this time. But where a moment before had been a hole that might have been stopped with a bag of sawdust (and Patrick Murtha was there attempting to do it) was now a rapidly widening gap through which was pouring a small niagara of foul river water, ooze and slime. As Cavanaugh reached it and seized a bag to stay it, another mass of muddy earth fell, striking both him and

Murtha, and half blinding them both. Murtha scrambled away for his life. McGlathery, who had been out in the front of the fatal tunnel with others, now came staggering back horribly frightened, scarcely knowing what to do.

"Quick, Dennis! Into the lock!" Cavanaugh called to him, while he himself held his ground. "Hurry!" and realizing the hopelessness of it and his own danger, Dennis thought to run past, but was stopped by the downpour of water and mud.

"Quick! Quick! Into the lock! For Christ's sake, can't ye see what's happenin'? Through with ye!"

McGlathery, hesitating by his chief's side, fearful to move lest he be killed, uncertain this time whether to leave his chief or not, was seized by Cavanaugh and literally thrown through, as were others after him, the blinding ooze and water choking them, but placing them within range of safety. When the last man was through Cavanaugh himself plunged after, wading knee-deep in mud and water.

"Quick! Quick! Into the lock!" he called, and then seeing McGlathery, who was now near it but waiting for him, added, "In, in!" There was a mad scramble about the door, floating timbers and bags interfering with many, and then, just as it seemed as if all would reach safety, an iron roof plate overhead, loosened by the breaking of plates beyond, gave way, felling one man in the half-open doorway of the lock and blocking and pinning it in such a way that it could be neither opened nor closed. Cavanaugh and others who came up after were shut out. McGlathery, who had just entered and saw it, could do nothing. But in this emergency, and unlike his previous attitude, he and several others on the inside seized upon the dead man and tried to draw him in, at the same time calling to Cavanaugh to know what to do. The latter, dumbfounded, was helpless. He saw very clearly and sadly that very little if anything could be done. The plate across the dead man was too heavy, and besides, the ooze was already pouring over him into the lock. At the same time the men in the lock, conscious that although they were partially on the road to safety they were still in danger of losing their lives, were frantic with fear.

Actually there were animal roars of terror. At the same time

McGlathery, once more realizing that his Nemesis, water, had overtaken him and was likely to slay him at last, was completely paralyzed with fear. St. Columba had promised him, to be sure, but was not this that same vision that he had had in his dreams, that awful sense of encroaching ooze and mud? Was he not now to die this way, after all? Was not his patron saint truly deserting him? It certainly appeared so.

"Holy Mary! Holy St. Columba!" he began to pray, "what shall I do now? Mother of God! Our Father, who art in Heaven! Bejasus, it's a tight place I'm in now! I'll never get out of this! Tower of Ivory! House of Gold! Can't we git him in, boys? Ark of the Covenant! Gate of Heaven!"

As he gibbered and chattered, the others screaming about him, some pulling at the dead man, others pulling at the other door, the still eye of Cavanaugh outside the lock waist-deep in mud and water was surveying it all.

"Listen to me, men!" came his voice in rich, heavy, guttural tones. "You, McGlathery! Dennis! Arr ye all crazy! Take aaf your clothes and stop up the doorway! It's yer only chance! Aaf with yer clothes, quick! And those planks there—stand them up! Never mind us. Save yerselves first. Maybe ye can do something for us afterwards."

As he argued, if only the gap in the door could be closed and the compressed air pushing from the tunnel outward toward the river allowed to fill the chamber, it would be possible to open the other door which gave into the next section shoreward, and so they could all run to safety.

His voice, commanding, never quavering, even in the face of death, subsided. About and behind him were a dozen men huddled like sheep, waist-deep in mud and water, praying and crying. They had got as close to him as might be, still trying to draw upon the sustaining force of his courage, but moaning and praying just the same and looking at the lock.

"Yis! Yis!" exclaimed McGlathery of a sudden, awakening at last to a sense of duty and that something better in conduct and thought which he had repeatedly promised himself and his saint that he would achieve. He had been forgetting. But now it seemed to him once more that he had been guilty of that same great wrong to his foreman which had marked his attitude on the previous occasion—that is, he had not helped him or any one but himself. He was a horrible coward. But what could he do? he asked himself. What could he do? Tearing off his coat and vest and shirt as commanded, he began pushing them into the opening, calling to the others to do the same. In a twinkling, bundles were made of all as well as of the sticks and beams afloat in the lock, and with these the gap in the door was stuffed, sufficiently to prevent the air from escaping, but shutting out the foreman and his men completely.

"It's awful. I don't like to do it," McGlathery kept crying to his foreman but the latter was not so easily shaken.

"It's all right, boys," he kept saying. "Have ye no courage at aal?" And then to the others outside with him, "Can't ye stand still and wait? They may be comin' back in time. Kape still. Say yer prayers if ye know any, and don't be afraid."

But, although the air pressing outward toward Cavanaugh held the bundles in place, still was not sufficient to keep all the air in or all the water out. It poured about the dead man and between the chinks, rising inside to their waists also. Once more it threatened their lives and now their one hope was to pull open the shoreward door and so release themselves into the chamber beyond, but this was not to be done unless the escaping air was completely blocked or some other method devised.

Cavanaugh, on the outside, his whole mind still riveted on the men whom he was thus aiding to escape, was the only one who realized what was to be done. In the panel of the door which confronted him, and the other, which they were trying to break open, were thick glass plates, or what were known as bull's eyes, through which one could see, and it was through the one at his end that Cavanaugh was peering. When it became apparent to him that the men were not going to be able to open the farthest door, a new thought occurred to him. Then it was that his voice was heard above the tumult, shouting:

"Break open the outside bull's eye! Listen to me, Dennis! Listen to me! Break open the outside bull's eye!"

Why did he call to Dennis, the latter often asked himself afterwards. And why did Dennis hear him so clearly? Through a bedlam of cries within, he heard, but also realized that if he ᴗ they knocked out the bull's eye in the other door, and the air escaped through it inward, the chances of their opening it would be improved, but the life of Cavanaugh and his helpless companions would certainly be destroyed. The water would rush inward from the river filling up this chamber and the space in which stood Cavanaugh. Should he? So he hesitated.

"Knock it out!" came the muffled voice of his foreman from within where he was eyeing him calmly. "Knock it out, Dennis! It's yer only chance! Knock it out!" And then, for the first time in all the years he had been working for him, McGlathery heard the voice of his superior waver slightly: "If ye're saved," it said, "try and do what ye can fer the rest av us."

In that moment McGlathery was reborn spiritually. Although he could have wept, something broke in him—fear. He was not afraid now for himself. He ceased to tremble, almost to hurry and awoke to a new idea, one of undying, unfaltering courage. What! There was Cavanaugh outside there, unafraid, and here was he, Dennis McGlathery, scrambling about like a hare for his life! He wanted to go back, to do something, but what could he? It was useless. Instead, he assumed partial command in here. The spirit of Cavanaugh seemed to come over to him and possess him. He looked about, saw a great stave, and seized it.

"Here, men!" he called with an air of command. "Help knock it out!" and with a will born of terror and death a dozen brawny hands were laid on it. With a mighty burst of energy they assaulted the thick plate and burst it through. Air rushed in, and at the same time the door gave way before them, causing them to be swept outward by the accumulated water like straws. Then, scrambling to their feet, they tumbled into the next lock, closing the door behind them. Once in, they heaved a tremendous sigh of relief, for here they were safe enough for the time being anyhow. McGlathery, the new spirit of Cavanaugh in him, even turned and looked back through the bull's eye into the chamber they had just left. Even as they waited for the pressure here to lower sufficiently to permit them to open the inner door he saw this last chamber they had left his foreman and a dozen fellow workers buried beyond. But what could he do? Only God, only St. Columba, could tell him, perhaps, and St. Columba had saved him—or had he?—him and fifteen other men, the while he had chosen to allow Cavanaugh and twelve men to perish! Had St. Columba done that—or God—or who?

" 'Tis the will av God," he murmured humbly—but why had God done that?

IV

But somehow, the river was not done with him yet, and that, seemingly, in spite of himself. Although he prayed constantly for the repose of the soul of Thomas Cavanaugh and his men, and avoided the water, until five years later, still there was a sequel. By now McGlathery was the father of eight children and as poor as any average laborer. With the death of Cavanaugh and this accident, as has been said, he had forsworn the sea—or water—and all its works. Ordinary house shoring and timbering were good enough for him, only—only—it was so hard to get enough of this at good pay. He was never faring as well as he should. And then one day when he was about as hard up as ever and as earnest, from somewhere was wafted a new scheme in connection with this same old tunnel.

A celebrated engineer of another country—England, no less—had appeared on the scene with a new device, according to the papers. Greathead was his name, and he had invented what was known as "The Greathead Shield," which finally, with a few changes and adaptations, was to rid tunnel work of all its dangers. McGlathery, sitting outside the door of his cottage overlooking Bergen Bay, read it all in the Evening *Clarion*, and wondered whether it could be true. He did not understand very much about this new shield idea even now, but even so, and in spite of himself, some of the old zest for tunneling came back to him. What times he had had, to be sure! What a life it had been, if a dog's one—and Cavanaugh—what a foreman! And his body was still down there entombed—erect, no doubt, as he was left. He wondered. It would be only fair to dig him out and honor his memory with a decent grave if it could be done. His wife and children were still living in Flatbush. It stirred up all the memories, old fears, old enthusiasms, but no particular desire to return. Still, here he was now, a man with a wife and eight children, earning three a day, no less—mostly less—

whereas tunneling paid seven and eight to such as himself, and he kept thinking that if this should start up again and men were advertised for, why shouldn't he go? His life had been almost miraculously saved these two times—but would it be again?— that was the great question. Almost unceasingly he referred the matter to his saint on Sundays in his church, but receiving no definite advice as yet and there being no work doing on the tunnel, he did nothing.

But then one day the following spring the papers were full of the fact that work would soon actually be resumed, and shortly thereafter, to his utter amazement, McGlathery received a note from that same Mr. Henderson under whom Cavanaugh had worked, asking him to call and see him. Feeling sure that it was the river that was calling him, he went over to St. Columba's and prayed before his saint, putting a dollar in his Orphan's box and a candle on his shrine, and then arising greatly refreshed and reassured, and after consulting with his wife, journeyed over to the river, where he found the old supervisor as before in a shed outside, considering one important matter and another.

What he wanted to know was this—did McGlathery want to take an assistant-foremanship under a new foreman who was going to be in charge of the day work here, one Michael Laverty by name, an excellent man, at seven dollars a day, seeing that he had worked here before and understood the difficulties, etc.? McGlathery stared in amazement. He an assistant-foreman in charge of timbering! And at seven dollars a day! He!

Mr. Henderson neglected to say that because there had been so much trouble with the tunnel and the difficulties so widely advertised, it was rather difficult to get just the right sort of men at first, although McGlathery was good enough any time. But the new shield made everything safe, he said. There could be no calamity this time. The work would be pushed right through. Mr. Henderson even went so far as to explain the new shield to him, its excellent points.

But McGlathery, listening, was dubious, and yet he was not thinking of the shield exactly now, nor of the extra pay he would receive, although that played a big enough part in his calculations, but of one Thomas Cavanaugh, mason foreman, and his twelve men, buried down below there in the ooze, and how he had left him, and how it would only be fair to take his bones out, his and the others', if they could be found, and give them a decent Christian burial. For by now he was a better Catholic than ever, and he owed that much to Cavanaugh, for certainly Cavanaugh had been very good to him—and anyhow, had not St. Columba protected him so far? And might he not in the future, seeing the position he was in? Wasn't this a call, really? He felt that it was.

Just the same, he was nervous and troubled, and went home and consulted with his wife again, and thought of the river and went over and prayed in front of the shrine of St. Columba. Then, once more spiritualized and strengthened, he returned and told Mr. Henderson that he would come back. Yes, he would come.

He felt actually free of fear, as though he had a mission, and the next day began by assisting Michael Laverty to get out the solid mass of earth which filled the tunnel from the second lock outward. It was slow work, well into the middle of the summer before the old or completed portion was cleared and the bones of Cavanaugh and his men reached. That was a great if solemn occasion—the finding of Cavanaugh and his men. They could recognize him by his big boots, his revolver, his watch, and a bunch of keys, all in position near his bones. These same bones and boots were then reverently lifted and transferred to a cemetery in Brooklyn, McGlathery and a dozen workers accompanying them, after which everything went smoothly. The new shield worked like a charm. It made eight feet a day in soft mud, and, although McGlathery, despite his revived courage, was intensely suspicious of the river, he was really no longer afraid of it in the old way. Something kept telling him that from now on he would be all right—not to fear. The river could never hurt him any more, really.

But just the same, a few months later—eight, to be exact— the river did take one last slap at him, but not so fatally as might have appeared on the surface, although in a very peculiar way, and whether with or without St. Columba's aid or consent, he never could make out. The circumstances were so very odd. This new cutting shield, as it turned out, was a cylinder thirteen feet long, twenty feet in diameter, and with a hardened steel cutting edge out on front, an apron, fifteen inches in length and three inches thick at the cutting edge. Behind this came what was known as an "outside diaphragm," which had several openings to let in the mud displaced by the shield's advance.

Back of these openings were chambers four feet in length, one chamber for each opening, through which the mud was passed. These chambers in turn had hinged doors, which regulated the quantity of mud admitted, and were water tight and easily closed. It was all very shipshape.

Behind these little chambers, again, were many steel jacks, fifteen to thirty, according to the size of the shield, driven by an air pressure of five thousand pounds to the square inch, which were used to push the shield forward. Back of them came what was known as the tail end of the shield, which reached back into the completed tunnel and was designed to protect the men who were at work putting in the new plates (at that danger point which had killed Cavanaugh) whenever the shield had been driven sufficiently forward to permit of a new ring of them.

The only danger involved in this part of the work lay in the fact that between this lining and the tail end of the shield was always a space of an inch to an inch and a half which was left unprotected. This small opening would, under ordinary circumstances, be insignificant, but in some instances where the mud covering at the top was very soft and not very thick, there was danger of the compressed air from within, pushing at the rate of several thousand pounds to the square inch, blowing it away and leaving the aperture open to the direct action of the water above. This was not anticipated, of course, not even thought of. The shield was going rapidly forward and it was predicted by Henderson and Laverty at intervals that the tunnel would surely go through within the year.

Some time the following winter, however, when the shield was doing such excellent work, it encountered a rock which turned its cutting edge and, in addition, necessitated the drilling out of the rock in front. A bulkhead had to be built, once sufficient stone had been cut away, to permit the repairing of the edge. This took exactly fifteen days. In the meantime, at the back of the shield, at the little crevice described, compressed air, two thousand pounds to the square inch, was pushing away at the mud outside, gradually hollowing out a cup-like depression eighty-five feet long (Mr. Henderson had soundings taken afterwards), which extended backward along the top of the completed tunnel toward the shore. There was then nothing but water overhead.

It was at this time that the engineers, listening to the river, which, raked by the outpouring of air from below, was rolling gravel and stones above the tunnel top and pounding on it like a drum, learned that such was the case. It was easy enough to fix it temporarily by stuffing the crevice with bags, but one of these days when the shield was repaired it would have to be moved forward to permit the insertion of a new ring of plates, and then, what?

At once McGlathery scented trouble. It was the wretched river again (water), up to its old tricks with him. He was seriously disturbed, and went to pray before St. Columba, but incidentally, when he was on duty, he hovered about this particular opening like a wasp. He wanted to know what was doing there every three minutes in the day, and he talked to the night foreman about it, as well as Laverty and Mr. Henderson. Mr. Henderson, at Laverty's and McGlathery's request, came down and surveyed it and meditated upon it.

"When the time comes to move the shield," he said, "you'll just have to keep plenty of bags stuffed around that opening, everywhere, except where the men are putting in the plates. We'll have extra air pressure that day, all we can stand, and I think that'll fix everything all right. Have plenty of men here to keep those bags in position, but don't let 'em know there's anything wrong, and we'll be all right. Let me know when you're ready to start, and I'll come down."

When the shield was eventually repaired and the order given to drive it just twenty-five inches ahead in order to permit the insertion of a new ring of plates, Mr. Henderson was there, as well as Laverty and McGlathery. Indeed, McGlathery was in charge of the men who were to stuff the bags and keep out the water. If you have ever seen a medium-sized red-headed Irishman when he is excited and determined, you have a good picture of McGlathery. He was seemingly in fifteen places at once, commanding, exhorting, persuading, rarely ever soothing—and worried. Yes, he was worried, in spite of St. Columba.

The shield started. The extra air pressure was put on, the water began to pour through the crevice, and then the bags were put in place and stopped most of it, only where the ironworkers were riveting on the plates it poured, poured so heavily at times that the workers became frightened.

"Come now! What's the matter wid ye! What arr ye standin' there fer? What arr ye afraid av? Give me that bag! Up with it! That's the idea! Do ye think ye're goin' to be runnin' away now?"

It was McGlathery's voice, if you please, commanding!—McGlathery, after his two previous experiences! Yet in his vitals he was really afraid of the river at this very moment.

What was it that happened? For weeks after, he himself, writhing with "bends" in a hospital, was unable to get it straight. For four of the bags of sawdust burst and blew through, he remembered that—it was a mistake to have sawdust bags at all. And then (he remembered that well enough), in stuffing others in, they found that they were a bag short, and until something was secured to put in its place, for the water was streaming in like a waterfall and causing a flood about their ankles, he, McGlathery, defiant to the core, not to be outdone by the river this time, commanded the great thing to be done.

"Here!" he shouted, "the three av ye," to three gaping men near at hand, "up with me! Put me there! I'm as good as a bag of sawdust any day. Up with me!"

Astonished, admiring, heartened, the three of them jumped forward and lifted him. Against the small breach, through which the water was pouring, they held him, while others ran off for more bags. Henderson and Laverty and the ironworkers, amazed and amused and made braver themselves because of this very thing—filled with admiration, indeed, by the sheer resourcefulness of it, stood by to help. But then, if you will believe it, while they were holding him there, and because now there was nothing but water above it, one end of the shield itself—yes, that great iron invention—was lifted by the tremendous air pressure below—eleven or thirteen or fourteen inches, whatever space you can imagine a medium sized man being forced through—and out he went, McGlathery, and all the bags, up into the river above, the while the water poured down, and the men fled for their lives.

A terrific moment, as you can well imagine, not long in duration, but just long enough to swallow up McGlathery, and then the shield, having responded at first to too much air pressure, now responding to too little (the air pressure having been lessened by the escape), shut down like a safety valve, shutting off most of the water and leaving the tunnel as it was before.

But McGlathery!

Yes, what of him?

Reader—a miracle!

A passing tug captain, steaming down the Hudson at three one bright December afternoon was suddenly astonished to see a small geyser of water lift its head some thirty feet from his boat, and at the top of it, as it were lying on it, a black object which at first he took to be a bag or a log. Later he made it out well enough, for it plunged and bellowed.

"Fer the love av God! Will no one take me out av this? Git me out av this! Oh! Oh! Oh!"

It was McGlathery right enough, alive and howling lustily and no worse for his blow-out save that he was suffering from a fair case of the "bends" and suffering mightily. He was able to scream, though, and was trying to swim. That old haunting sensation!—he had had it this time, sure enough. For some thirty or forty seconds or more he had been eddied swiftly along the top of the tunnel at the bottom of the river, and then coming to where the air richocheted upward had been hustled upward like a cork and literally blown through the air at the top of the great volume of water, out into space. The sudden shift from two thousand pounds of air pressure to none at all, or nearly none, had brought him down again, and in addition induced the severe case of "bends" from which he was now suffering. But St. Columba had not forgotten him entirely. Although he was suffering horribly, and was convinced that he was a dead man, still the good saint must have placed the tug conveniently near, and into this he was now speedily lifted.

"Well, of all things!" exclaimed Captain Hiram Knox, seeing him thoroughly alive, if not well, and eyeing him in astonishment. "Where do you come from?"

"Oh! Oh! Oh!" bawled McGlathery. "Me arms! Me ribs! Oh! Oh! Oh! The tunnel! The tunnel below, av course! Quick! Quick! It's dyin' av the bends I am! Git me to a hospital, quick!"

The captain, truly moved and frightened by his groans, did as requested. He made for the nearest dock. It took him but a few moments to call an ambulance, and but a few more before McGlathery was carried into the nearest hospital.

The house physician, having seen a case of this same disease two years before, and having meditated on it, had decided that the hair of the dog must be good for the bite. In consequence of this McGlathery was once more speedily carted off to one of the locks of this very tunnel, to the amazement of all who had known of him (his disappearance having aroused general excitement), and he was stared at as one who had risen from the grave. But, what was better yet, under the pressure of two thousand pounds now applied he recovered himself sufficiently to be host here and tell his story—another trick of his guardian saint, no doubt—and one rather flattering to his vanity, for he was now in no least danger of dying.

The whole city, if not the whole country, indeed, was astounded by the accident, and he was a true nine days' wonder, for the papers were full of the strange adventure. And with large pictures of McGlathery ascending heavenward, at the top of a geyser of water. And long and intelligent explanations as to the way and why of it all.

But, better yet, four of the happiest weeks of his life were subsequently spent in that same hospital to which he had first been taken relating to all and sundry his amazing adventure, he being interviewed by no less than five representatives of Sunday editors and eleven reporters for city dailies, all anxious to discover just how it was that he had been blown through water and air up through so great a thing as a river, and how he felt while en route. A triumph.

Rivers may be smart, but saints are smarter, thanks be.

And, to top it all, seeing that his right hand and arm might possibly be crippled for life, or at least an indefinite period (the doctors did not know), and in grateful appreciation of the fact that he had refused to deal with various wolfish lawyers who had now descended on him and urged him to sue for a large sum, he was offered a substantial pension by the company, or its equivalent, work with the company, no less, at good pay for the rest of his life, and a cash bonus into the bargain, a thing which seemed to solve his very uncertain future for him and put him at his ease. Once more the hand of the saint, you will certainly admit.

But, lastly, there was the peculiar spiritual consolation that comes with the feeling that you have done your duty and that a great saint is on your side. For if all these things did not prove that the good St. Columba had kept faith with him, what could? To be sure the river had attempted to do its worst, and had caused him considerable fear and pain, and perhaps St. Columba did not have as much control over the river as he should or as he might like to have, or—and this was far more likely—it was entirely possible that he (McGlathery) had not at all times deserved the good saint's support. But none the less, in the final extremity, had he not acted? And if not, how would you explain the fact that the tug *Mary Baker* was just at hand as he arose out of the water two thousand feet from shore? And why was it, if the saint had not been trying to help him, that the hospital doctor had seen to it that he was hustled off to a lock just in time—had seen, indeed, just such a case as this before, and known how to handle it? Incontrovertible facts all, aren't they?—or if not, why not?

At any rate McGlathery thought so, and on Sundays and holidays, whether there was or was not anything of importance being celebrated in his church, he might have been seen there kneeling before his favorite saint and occasionally eyeing him with both reverence and admiration. For, "Glory be," as he frequently exclaimed in narrating the wonderful event afterward, "I wasn't stuck between the shield and the tunnel, as I might 'a' been, and killed entirely, and sure, I've aaften thought 'tis a miracle that not enough water come in, just then, to drown 'em aal. It lifted up just enough to let me go out like a cork, and up I went, and then, God be praised, it shut down again. But, glory be, here I am, and I'm no worse fer it, though it do be that me hand wrenches me now and then."

And as for the good St. Columba—

Well, what about the good St. Columba?

McEwen of the Shining Slave Makers

It was a hot day in August. The parching rays of a summer
sun had faded the once sappy green leaves of the trees to a dull
and dusty hue. The grass, still good to look upon in shady places,
spread sere and dry where the light had fallen unbroken. The
roads were hot with thick dust, and wherever a stone path led,
it reflected heat to weary body and soul.

Robert McEwen had taken a seat under a fine old beech tree
whose broad arms cast a welcome shade. He had come here
out of the toil of the busy streets.

For a time he gave himself over to blank contemplation of
the broad park and the occasional carriages that jingled by.
Presently his meditation was broken by an ant on his trousers,
which he flipped away with his finger. This awoke him to the
thought that there might be more upon him. He stood up,
shaking and brushing himself. Then he noticed an ant running
along the walk in front of him. He stamped on it.

"I guess that will do for you," he said, half aloud, and sat
down again.

Now only did he really notice the walk. It was wide and hard
and hot. Many ants were hurrying about, and now he saw that
they were black. At last, one more active than the others fixed
his eye. He followed it with his glance for more than a score of
feet.

This particular ant was progressing urgently, now to the right, now to the left, stopping here and there, but never for more than a second. Its energy, the zig-zag course it pursued, the frequency with which it halted to examine something, enlisted his interest. As he gazed, the path grew in imagination until it assumed immense proportions.

Suddenly he bestirred himself, took a single glance and then jumped, rubbing his eyes. He was in an unknown world, strange in every detail. The branched and many-limbed trees had disappeared. A forest of immense flat swords of green swayed in the air above him. The ground between lacked its carpet of green and was roughly strewn with immense boulders of clay. The air was strong with an odor which seemed strange and yet familiar. Only the hot sun streaming down and a sky of faultless blue betokened a familiar world. In regard to himself McEwen felt peculiar and yet familiar. What was it that made these surroundings and himself seem odd and yet usual? He could not tell. His three pairs of limbs and his vigorous mandibles seemed natural enough. The fact that he sensed rather than saw things was natural and yet odd. Forthwith moved by a sense of duty, necessity, and a kind of tribal obligation which he more felt than understood, he set out in search of food and prey and presently came to a broad plain, so wide that his eye could scarce command more than what seemed an immediate portion of it. He halted and breathed with a feeling of relief. Just then a voice startled him.

"Anything to eat hereabout?" questioned the newcomer in a friendly and yet self-interested tone.

McEwen drew back.

"I do not know," he said, "I have just——"

"Terrible," said the stranger, not waiting to hear his answer. "It looks like famine. You know the Sanguineæ have gone to war."

"No," answered McEwen mechanically.

"Yes," said the other, "they raided the Fuscæ yesterday. They'll be down on us next."

With that the stranger made off. McEwen was about to exclaim at the use of the word *us* when a ravenous craving for food, brought now forcibly to his mind by the words of the other, made him start in haste after him.

Then came another who bespoke him in passing.

"I haven't found a thing to-day, and I've been all the way to the Pratensis region. I didn't dare go any further without having some others with me. They're hungry, too, up there, though they've just made a raid. You heard the Sanguineæ went to war, didn't you?"

"Yes, he told me," said McEwen, indicating the retreating figure of the stranger.

"Oh, Ermi. Yes, he's been over in their territory. Well, I'll be going now."

McEwen hastened after Ermi at a good pace, and soon overtook him. The latter had stopped and was gathering in his mandibles a jagged crumb, almost as large as himself.

"Oh!" exclaimed McEwen eagerly, "where did you get that?"

"Here," said Ermi.

"Will you give me a little?"

"I will not," said the other, and a light came in his eye that was almost evil.

"All right," said McEwen, made bold by hunger and yet cautious by danger, "which way would you advise me to look?"

"Wherever you please," said Ermi, "why ask me? You are not new at seeking," and strode off.

"The forest was better than this," thought McEwen; "there I would not die of the heat, anyhow, and I might find food. Here is nothing," and he turned and glanced about for a sight of the jungle whence he had come.

Far to the left and rear of him he saw it, those great up-standing swords. As he gazed, revolving in his troubled mind whether he should return or not, he saw another like himself hurrying toward him out of the distance.

He eagerly hailed the newcomer, who was yet a long way off.

"What is it?" asked the other, coming up rapidly.

"Do you know where I can get something to eat?"

"Is that why you called me?" he answered, eyeing him angrily. "Do you ask in time of famine? Certainly not. If I had anything for myself, I would not be out here. Go and hunt for it like the rest of us. Why should you be asking?"

"I have been hunting," cried McEwen, his anger rising. "I have searched here until I am almost starved."

"No worse off than any of us, are you?" said the other. "Look at me. Do you suppose I am feasting?"

He went off in high dudgeon, and McEwen gazed after him in astonishment. The indifference and sufficiency were at once surprising and yet familiar. Later he found himself falling rapidly into helpless lassitude from both hunger and heat, when a voice, as of one in pain, hailed him.

"Ho!" it cried.

"Hello!" he answered.

"Come, come!" was the feeble reply.

McEwen started forward at once. When he was still many times his own length away he recognized the voice as that of his testy friend of a little while before, but now sadly changed. He was stretched upon the earth, working his mandibles feebly.

"What is it?" asked McEwen solicitously. "What ails you? How did this happen?"

"I don't know," said the other. "I was passing along here when that struck me," indicating a huge boulder. "I am done for, though. You may as well have this food now, since you are one of us. The tribe can use what you do not eat," he sighed.

"Oh, nothing of the sort," said McEwen solicitously, the while he viewed the crushed limbs and side of the sufferer. "You'll be all right. Why do you speak of death? Just tell me where to take you, or whom to go for."

"No," said the other, "it would be no use. You see how it is. They could do nothing for me. I did not want your aid. I merely wanted you to have this food here. I shall not want it now."

"Don't say that," returned McEwen. "You mustn't talk about dying. There must be something I can do. Tell me. I don't want your food."

"No, there isn't anything you could do. There isn't any cure, you know that. Report, when you return, how I was killed. Just leave me now and take that with you. They need it, if you do not."

McEwen viewed him silently. This reference to a colony or

tribe or home seemed to clarify many things for him. He remembered now apparently the long road he had come, the immense galleries of the colony to which he belonged under the earth, the passages by which he had made his way in and out, the powerful and revered ant mother, various larvæ to be fed and eggs to be tended. To be sure. That was it. He was a part of this immense colony or group. The heat must have affected his sensory powers. He must gather food and return there—kill spiders, beetles, grubs, and bring them back to help provision the colony. That was it. Only there were so few to be found here, for some reason.

The sufferer closed his eyes in evident pain, and trembled convulsively. Then he fell back and died.

McEwen gazed upon the now fast stiffening body, with all but indifference, and wondered. The spectacle seemed so familiar as to be all but commonplace. Apparently he had seen so many die that way. Had he not, in times past, reported the deaths of hundreds?

"Is he dead?" asked a voice at his side.

"Yes," said McEwen, scarcely bringing himself out of his meditation sufficiently to observe the newcomer.

"Well, then, he will not need this, I guess," said the other, and he seized upon the huge lump with his mandibles, but McEwen was on the alert and savage into the bargain, on the instant. He, too, gripped his mandibles upon it.

"I was called by him to have this, before he died," he shouted "and I propose to have it. Let go."

"That I will not," said the other with great vigor and energy. "I'll have some of it at least," and, giving a mighty wrench, which sent both himself and McEwen sprawling, he tore off a goodly portion of it and ran, gaining his feet so quickly that he was a good length off before McEwen arose. The latter was too hungry, however, to linger in useless rage, and now fell to and ate before any other should disturb him. Then, feeling partially satisfied, he stretched himself languorously and continued more at his leisure. After a time he shook himself out of his torpor which had seized on him with his eating, and made off for the distant jungle, in which direction, as he now felt, lay the colony home.

He was in one of the darkest and thickest portions of the route thither when there was borne to him from afar the sound of feet in marching time, and a murmuring as of distant voices. He stopped and listened. Presently the sounds grew louder and more individual. He could now tell that a great company was nearing him. The narrow path which he followed was clear for some distance, and open to observation. Not knowing what creatures he was about to meet, he stepped out of it into a thicket, at one side and took up a position behind a great boulder. The tramp of many feet was now so close as to bode contact and discovery, and he saw, through the interstices of green stalks, a strange column filing along the path he had left. They were no other than a company of red warriors—slave makers like himself, only of a different species, the fierce Sanguineæ that Ermi had spoken of as having gone to war.

To war they certainly had been, and no doubt were going again. Nearly every warrior carried with him some mark of plunder or of death. Many bore in their mandibles dead bodies of the enemy or their larvae captured from a Fuscan colony. Others bore upon their legs the severed heads of the poor blacks who had been slain in the defense of their home, and whose jaws still clung to their foes, fixed in the rigor of death. Still others dragged the bodies of their victims, and shouted as they went, making the long, lonely path to ring with uncanny sounds as they disappeared in the distance.

McEwen came furtively out after a time and looked after them. He had gotten far to the left of the warriors and somewhat to the front of them, and was just about to leave the shadow of one clump of bushes to hurry to a neighboring stone, when there filed out from the very shelter upon which he had his eye fixed, the figure of one whom he immediately recognized as Ermi. The latter seemed to await a favorable opportunity when he should not be observed, and then started running. McEwen followed. In the distance could be seen a group of the Sanguineæ, who had evidently paused for something, moving about in great excitement, in groups of two or three, gesticulating and talking. Some of those not otherwise engaged displayed a sensibility of danger or a lust of war by working their jaws and sawing at heavy stones with their mandibles. Presently one gazed in the direction of Ermi, and shouted to the others.

Immediately four warriors set out in pursuit. McEwen hastened after Ermi, to see what would become of him. Discreetly hidden himself, he could do this with considerable equanimity. As he approached, he saw Ermi moving backward and forward, endeavoring to close the entrance to a cave in which he had now taken refuge. Apparently that warrior had become aware that no time was to be lost, since he also could see the pursuing Sanguineæ. With a swiftness born of daring and a keen realization of danger, he arranged a large boulder at the very edge of the portal as a key, and then others in such position that when the first should topple in the others would follow. Then he crawled deftly inside the portal, and pulling the keystone, toppled the whole mass in after him.

This was hardly done when the Sanguineæ were upon him. They were four cruel, murderous fighters, deeply scarred. One, called by the others Og, had a black's head at his thigh. One of his temples bore a scar, and the tip of his left antenna was broken. He was a keen old warrior, however, and scented the prey at once.

"Hi, you!" he shouted to the others. "Here's the place."

Just then another drew near to the portal which Ermi had barricaded. He looked at it closely, walked about several times, sounded with his antennæ and then listened. There was no answer.

"Hist!" he exclaimed to the others.

Now they came up. They also looked, but so well had Ermi done his work that they were puzzled.

"I'm not sure," said Og, "it looks to me more like an abandoned cave than an entrance."

"Tear it open, anyway," advocated Ponan, the second of the quartette, speaking for the first time. "There may be no other exit."

"Aha!" cried Og, "Good! We will see anyhow."

"Come on!" yelled Maru, a third, seizing the largest boulder, "Mandibles to!"

"Out with him!" cried Om, jumping eagerly to work. "We will have him out in a jiffy!"

It was not an easy task, as the boulders were heavy and deep, but they tore them out. Later they dragged forth Ermi, who, finding himself captured, seized the head of Maru with his mandibles. Og, on the other hand, seized one of Ermi's legs in his powerful jaws. The others also had taken hold. The antennæ of all were thrown back, and the entire mass went pushing and shoving, turning and tumbling in a whirl.

McEwen gazed, excited and sympathetic. At first he thought to avoid it all, having a horror of death, but a moment later decided to come to his friend's rescue, a feeling of tribal relationship which was overwhelming coming over him. Springing forward, he clambered upon the back of Og, at whose neck he began to saw with his powerful teeth. Og, realizing a new adversary, released his hold upon Ermi's limb and endeavored to shake off his new enemy. McEwen held tight, however. The others, however, too excited to observe the newcomer, still struggled to destroy Ermi. The latter had stuck steadily to his labor of killing Maru, and now, when Og's hold was loosened, he gave a powerful crush and Maru breathed his last. This advantaged him little, however, for both Ponan and Om were attacking his sides.

"Take that!" shouted Om, throwing himself violently upon Ermi and turning him over. "Saw off his head, Ponan."

Ponan released his hold and sprang for Ermi's head. There was a kicking and crushing of jaws, and Ponan secured his grip.

"Kill him!" yelled Om. "Come, Og! Come!"

At this very moment Og's severed head fell to the ground, and McEwen leaping from his back, sprang to the aid of Ermi.

"Come!" he shouted at Ponan, who was sawing at Ermi's head. "It's two to two now," and McEwen gave such a wrench to Ponan's side that he writhed in pain, and released his hold on Ermi.

But recovering himself he leaped upon McEwen, and bore him down, sprawling.

The fight was now more desperate than ever. The combatants rolled and tossed. McEwen's right antenna was broken by his fall, and one of his legs was injured. He could seem to get no hold upon his adversary, whom he now felt to be working toward his neck.

"Let go!" he yelled, gnashing at him with his mandibles, but Ponan only tightened his murderous jaws.

Better fortune was now with Ermi, however, who was a more experienced fighter. Getting a grip upon Om's body, he hurled him to the ground and left him stunned and senseless.

Seeing McEwen's predicament, he now sprang to his aid. The latter was being sadly worsted and but for the generous aid of Ermi, would have been killed. The latter struck Ponan a terrific blow with his head and having stunned him, dragged him off. The two, though much injured, now seized upon the unfortunate Sanguineæ and tore him in two, and would have done as much for Om, had they not discovered that that bedraggled warrior had recovered sufficiently to crawl away and hide.

McEwen and Ermi now drew near to each other in warm admiration.

"Come with me," said Ermi. "They are all about here now and that coward who escaped will have them upon us. There is a corridor into our home from here, only I was not able to reach it before they caught me. Help me barricade this entrance."

Together they built up the stones more effectually than before, and then entered, toppling the mass in behind them. With considerable labor, they built up another barricade below.

"You watch a moment, now," said Ermi to McEwen, and then hurried down a long passage through which he soon returned bringing with him a sentinel, who took up guard duty at the point where the fight had occurred. "He will stay here and give the alarm in case another attack is made," he commented.

"Come now," he added, touching McEwen affectionately with his antennæ. Leading the way, Ermi took him along a long winding corridor with which, somehow, he seemed to be familiar, and through various secret passages into the colony house.

"You see," he said to McEwen familiarly, as they went, "they could not have gotten in here, even if they had killed me, without knowing the way. Our passageways are too intricate. But it is as well to keep a picket there, now that they are about.

Where have you been? You do not belong to our colony, do you?"

McEwen related his experiences since their meeting in the desert, without explaining where he came from. He knew that he was a member of some other colony of this same tribe without being sure of which one. A strange feeling of wandering confusion possessed him, as though he had been injured in some way, somewhere, and was lost for the moment.

"Well, you might as well stay with us, now," said Ermi. "Are you hungry?"

"Very," said McEwen.

"Then we will eat at once."

McEwen now gazed upon a domed chamber of vast proportions, with which, also, he seemed familiar, an old inhabitant of one such, no less. It had several doors that opened out into galleries, and corridors leading to other chambers and store rooms, a home for thousands.

Many members of this allied family now hurried to meet them, all genially enough.

"You have had an encounter with them?" asked several at once.

"Nothing to speak of," said Ermi, who, fighter that he was, had also a touch of vanity. "Look after my friend here, who has saved my life."

"Not I!" cried McEwen warmly.

They could not explain, however, before they were seized by their admirers and carried into a chamber where none of the din of preparation penetrated, and where was a carpet of soft grass threads upon which they might lie.

Injured though they were, neither could endure lying still for long, and were soon poking about, though unable to do anything. McEwen was privileged to idle and listlessly watch an attack on one portal of the cave which lasted an entire day, resulting in failure for the invaders. It was a rather broken affair, the principal excitement occurring about the barricaded portals and secret exits at the end of the long corridors, where McEwen often found himself in the way. The story of his prowess had been well told by Ermi, and he was a friend and hero whom many served. A sort of ambulance service was established which not only looked to the bringing in of the injured, but also to the removal of the dead. A graveyard was prepared just outside one of the secret entrances, far from the scene of the siege, and here the dead were laid in orderly rows.

The siege having ended temporarily the same day it began, the household resumed its old order. Those who had remained within went forth for forage. The care of the communal young, which had been somewhat interrupted, was now resumed. Larvæ and chrysalis, which had been left almost unattended in the vast nurseries, were moved to and fro between the rooms where the broken sunlight warmed, and the shadow gave them rest.

"There is war ahead," said Ermi to McEwen one day not long after this. "These Sanguineæ will never let us alone until we give them battle. We shall have to stir up the whole race of Shining Slave Makers and fight all the Sanguineæ before we have peace again."

"Good," said McEwen. "I am ready."

"So am I," answered Ermi, "but it is no light matter. They are our ancient enemy and as powerful as we. If we meet again you will see war that is war."

Not long after this McEwen and Ermi, foraging together, encountered a Sanguinea, who fought with them and was slain. Numerous Lucidi, of which tribe he found himself to be a member, left the community of a morning to labor and were never heard of again. Encounters between parties of both camps were frequent, and orderly living ceased.

At last the entire community was in a ferment, and a council was called. It was held in the main saloon of the formicary, a vast chamber whose hollowed dome rose like the open sky above them. The queen of the community was present, and all the chief warriors, including Ermi and McEwen. Loud talking and fierce comment were indulged in to no point, until Yumi, long a light in the councils of the Lucidi, spoke. He was short and sharp of speech.

"We must go to war," he said. "Our old enemies will give us no peace. Send couriers to all the colonies of the Shining Slave Makers. We will meet the Red Slave Makers as we did before."

"Ah," said an old Lucidi, who stood at McEwen's side, "that was a great battle. You don't remember. You were too young.

There were thousands and thousands in that. I could not walk for the dead."

"Are we to have another such?" asked McEwen.

"If the rest of us come. We are a great people. The Shining Slave Makers are numberless."

Just then another voice spoke, and Ermi listened.

"Let us send for them to come here. When the Sanguineæ again lay siege let us pour out and destroy them. Let none escape."

"Let us first send couriers and hear what our people say," broke in Ermi loudly. "The Sanguineæ are a vast people also. We must have numbers. It must be a decisive battle."

"Ay, ay," answered many. "Send the couriers!"

Forthwith messengers were dispatched to all parts, calling the hordes of the Shining Slave Makers to war. In due course they returned, bringing information that they were coming. Their colonies also had been attacked. Later the warriors of the allied tribes began to put in an appearance.

It was a gathering of legions. The paths in the forests about resounded with their halloos. With the arrival of the first cohorts of these friendly colonies, there was a minor encounter with an irritant host of the Sanguineæ foraging hereabout, who were driven back and destroyed. Later there were many minor encounters and deaths before the hosts were fully assembled, but the end was not yet. All knew that. The Sanguineæ had fled, but not in cowardice. They would return.

The one problem with this vast host, now that it was assembled, was food. Eventually they expected to discover this in the sacked homes of the Sanguineæ, but temporarily other provision must be made. The entire region had to be scoured. Colonies of Fuscæ and Schauffusi living in nearby territory were attacked and destroyed. Their storehouses were ransacked and the contents distributed. Every form of life was attacked and still there was not enough.

Both McEwen and Ermi, now inseparable, joined in one of these raids. It was upon a colony of Fuscæ, who had their home in a neighboring forest. The company went singing on their way until within a short distance of the colony, when they became silent.

"Let us not lose track of one another," said McEwen.

"No," said Ermi, "but they are nothing. We will take all they possess without a struggle. See them running."

As he said this, he motioned in the direction of several Fuscæ that were fleeing toward their portals in terror. The Lucidi set up a shout, and darted after, plunging into the open gates, striking and slaying as they went. In a few minutes those first in came out again carrying their booty. Others were singly engaged in fiercest battle with large groups of the weaker Fuscæ. Only a few of the latter were inclined to fight. They seemed for the most part dazed by their misfortunes. Numbers hung from the topmost blades of the towering sword-trees, and the broad, floor-like leaves of the massive weeds, about their caves where they had taken refuge, holding in their jaws baby larvæ and cocoons rescued from the invaders, with which they had hurriedly fled to these nearest elevated objects.

Singly, McEwen pursued a dozen, and reveled in the sport of killing them. He tumbled them with rushes of his body, crushed them with his mandibles, and poisoned them with his formic sting.

"Do you need help?" called Ermi once, who was always near and shouting.

"Yes," called McEwen scornfully, "bring me more of them."

Soon the deadly work was over and the two comrades, gathering a mass of food, joined the returning band, singing as they went.

"To-morrow," said Ermi, as they went along, "we will meet the Sanguineæ. It is agreed. The leaders are conferring now."

McEwen did not learn where these latter were, but somehow he was pleased. An insane lust of combat was now upon him.

"They will not be four to two this time," he laughed exultingly.

"No, and we will not be barricading against them, either," laughed Ermi, the lust of war simmering in his veins.

As they came near their camp, however, they found a large number of the assembled companies already in motion. Thousands upon thousands of those who had arrived were already assembled in one group or another and were prepared for action.

There were cries and sounds of fighting, and long lines of Lucidi hurrying hither and thither.

"What's the matter?" asked Ermi excitedly.

"The Sanguineæ," was the answer. "They are returning."

Instantly McEwen became sober. Ermi turned to him affectionately.

"Now," he said solemnly, "courage. We're in for it."

A tremendous hubbub followed. Already vast legions of the Lucidi were bearing away to the east. McEwen and Ermi, not being able to find their own, fell in with a strange company.

"Order!" shouted a voice in their ears. "Fall in line. We are called."

The twain mechanically obeyed, and dropped behind a regular line. Soon they were winding along with other long lines of warriors through the tall sword trees, and in a little while reached a huge, smooth, open plain where already the actual fighting had begun. Thousands were here, apparently hundreds of thousands. There was little order, and scarcely any was needed apparently, since all contacts were individual or between small groups. It all depended now on numbers, and the results of the contests between individuals, or at the most, these small groups. Ermi, McEwen, and several other Lucidi were about to seize upon one Sanguinea, who was approaching them, when an amazing rush of the latter broke them, and McEwen found himself separated from Ermi with a red demon snapping at his throat. Dazed by the shock and clamor, he almost fell a prey to this first charge. A moment later, however, his courage and daring returned. With a furious bound, he recovered himself and forced himself upon his adversary, snapping his jaws in his neck.

"Take that!" he said to the tumbling carcass.

He had no sooner ended one foe, however, than another clutched him. They were on every hand, hard, merciless fighters like himself and Ermi who rushed and tore and sawed with amazing force. McEwen faced his newest adversary swiftly. While the latter was seeking for McEwen's head and antennæ with his mandibles, the former with a quick snap seized his foe by the neck. Turning up his abdomen, he ejected formic acid into the throat of the other. That finished him.

Meanwhile the battle continued on every hand with the same mad vehemence. Already the dead clogged the ground. Here, single combatants struggled—there, whole lines moved and swayed in deadly combat. Ever and anon new lines were formed, and strange hosts of friends or enemies came up, falling upon the combatants of both sides with murderous enthusiasm. McEwen, in a strange daze and lust of death, seemed to think nothing of it. He was alone now—lost in a tossing sea of war, and terror seemed to have forsaken him. It was wonderful, he thought, mysterious——

As enemy after enemy assailed him, he fought them as he best knew, an old method to him, apparently, and as they died, he wished them to die—broken, poisoned, sawed in two. He began to count and exult in the numbers he had slain. It was at last as though he were dreaming, and all around was a vain, dark, surging mass of enemies.

Finally, four of the Sanguineæ seized upon him in a group, and he went down before them, almost helpless. Swiftly they tore at his head and body, endeavoring to dispose of him quickly. One seized a leg, another an antenna. A third jumped and sawed at his neck. Still he did not care. It was all war, and he would struggle to the last shred of his strength, eagerly, enthusiastically. At last he seemed to lose consciousness.

When he opened his eyes again, Ermi was beside him.

"Well?" said Ermi.

"Well?" answered McEwen.

"You were about done for, then."

"Was I?" he answered. "How are things going?"

"I cannot tell yet," said Ermi. "All I know is that you were faring badly when I came up. Two of them were dead, but the other two were killing you."

"You should have left me to them," said McEwen, noticing now for the first time Ermi's wounds. "It does not matter so much—one Lucidi more or less—what of it? But you have been injured."

"I—oh, nothing. You are the one to complain. I fear you are badly injured."

"Oh, I," returned McEwen heavily, feeling at last the weight of death upon him, "I am done for. I cannot live. I felt myself dying some time ago."

He closed his eyes and trembled. In another moment——

II

McEwen opened his eyes. Strangely enough he was looking out upon jingling carriages and loitering passersby in the great city park. It was all so strange, by comparison with that which he had so recently seen, the tall buildings in the distance, instead of the sword trees, the trees, the flowers. He jumped to his feet in astonishment, then sank back again in equal amaze, a passerby eyeing him curiously the while.

"I have been asleep," he said in a troubled way. "I have been dreaming. And what a dream!"

He shut his eyes again, wishing, for some strange reason—charm, sympathy, strangeness—to regain the lost scene. An odd longing filled his heart, a sense of comradeship lost, of some friend he knew missing. When he opened his eyes again he seemed to realize something more of what had been happening but it was fading, fading.

At his feet lay the plain and the ants with whom he had recently been—or so he thought. Yes, there, only a few feet away in the parched grass, was an arid spot, over-run with insects. He gazed upon it, in amazement, searching for the details of a lost world. Now, as he saw, coming closer, a giant battle was in progress, such a one, for instance, as that in which he had been engaged in his dream. The ground was strewn with dead ants. Thousands upon thousands were sawing and striking at each other quite in the manner in which he had dreamed. What was this?—a revelation of the spirit and significance of a lesser life or of his own—or what? And what was life if the strange passions, moods and necessities which conditioned him here could condition those there on so minute a plane?

"Why, I was there," he said dazedly and a little dreamfully, "a little while ago. I died there—or as well as died there—in my dream. At least I woke out of it into this or sank from that into this."

Stooping closer he could see where lines were drawn, how in

places the forces raged in confusion, and the field was cluttered with the dead. At one moment an odd mad enthusiasm such as he had experienced in his dream-world lay hold of him, and he looked for the advantage of the Shining Slave Makers—the blacks—as he thought of the two warring hosts as against the reds. But finding it not, the mood passed, and he stood gazing, lost in wonder. What a strange world! he thought. What worlds within worlds, all apparently full of necessity, contention, binding emotions and unities—and all with sorrow, their sorrow— a vague, sad something out of far-off things which had been there, and was here in this strong bright city day, had been there and would be here until this odd, strange thing called *life* had ended.

The Shadow

What had given him his first hint that all might not be as well at home as he imagined was the incident of the automobile. Up to that time he had not had a troubled thought about her, not one. But after— Well, it was a year and a half now and although suspicion still lingered it was becoming weaker. But it had not been obliterated even though he could not help being fond of Beryl, especially since they had Tickles to look after between them. But anyhow, in spite of all his dark thoughts and subtle efforts to put two and two together, he had not been able to make anything of it. Perhaps he was being unjust to her to go on brooding about it. . . . But how was it possible that so many suspicious-looking things could happen in a given time, and one never be able to get the straight of them?

The main thing that had hampered him was his work. He was connected with the Tri-State Paper Company, at the City Order desk, and as a faithful employé he was not supposed to leave during working hours without permission, and it was not always easy to get permission. It was easy to count the times he had been off —once to go to the dentist, and two or three times to go home when Beryl was ill. Yet it just happened that on that particular afternoon his superior, Mr. Baggott, had suggested that he, in the place of Naigly who always attended to such matters but was away at the time, should run out to the Detts-Scanlon store and ask Mr. Pierce just what was wrong with that last order that had been shipped. There was a mix-up somewhere, and it had been impossible to get the thing straight over the telephone.

Well, just as he was returning to the office, seated in one of those comfortable cross seats of the Davenant Avenue line and looking at the jumble of traffic out near Blakely Avenue, and just as the car was nearing the entrance to Briscoe Park he saw a tan-and-chocolate-colored automobile driven by a biggish man in a light tan overcoat and cap swing into view, cross in front of the car, and enter the park. It was all over in a flash. But just as the car swung near him who should he see sitting beside the man but Beryl, or certainly a woman who was enough like her to be her twin sister. He would have sworn it was Beryl. And what was more, and worse, she was smiling up at this man as though they were on the best of terms and had known each other a long time! Of course he had only had a glimpse, and might have been mistaken. Beryl had told him that morning that she was going to spend the afternoon with her mother. She often did that, sometimes leaving Tickles there while she did her mother's marketing. Or, she and her mother, or she and her sister Alice, if she chanced to be there, would take the baby for a walk in the park. Of course he might have been mistaken.

But that hat with the bunch of bright green grapes on the side. . . . And that green-and-white striped coat. . . . And that peculiar way in which she always held her head when she was talking. Was it really Beryl? If it wasn't, why should he have had such a keen conviction that it was?

Up to that time there never had been anything of a doubtful character between them—that is, nothing except that business of the Raskoffsky picture, which didn't amount to much in itself. Anybody might become interested in a great violinist and write him for his photo, though even that couldn't be *proved* against Beryl. It was inscribed to Alice. But even if she had written him, that wasn't a patch compared to this last, her driving about in a car with a strange man. Certainly that would justify him in any steps that he chose to take, even to getting a divorce.

But what had he been able to prove so far? Nothing. He had tried to find her that afternoon, first at their own house, then at her mother's, and then at Winton & Marko's real estate office, where Alice sometimes helped out, but he couldn't find a trace of her. Still, did that prove anything once and for all? She might have been to the concert as she said, she and Alice. It must be dull to stay in the house all day long, anyhow, and he couldn't blame her for doing the few things she did within their means. Often he tried to get in touch with her of a morning or after-noon, and there was no answer, seeing that she was over to her mother's or out to market, as she said. And up to the afternoon of the automobile it had never occurred to him that there was anything queer about it. When he called up Beryl's mother she had said that Beryl and Alice had gone to a concert and it wasn't believable that Mrs. Dana would lie to him about anything. Maybe the two of them were doing something they shouldn't, or maybe Alice was helping Beryl to do something she shouldn't, without their mother knowing anything about it. Alice was like that, sly. It was quite certain that if there had been any cor-respondence between Beryl and that man Raskoffsky, that time he had found the picture inscribed to Alice, it had been Alice who had been the go-between. Alice had probably allowed her name and address to be used for Beryl's pleasure—that is, if there was anything to it at all. It wasn't likely that Beryl would have attempted anything like that without Alice's help.

But just the same he had never been able to prove that they had been in league, at that time or any other. If there was any-thing in it they were too clever to let him catch them. The day he thought he had seen her in the car he had first tried to get her by telephone and then had gone to the office, since it was on his way, to get permission to go home for a few minutes. But what had he gained by it? By the time he got there, Beryl and her mother were already there, having just walked over from Mrs. Dana's home, according to Beryl. And Beryl was not wear-ing the hat and coat he had seen in the car, and that was what he wanted to find out. But between the time he had called up her mother and the time he had managed to get home she had had time enough to return and change her clothes and go over to her mother's if there was any reason why she should. That was what had troubled him and caused him to doubt ever since. She would have known by then that he had been trying to get her on the telephone and would have had any answer ready for him. And that may have been exactly what happened, assuming that she had been in the car and gotten home ahead of him, and presuming her mother had lied for her, which she would not do—not Mrs. Dana. For when he had walked in, a little flushed and excited, Beryl had exclaimed: "Whatever is the matter, Gil?" And then: "What a crazy thing, to come hurrying home just to ask me about this! Of course I haven't been in any car. How ridiculous! Ask Mother. You wouldn't expect her to fib for me, would you?" And then to clinch the matter she had added: "Alice and I left Tickles with her and went to the concert after going into the park for a while. When we returned, Alice stopped home so Mother could walk over here with me. What are you so excited about." And for the life of him, he had not been able to say anything except that he had seen a woman going into Briscoe Park in a tan-and-chocolate car, seated beside a big man who looked like—well, he couldn't say exactly whom he did look like. But the woman beside him certainly looked like Beryl. And she had had on a hat with green grapes on one side and a white-and-green striped sports coat, just like the one she had. Taking all that into consideration, what would any one think? But she had laughed it off, and what was he to say? He certainly couldn't accuse Mrs. Dana of not knowing what she was talking about, or Beryl of lying, unless he was sure of what he was saying. She was too strong-minded and too strong-willed for that. She had only married him after a long period of begging on his part; and she wasn't any too anxious to live with him now unless they could get along comfortably together.

Yet taken along with that Raskoffsky business of only a few months before, and the incident of the Hotel Deming of only the day before (but of which he had thought nothing until he had seen her in the car), and the incident of the letters in the ashes, which followed on the morning after he had dashed home that day, and then that business of the closed car in Bergley Place, just three nights afterwards—well, by George! when one put such things together—

It was very hard to put these things in the order of their

effect on him, though it was easy to put them in their actual order as to time. The Hotel Deming incident had occurred only the day before the automobile affair and taken alone, meant nothing, just a chance encounter with her on the part of Naigly, who had chosen to speak of it. But joined afterwards with the business of the partly burned letters and after seeing her in that car or thinking he had— Well— After that, naturally his mind had gone back to that Hotel Deming business, and to the car, too. Naigly, who had been interested in Beryl before her marriage (she had been Baggott's stenographer), came into the office about four—the day before he had seen Beryl, or thought he had, in the car, and had said to him casually: "I saw your wife just now, Stoddard." "That so? Where?" "She was coming out of the Deming ladies' entrance as I passed just now." Well, taken by itself, there was nothing much in that, was there? There was an arcade of shops which made the main entrance to the Deming, and it was easy to go through that and come out of one of the other entrances. He knew Beryl had done it before, so why should he have worried about it then? Only, for some reason, when he came home that evening Beryl didn't mention that she had been downtown that day until he asked her. "What were you doing about four to-day?" "Downtown, shopping. Why? Did you see me? I went for Mother." "Me? No. Who do you know in the Deming?" "No one"—this without a trace of self-consciousness, which was one of the things that made him doubt whether there had been anything wrong. "Oh, yes; I remember now. I walked through to look at the hats in Anna McCarty's window, and came out the ladies' entrance. Why?" "Oh, nothing. Naigly said he saw you, that's all. You're getting to be a regular gadabout these days." "Oh, what nonsense! Why shouldn't I go through the Deming Arcade? I would have stopped in to see you, only I know you don't like me to come bothering around there."

And so he had dismissed it from his mind—until the incident of the car.

And then the matter of the letters . . . and Raskoffsky . . .

Beryl was crazy about music, although she couldn't play except a little by ear. Her mother had been too poor to give her anything more than a common school education, which was about all that he had had. But she was crazy about the violin and any-body who could play it, and when any of the great violinists came to town she always managed to afford to go. Raskoffsky was a big blond Russian who played wonderfully, so she said. She and Alice had gone to hear him, and for weeks afterward they had raved about him. They had even talked of writing to him, just to see if he would answer, but he had frowned on such a proceeding because he didn't want Beryl writing to any man. What good would it do her? A man like that wouldn't bother about answering her letter, especially if all the women were as crazy about him as the papers said. Yet later he had found Raskoffsky's picture in Beryl's room, only it was inscribed to Alice. . . . Still, Beryl might have put Alice up to it, might even have sent her own picture under Alice's name, just to see if he would answer. They had talked of sending a picture. Besides, if Alice had written and secured this picture, why wasn't it in her rather than Beryl's possession. He had asked about that. Yet the one flaw in that was that Alice wasn't really good-looking enough to send her picture and she knew it. Yet Beryl had sworn that she hadn't written. And Alice had insisted that it was she and not Beryl who had written. But there was no way of proving that she hadn't or that Beryl had.

Yet why all the secrecy? Neither of them had said anything more about writing Raskoffsky after that first time. And it was only because he had come across Raskoffsky's picture in one of Beryl's books that he had come to know anything about it at all. "To my fair little western admirer who likes my 'Dance Macabre' so much. The next time I play in your city you must come and see me." But Alice wasn't fair or good-looking. Beryl was. And it was Beryl and not Alice, who had first raved over that dance; Alice didn't care so much for music. And wasn't it Beryl, and not Alice, who had proposed writing him. Yet it was Alice who had received the answer. How was that? Very likely it was Beryl who had persuaded Alice to write for her, sending her own instead of Alice's picture, and getting Alice to receive Raskoffsky's picture for her when it came. Something in their manner the day he had found the picture indicated as much. Alice had been so quick to say: "Oh yes. I wrote him." But Beryl had looked a little queer when she caught him looking at her, had even flushed slightly, although she had kept her indifferent manner. At that time the incident of the car hadn't occurred. But afterwards,—after he had imagined he had seen Beryl in the car—it had occurred to him that maybe it was Raskoffsky with whom she was with that day. He was playing in Columbus, so the papers said, and he might have been passing through the city. He was a large man too, as he now recalled, by George! If only he could find a way to prove that!

Still, even so and when you come right down to it, was there anything so terrible about her writing a celebrity like that and asking for his picture, if that was all she had done. But was it? Those long-enveloped gray letters he had found in the fireplace that morning, after that day in which he had seen her in the car (or thought he had)—or at least traces of them. And the queer way she had looked at him when he brought them up in connection with that closed car in Bergley Place. She had squinted her eyes as if to think, and had then laughed rather shakily when he charged her with receiving letters from Raskoffsky, and with his having come here to see her. His finding them had been entirely by accident. He always got up early to "start things," for Beryl was a sleepyhead, and he would start the fire in the grate and put on the water to boil in the kitchen. And this morning as he was bending over the grate to push away some scraps of burnt wood so as to start a new fire, he came across five or six letters, or the ashes of them, all close together as though they might have been tied with a ribbon or something. What was left of them looked as though they had been written on heavy stationery such as a man of means might use, the envelopes long and thick. The top one still showed the address —"Mrs. Beryl Stoddard, Care of——" He was bending over to see the rest when a piece of wood toppled over and destroyed it. He rescued one little scrap, the half-charred corner of one page, and the writing on this seemed to be like that on Raskoffsky's picture, or so he thought, and he read: "to see you." Just that and nothing more, part of a sentence that ended the page and went to the next. And that page was gone, of course!

But it was funny wasn't it, that at sight of them the thought of Raskoffsky should have come to him? And that ride in the park. Come to think of it, the man in the car had looked a little like Raskoffsky's picture. And for all he knew, Raskoffsky might have then been in town—returned for this especial purpose— and she might have been meeting him on the sly. Of course. At the Deming. That was it. He had never been quite able to believe her. All the circumstances at the time pointed to something of the kind, even if he had never been able to tie them together and make her confess to the truth of them.

But how he had suffered after that because of that thought! Things had seemed to go black before him. Beryl unfaithful? Beryl running around with a man like that, even if he was a great violinist? Everybody knew what kind of a man he was— all those men. The papers were always saying how crazy women were over him, and yet that he should come all the way to C—— to make trouble between him and Beryl! (If only he could prove that!) But why should she, with himself and Tickles to look after, and a life of her own which was all right —why should she be wanting to run around with a man like that, a man who would use her for a little while and then drop her. And when she had a home of her own? And her baby? And her mother and sister right here in C——? And him? And working as hard as he was and trying to make things come out right for them? That was the worst of it. That was the misery of it. And all for a little notice from a man who was so far above her or thought he was, anyhow, that he couldn't care for her or any one long. The papers had said so at the time. But that was the whole secret. She was so crazy about people who did anything in music or painting or anything like that, that she couldn't reason right about them. And she might have done a thing like that on that account. Personally he wouldn't give a snap of his finger for the whole outfit. They weren't ordinary, decent people anyhow. But making herself as common as that! And right here in C——, too, where they were both known, Oh, if only he had been able to prove that! If only he had been able to at that time!

When he had recovered himself a little that morning after he had found the traces of the letters in the ashes he had wanted to go into the bedroom where she was still asleep and drag her out by the hair and beat her and make her confess to these things. Yes, he had. There had been all but murder in his heart that morning. He would show her. She couldn't get away with any such raw stuff as that even if she did have her mother and sister to help her. (That sly little Alice, always putting her sister up to something and never liking him from the first, anyhow.) But then the thought had come to him that after all he might be wrong. Supposing the letters weren't from Raskoffsky? And supposing she had told the truth when she said she hadn't been in the car? He had nothing to go on except what he imagined, and up to then everything had been as wonderful as could be between them. Still . . .

Then another thought had come: if the letters weren't from Raskoffsky who were they from? He didn't know of anybody who would be writing her on any such paper as that. And if not Raskoffsky whom did she know? And why should she throw them in the fire, choosing a time when he wasn't about? That was strange, especially after the automobile incident of the day before. But when he taxed her with this the night of the Bergley Place car incident—she had denied everything and said they were from Claire Haggerty, an old chum who had moved to New York just about the time they were married and who had been writing her at her mother's because at that time he and she didn't have a home of their own and that was the only address she could give. She had been meaning to destroy them but had been putting it off. But only the night before she had come across them in a drawer and had tossed them in the fire, and that was all there was to that.

But was that all there was to it?

For even as he had been standing there in front of the grate wondering what to do the thought had come to him that he was not going about this in the right way. He had had the thought that he should hire a detective at once and have her shadowed and then if she were doing anything, it might be possible to find it out. That would have been better. That was really the way. Yet instead of doing that he had gone on quarreling with her, had burst in on her with everything that he suspected or saw, or thought he saw, and that it was, if anything, that had given her warning each time and had allowed her to get the upper hand of him, if she had got the upper hand of him. That was it. Yet he had gone on and quarreled with her that day just the same, only, after he had thought it all over, he had decided to consult the Sol Cohn Detective Service and have her watched. But that very night, coming back from the night conference with Mr. Harris Cohn, which was the only time he could get to give it, was the night he had seen the car in Bergley Place, and Beryl near it.

Bergley Place was a cross street two doors from where they lived on Winton. And just around the corner in Bergley, was an old vacant residence with a deal of shrubbery and four over-arching trees in front, which made it very dark there at night. That night as he was coming home from Mr. Harris Cohn's— (he had told Beryl that he was going to the lodge, in order to throw her off and had come home earlier in order to see what he might see) and just as he was stepping off the Nutley Avenue car which turned into Marko Street, about half a block above where they lived whom should he see— But, no, let us put it this way. Just at that moment or a moment later as he turned toward his home an automobile that had been going the same way he was along Winton swung into Bergley Place and threw its exceptionally brilliant lights on a big closed automobile that was standing in front of the old house aforementioned. There were two vacant corner lots opposite the old house at Bergley and Winton and hence it was that he could see what was going on. Near the rear of the automobile, just as though she had stepped out of it and was about to leave, stood Beryl—or, he certainly thought it was Beryl, talking to some one in the car, just as one would before parting and returning into the house. She had on a hooded cape exactly like the one she wore at times though not often. She did not like hooded capes any more. They were out of style. Just the same so sure had he been that it was Beryl and that at last he had trapped her that he hurried on to the house or, rather, toward the car. But just as he neared the corner the lights of the car that had been standing there lightless flashed on for a second—then off and then sped away. Yet even with them on there had not been enough light to see whether it was Beryl, or who. Or what the number on the license plate was. It was gone and with it Beryl, presumably up the alley way and into the back door or so he had believed. So sure was he that she had gone that way that he himself had gone that way. Yet when he reached the rear door following her, as he chose to do, it was locked and the kitchen was dark. And he had to rap and pound even before she came to let him in. And when she did there she was looking as though she had not been out at all, undressed, ready for bed and wanting to know why he chose to come that way! And asking him not to make so much noise for fear of waking Tickles. . . .!

Think of it. Not a trace of excitement. No cape with a hood on. The light up in the dining-room and a book on the table as though she might have been reading—one of those novels by that fellow Barclay. And not a sign about anywhere that she might have been out—that was the puzzling thing. And denying that she had been out or that she had seen any car, or anything. Now what would you make of that!

Then it was, though, that he had burst forth in a fury of suspicion and anger and had dealt not only with this matter of the car in Bergley Place but the one in Briscoe Park, the letters in the ashes and the matter of Naigly seeing her come out of the Deming, to say nothing of her writing to Raskoffsky for his picture. For it was Raskoffsky, of course, if it was anybody. He was as positive as to that as any one could be. Who else could it have been? He had not even hesitated to insist that he knew who it was—Raskoffsky, of course—and that he had seen him and had been able to recognize him from his pictures. Yet she had denied that vehemently—even laughingly—or that he had seen any one, or that there had been a car there for her. And she did show him a clipping a week later which said that Raskoffsky was in Italy.

But if it wasn't Raskoffsky then who was it—if it was any one. "For goodness' sake, Gil," was all she would say at that or any other time, "I haven't been out with Raskoffsky or any one and I don't think you ought to come in here and act as you do. It seems to me you must be losing your mind. I haven't seen or heard of any old car. Do you think I could stand here and say that I hadn't if I had? And I don't like the way you have of rushing in here of late every little while and accusing me of something that I haven't done. What grounds have you for thinking that I have done anything wrong anyhow? That silly picture of Raskoffsky that Alice sent for. And that you think you saw me in an automobile. Not another thing. If you don't stop now and let me alone I will leave you I tell you and that is all there is to it. I won't be annoyed in this way and especially when you have nothing to go on." It was with that type of counter-argument that she had confronted him.

Besides, at that time—the night that he thought he saw her in Bergley Place—and as if to emphasize what she was saying, Tickles in the bedroom had waked up and begun to call "Mama, Mama." And she had gone in to him and brought him out even as she talked. And she had seemed very serious and defiant, then —very much more like her natural self and like a person who had been injured and was at bay. So he had become downright doubtful, again, and had gone back into the dining-room. And there was the light up and the book that she had been reading. And in the closet as he had seen when he had hung up his own coat was her hooded cape on the nail at the back where it always hung.

And yet how could he have been mistaken as to all of those things? Surely there must have been something to some of them. He could never quite feel, even now, that there hadn't been. Yet outside of just that brief period in which all of these things had occurred there had never been a thing that he could put his hands on, nothing that he could say looked even suspicious before or since. And the detective agency had not been able to find out anything about her either—not a thing. That had been money wasted: one hundred dollars. Now how was that?

II

The trouble with Gil was that he was so very suspicious by nature and not very clever. He was really a clerk, with a clerk's mind and a clerk's point of view. He would never rise to bigger things, because he couldn't, and yet she could not utterly dislike him either. He was always so very much in love with her, so generous—to her, at least—and he did the best he could to support her and Tickles which was something, of course. A lot of the trouble was that he was too affectionate and too clinging. He was always hanging around whenever he was not working. And with never a thought of going any place without her except to his lodge or on a business errand that he couldn't possibly escape. And if he did go he was always in such haste to get back! Before she had ever thought of marrying him, when he was shipping clerk at the Tri-State and she was Mr. Baggott's stenographer, she had seen that he was not very remarkable as a man. He hadn't the air or the force of Mr. Baggott, for whom she worked then and whose assistant Gil later became. Indeed, Mr. Baggott had once said: "Gilbert is all right, energetic and faithful enough, but he lacks a large grasp of things." And yet in spite of all that she had married him.

Why?

Well, it was hard to say. He was not bad-looking, rather handsome, in fact, and that had meant a lot to her then. He had fine, large black eyes and a pale forehead and pink cheeks, and such nice clean hands. And he always dressed so well for a young man in his position. He was so faithful and yearning, a very dog at her heels. But she shouldn't have married him, just the same. It was all a mistake. He was not the man for her. She knew that now. And, really, she had known it then, only she had not allowed her common sense to act. She was always too sentimental then—not practical enough as she was now. It was only after she was married and surrounded by the various problems that marriage includes that she had begun to wake up. But then it was too late.

Yes, she had married, and by the end of the first year and a half, during which the original glamour had had time to subside, she had Tickles, or Gilbert, Jr., to look after. And with him had come a new mood such as she had never dreamed of in connection with herself. Just as her interest in Gil had begun to wane a little her interest in Tickles had sprung into flame. And for all of three years now it had grown stronger rather than weaker. She fairly adored her boy and wouldn't think of doing anything to harm him. And yet she grew so weary at times of the humdrum life they were compelled to live. Gil only made forty-five dollars a week, even now. And on that they had to clothe and feed and house the three of them. It was no easy matter. She would rather go out and work. But it was not so easy with a three-year-old baby. And besides Gil would never hear of such a thing. He was just one of those young husbands who thought the wife's place was in the home, even when he couldn't provide a very good home for her to live in.

Still, during these last few years she had had a chance to read and think, two things which up to that time she had never seemed to have time for. Before that it had always been beaux and other girls. But most of the girls were married now and so there was an end to them. But reading and thinking had gradually taken up all of her spare time, and that had brought about such a change in her. She really wasn't the same girl now that Gil had married at all. She was wiser. And she knew so much more about life now than he did. And she thought so much more, and so differently. He was still at about the place mentally that he had been when she married him, interested in making a better place for himself in the Tri-State office and in playing golf or tennis out at the country club whenever he could afford the time to go out there. And he expected her to curry favor with Dr. and Mrs. Realk, and Mr. and Mrs. Stofft, because they had a car and because Mr. Stofft and Gil liked to play cards together. But beyond that he thought of nothing, not a thing.

But during all of this time she had more and more realized that Gil would never make anything much of himself. Alice had cautioned her against him before ever they had married. He was not a business man in any true sense. He couldn't think of a single thing at which he could make any money except in the paper business, and that required more capital than ever he would have. Everybody else they knew was prospering. And perhaps it was that realization that had thrown her back upon books and pictures and that sort of thing. People who did things in those days were so much more interesting than people who just made money, anyhow.

Yet she would never have entered upon that dangerous affair with Mr. Barclay if it hadn't been for the awful mental doldrums she found herself in about the time Tickles was two years old and Gil was so worried as to whether he would be able to keep his place at the Tri-State any longer. He had put all the money they had been able to save into that building and loan scheme, and when that had failed they were certainly up against it for a time. There was just nothing to do with, and there was no prospect of relief. To this day she had no clothes to speak of. And there wasn't much promise of getting them now. And she wasn't getting any younger. Still, there was Tickles, and she was brushing up on her shorthand again. If the worst came—

But she wouldn't have entered upon that adventure that had come so near to ending disastrously for herself and Tickles—for certainly if Gil had ever found out he could have taken Tickles away from her—if it hadn't been for that book *Heyday* which Mr. Barclay wrote and which she came across just when she was feeling so out of sorts with life and Gil and everything. That had pictured her own life so keenly and truly; indeed, it seemed to set her own life before her just as it was and as though some one were telling her about herself. It was the story of a girl somewhat like herself who had dreamed her way through a rather pinched girlhood, having to work for a living from the age of fourteen. And then just as she was able to make her own way had made a foolish marriage with a man of no import in any way—a clerk, just like Gil. And he had led her through more years of meagre living, until at last, very tired of it all, she had been about to yield herself to another man who didn't care very much about her but who had money and could do the things for her that her husband couldn't. Then of a sudden in this story her husband chose to disappear and leave her to make her way as best she might. The one difference between that story and her own life was that there was no little Tickles to look after. And Gil would never disappear, of course. But the heroine of the story had returned to her work without compromising herself. And in the course of time had met an architect who had the good sense or the romance to fall in love with and marry her. And so the story, which was so much like hers, except for Tickles and the architect, had ended happily.

But hers—well—

But the chances she had taken at that time! The restless and yet dreamy mood in which she had been and moved and which eventually had prompted her to write Mr. Barclay, feeling very doubtful as to whether he would be interested in her and yet drawn to him because of the life he had pictured. Her thought had been that if he could take enough interest in a girl like the one in the book to describe her so truly he might be a little interested in her real life. Only her thought at first had been not to entice him; she had not believed that she could. Rather, it was more the feeling that if he would he might be of some help to her, since he had written so sympathetically of Lila, the heroine. She was faced by the problem of what to do with her life, as Lila had been, but at that she hadn't expected him to solve it for her—merely to advise her.

But afterwards, when he had written to thank her, she feared that she might not hear from him again and had thought of that picture of herself, the one Dr. Realk had taken of her laughing so heartily, the one that everybody liked so much. She had felt that that might entice him to further correspondence with her, since his letters were so different and interesting, and she had sent it and asked him if his heroine looked anything like her, just as an excuse for sending it. Then had come that kindly letter in which he had explained his point of view and advised her, unless she were very unhappy, to do nothing until she should be able to look after herself in the great world. Life was an economic problem. As for himself, he was too much the rover to be more than a passing word to any one. His work came first. Apart from that, he said he drifted up and down the world trying to make the best of a life that tended to bore him. However if ever he came that way he would be glad to look her up and advise her as best he might, but that she must not let him compromise her in any way. It was not advisable in her very difficult position.

Even then she had not been able to give him up, so interested had she been by all he had written. And besides, he had eventually come to U—— only a hundred and fifty miles away, and had written from there to know if he might come over to see her. She couldn't do other than invite him, although she had known at the time that it was a dangerous thing to do. There was no solution, and it had only caused trouble—and how much trouble! And yet in the face of her mood then, anything had been welcome as a relief. She had been feeling that unless something happened to break the monotony she would do something desperate. And then something did happen. He had come, and there was nothing but trouble, and very much trouble, until he had gone again.

You would have thought there was some secret unseen force attending her and Gil at that time and leading him to wherever she was at just the time she didn't want him to be there. Take for example, that matter of Gil finding Mr. Barclay's letters in the fire after she had taken such care to throw them on the live coals behind some burning wood. He had evidently been able to make out a part of the address, anyhow, for he had said they were addressed to her in care of somebody he couldn't make out. And yet he was all wrong, as to the writer, of course. He had the crazy notion, based on his having found that picture of Raskoffsky inscribed to Alice, some months before, that they must be from him, just because he thought she had used Alice to write and ask Raskoffsky for his picture—which she had. But that was before she had ever read any of Mr. Barclay's books. Yet if it hadn't been for Gil's crazy notion that it was Raskoffsky she was interested in she wouldn't have had the courage to face it out the way she had, the danger of losing Tickles, which had come to her the moment Gil had proved so suspicious and watchful, frightening her so. Those three terrible days! And imagine him finding those bits of letters in the ashes and making something out of them! The uncanniness of it all.

And then that time he saw her speeding through the gate into Briscoe Park. They couldn't have been more than a second passing there, anyhow, and yet he had been able to pick her out! Worse, Mr. Barclay hadn't even intended coming back that way; they had just made the mistake of turning down Ridgley instead of Warren. Yet, of course, Gil had to be there, of all places, when as a rule he was never out of the office at any time. Fortunately for her she was on her way home, so there was no chance of his getting there ahead of her as, plainly, he planned afterwards. Still, if it hadn't been for her mother whom everybody believed, and who actually believed that she and Alice had been to the concert, she would never have had the courage to face him. She hadn't expected him home in the first place, but when he did come and she realized that unless she faced him out then and there in front of her mother who believed in her, that *she* as well as he would know, there was but one thing to do —brave it. Fortunately her mother hadn't seen her in that coat and hat which Gil insisted that she had on. For before going she and Alice had taken Tickles over to her mother's and then she had returned and changed her dress. And before Gil had arrived Alice had gone on home and told her mother to bring over the baby, which was the thing that had so confused Gil really. For he didn't know about the change and neither did her mother. And her mother did not believe that there had been any, which made her think that Gil was a little crazy, talking that way. And her mother didn't know to this day—she was so unsuspecting.

And then that terrible night on which he thought he had seen her in Bergley Place and came in to catch her. Would she ever forget that? Or that evening, two days before, when he had come home and said that Naigly had seen her coming out of the Deming. She could tell by his manner that time that he thought nothing of that then—he was so used to her going downtown in the daytime anyhow. But that Naigly should have seen her just then when of all times she would rather he would not have!

To be sure it had been a risky thing—going there to meet Mr. Barclay in that way, only from another point of view it had not seemed so. Every one went through the Deming Arcade for one reason or another and that made any one's being seen there rather meaningless. And in the great crowd that was always there it was the commonest thing for any one to meet any one else and stop and talk for a moment anyhow. That was all she was there for that day—to see Mr. Barclay on his arrival and make an appointment for the next day. She had done it because she knew she couldn't stay long and she knew Gil wouldn't be out at that time and that if any one else saw her she could say that it was almost any one they knew casually between them. Gil was like that, rather easy at times. But to think that Naigly should have been passing the Deming just as she was coming out— alone, fortunately—and should have run and told Gil. That was like him. It was pure malice. He had never liked her since she had turned him down for Gil. And he would like to make trouble for her if he could, that was all. That was the way people did who were disappointed in love.

But the worst and the most curious thing of all was that last evening in Bergley Place, the last time she ever saw Mr. Barclay anywhere. That *was* odd. She had known by then, of course, that Gil was suspicious and might be watching her and she hadn't intended to give him any further excuse for complaint. But that was his lodge night and he had never missed a meeting since they had been married—not one. Besides she had only intended to stay out about an hour and always within range of the house so that if Gil got off the car or any one else came she would know of it. She had not even turned out the light in the dining-room, intending to say if Gil came back unexpectedly or any one else called, that she had just run around the corner in the next block to see Mrs. Stofft. And in order that that statement might not be questioned, she had gone over there for just a little while before Mr. Barclay was due to arrive with his car. She had even asked Mr. Barclay to wait in the shadow of the old Dalrymple house in Bergley Place, under the trees, in order that the car might not be seen. So few people went up that street, anyhow. And it was always so dark in there. Besides it was near to raining which made it seem safer still. And yet he had seen her. And just as she was about to leave. And when she had concluded that everything had turned out so well.

But how could she have foreseen that a big car with such powerful lights as that would have turned in there just then. Or that Gil would step off the car and look up that way? Or that he would be coming home an hour earlier when he never did —not from lodge meeting. And besides she hadn't intended to go out that evening at all until Mr. Barclay called up and said he must leave the next day, for a few days anyhow, and wanted to see her before he went. She had thought that if they stayed somewhere in the neighborhood in a closed car, as he suggested, it would be all right. But, no. That big car had to turn to there just when it did, and Gil had to be getting off the car and looking up Bergley Place just when it did, and she had to be standing there saying good-bye, just as the lights flashed on that spot. Some people might be lucky, but certainly she was not one of them. The only thing that had saved her was the fact that she had been able to get in the house ahead of Gil, hang up her cape and go in to her room and undress and see if Tickles was still asleep. And yet when he did burst in she had felt that she could not face him—he was so desperate and angry. And yet, good luck, it had ended in his doubting whether he had really seen her or not, though even to this day he would never admit that he doubted.

But the real reason why she hadn't seen Mr. Barclay since (and that in the face of the fact that he had been here in the city once since, and that, as he wrote, he had taken such a fancy to her and wanted to see her and help her in any way she chose), was not that she was afraid of Gil or that she liked him more than she did Mr. Barclay (they were too different in all their thoughts and ways for that) or that she would have to give up her life here and do something else, if Gil really should have found out (she wouldn't have minded that at all)—but because only the day before Mr. Barclay's last letter she had found out that under the law Gil would have the power to take Tickles away from her and not let her see him any more if he caught her in any wrongdoing. That was the thing that had frightened her more than anything else could have and had decided her, then and there, that whatever it was she was thinking she might want to do, it could never repay her for the pain and agony that the loss of Tickles would bring her. She had not really stopped to think of that before. Besides on the night of that quarrel with Gil, that night he thought he saw her in Bergley Place and he had sworn that if ever he could prove anything he would take Tickles away from her, or, that he would kill her and Tickles and himself and Raskoffsky (Raskoffsky!), it was then really that she had realized that she couldn't do without Tickles—no, not for a time even. Her dream of a happier life would be nothing without him—she knew that. And so it was that she had fought there as she had to make Gil believe he was mistaken, even in the face of the fact that he actually knew he had seen her. It was the danger of the loss of Tickles that had given her the courage and humor and calmness, the thought of what the loss of him would mean, the feeling that life would be colorless and blank unless she could take him with her wherever she went, whenever that might be, if ever it was.

And so when Gil had burst in as he did she had taken up Tickles and faced him, after Gil's loud talk had waked him. And Tickles had put his arms about her neck and called "Mama! Mama!" even while she was wondering how she was ever to get out of that scrape. And then because he had fallen asleep again, lying close to her neck, even while Gil was quarreling, she had told herself then that if she came through that quarrel safely she would never do anything more to jeopardize her claim to Tickles, come what might. And with that resolution she had been able to talk to Gil so convincingly and defiantly that he had finally begun to doubt his own senses, as she could see. And so it was that she had managed to face him out and to win completely.

And then the very next day she had called up Mr. Barclay and told him that she couldn't go on with that affair, and why— that Tickles meant too much to her, that she would have to wait and see how her life would work out. And he had been so nice about it then and had sympathized with her and had told her that, all things considered, he believed she was acting wisely and for her own happiness. And so she had been. Only since he had written her and she had had to say no to him again. And now he had gone for good. And she admired him so much. And she never heard from him since, for she had asked him not to write to her unless she first wrote to him.

But with how much regret she had done that! And how commonplace and humdrum this world looked at times now, even with the possession of Tickles. Those few wonderful days. . . . And that dream that had mounted so high. Yet she had Tickles. And in the novel the husband had gone away and the architect had appeared.

A Doer of the Word

Noank is a little played-out fishing town on the southeastern coast of Connecticut, lying half-way between New London and Stonington. Once it was a profitable port for mackerel and cod fishing. Today its wharves are deserted of all save a few lobster smacks. There is a shipyard, employing three hundred and fifty men, a yacht-building establishment, with two or three hired hands; a sail-loft, and some dozen, or so shops or sheds, where the odds and ends of fishing life are made and sold. Everything is peaceful. The sound of the shipyard axes and hammers can be heard for miles over the quiet waters of the bay. In the sunny lane which follows the line of the shore, and along which a few shops struggle in happy-go-lucky disorder, may be heard the voices and noises of the workers at their work. Water gurgling about the stanchions of the docks, the whistle of some fisherman as he dawdles over his nets, or puts his fish ashore, the whirr of the single high-power sewing machine in the sail-loft, often mingle in pleasant harmony, and invite the mind to repose and speculation.

I was in a most examining and critical mood that summer, looking into the nature and significance of many things, and was sitting one day in the shed of the maker of sailboats, where a half-dozen characters of the village were gathered, when some turn in the conversation brought up the nature of man. He is queer, he is restless; life is not so very much when you come to look upon many phases of it.

"Did any of you ever know a contented man?" I inquired idly, merely for the sake of something to say.

There was silence for a moment, and one after another met my roving glance with a thoughtful, self-involved and retrospective eye.

Old Mr. Main was the first to answer.

"Yes, I did. One."

"So did I," put in the sailboat maker, as he stopped in his work to think about it.

"Yes, and I did," said a dark, squat, sunny, little old fisherman, who sold cunners for bait in a little hut next door.

"Maybe you and me are thinking of the same one, Jacob," said old Mr. Main, looking inquisitively at the boat-builder.

"I think we've all got the same man in mind, likely," returned the builder.

"Who is he?" I asked.

"Charlie Potter," said the builder.

"That's the man!" exclaimed Mr. Main.

"Yes, I reckon Charlie Potter is contented, if anybody be," said an old fisherman who had hitherto been silent.

Such unanimity of opinion struck me forcibly. Charlie Potter—what a humble name! not very remarkable, to say the least. And to hear him so spoken of in this restless, religious, quibbling community made it all the more interesting.

"So you really think he is contented, do you?" I asked.

"Yes, sir! Charlie Potter is a contented man," replied Mr. Main, with convincing emphasis.

"Well," I returned, "that's rather interesting. What sort of a man is he?"

"Ah, he's just an ordinary man, not much of anybody. Fishes and builds boats occasionally," put in the boat-builder.

"Is that all? Nothing else?"

"He preaches now and then—not regularly," said Mr. Main.

A-ha! I thought. A religionist!

"A preacher is expected to set a good example," I said.

"He ain't a regular preacher," said Mr. Main, rather quickly. "He's just kind of around in religious work."

"What do you mean?" I asked curiously, not quite catching the import of this "around."

"Well," answered the boat-builder, "he don't take any money for what he does. He ain't got anything."

"What does he live on then?" I persisted, still wondering at the significance of "around in religious work."

"I don't know. He used to fish for a living. Fishes yet once in a while, I believe."

"He makes models of yachts," put in one of the bystanders. "He sold the New Haven Road one for two hundred dollars here not long ago."

A vision of a happy-go-lucky Jack-of-all-trades arose before me. A visionary—a theorist.

"What else?" I asked, hoping to draw them out. "What makes you all think he is contented? What does he do that makes him so contented?"

"Well," said Mr. Main, after a considerable pause and with much of sympathetic emphasis in his voice, "Charlie Potter is just a good man, that's all. That's why he's contented. He does as near as he can what he thinks he ought to by other people —poor people."

"You won't find anybody with a kinder heart than Charlie Potter," put in the boat-builder. "That's the trouble with him, really. He's too good. He don't look after himself right, I say. A fellow has to look out for himself some in this world. If he don't, no one else will."

"Right you are, Henry," echoed a truculent sea voice from somewhere.

I was becoming both amused and interested, intensely so.

"If he wasn't that way, he'd be a darned sight better off than he is," said a thirty-year-old helper, from a far corner of the room.

"What makes you say that?" I queried. "Isn't it better to be kind-hearted and generous than not?"

"It's all right to be kind-hearted and generous, but that ain't sayin' that you've got to give your last cent away and let your family go hungry."

"Is that what Charlie Potter does?"

"Well, no, maybe he don't, but he comes mighty near to it at times. He and his wife and his adopted children have been pretty close to it at times."

You see, this was the center, nearly, for all village gossip and philosophic speculation, and many of the most important local problems, morally and intellectually speaking, were here thrashed out.

"There's no doubt but that's where Charlie is wrong," put in old Mr. Main a little later. "He don't always stop to think of his family."

"What did he ever do that struck you as being over-generous?" I asked of the young man who had spoken from the corner.

"That's all right," he replied in a rather irritated and peevish tone; "I ain't going to go into details now, but there's people around here that hang on him, and that he's give to, that he hadn't orter."

"I believe in lookin' out for Number One, that's what I believe in," interrupted the boat-maker, laying down his rule and line. "This givin' up everything and goin' without yourself may be all right, but I don't believe it. A man's first duty is to his wife and children, that's what I say."

"That's the way it looks to me," put in Mr. Main.

"Well, does Potter give up everything and go without things?" I asked the boat-maker.

"Purty blamed near it at times," he returned definitely, then addressing the company in general he added, "Look at the time he worked over there on Fisher's Island, at the Ellersbie farm—the time they were packing the ice there. You remember that, Henry, don't you?"

Mr. Main nodded.

"What about it?"

"What about it! Why, he give his rubber boots away, like a darned fool, to old drunken Jimmy Harper, and him loafin' around half the year drunk, and worked around on the ice without any shoes himself. He might 'a' took cold and died."

"Why did he do it?" I queried, very much interested by now.

"Oh, Charlie's naturally big-hearted," put in the little old man who sold cunners. "He believes in the Lord and the Bible. Stands right square on it, only he don't belong to no church like. He's got the biggest heart I ever saw in a livin' being."

"Course the other fellow didn't have any shoes for to wear," put in the boat-maker explanatory, "but he never would work, anyhow."

They lapsed into silence while the latter returned to his measuring, and then out of the drift of thought came this from the helper in the corner:

"Yes, and look at the way Bailey used to sponge on him. Get his money Saturday night and drink it all up, and then Sunday morning, when his wife and children were hungry, go cryin' around Potter. Dinged if I'd 'a' helped him. But Potter'd take the food right off his breakfast table and give it to him. I saw him do it! I don't think that's right. Not when he's got four or five orphans of his own to care for."

"His own children?" I interrupted, trying to get the thing straight.

"No, sir; just children he picked up around, here and there."

Here is a curious character, sure enough, I thought—one well worth looking into.

Another lull, and then as I was leaving the room to give the matter a little quiet attention, I remarked to the boat-builder:

"Outside of his foolish giving, you haven't anything against Charlie Potter, have you?"

"Not a thing," he replied, in apparent astonishment. "Charlie Potter's one of the best men that ever lived. He's a good man."

I smiled at the inconsistency and went my way.

A day or two later the loft of the sail-maker, instead of the shed of the boat-builder, happened to be my lounging place, and thinking of this theme, now uppermost in my mind, I said to him:

"Do you know a man around here by the name of Charlie Potter?"

"Well, I might say that I do. He lived here for over fifteen years."

"What sort of a man is he?"

He stopped in his stitching a moment to look at me, and then said:

"How d'ye mean? By trade, so to speak, or religious-like?"

"What is it he has done," I said, "that makes him so popular with all you people? Everybody says he's a good man. Just what do you mean by that?"

"Well," he said, ceasing his work as though the subject were one of extreme importance to him, "he's a peculiar man, Charlie is. He believes in giving nearly everything he has away if any one else needs it. He'd give the coat off his back if you asked him for it. Some folks condemn him for this, and for not giving everything to his wife and them orphans he has, but I always thought the man was nearer right than most of us. I've got a family myself—but, then, so's he, now, for that matter. It's pretty hard to live up to your light always."

He looked away as if he expected some objection to be made to this, but hearing none, he went on. "I always liked him personally very much. He ain't around here now any more—lives up in Norwich, I think. He's a man of his word, though, as truthful as kin be. He ain't never done nothin' for me, I not bein' a takin' kind, but that's neither here nor there."

He paused, in doubt apparently, as to what else to say.

"You say he's so good," I said. "Tell me one thing that he ever did that struck you as being preëminently good."

"Well, now, I can't say as I kin, exactly, offhand," he replied, "there bein' so many of them from time to time. He was always doin' things one way and another. He give to everybody around here that asked him, and to a good many that didn't. I remember once"—and a smile gave evidence of a genial memory—"he give away a lot of pork that he'd put up for the winter to some colored people back here—two or three barrels, maybe. His wife didn't object, exactly, but my, how his mother-in-law did go on about it. She was livin' with him then. She went and railed against him all around."

"She didn't like to give it to them, eh?"

"Well, I should say not. She didn't set with his views, exactly—never did. He took the pork, though—it was right in the coldest weather we had that winter—and hauled it back about seven miles here to where they lived, and handed it all out himself. Course they were awful hard up, but then they might 'a' got along without it. They do now, sometimes. Charlie's too good that way. It's his one fault, if you might so speak of it."

I smiled as the evidence accumulated. Houseless wayfarers, stopping to find food and shelter under his roof, an orphan child carried seven miles on foot from the bedside of a dead mother and cared for all winter, three children, besides two of his own, being raised out of a sense of affection and care for the fatherless.

One day in the local postoffice I was idling a half hour with the postmaster, when I again inquired:

"Do you know Charlie Potter?"

"I should think I did. Charlie Potter and I sailed together for something over eleven years."

"How do you mean sailed together?"

"We were on the same schooner. This used to be a great port for mackerel and cod. We were wrecked once together."

"How was that?"

"Oh, we went on rocks."

"Any lives lost?"

"No, but there came mighty near being. We helped each other in the boat. I remember Charlie was the last one in that time. Wouldn't get in until all the rest were safe."

A sudden resolution came to me.

"Do you know where he is now?"

"Yep, he's up in Norwich, preaching or doing missionary work. He's kind of busy all the time among the poor people, and so on. Never makes much of anything out of it for himself, but just likes to do it, I guess."

"Do you know how he manages to live?"

"No, I don't, exactly. He believes in trusting to Providence for what he needs. He works though, too, at one job and another. He's a carpenter for one thing. Got an idea the Lord will send 'im whatever he needs."

"Well, and does He?"

"Well, he lives." A little later he added:

"Oh, yes. There's nothing lazy about Charlie. He's a good worker. When he was in the fishing line here there wasn't a man worked harder than he did. They can't anybody lay anything like that against him."

"Is he very difficult to talk to?" I asked, meditating on seeking him out. I had so little to do at the time, the very idlest of summers, and the reports of this man's deeds were haunting me. I wanted to discover for myself whether he was real or not—

whether the reports were true. The Samaritan in people is so easily exaggerated at times.

"Oh, no. He's one of the finest men that way I ever knew. You could see him, well enough, if you went up to Norwich, providing he's up there. He usually is, though, I think. He lives there with his wife and mother, you know."

I caught an afternoon boat for New London and Norwich at one-thirty, and arrived in Norwich at five. The narrow streets of the thriving little mill city were alive with people. I had no address, could not obtain one, but through the open door of a news-stall near the boat landing I called to the proprietor:

"Do you know any one in Norwich by the name of Charlie Potter?"

"The man who works around among the poor people here?"

"That's the man."

"Yes, I know him. He lives out on Summer Street, Number Twelve, I think. You'll find it in the city directory."

The ready reply was rather astonishing. Norwich has something like thirty thousand people.

I walked out in search of Summer Street and finally found a beautiful lane of that name climbing upward over gentle slopes, arched completely with elms. Some of the pretty porches of the cottages extended nearly to the sidewalk. Hammocks, rocking-chairs on verandas, benches under the trees—all attested the love of idleness and shade in summer. Only the glimpse of mills and factories in the valley below evidenced the grimmer life which gave rise mayhap to the need of a man to work among the poor.

"Is this Summer Street?" I inquired of an old darky who was strolling cityward in the cool of the evening. An umbrella was under his arm and an evening paper under his spectacled nose.

"Bress de Lord!" he said, looking vaguely around. "Ah couldnt' say. Ah knows dat street—been on it fifty times—but Ah never did know de name. Ha, ha, ha!"

The hills about echoed his hearty laugh.

"You don't happen to know Charlie Potter?"

"Oh, yas, sah. Ah knows Charlie Potter. Dat's his house right ovahdar."

The house in which Charlie Potter lived was a two-story frame, overhanging a sharp slope, which descended directly to the waters of the pretty river below. For a mile or more, the valley of the river could be seen, its slopes dotted with houses, the valley itself lined with mills. Two little girls were upon the sloping lawn to the right of the house. A stout, comfortable-looking man was sitting by a window on the left side of the house, gazing out over the valley.

"Is this where Charlie Potter lives?" I inquired of one of the children.

"Yes, sir."

"Did he live in Noank?"

"Yes, sir."

Just then a pleasant-faced woman of forty-five or fifty issued from a vine-covered door.

"Mr. Potter?" she replied to my inquiry. "He'll be right out."

She went about some little work at the side of the house, and in a moment Charlie Potter appeared. He was short, thick-set, and weighed no less than two hundred pounds. His face and hands were sunburned and brown like those of every fisherman of Noank. An old wrinkled coat and a baggy pair of gray trousers clothed his form loosely. Two inches of a spotted, soft-brimmed hat were pulled carelessly over his eyes. His face was round and full, but slightly seamed. His hands were large, his walk uneven, and rather inclined to a side swing, or the sailor's roll. He seemed an odd, pudgy person for so large a fame.

"Is this Mr. Potter?"

"I'm the man."

"I live on a little hummock at the east of Mystic Island, off Noank."

"You do?"

"I came up to have a talk with you."

"Will you come inside, or shall we sit out here?"

"Let's sit on the step."

"All right, let's sit on the step."

He waddled out of the gate and sank comfortably on the little low doorstep, with his feet on the cool bricks below. I dropped into the space beside him, and was greeted by as sweet and kind a look as I have ever seen in a man's eyes. It was one of perfect courtesy and good nature—void of all suspicion.

"We were sitting down in the sailboat maker's place at Noank the other day, and I asked a half-dozen of the old fellows whether they had ever known a contented man. They all thought a while, and then they said they had. Old Mr. Main and the rest of them agreed that Charlie Potter was a contented man. What I want to know is, are you?"

I looked quizzically into his eyes to see what effect this would have, and if there was no evidence of a mist of pleasure and affection being vigorously restrained I was very much mistaken. Something seemed to hold the man in helpless silence as he gazed vacantly at nothing. He breathed heavily, then drew himself together and lifted one of his big hands, as if to touch me, but refrained.

"Yes, brother," he said after a time, "I *am*."

"Well, that's good," I replied, taking a slight mental exception to the use of the word brother. "What makes you contented?"

"I don't know, unless it is that I've found out what I ought to do. You see, I need so very little for myself that I couldn't be very unhappy."

"What ought you to do?"

"I ought to love my fellowmen."

"And do you?"

"Say, brother, but I do," he insisted quite simply and with no evidence of chicane or make-believe—a simple, natural enthusiasm. "I love everybody. There isn't anybody so low or so mean but I love him. I love you, yes, I do. I love you."

He reached out and touched me with his hand, and while I was inclined to take exception to this very moral enthusiasm, I thrilled just the same as I have not over the touch of any man in years. There was something effective and electric about him, so very warm and foolishly human. The glance which accompanied it spoke, it seemed, as truthfully as his words. He probably did love me—or thought he did. What difference?

We lapsed into silence. The scene below was so charming

that I could easily gaze at it in silence. This little house was very simple, not poor, by no means prosperous, but well-ordered —such a home as such a man might have. After a while I said:

"It is very evident that you think the condition of some of your fellowmen isn't what it ought to be. Tell me what you are trying to do. What method have you for improving their condition?"

"The way I reason is this-a-way," he began. "All that some people have is their feelings, nothing else. Take a tramp, for instance, as I often have. When you begin to sum up to see where to begin, you find that all he has in the world, besides his pipe and a little tobacco, is his feelings. It's all most people have, rich or poor, though a good many think they have more than that. I try not to injure anybody's feelings."

He looked at me as though he had expressed the solution of the difficulties of the world, and the wonderful, kindly eyes beamed in rich romance upon the scene.

"Very good," I said, "but what do you do? How do you go about it to aid your fellowmen?"

"Well," he answered, unconsciously overlooking his own personal actions in the matter, "I try to bring them the salvation which the Bible teaches. You know I stand on the Bible, from cover to cover."

"Yes, I know you stand on the Bible, but what do you do? You don't merely preach the Bible to them. What do you do?"

"No, sir, I don't preach the Bible at all. I stand on it myself. I try as near as I can to do what it says. I go wherever I can be useful. If anybody is sick or in trouble, I'm ready to go. I'll be a nurse. I'll work and earn them food. I'll give them anything I can—that's what I do."

"How can you give when you haven't anything? They told me in Noank that you never worked for money."

"Not for myself alone. I never take any money for myself alone. That would be self-seeking. Anything I earn or take is for the Lord, not me. I never keep it. The Lord doesn't allow a man to be self-seeking."

"Well, then, when you get money what do you do with it? You can't do and live without money."

He had been looking away across the river and the bridge to the city below, but now he brought his eyes back and fixed them on me.

"I've been working now for twenty years or more, and, although I've never had more money than would last me a few days at a time, I've never wanted for anything and I've been able to help others. I've run pretty close sometimes. Time and time again I've been compelled to say, 'Lord, I'm all out of coal,' or 'Lord, I'm going to have to ask you to get me my fare to New Haven tomorrow,' but in the moment of my need He has never forgotten me. Why, I've gone down to the depot time and time again, when it was necessary for me to go, without five cents in my pocket, and He's been there to meet me. Why, He wouldn't keep you waiting when you're about His work. He wouldn't forget you—not for a minute."

I looked at the man in open-eyed amazement.

"Do you mean to say that you would go down to a depot without money and wait for money to come to you?"

"Oh, brother," he said, with the softest light in his eyes, "if you only knew what it is to have faith!"

He laid his hand softly on mine.

"What is car-fare to New Haven or to anywhere, to Him?"

"But," I replied materially, "you haven't any car-fare when you go there—how do you actually get it? Who gives it to you? Give me one instance."

"Why, it was only last week, brother, that a woman wrote me from Malden, Masachusetts, wanting me to come and see her. She's very sick with consumption, and she thought she was going to die. I used to know her in Noank, and she thought if she could get to see me she would feel better.

"I didn't have any money at the time, but that didn't make any difference.

"'Lord,' I said, 'here's a woman sick in Malden, and she wants me to come to her. I haven't got any money, but I'll go right down to the depot, in time to catch a certain train,' and I went. And while I was standing there a man came up to me and said, 'Brother, I'm told to give you this,' and he handed me ten dollars."

"Did you know the man?" I exclaimed.

"Never saw him before in my life," he replied, smiling genially.

"And didn't he say anything more than that?"

"No."

I stared at him, and he added, as if to take the edge off my astonishment:

"Why, bless your heart, I knew he was from the Lord, just the moment I saw him coming."

"You mean to say you were standing there without a cent, expecting the Lord to help you, and He did?"

"'He shall call upon me, and I shall answer him,'" he answered simply, quoting the Ninety-first Psalm.

This incident was still the subject of my inquiry when a little colored girl came out of the yard and paused a moment before us.

"May I go down across the bridge, papa?" she asked.

"Yes," he answered, and then as she tripped away, said:

"She's one of my adopted children." He gazed between his knees at the sidewalk.

"Have you many others?"

"Three."

"Raising them, are you?"

"Yes."

"They seem to think, down in Noank, that living as you do and giving everything away is satisfactory to you but rather hard on your wife and children."

"Well, it is true that she did feel a little uncertain in the beginning, but she's never wanted for anything. She'll tell you herself that she's never been without a thing that she really needed, and she's been happy."

He paused to meditate, I presume, over the opinion of his former fellow townsmen, and then added:

"It's true, there have been times when we have been right where we had to have certain things pretty badly, before they came, but they never failed to come."

While he was still talking, Mrs. Potter came around the corner of the house and out upon the sidewalk. She was going to the Saturday evening market in the city below.

"Here she is," he said. "Now you can ask her."

"What is it?" she inquired, turning a serene and smiling face to me.

"They still think, down in Noank, that you're not very happy with me," he said. "They're afraid you want for something once in a while."

She took this piece of neighborly interference in better fashion than most would, I fancy.

"I have never wanted for anything since I have been married to my husband," she said. "I am thoroughly contented."

She looked at him and he at her, and there passed between them an affectionate glance.

"Yes," he said, when she had passed after a pleasing little conversation, "my wife has been a great help to me. She has never complained."

"People are inclined to talk a little," I said.

"Well, you see, she never complained, but she did feel a little bit worried in the beginning."

"Have you a mission or a church here in Norwich?"

"No, I don't believe in churches."

"Not in churches?"

"No. The sight of a minister preaching the word of God for so much a year is all a mockery to me."

"What do you believe in?"

"Personal service. Churches and charitable institutions and societies are all valueless. You can't reach your fellowman that way. They build up buildings and pay salaries—but there's a better way." (I was thinking of St. Francis and his original dream, before they threw him out and established monasteries and a costume or uniform—the thing he so much objected to.) "This giving of a few old clothes that the moths will get anyhow, that won't do. You've got to give something of yourself, and that's affection. Love is the only thing you can really give in all this world. When you give love, you give everything. Everything comes with it in some way or other."

"How do you say?" I queried. "Money certainly comes handy sometimes."

"Yes, when you give it with your own hand and heart—in no other way. It comes to nothing just contributed to something. Ah!" he added, with sudden animation, "the tangles men can get themselves into, the snarls, the wretchedness! Troubles with women, with men whom they owe, with evil things they say and think, until they can't walk down the street any more without peeping about to see if they are followed. They can't look you in the face; can't walk a straight course, but have got to sneak around corners. Poor, miserable, unhappy —they're worrying and crying and dodging one another!"

He paused, lost in contemplation of the picture he had conjured up.

"Yes," I went on catechistically, determined, if I could, to rout out this matter of giving, this actual example of the modus operandi of Christian charity. "What do you do? How do you get along without giving them money?"

"I don't get along without giving them some money. There are cases, lots of them, where a little money is necessary. But, brother, it is so little necessary at times. It isn't always money they want. You can't reach them with old clothes and charity societies," he insisted. "You've got to love them, brother. You've got to go to them and love them, just as they are, scarred and miserable and bad-hearted."

"Yes," I replied doubtfully, deciding to follow this up later. "But just what is it you do in a needy case? One instance?"

"Why, one night I was passing a little house in this town," he went on, "and I heard a woman crying. I went right up to the door and opened it, and when I got inside she just stopped and looked at me.

" 'Madam,' I said, 'I have come to help you, if I can. Now you tell me what you're crying for.'

"Well, sir, you know she sat there and told me how her husband drank and how she didn't have anything in the house to eat, and so I just gave her all I had and told her I would see her husband for her, and the next day I went and hunted him up and said to him, 'Oh, brother, I wish you would open your eyes and see what you are doing. I wish you wouldn't do that any more. It's only misery you are creating.' And, you know, I got to telling about how badly his wife felt about it, and how I intended to work and try and help her, and bless me if he didn't up and promise me before I got through that he wouldn't do that any more. And he didn't. He's working today, and it's been two years since I went to him, nearly."

His eyes were alight with his appreciation of personal service.

"Yes, that's one instance," I said.

"Oh, there are plenty of them," he replied. "It's the only way. Down here in New London a couple of winters ago we had a terrible time of it. That was the winter of the panic, you know. Cold—my, but that was a cold winter, and thousands of people out of work—just thousands. It was awful. I tried to do what I could here and there all along, but finally things got so bad there that I went to the mayor. I saw they were raising some kind of a fund to help the poor, so I told him that if he'd give me a little of the money they were talking of spending that I'd feed the hungry for a cent-and-a-half a meal."

"A cent-and-a-half a meal!"

"Yes, sir. They all thought it was rather curious, not possible at first, but they gave me the money and I fed 'em."

"Good meals?"

"Yes, as good as I ever eat myself," he replied.

"How did you do it?" I asked.

"Oh, I can cook. I just went around to the markets, and told the market-men what I wanted—heads of mackerel, and the part of the halibut that's left after the rich man cuts off his steak—it's the poorest part that he pays for, you know. And I went fishing myself two or three times—borrowed a big boat and got men to help me—oh, I'm a good fisherman, you know. And then I got the loan of an old covered brick-yard that no one was using any more, a great big thing that I could close up and build fires in, and I put my kettle in there and rigged up tables out of borrowed boards, and got people to loan me plates and spoons and knives and forks and cups. I made fish chowder, and fish dinners, and really I set a very fine table, I did, that winter."

"For a cent-and-a-half a meal!"

"Yes, sir, a cent-and-a-half a meal. Ask any one in New London. That's all it cost me. The mayor said he was surprised at the way I did it."

"Well, but there wasn't any particular personal service in the money they gave you?" I asked, catching him up on that point. "They didn't personally serve—those who gave you the money?"

"No, sir, they didn't," he replied dreamily, with unconscious simplicity. "But they gave through me, you see. That's the way it was. I gave the personal service. Don't you see? That's the way."

"Yes, that's the way," I smiled, avoiding as far as possible a further discussion of this contradiction, so unconscious on his part, and in the drag of his thought he took up another idea.

"I clothed 'em that winter, too—went around and got barrels and boxes of old clothing. Some of them felt a little ashamed to put on the things, but I got over that, all right. I was wearing them myself, and I just told them, 'Don't feel badly, brother. I'm wearing them out of the same barrel with you—I'm wearing them out of the same barrel.' Got my clothes entirely free for that winter."

"Can you always get all the aid you need for such enterprises?"

"Usually, and then I can earn a good deal of money when I work steadily. I can get a hundred and fifty dollars for a little yacht, you know, every time I find time to make one; and I can make a good deal of money out of fishing. I went out fishing here on the Fourth of July and caught two hundred blackfish—four and five pounds, almost, every one of them."

"That ought to be profitable," I said.

"Well, it was," he replied.

"How much did you get for them?"

"Oh, I didn't sell them," he said. "I never take money for my work that way. I gave them all away."

"What did you do?" I asked, laughing—"advertise for people to come for them?"

"No. My wife took some, and my daughters, and I took the rest and we carried them around to people that we thought would like to have them."

"Well, that wasn't so profitable, was it?" I commented amusedly.

"Yes, they were fine fish," he replied, not seeming to have heard me.

We dropped the subject of personal service at this point, and I expressed the opinion that his service was only a temporary expedient. Times changed, and with them, people. They forgot. Perhaps those he aided were none the better for accepting his charity.

"I know what you mean," he said. "But that don't make any difference. You just have to keep on giving, that's all, see? Not all of 'em turn back. It helps a lot. Money is the only dangerous thing to give—but I never give money—not very often. I give myself, rather, as much as possible. I give food and clothing, too, but I try to show 'em a new way—that's not money, you know. So many people need a new way. They're looking for it often, only they don't seem to know how. But God, dear brother, however poor or mean they are—He knows. You've got to reach the heart, you know, and I let Him help me. You've got to make a man over in his soul, if you want to help him, and money won't help you to do that, you know. No, it won't."

He looked up at me in clear-eyed faith. It was remarkable.

"Make them over?" I queried, still curious, for it was all like a romance, and rather fantastic to me. "What do you mean? How do you make them over?"

"Oh, in their attitude, that's how. You've got to change a man and bring him out of self-seeking if you really want to make him good. Most men are so tangled up in their own errors and bad ways, and so worried over their seekings, that unless you can set them to giving it's no use. They're always seeking, and they don't know what they want half the time. Money isn't the thing. Why, half of them wouldn't understand how to use it if they had it. Their minds are not bright enough. Their perceptions are not clear enough. All you can do is to make them content with themselves. And that, giving to others will do. I never saw the man or the woman yet who couldn't be happy if you could make them feel the need of living for others, of doing something for somebody besides themselves. It's a fact. Selfish people are never happy."

He rubbed his hands as if he saw the solution of the world's difficulties very clearly, and I said to him:

"Well, now, you've got a man out of the mire, and 'saved,' as you call it, and then what? What comes next?"

"Well, then he's saved," he replied. "Happiness comes next —content."

"I know. But must he go to church, or conform to certain rules?"

"No, no, no!" he replied sweetly. "Nothing to do except to be good to others. 'True religion and undefiled before our God and Father is this'" he quoted, "'to visit the widow and the orphan in their affliction and to keep unspotted from the world. Charity is kind,'" you know. "'Charity vaunteth not itself, is not puffed up, seeketh not its own.'"

"Well," I said, rather aimlessly, I will admit, for this high faith staggered me. (How high! How high!) "And then what?"

"Well, then the world would come about. It would be so much better. All the misery is in the lack of sympathy one with another. When we get that straightened out we can work in peace. There are lots of things to do, you know."

Yes, I thought, looking down on the mills and the driving force of self-interest—on greed, lust, love of pleasure, all their fantastic and yet moving dreams.

"I'm an ignorant man myself, and I don't know all," he went on, "and I'd like to study. My, but I'd like to look into all things, but I can't do it now. We can't stop until this thing is straightened out. Some time, maybe," and he looked peacefully away.

"By the way," I said, "whatever became of the man to whom you gave your rubber boots over on Fisher's Island?"

His face lit up as if it were the most natural thing that I should know about it.

"Say," he exclaimed, in the most pleased and confidential way, as if we were talking about a mutual friend, "I saw him not long ago. And, do you know, he's a good man now—really, he is. Sober and hard-working. And, say, would you believe it, he told me that I was the cause of it—just that miserable old pair of rubber boots—what do you think of that?"

I shook his hand at parting, and as we stood looking at each other in the shadow of the evening I asked him:

"Are you afraid to die?"

"Say, brother, but I'm not," he returned. "It hasn't any terror for me at all. I'm just as willing. My, but I'm willing."

He smiled and gripped me heartily again, and, as I was starting to go, said:

"If I die tonight, it'll be all right. He'll use me just as long as He needs me. That I know. Good-by."

"Good-by," I called back.

He hung by his fence, looking down upon the city. As I turned the next corner I saw him awakening from his reflection and waddling stolidly back into the house.

Nigger Jeff

THE city editor was waiting for one of his best reporters, Elmer Davies by name, a vain and rather self-sufficient youth who was inclined to be of that turn of mind which sees in life only a fixed and ordered process of rewards and punishments. If one did not do exactly right, one did not get along well. On the contrary, if one did, one did. Only the so-called evil were really punished, only the good truly rewarded—or Mr. Davies had heard this so long in his youth that he had come nearly to believe it. Presently he appeared. He was dressed in a new spring suit, a new hat and new shoes. In the lapel of his coat was a small bunch of violets. It was one o'clock of a sunny spring afternoon, and he was feeling exceedingly well and good-natured—quite fit, indeed. The world was going unusually well with him. It seemed worth singing about.

"Read that, Davies," said the city editor, handing him the clipping. "I'll tell you afterward what I want you to do."

The reporter stood by the editorial chair and read:

Pleasant Valley, Ko., April 16.
"A most dastardly crime has just been reported here. Jeff Ingalls, a negro, this morning assaulted Ada Whitaker, the nineteen-year-old daughter of Morgan Whitaker, a well-to-do farmer, whose home is four miles south of this place. A posse, headed by Sheriff Mathews, has started in pursuit. If he is caught, it is thought he will be lynched."

The reporter raised his eyes as he finished. What a terrible crime! What evil people there were in the world! No doubt such a creature ought to be lynched, and that quickly.

"You had better go out there, Davies," said the city editor. "It looks as if something might come of that. A lynching up here would be a big thing. There's never been one in this state."

Davies smiled. He was always pleased to be sent out of town. It was a mark of appreciation. The city editor rarely sent any of the other men on these big stories. What a nice ride he would have!

As he went along, however, a few minutes later he began to meditate on this. Perhaps, as the city editor had suggested, he might be compelled to witness an actual lynching. That was by no means so pleasant in itself. In his fixed code of rewards and punishments he had no particular place for lynchings, even for crimes of the nature described, especially if he had to witness the lynching. It was too horrible a kind of reward or punishment. Once, in line of duty, he had been compelled to witness a hanging, and that had made him sick—deathly so—even though carried out as a part of the due process of law of his day and place. Now, as he looked at this fine day and his excellent clothes, he was not so sure that this was a worthwhile assignment. Why should he always be selected for such things —just because he could write? There were others—lots of men on the staff. He began to hope as he went along that nothing really serious would come of it, that they would catch the man before he got there and put him in jail—or, if the worst had to be—painful thought!—that it would be all over by the time he got there. Let's see—the telegram had been filed at nine a.m. It was now one-thirty and would be three by the time he got out there, all of that. That would give him time enough, and then, if all were well, or ill, as it were, he could just gather the details of the crime and the—aftermath—and return. The mere thought of an approaching lynching troubled him greatly, and the farther he went the less he liked it.

He found the village of Pleasant Valley a very small affair indeed, just a few dozen houses nestling between green slopes of low hills, with one small business corner and a rambling array of lanes. One or two merchants of K——, the city from which he had just arrived, lived out here, but otherwise it was very rural. He took notes of the whiteness of the little houses, the shimmering beauty of the small stream one had to cross in going from the depot. At the one main corner a few men were gathered about a typical village barroom. Davies headed for this as being the most likely source of information.

In mingling with this company at first he said nothing about his being a newspaper man, being very doubtful as to its effect upon them, their freedom of speech and manner.

The whole company was apparently tense with interest in the crime which still remained unpunished, seemingly craving excitement and desirous of seeing something done about it. No such opportunity to work up wrath and vent their stored-up animal propensities had probably occurred here in years. He took this occasion to inquire into the exact details of the attack, where it had occurred, where the Whitakers lived. Then, seeing that mere talk prevailed here, he went away thinking that he had best find out for himself how the victim was. As yet she had not been described, and it was necessary to know a little something about her. Accordingly, he sought an old man who kept a stable in the village, and procured a horse. No carriage was to be had. Davies was not an excellent rider, but he made a shift of it. The Whitaker home was not so very far away—about four miles out—and before long he was knocking at its front door, set back a hundred feet from the rough country road.

"I'm from the *Times*," he said to the tall, rawboned woman who opened the door, with an attempt at being impressive. His position as reporter in this matter was a little dubious; he might be welcome, and he might not. Then he asked if this were Mrs. Whitaker, and how Miss Whitaker was by now.

"She's doing very well," answered the woman, who seemed decidedly stern, if repressed and nervous, a Spartan type. "Won't you come in? She's rather feverish, but the doctor says she'll probably be all right later on." She said no more.

Davies acknowledged the invitation by entering. He was very anxious to see the girl, but she was sleeping under the influence of an opiate, and he did not care to press the matter at once.

"When did this happen?" he asked.

"About eight o'clock this morning," said the woman. "She

started to go over to our next door neighbor here, Mr. Edmonds, and this negro met her. We didn't know anything about it until she came crying through the gate and dropped down in here."

"Were you the first one to meet her?" asked Davies.

"Yes, I was the only one," said Mrs. Whitaker. "The men had all gone to the fields."

Davies listened to more of the details, the type and history of the man, and then rose to go. Before doing so he was allowed to have a look at the girl, who was still sleeping. She was young and rather pretty. In the yard he met a country man who was just coming to get home news. The latter imparted more information.

"They're lookin' all around south of here," he said, speaking of a crowd which was supposed to be searching. "I expect they'll make short work of him if they get him. He can't get away very well, for he's on foot, wherever he is. The sheriff's after him too, with a deputy or two, I believe. He'll be tryin' to save him an' take him over to Clayton, but I don't believe he'll be able to do it, not if the crowd catches him first."

So, thought Davies, he would probably have to witness a lynching after all. The prospect was most unhappy.

"Does any one know where this negro lived?" he asked heavily, a growing sense of his duty weighing upon him.

"Oh, right down here a little way," replied the farmer. "Jeff Ingalls was his name. We all know him around here. He worked for one and another of the farmers hereabouts, and don't appear to have had such a bad record, either, except for drinkin' a little now and then. Miss Ada recognized him, all right. You follow this road to the next crossing and turn to the right. It's a little log house that sets back off the road—something like that one you see down the lane there, only it's got lots o' chips scattered about."

Davies decided to go there first, but changed his mind. It was growing late, and he thought he had better return to the village. Perhaps by now developments in connection with the sheriff or the posse were to be learned.

Accordingly, he rode back and put the horse in the hands of its owner, hoping that all had been concluded and that he might learn of it here. At the principal corner much the same company was still present, arguing, fomenting, gesticulating. They seemed parts of different companies that earlier in the day had been out searching. He wondered what they had been doing since, and then decided to ingratiate himself by telling them he had just come from the Whitakers and what he had learned there of the present condition of the girl and the movements of the sheriff.

Just then a young farmer came galloping up. He was coatless, hatless, breathless.

"They've got him!" he shouted excitedly. "They've got him!"

A chorus of "whos," "wheres" and "whens" greeted this information as the crowd gathered about the rider.

"Why, Mathews caught him up here at his own house!" exclaimed the latter, pulling out a handkerchief and wiping his face. "He must 'a' gone back there for something. Mathews's takin' him over to Clayton, so they think, but they don't project he'll ever get there. They're after him now, but Mathews says he'll shoot the first man that tries to take him away."

"Which way'd he go?" exclaimed the men in chorus, stirring as if to make an attack.

" 'Cross Sellers' Lane," said the rider. "The boys think he's goin' by way of Baldwin."

"Whoopee!" yelled one of the listeners. "We'll get him away from him, all right! Are you goin', Sam?"

"You bet!" said the latter. "Wait'll I get my horse!"

"Lord!" thought Davies. "To think of being (perforce) one of a lynching party—a hired spectator!"

He delayed no longer, however, but hastened to secure his horse again. He saw that the crowd would be off in a minute to catch up with the sheriff. There would be information in that quarter, drama very likely.

"What's doin'?" inquired the liveryman as he noted Davies' excited appearance.

"They're after him," replied the latter nervously. "The sheriff's caught him. They're going now to try to take him away from him, or that's what they say. The sheriff is taking him over to Clayton, by way of Baldwin. I want to get over there if I can. Give me the horse again, and I'll give you a couple of dollars more."

The liveryman led the horse out, but not without many

provisionary cautions as to the care which was to be taken of him, the damages which would ensue if it were not. He was not to be ridden beyond midnight. If one were wanted for longer than that Davies must get him elsewhere or come and get another, to all of which Davies promptly agreed. He then mounted and rode away.

When he reached the corner again several of the men who had gone for their horses were already there, ready to start. The young man who had brought the news had long since dashed off to other parts.

Davies waited to see which road this new company would take. Then through as pleasant a country as one would wish to see, up hill and down dale, with charming vistas breaking upon the gaze at every turn, he did the riding of his life. So disturbed was the reporter by the grim turn things had taken that he scarcely noted the beauty that was stretched before him, save to note that it was so. Death! Death! The proximity of involuntary and enforced death was what weighed upon him now.

In about an hour the company had come in sight of the sheriff, who, with two other men, was driving a wagon he had borrowed along a lone country road. The latter was sitting at the back, a revolver in each hand, his face toward the group, which at sight of him trailed after at a respectful distance. Excited as every one was, there was no disposition, for the time being at least, to halt the progress of the law.

"He's in that wagon," Davies heard one man say. "Don't you see they've got him in there tied and laid down?"

Davies looked.

"That's right," said another. "I see him now."

"What we ought to do," said a third, who was riding near the front, "is to take him away and hang him. That's just what he deserves, and that's what he'll get before we're through to-day."

"Yes!" called the sheriff, who seemed to have heard this. "You're not goin' to do any hangin' this day, so you just might as well go on back." He did not appear to be much troubled by the appearance of the crowd.

"Where's old man Whitaker?" asked one of the men who seemed to feel that they needed a leader. "He'd get him quick enough!"

"He's with the other crowd, down below Olney," was the reply.

"Somebody ought to go an' tell him."

"Clark's gone," assured another, who hoped for the worst.

Davies rode among the company a prey to mingled and singular feelings. He was very much excited and yet depressed by the character of the crowd which, in so far as he could see, was largely impelled to its jaunt by curiosity and yet also able under sufficient motivation on the part of some one—any one, really—to kill too. There was not so much daring as a desire to gain daring from others, an unconscious wish or impulse to organize the total strength or will of those present into one strength or one will, sufficient to overcome the sheriff and inflict death upon his charge. It was strange—almost intellectually incomprehensible—and yet so it was. The men were plainly afraid of the determined sheriff. They thought something ought to be done, but they did not feel like getting into trouble.

Mathews, a large solemn, sage, brown man in worn clothes and a faded brown hat, contemplated the recent addition to his trailers with apparent indifference. Seemingly he was determined to protect his man and avoid mob justice, come what may. A mob should not have him if he had to shoot, and if he shot it would be to kill. Finally, since the company thus added to did not dash upon him, he seemingly decided to scare them off. Apparently he thought he could do this, since they trailed like calves.

"Stop a minute!" he called to his driver.

The latter pulled up. So did the crowd behind. Then the sheriff stood over the prostrate body of the negro, who lay in the jolting wagon beneath him, and called back:

"Go 'way from here, you people! Go on, now! I won't have you follerin' after me!"

"Give us the nigger!" yelled one in a half-bantering, half-derisive tone of voice.

"I'll give ye just two minutes to go on back out o' this road," returned the sheriff grimly, pulling out his watch and looking at it. They were about a hundred feet apart. "If you don't, I'll clear you out!"

"Give us the nigger!"

"I know you, Scott," answered Mathews, recognizing the voice. "I'll arrest every last one of ye tomorrow. Mark my word!"

The company listened in silence, the horses champing and twisting.

"We've got a right to foller," answered one of the men.

"I give ye fair warning," said the sheriff, jumping from his wagon and leveling his pistols as he approached. "When I count five I'll begin to shoot!"

He was a serious and stalwart figure as he approached, and the crowd fell back a little.

"Git out o' this now!" he yelled. "One—Two——"

The company turned completely and retreated, Davies among them.

"We'll foller him when he gits further on," said one of the men in explanation.

"He's got to do it," said another. "Let him git a little ways ahead."

The sheriff returned to his wagon and drove on. He seemed, however, to realize that he would not be obeyed and that safety lay in haste alone. His wagon was traveling fast. If only he could lose them or get a good start he might possibly get to Clayton and the strong county jail by morning. His followers, however, trailed him swiftly as might be, determined not to be left behind.

"He's goin' to Baldwin," said one of the company of which Davies was a member.

"Where's that?" asked Davies.

"Over west o' here, about four miles."

"Why is he going there?"

"That's where he lives. I guess he thinks if he kin git 'im over there he kin purtect 'im till he kin get more help from Clayton. I cal'late he'll try an' take 'im over yet to-night, or early in the mornin' shore."

Davies smiled at the man's English. This country-side lingo always fascinated him.

Yet the men lagged, hesitating as to what to do. They did not want to lose sight of Mathews, and yet cowardice controlled them. They did not want to get into direct altercation with the law. It wasn't their place to hang the man, although plainly they felt that he ought to be hanged, and that it would be a stirring and exciting thing if he were. Consequently they desired to watch and be on hand—to get old Whitaker and his son Jake, if they could, who were out looking elsewhere. They wanted to see what the father and brother would do.

The quandary was solved by one of the men, who suggested that they could get to Baldwin by going back to Pleasant Valley and taking the Sand River Pike, and that in the meantime they might come upon Whitaker and his son en route, or leave word at his house. It was a shorter cut than this the sheriff was taking, although he would get there first now. Possibly they could beat him at least to Clayton, if he attempted to go on. The Clayton road was back via Pleasant Valley, or near it, and easily intercepted. Therefore, while one or two remained to trail the sheriff and give the alarm in case he did attempt to go on to Clayton, the rest, followed by Davies, set off at a gallop to Pleasant Valley. It was nearly dusk now when they arrived and stopped at the corner store—supper time. The fires of evening meals were marked by upcurling smoke from chimneys. Here, somehow, the zest to follow seemed to depart. Evidently the sheriff had worsted them for the night. Morg Whitaker, the father, had not been found; neither had Jake. Perhaps they had better eat. Two or three had already secretly fallen away.

They were telling the news of what had occurred so far to one of the two storekeepers who kept the place, when suddenly Jake Whitaker, the girl's brother, and several companions came riding up. They had been scouring the territory to the north of the town, and were hot and tired. Plainly they were unaware of the developments of which the crowd had been a part.

"The sheriff's got 'im!" exclaimed one of the company, with that blatance which always accompanies the telling of great news in small rural companies. "He taken him over to Baldwin in a wagon a coupla hours ago."

"Which way did he go?" asked the son, whose hardy figure, worn, hand-me-down clothes and rakish hat showed up picturesquely as he turned here and there on his horse.

" 'Cross Seller Lane. You won't git 'em that-a-way, though, Jake. He's already over there by now. Better take the short cut."

A babble of voices now made the scene more interesting. One told how the negro had been caught, another that the sheriff was defiant, a third that men were still tracking him or over there watching, until all the chief points of the drama had been spoken if not heard.

Instantly suppers were forgotten. The whole customary order of the evening was overturned once more. The company started off on another excited jaunt, up hill and down dale, through the lovely country that lay between Baldwin and Pleasant Valley.

By now Davies was very weary of this procedure and of his saddle. He wondered when, if ever, this story was to culminate, let alone he write it. Tragic as it might prove, he could nevertheless spend an indefinite period trailing a possibility, and yet, so great was the potentiality of the present situation, he dared not leave. By contrast with the horror impending, as he now noted, the night was so beautiful that it was all but poignant. Stars were already beginning to shine. Distant lamps twinkled like yellow eyes from the cottages in the valleys and on the hillsides. The air was fresh and tender. Some pea-fowls were crying afar off, and the east promised a golden moon.

Silently the assembled company trotted on—no more than a score in all. In the dusk, and with Jake ahead, it seemed too grim a pilgrimage for joking. Young Jake, riding silently toward the front, looked as if tragedy were all he craved. His friends seemed considerately to withdraw from him, seeing that he was the aggrieved.

After an hour's riding Baldwin came into view, lying in a sheltering cup of low hills. Already its lights were twinkling softly and there was still an air of honest firesides and cheery suppers about it which appealed to Davies in his hungry state. Still, he had no thought now of anything save this pursuit.

Once in the village, the company was greeted by calls of recognition. Everybody seemed to know what they had come for. The sheriff and his charge were still there, so a dozen citizens volunteered. The local storekeepers and loungers followed the cavalcade up the street to the sheriff's house, for the riders had now fallen into a solemn walk.

"You won't get him though, boys," said one whom Davies later learned was Seavey, the village postmaster and telegraph operator, a rather youthful person of between twenty-five and thirty, as they passed his door. "He's got two deputies in there with him, or did have, and they say he's going to take him over to Clayton."

At the first street corner they were joined by the several men who had followed the sheriff.

"He tried to give us the slip," they volunteered excitedly, "but he's got the nigger in the house, there, down in the cellar. The deputies ain't with him. They've gone somewhere for help—Clayton, maybe."

"We saw 'em go out that back way. We think we did, anyhow."

A hundred feet from the sheriff's little white cottage, which backed up against a sloping field, the men parleyed. Then Jake announced that he proposed to go boldly up to the sheriff's door and demand the negro.

"If he don't turn him out I'll break in the door an' take him!" he said.

"That's right! We'll stand by you, Whitaker," commented several.

By now the throng of unmounted natives had gathered. The whole village was up and about, its one street alive and running with people. Heads appeared at doors and windows. Riders pranced up and down, hallooing. A few revolver shots were heard. Presently the mob gathered even closer to the sheriff's gate, and Jake stepped forward as leader. Instead, however, of going boldly up to the door as at first it appeared he would, he stopped at the gate, calling to the sheriff.

"Hello, Mathews!"

"Eh, eh, eh!" bellowed the crowd.

The call was repeated. Still no answer. Apparently to the sheriff delay appeared to be his one best weapon.

Their coming, however, was not as unexpected as some might have thought. The figure of the sheriff was plainly to be seen close to one of the front windows. He appeared to be holding a double-barreled shotgun. The negro, as it developed later, was cowering and chattering in the darkest corner of the cellar, hearkening no doubt to the voices and firing of the revolvers outside.

Suddenly, and just as Jake was about to go forward, the front door of the house flew open, and in the glow of a single lamp inside appeared first the double-barreled end of the gun, followed immediately by the form of Mathews, who held the weapon poised ready for a quick throw to the shoulder. All except Jake fell back.

"Mr. Mathews," he called deliberately, "we want that nigger!"

"Well, you can't git 'em!" replied the sheriff. "He's not here."

"Then what you got that gun fer?" yelled a voice.

Mathews made no answer.

"Better give him up, Mathews," called another, who was safe in the crowd, "or we'll come in an' take him!"

"No you won't," said the sheriff defiantly. "I said the man wasn't here. I say it ag'in. You couldn't have him if he was, an' you can't come in my house! Now if you people don't want trouble you'd better go on away."

"He's down in the cellar!" yelled another.

"Why don't you let us see?" asked another.

Mathews waved his gun slightly.

"You'd better go away from here now," cautioned the sheriff. "I'm tellin' ye! I'll have warrants out for the lot o' ye, if ye don't mind!"

The crowd continued to simmer and stew, while Jake stood as before. He was very pale and tense, but lacked initiative.

"He won't shoot," called some one at the back of the crowd. "Why don't you go in, Jake, an' git him?"

"Sure! Rush in. That's it!" observed a second.

"He won't, eh?" replied the sheriff softly. Then he added in a lower tone, "The first man that comes inside that gate takes the consequences."

No one ventured inside the gate; many even fell back. It seemed as if the planned assault had come to nothing.

"Why not go around the back way?" called some one else.

"Try it!" replied the sheriff. "See what you find on that side! I told you you couldn't come inside. You'd better go away from here now before ye git into trouble," he repeated. "You can't come in, an' it'll only mean bloodshed."

There was more chattering and jesting while the sheriff

stood on guard. He, however, said no more. Nor did he allow the banter, turmoil and lust for tragedy to disturb him. Only, he kept his eye on Jake, on whose movements the crowd seemed to hang.

Time passed, and still nothing was done. The truth was that young Jake, put to the test, was not sufficiently courageous himself, for all his daring, and felt the weakness of the crowd behind him. To all intents and purposes he was alone, for he did not inspire confidence. He finally fell back a little, observing, "I'll git 'im before mornin', all right," and now the crowd itself began to disperse, returning to its stores and homes or standing about the postoffice and the one village drugstore. Finally, Davies smiled and came away. He was sure he had the story of a defeated mob. The sheriff was to be his great hero. He proposed to interview him later. For the present, he meant to seek out Seavey, the telegraph operator, and arrange to file a message, then see if something to eat was not to be had somewhere.

After a time he found the operator and told him what he wanted—to write and file a story as he wrote it. The latter indicated a table in the little postoffice and telegraph station which he could use. He became very much interested in the reporter when he learned he was from the *Times*, and when Davies asked where he could get something to eat said he would run across the street and tell the proprietor of the only boarding house to fix him something which he could consume as he wrote. He appeared to be interested in how a newspaper man would go about telling a story of this kind over a wire.

"You start your story," he said, "and I'll come back and see if I can get the *Times* on the wire."

Davies sat down and began his account. He was intent on describing things to date, the uncertainty and turmoil, the apparent victory of the sheriff. Plainly the courage of the latter had won, and it was all so picturesque. "A foiled lynching," he began, and as he wrote the obliging postmaster, who had by now returned, picked up the pages and carefully deciphered them for himself.

"That's all right. I'll see if I can get the *Times* now," he commented.

"Very obliging postmaster," thought Davies as he wrote, but he had so often encountered pleasant and obliging people on his rounds that he soon dropped that thought.

The food was brought, and still Davies wrote on, munching as he did so. In a little while the *Times* answered an often-repeated call.

"Davies at Baldwin," ticked the postmaster, "get ready for quite a story!"

"Let 'er go!" answered the operator at the *Times*, who had been expecting this dispatch.

As the events of the day formulated themselves in his mind, Davies wrote and turned over page after page. Between whiles he looked out through the small window before him where afar off he could see a lonely light twinkling against a hillside. Not infrequently he stopped his work to see if anything new was happening, whether the situation was in any danger of changing, but apparently it was not. He then proposed to remain until all possibility of a tragedy, this night anyhow, was eliminated. The operator also wandered about, waiting for an accumulation of pages upon which he could work but making sure to keep up with the writer. The two became quite friendly.

Finally, his dispatch nearly finished, he asked the postmaster to caution the night editor at K—— to the effect, that if anything more happened before one in the morning he would file it, but not to expect anything more as nothing might happen. The reply came that he was to remain and await developments. Then he and the postmaster sat down to talk.

About eleven o'clock, when both had about convinced themselves that all was over for this night anyhow, and the lights in the village had all but vanished, a stillness of the purest, summery-est, country-est quality having settled down, a faint beating of hoofs, which seemed to suggest the approach of a large cavalcade, could be heard out on the Sand River Pike as Davies by now had come to learn it was, back or northwest of the post-office. At the sound the postmaster got up, as did Davies, both stepping outside and listening. On it came, and as the volume increased, the former said, "Might be help for the sheriff, but I doubt it. I telegraphed Clayton six times to-day. They wouldn't come that way, though. It's the wrong road." Now, thought

Davies nervously, after all there might be something to add to his story, and he had so wished that it was all over! Lynchings, as he now felt, were horrible things. He wished people wouldn't do such things—take the law, which now more than ever he respected, into their own hands. It was too brutal, cruel. That negro cowering there in the dark probably, and the sheriff all taut and tense, worrying over his charge and his duty, were not happy things to contemplate in the face of such a thing as this. It was true that the crime which had been committed was dreadful, but still why couldn't people allow the law to take its course? It was so much better. The law was powerful enough to deal with cases of this kind.

"They're comin' back, all right," said the postmaster solemnly, as he and Davies stared in the direction of the sound which grew louder from moment to moment.

"It's not any help from Clayton, I'm afraid."

"By George, I think you're right!" answered the reporter, something telling him that more trouble was at hand. "Here they come!"

As he spoke there was a clattering of hoofs and crunching of saddle girths as a large company of men dashed up the road and turned into the narrow street of the village, the figure of Jake Whitaker and an older bearded man in a wide black hat riding side by side in front.

"There's Jake," said the postmaster, "and that's his father riding beside him there. The old man's a terror when he gets his dander up. Sompin's sure to happen now."

Davies realized that in his absence writing a new turn had been given to things. Evidently the son had returned to Pleasant Valley and organized a new posse or gone out to meet his father.

Instantly the place was astir again. Lights appeared in doorways and windows, and both were thrown open. People were leaning or gazing out to see what new movement was afoot. Davies noted at once that there was none of the brash enthusiasm about this company such as had characterized the previous descent. There was grimness everywhere, and he now began to feel that this was the beginning of the end. After the cavalcade had passed down the street toward the sheriff's house, which was quite dark now, he ran after it, arriving a few moments after the former which was already in part dismounted. The towns-people followed. The sheriff, as it now developed, had not re-laxed any of his vigilance, however; he was not sleeping, and as the crowd reappeared the light inside reappeared.

By the light of the moon, which was almost overhead, Davies was able to make out several of his companions of the afternoon, and Jake, the son. There were many more, though, now, whom he did not know, and foremost among them this old man.

The latter was strong, iron-gray, and wore a full beard. He looked very much like a blacksmith.

"Keep your eye on the old man," advised the postmaster, who had by now come up and was standing by.

While they were still looking, the old man went boldly for-ward to the little front porch of the house and knocked at the door. Some one lifted a curtain at the window and peeped out.

"Hello, in there!" cried the old man, knocking again.

"What do you want?" asked a voice.

"I want that nigger!"

"Well, you can't have him! I've told you people that once."

"Bring him out or I'll break down the door!" said the old man.

"If you do it's at your own risk. I know you, Whitaker, an' you know me. I'll give ye two minutes to get off that porch!"

"I want that nigger, I tell ye!"

"If ye don't git off that porch I'll fire through the door," said the voice solemnly. "One—Two——"

The old man backed cautiously away.

"Come out, Mathews!" yelled the crowd. "You've got to give him up this time. We ain't goin' back without him."

Slowly the door opened, as if the individual within were very well satisfied as to his power to handle the mob. He had done it once before this night, why not again? It revealed his tall form, armed with his shotgun. He looked around very stolidly, and then addressed the old man as one would a friend.

"Ye can't have him, Morgan," he said. "It's ag'in' the law. You know that as well as I do."

"Law or no law," said the old man, "I want that nigger!"

"I tell you I can't let you have him, Morgan. It's ag'in' the law. You know you oughtn't to be comin' around here at this time o' night actin' so."

"Well, I'll take him then," said the old man, making a move.

"Stand back!" shouted the sheriff, leveling his gun on the instant. "I'll blow ye into kingdom come, sure as hell!"

A noticeable movement on the part of the crowd ceased. The sheriff lowered his weapon as if he thought the danger were once more over.

"You-all ought to be ashamed of yerselves," he went on, his voice sinking to a gentle neighborly reproof, "tryin' to upset the law this way."

"The nigger didn't upset no law, did he?" asked one derisively.

"Well, the law's goin' to take care of the nigger now," Mathews made answer.

"Give us that scoundrel, Mathews; you'd better do it," said the old man. "It'll save a heap o' trouble."

"I'll not argue with ye, Morgan. I said ye couldn't have him, an' ye can't. If ye want bloodshed, all right. But don't blame me. I'll kill the first man that tries to make a move this way."

He shifted his gun handily and waited. The crowd stood outside his little fence murmuring.

Presently the old man retired and spoke to several others. There was more murmuring, and then he came back to the dead line.

"We don't want to cause trouble, Mathews," he began explanatively, moving his hand oratorically, "but we think you ought to see that it won't do any good to stand out. We think that——"

Davies and the postmaster were watching young Jake, whose peculiar attitude attracted their attention. The latter was standing poised at the edge of the crowd, evidently seeking to remain unobserved. His eyes were on the sheriff, who was hearkening to the old man. Suddenly, as the father talked and when the sheriff seemed for a moment mollified and unsuspecting, he made a quick run for the porch. There was an intense movement all along the line as the life and death of the deed became apparent. Quickly the sheriff drew his gun to his shoulder. Both triggers were pressed at the same time, and the gun spoke, but not before

Jake was in and under him. The latter had been in sufficient time to knock the gun barrel upward and fall upon his man. Both shots blazed harmlessly, over the heads of the crowd in red puffs, and then followed a general onslaught. Men leaped the fence by tens and crowded upon the little cottage. They swarmed about every side of the house and crowded upon the porch, where four men were scuffling with the sheriff. The latter soon gave up, vowing vengeance and the law. Torches were brought, and a rope. A wagon drove up and was backed into the yard. Then began the calls for the negro.

As Davies contemplated all this he could not help thinking of the negro who during all this turmoil must have been crouching in his corner in the cellar, trembling for his fate. Now indeed he must realize that his end was near. He could not have dozed or lost consciousness during the intervening hours, but must have been cowering there, wondering and praying. All the while he must have been terrified lest the sheriff might not get him away in time. Now, at the sound of horses' feet and the new murmurs of contention, how must his body quake and his teeth chatter!

"I'd hate to be that nigger," commented the postmaster grimly, "but you can't do anything with 'em. The county oughta sent help."

"It's horrible, horrible!" was all Davies could say.

He moved closer to the house, with the crowd, eager to observe every detail of the procedure. Now it was that a number of the men, as eager in their search as bloodhounds, appeared at a low cellar entryway at the side of the house carrying a rope. Others followed with torches. Headed by father and son they began to descend into the dark hole. With impressive daring, Davies, who was by no means sure that he would be allowed but who was also determined if possible to see, followed.

Suddenly, in the farthest corner, he espied Ingalls. The latter in his fear and agony had worked himself into a crouching position, as if he were about to spring. His nails were apparently forced into the earth. His eyes were rolling, his mouth foaming.

"Oh, my Lawd, boss," he moaned, gazing almost as one blind, at the lights, "oh, my Lawd, boss, don't kill me! I won't do it no mo'. I didn't go to do it. I didn't mean to dis time. I was just drunk, boss. Oh, my Lawd! My Lawd!" His teeth chattered the while his mouth seemed to gape open. He was no longer sane really, but kept repeating monotonously, "Oh, my Lawd!"

"Here he is, boys! Pull him out," cried the father.

The negro now gave one yell of terror and collapsed, falling prone. He quite bounded as he did so, coming down with a dead chug on the earthen floor. Reason had forsaken him. He was by now a groveling, foaming brute. The last gleam of intelligence was that which notified him of the set eyes of his pursuers.

Davies, who by now had retreated to the grass outside before this sight, was standing but ten feet back when they began to reappear after seizing and binding him. Although shaken to the roots of his being, he still had all the cool observing powers of the trained and relentless reporter. Even now he noted the color values of the scene, the red, smoky heads of the torches, the disheveled appearance of the men, the scuffling and pulling. Then all at once he clapped his hands over his mouth, almost unconscious of what he was doing.

"Oh, my God!" he whispered, his voice losing power.

The sickening sight was that of the negro, foaming at the mouth, bloodshot as to his eyes, his hands working convulsively, being dragged up the cellar steps feet foremost. They had tied a rope about his waist and feet, and so had hauled him out, leaving his head to hang and drag. The black face was distorted beyond all human semblance.

"Oh, my God!" said Davies again, biting his fingers unconsciously.

The crowd gathered about now more closely than ever, more horror-stricken than gleeful at their own work. None apparently had either the courage or the charity to gainsay what was being done. With a kind of mechanical deftness now the negro was rudely lifted and like a sack of wheat thrown into the wagon. Father and son now mounted in front to drive and the crowd took to their horses, content to clatter, a silent cavalcade, behind. As Davies afterwards concluded, they were not so much hardened lynchers perhaps as curious spectators, the majority of them, eager for any variation—any excuse for one—to the dreary commonplaces of their existences. The task to most—

all indeed—was entirely new. Wide-eyed and nerve-racked, Davies ran for his own horse and mounting followed. He was so excited he scarcely knew what he was doing.

Slowly the silent company now took its way up the Sand River pike whence it had come. The moon was still high, pouring down a wash of silvery light. As Davies rode he wondered how he was to complete his telegram, but decided that he could not. When this was over there would be no time. How long would it be before they would really hang him? And would they? The whole procedure seemed so unreal, so barbaric that he could scarcely believe it—that he was a part of it. Still they rode on.

"Are they really going to hang him?" he asked of one who rode beside him, a total stranger who seemed however not to resent his presence.

"That's what they got 'im fer," answered the stranger.

And think, he thought to himself, to-morrow night he would be resting in his own good bed back in K——!

Davies dropped behind again and into silence and tried to recover his nerves. He could scarcely realize that he, ordinarily accustomed to the routine of the city, its humdrum and at least outward social regularity, was a part of this. The night was so soft, the air so refreshing. The shadowy trees were stirring with a cool night wind. Why should any one have to die this way? Why couldn't the people of Baldwin or elsewhere have bestirred themselves on the side of the law before this, just let it take its course? Both father and son now seemed brutal, the injury to the daughter and sister not so vital as all this. Still, also, custom seemed to require death in this way for this. It was like some axiomatic, mathematic law—hard, but custom. The silent company, an articulated, mechanical and therefore terrible thing, moved on. It also was axiomatic, mathematic. After a time he drew near to the wagon and looked at the negro again.

The latter, as Davies was glad to note, seemed still out of his sense. He was breathing heavily and groaning, but probably not with any conscious pain. His eyes were fixed and staring, his face and hands bleeding as if they had been scratched or trampled upon. He was crumpled limply.

But Davies could stand it no longer now. He fell back, sick at heart, content to see no more. It seemed a ghastly, murderous thing to do. Still the company moved on and he followed, past fields lit white by the moon, under dark, silent groups of trees, through which the moonlight fell in patches, up low hills and down into valleys, until at last a little stream came into view, the same little stream, as it proved, which he had seen earlier to-day and for a bridge over which they were heading. Here it ran now, sparkling like electricity in the night. After a time the road drew closer to the water and then crossed directly over the bridge, which could be seen a little way ahead.

Up to this the company now rode and then halted. The wagon was driven up on the bridge, and father and son got out. All the riders, including Davies, dismounted, and a full score of them gathered about the wagon from which the negro was lifted, quite as one might a bag. Fortunately, as Davies now told himself, he was still unconscious, an accidental mercy. Nevertheless he decided now that he could not witness the end, and went down by the waterside slightly above the bridge. He was not, after all, the utterly relentless reporter. From where he stood, however, he could see long beams of iron projecting out over the water, where the bridge was braced, and some of the men fastening a rope to a beam, and then he could see that they were fixing the other end around the negro's neck.

Finally the curious company stood back, and he turned his face away.

"Have you anything to say?" a voice demanded.

There was no answer. The negro was probably lolling and groaning, quite as unconscious as he was before.

Then came the concerted action of a dozen men, the lifting of the black mass into the air, and then Davies saw the limp form plunge down and pull up with a creaking sound of rope. In the weak moonlight it seemed as if the body were struggling, but he could not tell. He watched, wide-mouthed and silent, and then the body ceased moving. Then after a time he heard the company making ready to depart, and finally it did so, leaving him quite indifferently to himself and his thoughts. Only the black mass swaying in the pale light over the glimmering water seemed human and alive, his sole companion.

He sat down upon the bank and gazed in silence. Now the horror was gone. The suffering was ended. He was no longer afraid. Everything was summery and beautiful. The whole cavalcade had disappeared; the moon finally sank. His horse, tethered to a sapling beyond the bridge, waited patiently. Still he sat. He might now have hurried back to the small postoffice in Baldwin and attempted to file additional details of this story, providing he could find Seavey, but it would have done no good. It was quite too late, and anyhow what did it matter? No other reporter had been present, and he could write a fuller, sadder, more colorful story on the morrow. He wondered idly what had become of Seavey? Why had he not followed? Life seemed so sad, so strange, so mysterious, so inexplicable.

As he still sat there the light of morning broke, a tender lavender and gray in the east. Then came the roseate hues of dawn, all the wondrous coloring of celestial halls, to which the waters of the stream responded. The white pebbles shone pinkily at the bottom, the grass and sedges first black now gleamed a translucent green. Still the body hung there black and limp against the sky, and now a light breeze sprang up and stirred it visibly. At last he arose, mounted his horse and made his way back to Pleasant Valley, too full of the late tragedy to be much interested in anything else. Rousing his liveryman, he adjusted his difficulties with him by telling him the whole story, assuring him of his horse's care and handing him a five-dollar bill. Then he left, to walk and think again.

Since there was no train before noon and his duty plainly called him to a portion of another day's work here, he decided to make a day of it, idling about and getting additional details as to what further might be done. Who would cut the body down? What about arresting the lynchers—the father and son, for instance? What about the sheriff now? Would he act as he threatened? If he telegraphed the main fact of the lynching his city editor would not mind, he knew, his coming late, and the day here was so beautiful. He proceeded to talk with citizens and officials, rode out to the injured girl's home, rode to Baldwin to see the sheriff. There was a singular silence and placidity in that corner. The latter assured him that he knew nearly all of those who had taken part, and proposed to swear out warrants for them, but just the same Davies noted that he took his defeat as he did his danger, philosophically. There was no real activity in that corner later. He wished to remain a popular sheriff, no doubt.

It was sundown again before he remembered that he had not discovered whether the body had been removed. Nor had he heard why the negro came back, nor exactly how he was caught. A nine o'clock evening train to the city giving him a little more time for investigation, he decided to avail himself of it. The negro's cabin was two miles out along a pine-shaded road, but so pleasant was the evening that he decided to walk. En route, the last rays of the sinking sun stretched long shadows of budding trees across his path. It was not long before he came upon the cabin, a one-story affair set well back from the road and surrounded with a few scattered trees. By now it was quite dark. The ground between the cabin and the road was open, and strewn with the chips of a woodpile. The roof was sagged, and the windows patched in places, but for all that it had the glow of a home. Through the front door, which stood open, the blaze of a wood-fire might be seen, its yellow light filling the interior with a golden glow.

Hesitating before the door, Davies finally knocked. Receiving no answer he looked in on the battered cane chairs and aged furniture with considerable interest. It was a typical negro cabin, poor beyond the need of description. After a time a door in the rear of the room opened and a little negro girl entered carrying a battered tin lamp without any chimney. She had not heard his knock and started perceptibly at the sight of his figure in the doorway. Then she raised her smoking lamp above her head in order to see better, and approached.

There was something ridiculous about her unformed figure and loose gingham dress, as he noted. Her feet and hands were so large. Her black head was strongly emphasized by little pig-tails of hair done up in white twine, which stood out all over her head. Her dark skin was made apparently more so by contrast with her white teeth and the whites of her eyes.

Davies looked at her for a moment but little moved now by the oddity which ordinarily would have amused him, and asked, "Is this where Ingalls lived?"

The girl nodded her head. She was exceedingly subdued, and looked as if she might have been crying.

"Has the body been brought here?"

"Yes, suh," she answered, with a soft negro accent.

"When did they bring it?"

"Dis moanin'."

"Are you his sister?"

"Yes, suh."

"Well, can you tell me how they caught him? When did he come back, and what for?" He was feeling slightly ashamed to intrude thus.

"In de afternoon, about two."

"And what for?" repeated Davies.

"To see us," answered the girl. "To see my motha'."

"Well, did he want anything? He didn't come just to see her, did he?"

"Yes, suh," said the girl, "he come to say good-by. We doan know when dey caught him." Her voice wavered.

"Well, didn't he know he might get caught?" asked Davies sympathetically, seeing that the girl was so moved.

"Yes, suh, I think he did."

She still stood very quietly holding the poor battered lamp up, and looking down.

"Well, what did he have to say?" asked Davies.

"He didn' have nothin' much to say, suh. He said he wanted to see motha'. He was a-goin' away."

The girl seemed to regard Davies as an official of some sort, and he knew it.

"Can I have a look at the body?" he asked.

The girl did not answer, but started as if to lead the way.

"When is the funeral?" he asked.

"Tomorra'."

The girl then led him through several bare sheds of rooms strung in a row to the furthermost one of the line. This last seemed a sort of storage shed for odds and ends. It had several windows, but they were quite bare of glass and open to the moonlight save for a few wooden boards nailed across from the outside. Davies had been wondering all the while where the body was and at the lonely and forsaken air of the place. No one but this little pig-tailed girl seemed about. If they had any colored neighbors they were probably afraid to be seen here.

Now, as he stepped into this cool, dark, exposed outer room, the desolation seemed quite complete. It was very bare, a mere shed or wash-room. There was the body in the middle of the room, stretched upon an ironing board which rested on a box and a chair, and covered with a white sheet. All the corners of the room were quite dark. Only its middle was brightened by splotches of silvery light.

Davies came forward, the while the girl left him, still carrying her lamp. Evidently she thought the moon lighted up the room sufficiently, and she did not feel equal to remaining. He lifted the sheet quite boldly, for he could see well enough, and looked at the still, black form. The face was extremely distorted, even in death, and he could see where the rope had been tightened. A bar of cool moonlight lay just across the face and breast. He was still looking, thinking soon to restore the covering, when a sound, half sigh, half groan, reached his ears.

At it he started as if a ghost had made it. It was so eerie and unexpected in this dark place. His muscles tightened. Instantly his heart went hammering like mad. His first impression was that it must have come from the dead.

"Oo-o-ohh!" came the sound again, this time whimpering, as if some one were crying.

Instantly he turned, for now it seemed to come from a corner of the room, the extreme corner to his right, back of him. Greatly disturbed, he approached, and then as his eyes strained he seemed to catch the shadow of something, the figure of a woman, perhaps, crouching against the walls, huddled up, dark, almost indistinguishable.

"Oh, oh, oh!" the sound now repeated itself, even more plaintively than before.

Davies began to understand. He approached slowly, then more swiftly desired to withdraw, for he was in the presence of an old black mammy, doubled up and weeping. She was in the very niche of the two walls, her head sunk on her knees, her body quite still. "Oh, oh, oh!" she repeated, as he stood there near her.

Davies drew silently back. Before such grief his intrusion seemed cold and unwarranted. The guiltlessness of the mother —her love—how could one balance that against the other? The sensation of tears came to his eyes. He instantly covered the dead and withdrew.

Out in the moonlight he struck a brisk pace, but soon stopped and looked back. The whole dreary cabin, with its one golden eye, the door, seemed such a pitiful thing. The weeping mammy, alone in her corner—and he had come back to say "Good-by!" Davies swelled with feeling. The night, the tragedy, the grief, he saw it all. But also with the cruel instinct of the budding artist that he already was, he was beginning to meditate on the character of story it would make—the color, the pathos. The knowledge now that it was not always exact justice that was meted out to all and that it was not so much the business of the writer to indict as to interpret was borne in on him with distinctness by the cruel sorrow of the mother, whose blame, if any, was infinitesimal.

"I'll get it all in!" he exclaimed feelingly, if triumphantly at last. "I'll get it all in!"

The Old Neighborhood

H<small>E</small> came to it across the new bridge, from the south where the greater city lay—the older portion—and where he had left his car, and paused at the nearer bridgehead to look at it—the eddying water of the river below, the new docks and piers built on either side since he had left, twenty years before; the once grassy slopes on the farther shore, now almost completely covered with factories, although he could see too, among them, even now, traces of the old, out-of-the-way suburb which he and Marie had known. Chadds Bridge, now an integral part of the greater city, connected by car lines and through streets, was then such a simple, unpretentious affair, a little suburban village just on the edge of this stream and beyond the last straggling northward streets of the great city below, where the car lines stopped and from which one had to walk on foot across this bridge in order to take advantage of the rural quiet and the cheaper—much cheaper—rents, so all-important to him then.

Then he was poor—he and Marie—a mere stripling of a mechanic and inventor, a student of aeronautics, electricity, engineering, and what not, but newly married and without a dollar, and no clear conception of how his future was to eventuate, whereas now—but somehow he did not want to think of now. Now he was so very rich, comparatively speaking, older, wiser, such a forceful person commercially and in every other way, whereas then he was so lean and pathetic and worried and wistful—a mere uncertain stripling, as he saw himself now, with ideas and ambitions and dreams which were quite out of accord with his immediate prospects or opportunities. It was all right to say, as some one had—Emerson, he believed—"hitch your wagon to a star." But some people hitched, or tried to, before they were ready. They neglected some of the slower moving vehicles about them, and so did not get on at all—or did not seem to, for the time being.

And that had been his error. He was growing at the time, of course, but he was so restless, so dissatisfied with himself, so unhappy. All the world was apparently tinkling and laughing by, eating, drinking, dancing, growing richer, happier, every minute; whereas he—he and Marie, and the two babies which came a little later—seemed to make no progress at all. None. They were out of it, alone, hidden away in this little semi-rural realm, and it was all so disturbing when elsewhere was so much —to him, at least, if not to her—of all that was worth while— wealth, power, gayety, repute. How intensely, savagely almost, he had craved all of those things in those days, and how far off they still were at that time!

Marie was not like him, soft, clinging little thing that she was, inefficient in most big ways, and yet dear and helpful enough in all little ones—oh, so very much so.

When first he met her in Philadelphia, and later when he brought her over to New York, it seemed as though he could not possibly have made a better engagement for himself. Marie was so sweet, so gentle, with her waxy white pallor, delicately tinted cheeks, soft blackish brown eyes that sought his so gently always, as if seeming to ask, "And what can I do for my dearie now? What can he teach me to do for him?" She was never his equal, mentally or spiritually—that was the dreadful discovery he had made a few months after the first infatuation had worn off, after the ivory of her forehead, the lambent sweetness of her eyes, her tresses, and her delicately rounded figure, had ceased to befuddle his more poetical grain. But how delightful she seemed then in her shabby little clothes and her shabbier little home—all the more so because her delicate white blossom of a face was such a contrast to the drear surroundings in which it shone. Her father was no more than a mechanic, she a little store clerk in the great Rand department store in Philadelphia when he met her, he nothing more than an experimental assistant with the Culver Electrical Company, with no technical training of any kind, and only dreams of a technical course at some time or other. The beginnings of his career were so very vague.

His parents were poor too, and he had had to begin to earn his own living, or share, at fourteen. And at twenty-four he had contracted this foolish marriage when he was just beginning to dream of bigger things, to see how they were done, what steps were necessary, what studies, what cogitations and hard, grinding sacrifices even, before one finally achieved anything, especially in the electrical world. The facts which had begun to rise and take color and classify themselves in his mind had all then to develop under the most advantageous conditions thereafter. His salary did not rise at once by any means, just because he was beginning to think of bigger things. He was a no better practical assistant in a laboratory or the equipment department of the several concerns for which he worked, because in his brain were already seething dim outlines of possible improvements in connection with arms, the turbine gun, electro-magnetic distance control, and the rotary excavator. He had ideas, but also he realized at the time he would have to study privately and long in order to make them real; and his studies at night and Sundays and holidays in the libraries and everywhere else, made him no more helpful, if as much so, in his practical, everyday corporation labors. In fact, for a long time when their finances were at the lowest ebb and the two children had appeared, and they all needed clothes and diversion, and his salary had not been raised, it seemed as though he were actually less valuable to everybody.

But in the meantime Marie had worked for and with him, dear little thing, and although she had seemed so wonderful at first, patient, enduring, thoughtful, later because of their poverty and so many other things which hampered and seemed to interfere with his work, he had wearied of her a little. Over in Philadelphia, where he had accompanied her home of an evening and had watched her help her mother, saw her set the table, wash the dishes, straighten up the house after dinner, and then if it were pleasant go for a walk with him, she seemed ideal, just the wife for him, indeed. Later as he sensed the world, its hardness, its innate selfishness, the necessity for push, courage, unwillingness to be a slave and a drudge, these earlier qualities and charms were the very things that militated against her in his mind. Poor little Marie!

But in other ways his mind was not always on his work, either. Sometimes it was on his dreams of bigger things. Sometimes it was on his silly blindness in wanting to get married so soon, in being betrayed by the sweet innocence and beauty of Marie into saddling himself with this burden when he was scarcely prepared, as he saw after he was married, to work out his own life on a sensible, economic basis. A thought which he had encountered somewhere in some book of philosophy or other (he was always reading in those days) had haunted him—"He that hath wife and children hath given hostages to fortune"—and that painful thought seemed to grow with each succeeding day. Why had he been so foolish, why so very foolish, as to get married when he was so unsuitably young! That was a thing the folly of which irritated him all the time.

Not that Marie was not all she should be—far from it!— nor the two little boys (both boys, think of that!), intensely precious to him at first. No, that was not it, but this, that whatever the values and the charms of these (and they were wonderful at first), he personally was not prepared to bear or enjoy them as yet. He was too young, too restless, too nebulous, too inventively dreamful. He did not, as he had so often thought since, know what he wanted—only, when they began to have such a very hard time, he knew he did not want that. Why, after the first year of their marriage, when Peter was born, and because of better trade conditions in the electrical world, they had moved over here (he was making only twenty-two dollars a week at the time), everything had seemed to go wrong. Indeed, nothing ever seemed to go right any more after that, not one thing.

First it was Marie's illness after Peter's birth, which kept him on tenterhooks and took all he could rake and scrape and save to pay the doctor's bill, and stole half her beauty, if not more. She always looked a little pinched and weak after that. (And he had charged that up to her, too!) Then it was some ailment which affected Peter for months and which proved to be undernourishment, due to a defect in Marie's condition even after she had seemingly recovered. Then, two years later, it was the birth of Frank, due to another error, of course, he being not intended in Marie's frail state; and then his own difficulties with the manager of the insulating department of the International Electric, due to his own nervous state, his worries, his consciousness of error in the manipulation of his own career—and Marie's. Life was slipping away, as he saw it then and he kept thinking he was growing older, was not getting on as he had thought he should, was not achieving his technical education; he was saddled with a family which would prevent him from ever getting on. Here, in this neighborhood, all this had occurred—this quiet, run-down realm, so greatly changed since he had seen it last. Yes, it had all happened here.

But how peaceful it was to-day, although changed. How the water ran under this bridge now, as then, eddying out to sea. And how this late October afternoon reminded him of that other October afternoon when they had first walked up here—warm, pleasant, colorful. Would he ever forget that afternoon? He had thought he was going to do so much better—was praying that he would, and they had done so much worse. He, personally, had grown so restless and dissatisfied with himself and her and life. And things seemed to be almost as bad as they could be, drifting indefinitely on to nothing. Indeed, life seemed to gather as a storm and break. He was discharged from the International Electric, due supposedly to his taking home for a night a battery for an experiment he was making but in reality because of the opposition of his superior, based on the latter's contempt for his constantly (possibly) depressed and dissatisfied air, his brooding mien, and some minor inattentions due to the state of his mind at the time.

Then, quite as swiftly (out of black plotting or evil thoughts of his own, perhaps), Peter had died of pneumonia. And three days later Frank. There were two funerals, two dreary, one-carriage affairs—he remembered that so well!—for they had no money; and his pawned watch, five dollars from Marie's mother, and seven chemical and electrical works sold to an old book man had provided the cash advance required by the under-

taker! Then, spiritually, something seemed to break within him.
He could not see this world, this immediate life in which he was
involved, as having any significance in it for himself or any one
after that. He could not stand it any more, the weariness, the
boredom, the dissatisfaction with himself, the failure of himself,
the sickening chain of disasters which had befallen this earlier
adventure. And so—

But that was why he was here to-day, after all these years—
twenty-four, to be exact—with his interest in this old region so
keen, if so sad. Why, there—there!—was a flock of pigeons,
just like those of old Abijah Hargot's, flying around the sky
now, as then. And a curl of smoke creeping up from Tanzer's
blacksmith shop, or the one that had succeeded it, just one block
from this bridge. How well he remembered old Tanzer and
his forge, his swelling muscles and sooty face! He had always
nodded in such a friendly way as he passed and talked of the
pest of flies and heat in summer. That was why he was pausing
on this bridge to-day, just to see once more, to feel, standing
in the pleasant afternoon sun of this October day and gazing
across the swirling waters below at the new coal-pockets, the
enlarged lamp works of the George C. Woodruff Company, once
a mere shed hidden away at a corner of this nearest street and
rented out here no doubt because it was cheap and Woodruff
was just beginning—just as he did twenty-four years before.
Time had sped by so swiftly. One's ideals and ideas changed
so. Twenty years ago he would have given so much to be what
he was now—rich and fairly powerful—and now—now— The
beauty of this old neighborhood, to-day, even.

The buff school which crowned the rise beyond, and the
broad asphalt of Edgewood Avenue leading up to the old
five-story flat building—the only one out here, and a failure
financially—in which he and Marie had had their miserable
little apartment—here it was, still to be seen. Yes, it and so
many other things were all here; that group of great oaks
before old Hargot's door; the little red—if now rusted—
weather-vane over his carriage house; the tall romantic tower
of St. George's Episcopal Church—so far to the west over
the river, and the spars and masts of vessels that still docked
here for a while. But dark memories they generated, too, along

with a certain idyllic sweetness, which had seemed to envelop the whole at first. For though it had had sweetness and peace at first, how much that had been bitter and spiritually destroying had occurred here, too.

How well he recalled, for instance, the day he and Marie had wandered up here, almost hand in hand, across this very bridge and up Edgewood Avenue, nearly twenty-four years before! They had been so happy at first, dreaming their little dream of a wonderful future for them—and now—well, his secret agency had brought him all there was to know of her and her mother and her little world after he had left. They had suffered so much, apparently, and all on account of him. But somehow he did not want to think of that now. It was not for that he had come to-day, but to see, to dream over the older, the better, the first days.

He crossed over, following the old road which had then been a cobble wagon trail, and turned into Edgewood Avenue which led up past the line of semi-country homes which he used to dread so much, homes which because of their superior prosperity, wide lawns, flowers and walks, made the life which he and Marie were compelled to lead here seem so lean and meagre by contrast. Why, yes, here was the very residence of Gatewood, the dentist, so prosperous then and with an office downtown; and that of Dr. Newton, whom he had called in when Peter and Frank were taken ill that last time; and Temple, the druggist, and Stoutmeyer, the grocer—both of whom he had left owing money; and Dr. Newton, too, for that matter—although all had subsequently been paid. Not a sign of the names of either Gatewood or Newton on their windows or gates now; not a trace of Temple's drug store. But here was Stoutmeyer's grocery just the same. And Buchspiel, the butcher. (Could he still be alive, by any chance—was that his stout, aged figure within?) And Ortman, the baker—not a sign of change there. And over the way the then village school, now Public School No. 261, as he could see. And across from it, beyond, the slim little, almost accidental (for this region) five-story apartment house— built because of an error in judgment, of course, when they thought the city was going to grow out this way—a thing of grayish-white brick. On the fifth floor of this, in the rear, he

and Marie had at last found a tiny apartment of three rooms
and bath, cheap enough for them to occupy in the growing city
and still pay their way. What memories the mere sight of the
building evoked! Where were all the people now who used to
bustle about here of a summer evening when he and Marie
were here, boys and girls, grown men and women of the neighborhood? It had all been so pleasant at first, Marie up there
preparing dinner and he coming home promptly at seven and
sometimes whistling as he came! He was not always unhappy,
even here.

Yes, all was exactly as it had been in the old days in regard
to this building and this school, even—as he lived!—a "For
Rent" sign in that very same apartment, four flights up, as
it had been that warm October day when they had first come
up here seeking.

But what a change in himself—stouter, so much older, gray
now. And Marie—dying a few years after in this very region
without his ever seeing her again or she him—and she had
written him such pathetic letters. She had been broken, no doubt,
spiritually and in every other way when he left her,—no
pointless vanity in that, alas—it was too sad to involve vanity.
Yes, he had done that. Would it ever be forgiven him? Would
his error of ambition and self-dissatisfaction be seen anywhere
in any kindly light—on earth or in heaven? He had suffered
so from remorse in regard to it of late. Indeed, now that he
was rich and so successful the thought of it had begun to
torture him. Some time since—five years ago—he had thought
to make amends, but then—well, then he had found that she
wasn't any more. Poor little Marie!

But these walls, so strong and enduring (stone had this
advantage over human flesh!), were quite as he had left them,
quite as they were the day he and Marie had first come here—
hopeful, cheerful, although later so depressed, the two of them.
(And he had charged her spiritually with it all, or nearly so—
its fatalities and gloom, as though she could have avoided
them!)

The ruthlessness of it!

The sheer brutality!

The ignorance!

If she could but see him now, his great shops and factories, his hundreds of employés, his present wife and children, his great new home—and still know how he felt about her! If he could only call her back and tell her, apologize, explain, make some amends! But no; life did not work that way. Doors opened and doors closed. It had no consideration for eleventh-hour repentances. As though they mattered to life, or anything else! He could tell her something now, of course, explain the psychology, let her know how pathetically depressed and weary he had felt then. But would she understand, care, forgive? She had been so fond of him, done so much for him in her small, sweet way. And yet, if she only knew, he could scarcely have helped doing as he did then, so harried and depressed and eager for advancement had he been, self-convinced of his own error and failure before ever his life had a good start. If she could only see how little all his later triumphs mattered now, how much he would be glad to do for her now! if only—only— he could. Well, he must quit these thoughts. They did not help at all, nor his coming out here and feeling this way!

But life was so automatic and unconsciously cruel at times. One's disposition drove one so, shutting and bolting doors behind one, driving one on and on like a harried steer up a narrow runway to one's fate. He could have been happy right here with Marie and the children—as much so as he had ever been since. Or, if he had only taken Marie along, once the little ones were gone—they might have been happy enough together. They might have been! But no, no; something in him at that time would not let him. Really, he was a victim of his own grim impulses, dreams, passions, mad and illogical as that might seem. He was crazy for success, wild with a desire for a superior, contemptuous position in the world. People were so, at times. He had been. He had to do as he did, so horribly would he have suffered mentally if he had not, all the theories of the moralists to the contrary notwithstanding. The notions of one's youth were not necessarily those of age, and that was why he was here to-day in this very gloomy and contrite mood.

He went around the corner now to the side entrance of the old apartment house, and paused. For there, down the street, almost—not quite—as he had left it, was the residence of the quondam old Abijah Hargot, he of the pigeons,—iron manufacturer and Presbyterian, who even in his day was living there in spite of the fact that the truly princely residence suburbs had long since moved much farther out and he was being entirely surrounded by an element of cheaper life which could not have been exactly pleasant to him. In those days he and Marie had heard of the hardwood floors, the great chandeliers, the rugs and pictures of the house that had faced a wide sward leading down to the river's edge itself. But look at it now! A lumber-yard between it and the river! And some sort of a small shop or factory on this end of the lawn! And in his day, Abijah had kept a pet Jersey cow nibbling the grass under the trees and fantailed pigeons on the slate roof of his barn, at the corner where now was this small factory, and at the back of his house an immense patch of golden glow just outside the conservatory facing the east, and also two pagodas down near the river. But all gone! all gone, or nearly so. Just the house and a part of the lawn. And occupied now by whom? In the old days he had never dared dream, or scarcely so, that some day, years later—when he would be much older and sadder, really, and haunted by the ghosts of these very things—he would be able to return here and know that he had far more imposing toys than old Hargot had ever dreamed of, as rich as he was.

Toys!

Toys!

Yes, they were toys, for one played with them a little while, as with so many things, and then laid them aside forever.

Toys!

Toys!

But then, as he had since come to know, old Hargot had not been without his troubles, in spite of all his money. For, as rumor had it then, his oldest son, Lucien, his pride, in those days, a slim, artistic type of boy, had turned out a drunkard, gambler, night-life lover; had run with women, become afflicted with all sorts of ills, and after his father had cut him off and driven him out (refusing to permit him even to visit the home), had hung about here, so the neighbors had said, and stolen in to see his mother, especially on dark or rainy nights, in order to get aid from her. And, like all mothers, she had aided him secretly, or so they said, in spite of her fear of her husband. Mothers were like that—his mother, too. Neighbors testified that they had seen her whispering to him in the shade of the trees of the lawn or around the corner in the next street—a sad, brooding, care-worn woman, always in black or dark blue. Yes, life held its disappointments for every one, of course, even old Abijah and himself.

He went on to the door and paused, wondering whether to go up or not, for the atmosphere of this building and this neighborhood was very, very sad now, very redolent of old, sweet, dead and half-forgotten things. The river there, running so freshly at the foot of the street; the school where the children used to play and shout, while he worked on certain idle days when there was no work at the factory; the little church up the street to which so many commonplace adherents used to make their way on Sunday; the shabby cabin of the plumber farther up this same street, who used to go tearing off every Saturday and Sunday in a rattle-trap car which he had bought second-hand and which squeaked and groaned, for all the expert repairing he had been able to do upon it.

The color, the humor, the sunshine of those old first days, in spite of their poverty!

He hesitated as to whether to ring the bell or no—just as he and Marie had, twenty-odd years before. She was so gay then, so hopeful, so all-unconscious of the rough fate that was in store for her here. . . . How would it be inside? Would Marie's little gas stove still be near the window in the combined kitchen, dining-room and laundry—almost general living-room—which that one room was? Would the thin single gas jet still be hanging from the ceiling over their small dining-room table (or the ghost of it) where so often after their meals, to save heat in the other room—because there was no heat in the alleged radiator, and their oil stove cost money—he had sat and read or worked on plans of some of the things he hoped to perfect—and had since, years since, but long after he had left her and this place? How sad! He had never had one touch of luck or opportunity with her here,—not one. Yet, if only she could, and without pain because of it, know how brilliantly he had finished some of them, how profitably they had resulted for him if not her.

But he scarcely looked like one who would be wanting to see so small an apartment, he now felt, tall and robust and prosperous as he was. Still might he not be thinking of buying this place? Or renting quarters for a servant or a relative? Who should know? What difference did it make? Why should he care?

He rang the bell, thinking of the small, stupid, unfriendly and self-defensive woman who, twenty or more years before, had come up from the basement below, wiping her hands on a gingham apron and staring at them querulously. How well he remembered her—and how unfriendly she had always remained in spite of their efforts to be friendly, because they had no tips to give her. She could not be here any longer, of course; no, this one coming was unlike her in everything except stupidity and grossness. But they were alike in that, well enough. This one was heavy, beefy. She would make almost two of the other one.

"The rooms," he had almost said "apartment," "on the top floor—may I see them?"

"Dey are only t'ree an' bat'—fourteen by der mont'."

"Yes, I know," he now added almost sadly. So they had not raised the rent in all this time, although the city had grown so. Evidently this region had become worse, not better. "I'll look at them, if you please, just the same," he went on, feeling that the dull face before him was wondering why he should be looking at them at all.

"Vait; I getcha der key. You can go up py yerself."

He might have known that she would never climb any four flights save under compulsion.

She returned presently, and he made his way upward, remembering how the fat husband of the former janitress had climbed up promptly every night at ten, if you please, putting out the wee lights of gas on the return trip (all but a thin flame on the second floor: orders from the landlord, of course), and exclaiming as he did so, at each landing, "Ach Gott, I go me up py der secon' floor ant make me der lights out. Ach Gott, I go me py der t'ird floor ant make me der lights out. Ach Gott, I go me py der fourt' floor ant make me der lights out," and so on until he reached the fifth, where they lived. How often he had listened to him, puffing and moaning as he came!

Yes, the yellowish-brown paper that they had abhorred then, or one nearly as bad, covered all these hall walls today. The stairs squeaked, just as they had then. The hall gas jets were just as small and surmounted by shabby little pink imitation glass candles—to give the place an air, no doubt! He and Marie would never have taken this place at all if it had depended on the hall, or if the views from its little windows had not been so fine. In the old days he had trudged up these steps many a night, winter and summer, listening, as he came, for sounds of Marie in the kitchen, for the prattle of the two children after they were with them, for the glow of a friendly light (always shining at six in winter) under the door and through the key-hole. His light! His door! In those early dark winter days, when he was working so far downtown and coming home this way regularly, Marie, at the sound of his key in the lock, would always come running, her heavy black hair done in a neat braid about her brow, her trim little figure buttoned gracefully into a house-dress of her own making. And she always had a smile and a "Hello, dearie; back again?" no matter how bad things were with them, how lean the little larder or the family purse. Poor little Marie!

It all came back to him now as he trudged up the stairs and neared the door. God!

And here was the very door, unchanged—yellow, painted to imitate the natural grain of oak, but the job having turned out a dismal failure as he had noted years before. And the very lock the same! Could he believe? Scarcely any doubt of it. For here was that old hole, stuffed with putty and painted over, which he and Marie had noted as being the scar of some other kind of a lock or knob that had preceded this one. And still stuffed with paper! Marie had thought burglars (!) might make their way in via that, and he had laughed to think what they would steal if they should. Poor little Marie!

But now, now—well, here he was all alone, twenty-four years later, Marie and Peter and Frank gone this long time, and he the master of so many men and so much power and so much important property. What was life, anyhow? What was it?

Ghosts! Ghosts!

Were there ghosts?

Did spirits sometimes return and live and dream over old, sad scenes such as this? Could Marie? Would she? Did she?

Oh, Marie! . . . Marie! Poor little weak, storm-beaten, life-beaten soul. And he the storm, really.

Well, here was the inside now, and things were not a bit different from what they had been in his and her day, when they had both been so poor. No, just the same. The floor a little more nail-marked, perhaps, especially in the kitchen here, where no doubt family after family had tacked down oil-cloth in place of other pieces taken up—theirs, for instance. And here in the parlor—save the mark!—the paper as violent as it had ever been! Such paper—red, with great bowls of pinkish flowers arranged in orderly rows! But then they were paying so little rent that it was ridiculous for them to suggest that they wanted anything changed. The landlord would not have changed it anyhow.

And here on the west wall, between the two windows, over-looking Abijah Hargot's home and the river and the creeping city beyond, was where he had hung a wretched little picture, a print of an etching of a waterscape which he had admired so much in those days and had bought somewhere second-hand for a dollar—a house on an inlet near the sea, such a house as he would have liked to have occupied, or thought he would—then. Ah, these windows! The northernmost one had always been preferred by him and her because of the sweep of view west and north. And how often he had stood looking at a soft, or bleak, or reddening, sunset over the river; or, of an early night in winter, at the lights on the water below. And the outpost apart-ments and homes of the great city beyond. Life had looked very dark then, indeed. At times, looking, he had been very sad. He was like some brooding Hamlet of an inventor as he stood there then gazing at the sweet little river, the twinkling stars in a steely black sky overhead; or, in the fall when it was still light, some cold red island of a cloud in the sky over the river and the city, and wondering what was to become of him—what was in store for him! The fallacy of such memories as these! Their futility!

But things had dragged and dragged—here! In spite of the fact that his mind was full of inventions, inventions, inventions, and methods of applying them in some general way which would earn him money, place, fame—as they subsequently did—the strange mysteries of ironic or electronic action, for instance, of motion, of attraction and polarity, of wave lengths and tensile strengths and adhesions in metals, woods and materials of all kinds—his apparent error in putting himself in a position where failure might come to him had so preyed on his mind here, that he could do nothing. He could only dream, and do common, ordinary day labor—skeleton wiring and insulating, for instance, electrical mapping, and the like. Again, later, but while still here, since he had been reading, reading, reading after marriage, and working and thinking, life had gone off into a kind of welter of conflicting and yet organized and plainly directed powers which was confusing to him, which was not to be explained by anything man could think of and which no inventor had as yet fully used, however great he was—Edison, Kelvin, or Bell. Everything as he knew then and hoped to make use of in some way was alive, everything full of force, even so-called dead or decaying things. Life was force, that strange, seemingly (at times) intelligent thing, and there was apparently nothing but force—everywhere—amazing, perfect, indestructible. (He had thought of all that here in this little room and on the roof overhead where he made some of his experiments, watching old Hargot's pigeons flying about the sky, the sound of their wings coming so close at times that they were like a whisper of the waves of the sea, dreams in themselves.)

But the little boundaries of so-called health and decay, strength and weakness, as well as all alleged *fixity* or change-lessness of things,—how he had brooded on all that, at that time. And how all thought of fixity in anything had disappeared as a ridiculous illusion intended, maybe, by something to fool man into the belief that his world here, his physical and mental state, was real and enduring, a greater thing than anything else in the universe, when so plainly it was not. But not himself. A mere shadow—an illusion—nothing. On this little roof, here, sitting alone at night or by day in pleasant weather or gray, Saturdays and Sundays when it was warm and because they had no money and no particular place to go, and looking at the stars or the lights of the city or the sun shining on the waters of the little river below,—he had thought of all this. It had all come to him, the evanescence of everything, its slippery, protean changefulness. Everything was alive, and everything was nothing, in so far as its seeming reality was concerned. And yet everything was everything but still capable of being undermined, changed, improved, or come at in some hitherto undreamed-of way—even by so humble a creature as himself, an inventor—and used as chained force, if only one knew how. And that was why he had become a great inventor since—because he had thought so—had chained force and used it—even he. He had become conscious of anterior as well as ulterior forces and immensities and fathomless wells of wisdom and energy, and had enslaved a minute portion of them, that was all. But not here! Oh, no. Later!

The sad part of it, as he thought of it now, was that poor little Marie could not have understood a thing of all he was thinking, even if he had explained and explained, as he never attempted to do. Life was all a mystery to Marie—deep, dark, strange—as it was to him, only he was seeking and she was not. Sufficient to her to be near him, loving him in her simple, dumb way, not seeking to understand. Even then he had realized that and begun to condemn her for it in his mind, to feel that she was no real aid and could never be—just a mother-girl, a housewife, a social fixture, a cook, destined to be shoved back if ever he were really successful; and that was sad even then, however obviously true.

But to her, apparently, he was so much more than just a mere man—a god, really, a dream, a beau, a most wonderful person, dreaming strange dreams and thinking strange thoughts which would lead him heaven knows where; how high or how strange, though, she could never guess, nor even he then. And for that very reason—her blind, non-understanding adoration—she had bored him then, horribly at times. All that he could think of then, as he looked at her at times—after the first year or two or three, when the novelty of her physical beauty and charm had worn off and the children had come, and cares and worries due to his non-success were upon them—was that she was an honest, faithful, patient, adoring little drudge, but no more, and that was all she would ever be. Think of that! That was the way life was—the way it rewarded love! He had not begun to dislike her—no, that was not it—but it was because, as the philosopher had said, that in and through her and the babies he had given hostages to fortune, and that she was not exactly the type of woman who could further him as fast as he wished—that he had begun to weary of her. And that was practically the whole base of his objection to her,—not anything she did.

Yes, yes—it was that, *that*, that had begun to plague him as though he had consciously fastened a ball and chain on one foot and now never any more could walk quickly or well or be really free. Instead of being able to think on his inventions he was constantly being compelled to think on how he would make a living for her and them, or find ten more dollars, or get a new dress for Marie and shoes for the children! Or how increase his salary. That was the great and enduring problem all the time, and over and over here. Although healthy, vigorous and savagely ambitious, at that time, it was precisely because he was those things that he had rebelled so and had desired to be free. He was too strong and fretful as he could see now to endure so mean a life. It was that that had made him savage, curt, remote, indifferent so much of the time in these later days—here— And to her. And when she could not help it at all—poor little thing— did not know how to help it and had never asked him to marry her! Life had tinkled so in his ears then. It had called and called. And essentially, in his own eyes then, he was as much of a failure as a husband as he was at his work, and that was killing him. His mind had been too steadily depressed by his mistake in getting married, in having children so soon, as well as by his growing knowledge of what he might be fitted to do if only he had a chance to go off to a big technical school somewhere and work his way through alone and so get a new and better position somewhere else—to have a change of scene. For once, as he knew then, and with all his ideas, he was technically fitted for his work, with new light and experience in his mind, what wonders might he not accomplish! Sitting in this little room, or working or dreaming upstairs in the air, how often he had thought of all that!

But no; nothing happened for ever so long here. Days and weeks and months, and even years went by without perceptible change. Nature seemed to take a vicious delight in torturing him, then, in so far as his dreams were concerned, his hopes. Hard times came to America, blasting ones—a year and a half of panic really—in which every one hung on to his pathetic little place, and even he was afraid to relinquish the meagre one he had, let alone ask for more pay. At the same time his dreams, the passing of his youth, this unconscionable burden of a family, tortured him more and more. Marie did not seem to mind anything much, so long as she was with him. She suffered, of course, but more for him than for herself, for his unrest, and his dissatisfaction, which she feared. Would he ever leave her? Was he becoming unhappy with her? Her eyes so often asked what her lips feared to frame.

Once they had seventy dollars saved toward some inventive work of his. But then little Peter fell from the top of the washtub, where he had climbed for some reason, and broke his arm. Before it was healed and all the bills paid, the seventy was gone. Another time Marie's mother was dying, or so she thought, and she had to go back home and help her father and brother in their loneliness. Again, it was brother George who, broke, arrived from Philadelphia and lived with them a while because he had no place else to go. Also once he thought to better himself by leaving the International Electric, and joining the Winston Castro Generator Company. But when he had left the first, the manager of the second, to whom he had applied and by whom he had been engaged, was discharged ("let out," as he phrased it), and the succeeding man did not want him. So for three long months he had been without anything, and, like Job, finally, he had been ready to curse God and die.

And then—right here in these rooms it was—he had rebelled, spiritually, as he now recalled, and had said to himself that he could not stand this any longer, that he was ruining his life, and that however much it might torture Marie—ruin her even—he must leave and do something to better his state. Yes, quite definitely, once and for all, then, he had wished that he had not married Marie, that they had never been so foolish as to have children, that Marie was not dependent on him any more, that he was free to go, be, do, all the things he felt that he could go do, be—no matter where, so long as he went and was free. Yes, he had wished that in a violent, rebellious, prayerful way, and then—

Of all the winters of his life, the one that followed that was the blackest and bleakest, that last one with Marie. It seemed to bring absolutely nothing to either him or her or the children save disaster. Twenty-five dollars was all he had ever been able to make, apparently, while he was with her. The children were growing and constantly requiring more; Marie needed many things, and was skimping along on God knows what. Once she had made herself some corset slips and other things out of his cast-off underwear—bad as that was! And then once, when he was crossing Chadds Bridge, just below here, and had paused to meditate and dream, a new hat—his very best, needless to say, for he had worn his old one until it was quite gone—had blown off into the water, a swift wind and some bundles he was compelled to carry home aiding, and had been swiftly carried out by the tide. So much had he been harried in those days by one thing and another that at first he had not even raged, although he was accustomed so to do. Instead then he had just shut his teeth and trudged on in the biting wind, in danger of taking cold and dying of something or other—as he had thought at the time—only then he had said to himself that he did not really mind now. What difference did it make to himself or anybody whether he died or not? Did anybody care really, God or anybody else, what became of him? Supposing he did it? What of it? Could it be any worse than this? To hell with life itself, and its Maker,—this brutal buffeting of winds and cold and harrying hungers and jealousies and fears and brutalities, arranged to drive and make miserable these crawling, beggarly creatures— men! Why, what had he ever had of God or any creative force so far? What had God ever done for him or his life, or his wife and children?

So he had defiantly raged.

And then life—or God, or what you will—had seemed to strike at last. It was as if some Jinnee of humane or inhuman power had said, "Very well, then, since you are so dissatisfied and unhappy, so unworthy of all this (perhaps) that I have given you, you shall have your will, your dreams. You have prayed to be free. Even so—this thing that you see here now shall pass away. You have sinned against love and faith in your thoughts. You shall be free! Look! Behold! You shall be! Your dreams shall come true!"

And then, at once, as if in answer to this command of the Jinnee, as though, for instance, it had waved its hand, the final storm began which blew everything quite away. Fate struck. It was as if black angels had entered and stationed themselves at his doors and windows, armed with the swords of destruction, of death. Harpies and furies beset his path and perched on his roof. One night—it was a month before Peter and Frank died, only three days before they contracted their final illness—he was crossing this same bridge below here and was speculating, as usual, as to his life and his future, when suddenly, in spite of the wind and cold and some dust flying from a coal barge below, his eye was attracted by two lights which seemed to come dancing down the hill from the direction of his apartment and passed out over the river. They rose to cross over the bridge in front of him and disappeared on the other side. They came so close they seemed almost to brush his face, and yet he could not quite accept them as real. There was something too eerie about them. From the moment he first laid eyes on them in the distance they seemed strange. They came so easily, gracefully, and went so. From the first moment he saw them there below Tegetmiller's paint shop, he wondered about them. What were they? What could they mean? They were so bluish clear, like faint, grey stars, so pale and watery. Suddenly it was as if something whispered to him, "Behold! These are the souls of your children. They are going—never to return! See! Your prayers are being answered!"

And then it was that, struck with a kind of horror and numb despair, he had hurried home, quite prepared to ask Marie if the two boys were dead or if anything had happened to them. But, finding them up and playing as usual he had tried to put away all thought of this fact as a delusion, to say nothing. But the lights haunted him. They would not stay out of his mind. Would his boys really die? Yet the first and the second day went without change. But on the third both boys took sick, and he knew his dread was well founded.

For on the instant, Marie was thrown into a deep, almost inexplicable, depression, from which there was no arousing her, although she attempted to conceal it from him by waiting on and worrying over them. They had to put the children in the one little bedroom (theirs), while they used an extension cot in the "parlor," previously occupied by the children. Young Dr. Newton, the one physician of repute in the neighborhood, was called in, and old Mrs. Wertzel, the German woman in front, who, being old and lonely and very fond of Marie, had volunteered her services. And so they had weathered along, God only knows how. Marie prepared the meals—or nearly all of them—as best she could. He had gone to work each day, half in a dream, wondering what the end was to be.

And then one night, as he and Marie were lying on the cot pretending to sleep, he felt her crying. And taking her in his arms he had tried to unwish all the dark things he had wished, only apparently then it was too late. Something told him it was. It was as though in some dark mansion somewhere—some supernal court or hall of light or darkness—his prayer had been registered and answered, a decision made, and that that decision could not now be unmade. No. Into this shabby little room where they lay and where she was crying had come a final black emissary, scaled, knightly, with immense arms and wings and a glittering sword, all black, and would not leave until all this should go before him. Perhaps he had been a little deranged in his mind at the time, but so it had seemed.

And then, just a few weeks after he had seen the lights and a few days after Marie had cried so, Peter had died—poor weak little thing that he was—and, three days later, Frank. Those terrible hours! For by then he was feeling so strange and sad and mystical about it all that he could neither eat nor sleep nor weep nor work nor think. He had gone about, as indeed had Marie, in a kind of stupor of misery and despair. True, as he now told himself—and then too, really,—he had not loved the children with all the devotion he should have or he would never have had the thoughts he had had—or so he had reasoned afterward. Yet then as now he suffered because of the love he should have given them, *and had not*—and now could not any more, save in memory. He recalled how both boys looked in those last sad days, their pinched little faces and small weak hands! Marie was crushed, and yet dearer for the time being than ever before. But the two children, once gone, had seemed the victims of his own dark thoughts as though his own angry, resentful wishes had slain them. And so, for the time, his mood changed. He wished, if he could, that he might undo it all, go on as before with Marie, have other children to replace these lost ones in her affection—but no. It was apparently not to be, not ever any more.

For, once they were gone, the cords which had held him and Marie together were weaker, not stronger—almost broken, really. For the charm which Marie had originally had for him had mostly been merged in the vivacity and vitality and interest of these two prattling curly-headed boys. Despite the financial burden, the irritation and drain they had been at times, they had also proved a binding chain, a touch of sweetness in the relationship, a hope for the future, a balance which had kept even this uneven scale. With them present he had felt that however black the situation it must endure because of them, their growing interests; with them gone, it was rather plain that some modification of their old state was possible—just how, for the moment, he scarcely dared think or wish. It might be that he could go away and study for awhile now. There was no need of his staying here. The neighborhood was too redolent now of the miseries they had endured. Alone somewhere else, perhaps, he could collect his thoughts, think out a new program. If he went away he might eventually succeed in doing better by Marie. She could return to her parents in Philadelphia for a little while and wait for him, working there at something as she had before until he was ready to send for her. The heavy load of debts could wait until he was better able to pay them. In the meantime, also, he could work and whatever he made over and above his absolute necessities might go to her—or to clearing off these debts.

So he had reasoned.

But it had not worked out so of course. No. In the broken mood in which Marie then was it was not so easy. Plainly, since he had run across her that April day in Philadelphia when he was wiring for the great dry goods store, her whole life had become identified with his, although his had not become merged with hers. No. She was, and would be, as he could so plainly see, then, nothing without him, whereas he—he— Well, it had long since been plain that he would be better off without her—materially, anyhow. But what would she do if he stayed away a long time—or never came back? What become? Had he thought of that then? Yes, he had. He had even thought that once away he might not feel like renewing this situation which had proved so disastrous. And Marie had seemed to sense that, too. She was so sad. True he had not thought of all these things in any bold outright fashion then. Rather they were as sly, evasive shadows skulking in the remote recesses of his brain, things which scarcely dared show their faces to the light, although later, once safely away—they had come forth boldly enough. Only at that time, and later—even now, he could not help feeling that however much Marie might have lacked originally, or then, the fault for their might was his,—that if he himself had not been so dull in the first instance all these black things would not have happened to him or to her. But could she go on without him? Would she? he had asked himself then. And answered that it would be better for him to leave and build himself up in a different world, and then return and help her later. So he fretted and reasoned.

But time had solved all that, too. In spite of the fact that he could not help picturing her back there alone with her parents in Philadelphia, their poor little cottage in Leigh Street in which she and her parents had lived—not a cottage either, but a minute little brick pigeon-hole in one of those long lines of red, treeless, smoky barracks flanking the great mills of what was known as the Reffington District, where her father worked—he had gone. He had asked himself what would she be doing there? What thinking, all alone without him—the babies dead? But he had gone.

He recalled so well the day he left her—she to go to Philadelphia, he to Boston, presumably—the tears, the depression, the unbelievable sadness in her soul and his. Did she suspect? Did she foreknow? She was so gentle, even then, so trustful, so sad. "You will come back to me, dearie, won't you, soon?" she had said, and so sadly. "We will be happy yet, won't we?" she had asked between sobs. And he had promised. Oh yes;

he had done much promising in his life, before and since. That was one of the darkest things in his nature, his power of promising.

But had he kept that?

However much in after months and years he told himself that he wanted to, that he must, that it was only fair, decent, right, still he had not gone back. No. Other things had come up with the passing of the days, weeks, months, years, other forces, other interests. Some plan, person, desire had always intervened, interfered, warned, counseled, delayed. Were there such counselors? There had been times during the first year when he had written her and sent her a little money—money he had needed badly enough himself. Later there was that long period in which he felt that she must be getting along well enough, being with her parents and at work, and he had not written. A second woman had already appeared on the scene by then as a friend. And then—

The months and years since then in which he had not done so! After his college course—which he took up after he left Marie, working his way—he had left Boston and gone to K—— to begin a career as an assistant plant manager and a developer of ideas of his own, selling the rights to such things as he invented to the great company with which he was connected. And then it was that by degrees the idea of a complete independence and a much greater life had occurred to him. He found himself so strong, so interesting to others. Why not be free, once and for all? Why not grow greater? Why not go forward and work out all the things about which he had dreamed? The thing from which he had extricated himself was too confining, too narrow. It would not do to return. The old shell could not now contain him. Despite her tenderness, Marie was not significant enough. So— He had already seen so much that he could do, be, new faces, a new world, women of a higher social level.

But even so, the pathetic little letters which still followed from time to time—not addressed to him in his new world (she did not know where he was), but to him in the old one—saying how dearly she loved him, how she still awaited his return, that she knew he was having a hard time, that she prayed always, and that all would come out right yet, that they would be able to be together yet!—she was working, saving, praying for him! True, he had the excuse that for the first four years he had not really made anything much, but still he might have done something for her,—might he not have?—gone back, persuaded her to let him go, made her comfortable, brought her somewhat nearer him even? Instead he had feared, feared, reasoned, argued.

Yes, the then devil of his nature, his ambition, had held him completely. He was seeing too clearly the wonder of what he might be, and soon, what he was already becoming. Everything as he argued then and saw now would have had to be pushed aside for Marie, whereas what he really desired was that his great career, his greater days, his fame, the thing he was sure to be now—should push everything aside. And so— Perhaps he had become sharper, colder, harder, than he had ever been, quite ready to sacrifice everything and everybody, or nearly, until he should be the great success he meant to be. But long before this he might have done so much. And he had not—had not until very recently decided to revisit this older, sweeter world.

But in the meantime, as he had long since learned, how the tragedy of her life had been completed. All at once in those earlier years all letters had ceased, and time slipping by—ten years really—he had begun to grow curious. Writing back to a neighbor of hers in Philadelphia in a disguised hand and on nameless paper, he had learned that nearly two years before her father had died and that she and her mother and brother had moved away, the writer could not say where. Then, five years later, when he was becoming truly prosperous, he had learned, through a detective agency, that she and her mother and her ne'er-do-well brother had moved back into this very neighborhood—this old neighborhood of his and hers!—or, rather, a little farther out near the graveyard where their two boys were buried. The simplicity of her! The untutored homing instinct!

But once here, according to what he had learned recently, she and her mother had not prospered at all. They had occupied the most minute of apartments farther out, and had finally been compelled to work in a laundry in their efforts to get along—and he was already so well-to-do, wealthy, really! Indeed three years before his detectives had arrived, her mother had died, and two years after that, she herself, of pneumonia, as had their children. Was it a message from her that had made him worry at that time? Was that why, only six months since, although married and rich and with two daughters by this later marriage, he had not been able to rest until he had found this out, returned here now to see? Did ghosts still stalk the world?

Yes, to-day he had come back here, but only to realize once and for all now how futile this errand was, how cruel he had been, how dreary her latter days must have been in this poor, out-of-the-way corner where once, for a while at least, she had been happy—he and she.

"Been happy!"

"By God," he suddenly exclaimed, a passion of self-reproach and memory overcoming him, "I can't stand this! It was not right, not fair. I should not have waited so long. I should have acted long, long since. The cruelty—the evil! There is something cruel and evil in it all, in all wealth, all ambition, in love of fame—too cruel. I must get out! I must think no more—see no more."

And hurrying to the door and down the squeaking stairs, he walked swiftly back to the costly car that was waiting for him a few blocks away below the bridge—that car which was so representative of the realm of so-called power and success of which he was now the master—that realm which, for so long, had taken its meaningless lustre from all that had here preceded it—the misery, the loneliness, the shadow, the despair. And in it he was whirled swiftly and gloomily away.

Phantom Gold

You would have to have seen it to have gathered a true impression—the stubby roughness of the country, the rocks, the poverty of the soil, the poorness of the houses, barns, agricultural implements, horses and cattle and even human beings, in consequence—especially human beings, for why should they, any more than any other product of the soil, flourish where all else was so poor?

It was old Judge Blow who first discovered that "Jack," or zinc, was the real riches of Taney, if it could be said to have had any before "Jack" was discovered. Months before the boom began he had stood beside a smelter in far-off K—— one late winter afternoon and examined with a great deal of care the ore which the men were smelting, marveling at its resemblance to certain rocks or boulders known as "slug lumps" in his home county.

"What is this stuff?" he asked of one of the bare-armed men who came out from the blazing furnace after a time to wipe his dripping face.

"Zinc," returned the other, as he passed his huge, soiled palm over his forehead.

"We have stuff down in our county that looks like that," said the judge as he turned the dull-looking lump over and considered for a while. "I'm sure of it—any amount." Then he became suddenly silent, for a thought struck him.

"Well, if it's really 'Jack,' " said the workman, using the trade or mining name for it, "there's money in it, all right. This here comes from St. Francis."

The old judge thought of this for a little while and quietly turned away. He knew where St. Francis was. If this was so valuable that they could ship it all the way from southeast B——, why not from Taney? Had he not many holdings in Taney?

The result was that before long a marked if secret change began to manifest itself in Taney and regions adjacent thereto. Following the private manipulations and goings to and fro of the judge one or two shrewd prospectors appeared, and then after a time the whole land was rife with them. But before that came to pass many a farmer who had remained in ignorance of the value of his holdings was rifled of them.

Old Bursay Queeder, farmer and local ne'er-do-well in the agricultural line, had lived on his particular estate or farm for forty years, and at the time that Judge Blow was thus mysteriously proceeding to and fro and here and there upon the earth, did not know that the rocks against which his pair of extra large feet were being regularly and bitterly stubbed contained the very wealth of which he had been idly and rather wistfully dreaming all his life. Indeed, the earth was a very mysterious thing to Bursay, containing, as it did, everything he really did not know. This collection of seventy acres, for instance—which individually and collectively had wrung more sweat from his brow and more curses from his lips than anything else ever had—contained, unknown to him, the possibility of the fulfilment of all his dreams. But he was old now and a little queer in the head at times, having notions in regard to the Bible, when the world would come to an end, and the like, although still able to contend with nature, if not with man. Each day in the spring and summer and even fall seasons he could be seen on some portion or other of his barren acres, his stubby beard and sparse hair standing out roughly, his fingers like a bird's claws clutching his plough handles, turning the thin and meagre furrows of his fields and rattling the stony soil, which had long ceased to yield him even a modicum of profit. It was a bare living now which he expected, and a bare living which he received. The house, or cabin, which he occupied with his wife and son and daughter, was dilapidated beyond the use or even need of care. The fences were all decayed save for those which had been built of these same impediments of the soil which he had always considered a queer kind of stone, useless to man or beast—a "hendrance," as he would have said. His barn was a mere accumulation of patchboards, shielding an old wagon and some few scraps of machinery. And the alleged corn crib was so aged and lopsided that it was ready to fall. Weeds and desolation, bony horses and as bony children, stony fields and thin trees, and withal solitude and occasional want—such was the world of his care and his ruling.

Mrs. Queeder was a fitting mate for the life to which he was doomed. It had come to that pass with her that the monotony of deprivation was accepted with indifference. The absence or remoteness of even a single modest school, meeting house or town hall, to say nothing of convenient neighbors, had left her and hers all but isolated. She was irascible, cantankerous, peculiar; her voice was shrill and her appearance desolate. Queeder, whom she understood or misunderstood thoroughly, was a source of comfort in one way—she could "nag at him," as he said, and if they quarreled frequently it was in a fitting and harmonious way. Amid such a rattletrap of fields and fences bickering was to be expected.

"Why don't yuh take them thar slug lumps an' make a fence over thar?" she asked of Queeder for something like the thousandth time in ten years, referring to as many as thirty-five piles of the best and almost pure zinc lying along the edges of the nearest field, and piled there by Bursay,—this time because two bony cows had invaded one of their corn patches. The "slug lumps" to which she referred could not have been worth less than $2,000.

For as many as the thousandth time he had replied:

"Well, fer the land sakes, hain't I never got nuthin' else tuh do? Yuh'd think them thar blame-ding rocks wuz wuth more nor anythin' else. I do well enough ez 'tis to git 'em outen the sile, I say, 'thout tryin' tuh make fences outen 'em."

"So yuh say—yuh lazy, good-fer-nuthin' ole tobacco-chewin' ——," here a long list of expletives which was usually succeeded by a stove lid or poker or a fair-sized stick of wood, propelled by one party or the other, and which was as deftly dodged. Love and family affection, you see, due to unbroken and unbreakable propinquity, as it were.

But to proceed: The hot and rainy seasons had come and gone in monotonous succession during a period of years, and the lumps still lay in the field. Dode, the eldest child and only son—a huge, hulking, rugged and yet bony ignoramus, who had not inherited an especially delicate or agreeable disposition from his harried parents—might have removed them had he not been a "consarned lazy houn'," his father said, or like his father, as his mother said, and Jane, the daughter, might have helped, but these two partook of the same depressed indifference which characterized the father. And why not, pray? They had worked long, had had little, seen less and hoped for no particular outlet for their lives in the future, having sense enough to know that if fate had been more kind there might have been. Useless contention with an unyielding soil had done its best at hardening their spirits.

"I don't see no use ploughin' the south patch," Dode had now remarked for the third time this spring. "The blamed thing don't grow nuthin'."

"Ef yuh only half 'tended it instid o' settin' out thar under them thar junipers pickin' yer teeth an' meditatin', mebbe 'twould," squeaked Mrs. Queeder, always petulant or angry or waspish—a nature soured by long and hopeless and useless contention.

"No use shakin' up a lot uv rocks, ez I see," returned Dode, wearily and aimlessly slapping at a fly. "The hull place ain't wuth a hill o' beans," and from one point of view he was right.

"Why don't yuh git off'n hit then?" suggested Queeder in a tantalizing voice, with no particular desire to defend the farm, merely with an idle wish to vary the monotony. "Ef hit's good enough tuh s'port yuh, hit's good enough to work on, I say."

"S'port!" sniffed the undutiful Dode, wearily, and yet humorously and scornfully. "I ain't seed much s'port, ez I kin remember. Mebbe ye're thinkin' uv all the fine schoolin' I've had, er the places I've been." He slapped at another fly.

Old Queeder felt the sneer, but as he saw it it was scarcely his fault. He had worked. At the same time he felt the futility of quarreling with Dode, who was younger and stronger and no longer, owing to many family quarrels, bearing him any filial respect. As a matter of fact it was the other way about. From having endured many cuffs and blows in his youth Dode was now much the more powerful physically, and in any contest could easily outdo his father; and Queeder, from at first having ruled and seen his word law, was now compelled to take second, even third and fourth, place, and by contention and all but useless snarling gain the very little consideration that he received.

But in spite of all this they lived together indifferently. And day after day—once Judge Blow had returned to Taney—time was bringing nearer and nearer the tide of mining and the amazing boom that went with it. Indeed every day, like a gathering storm cloud, it might have been noted by the sensitive as approaching closer and closer, only these unwitting holders were not sensitive. They had not the slightest inkling as yet of all that was to be. Here in this roadless, townless region how was one to know. Prospectors passed to the north and the south of them; but as yet none had ever come directly to this wonderful patch upon which Queeder and his family rested. It was in too out-of-the-way a place—a briary, woodsy, rocky corner.

Then one sunny June morning—

"Hi, thar!" called Cal Arnold, their next neighbor, who lived some three miles further on, who now halted his rickety wagon and bony horses along the road opposite the field in which Queeder was working. "Hyur the news?" He spoke briskly, shifting his cud of tobacco and eyeing Queeder with the chirpiness of one who brings diverting information.

"No; what?" asked Queeder, ceasing his "cultivating" with a worn one-share plough and coming over and leaning on his zinc fence, rubbing a hand through his sparse hair the while.

"Ol' Dunk Porter down here to Newton's sold his farm," replied Cal, shrewdly and jubilantly, as though he were relating the tale of a great battle or the suspected approach of the end of the world. "An' he got three thousan' dollars fer it." He rolled the sum deliciously under his tongue.

"Yuh don't say!" said Queeder quietly but with profound and

amazed astonishment. "Three thousan'?" He stirred as one who hears of the impossible being accomplished and knows it can't be true. "Whut fer?"

"They 'low now ez how thar's min'l onto it," went on the farmer wisely. "They 'low ez how now this hyur hull kentry round hyur is thick an' spilin' with it. Hit's uvry-whar. They tell me ez how these hyur slug lumps"—and he flicked at one of the large piles of hitherto worthless zinc against which Queeder was leaning—"is this hyur min'l—er 'Jack,' ez they call hit—an' that hit's wuth two cents a pound when it's swelted" ("smelted," he meant) "an' even more. I see yuh got quite a bit uv hit. So've I. Thar's a lot layin' down around my place. I allus 'lowed ez how 'twant wuth much o' anythin,' but they say 'tis. I hyur from some o' the boys 'at's been to K—— that when hit's fixed up, swelted and like o' that, that hit's good fer lots of things."

He did not know what exactly, so he did not stop to explain. Instead he cocked a dreamful eye, screwed up his mouth preparatory to expectorating and looked at Queeder. The latter, unable to adjust his thoughts to this new situation, picked up a piece of the hitherto despised "slug" and looked at it. To think that through all these years of toil and suffering he should have believed it worthless and now all of a sudden it was worth two cents a pound when "swelted" and that neighbors were beginning to sell their farms for princely sums!—and his farm was covered with this stuff, this gold almost! Why, there were whole hummocks of it raising slaty-gray backs to the hot sun further on, a low wall in one place where it rose sheer out of the ground on this "prupetty," as he always referred to it. Think of that! Think of that! But although he thought much he said nothing, for in his starved and hungry brain was beginning to sprout and flourish a great and wondrous idea. He was to have money, wealth—ease, no less! Think of it! Not to toil and sweat in the summer sun any more, to loaf and dream at his ease, chew all the tobacco he wished, live in town, visit far-off, mysterious K——, see all there was to see!

"Well, I guess I'll be drivin' on," commented Arnold after a time, noting Queeder's marked abstraction. "I cal'late tuh git over tuh Bruder's an' back by sundown. He's got a little hay I traded him a pig fer hyur a while back," and he flicked his two bony horses and was off up the rubbly, dusty road.

For a time Queeder was scarcely satisfied to believe his senses. Was it really true? Had Porter really sold his place? For days thereafter, although he drove to Arno—sixteen miles away—to discover the real truth, he held his own counsel, nursing a wonderful fancy. This property was his, not his wife's, nor his two children's. Years before he had worked and paid for it, a few lone dollars at a time, or their equivalent in corn, pigs, wheat, before he had married. Now—now—soon one of those strange creatures—a "prowspector," Arnold had called him—who went about with money would come along and buy up his property. Wonderful! Wonderful! What would he get for it?—surely five thousand dollars, considering that Porter had received three for forty acres, whereas he had seventy. Four thousand, anyhow —a little more than Dunk. He could not figure it very well, but it would be more than Dunk's, whatever it was—probably five thousand!

The one flaw in all this though—and it was a great flaw—was the thought of his savage and unkindly family—the recalcitrant Dode, the angular Jane and his sour better half, Emma—who would now probably have to share in all this marvelous prosperity, might even take it away from him and push him into that background where he had been for so long. They were so much more dogmatic, forceful than he. He was getting old, feeble even, from long years of toil. His wife had done little this long time but sneer and jeer at him, as he now chose most emphatically to remember; his savage son the same. Jane, the indifferent, who looked on him as a failure and a ne'er-do-well, had done nothing but suggest that he work harder. Love, family tenderness, family unity—if these had ever existed they had long since withered in the thin, unnourishing air of this rough, poverty-stricken world. What did he owe any of them? Nothing. And now they would want to share in all this, of course. Having lived so long with them, and under such disagreeable conditions, he now wondered how they would dare suggest as much, and still he knew they would. Fight him, nag him, that's all they had ever done. But now that wealth was at his door they would be running after him, fawning upon him—demanding it of him,

perhaps! What should he do? How arrange for all of this?—
for wealth was surely close to his hands. It must be. Like a small,
half-intelligent rat he peeked and perked. His demeanor changed
to such an extent that even his family noticed it and began to
wonder, although (knowing nothing of all that had transpired
as yet) they laid it to the increasing queerness of age.

"Have yuh noticed how Pap acts these hyur days?" Dode
inquired of Jane and his mother one noontime after old Queeder
had eaten and returned to the fields. "He's all the time standin'
out thar at the fence lookin' aroun' ez if he wuz a-waitin' fer
somebody er thinkin' about somepin. Mebbe he's gittin' a little
queer, huh? Y' think so?"

Dode was most interested in anything which concerned his
father—or, rather, his physical or mental future—for once he
died this place would have to be divided or he be called upon
to run it, and in that case he would be a fitting catch for any
neighborhood farming maiden, and as such able to broach and
carry through the long-cherished dream of matrimony, now
attenuated and made all but impossible by the grinding necessities he was compelled to endure.

"Yes, I've been noticin' somepin," returned Mrs. Queeder.
"He hain't the same ez he wuz a little while back. Some new
notion he's got into his mind, I reckon, somepin he wants tuh
do an' kain't, er somepin new in 'ligion, mebbe. Yuh kain't ever
tell whut's botherin' him."

Jane " 'lowed" as much and the conversation ended. But still
Queeder brooded, trying to solve the knotty problem, which
depended, of course, on the open or secret sale of the land—
secret, if possible, he now finally decided, seeing that his family
had always been so unkind to him. They deserved nothing better.
It was his—why not?

In due time appeared a prospector, mounted on horseback
and dressed for rough travel, who, looking over the fields of
this area and noting the value of these particular acres, the
surface outcropping of a thick vein, became intensely interested.
Queeder was not to be seen at the time, having gone to some
remote portion of the farm, but Mrs. Queeder, wholly ignorant
of the value of the land and therefore of the half-suppressed
light in the stranger's eye, greeted him pleasantly enough.

"Would you let me have a drink of water?" inquired the stranger when she appeared at the door.

"Sartinly," she replied with a tone of great respect. Even comparatively well-dressed strangers were so rare here.

Old Queeder in a distant field observing him at the well, now started for the house.

"What is that stuff you make your fences out of?" asked the stranger agreeably, wondering if they knew.

"Well, now, I dunno," said Mrs. Queeder. "It's some kind 'o stone, I reckon—slug lumps, we uns always call hit aroun' hyur."

The newcomer suppressed a desire to smile and stooped to pick up a piece of the zinc with which the ground was scattered. It was the same as he had seen some miles back, only purer and present in much greater quantities. Never had he seen more and better zinc near the surface. It was lying everywhere exposed, cultivation, frosts and rains having denuded it, whereas in the next county other men were digging for it. The sight of these dilapidated holdings, the miserable clothing, old Queeder toiling out in the hot fields, and all this land valueless for agriculture because of its wondrous mineral wealth, was almost too much for him.

"Do you own all this land about here?" he inquired.

"'Bout seventy acres," returned Mrs. Queeder.

"Do you know what it sells at an acre?"

"No. It ain't wuth much, though, I reckon. I ain't heerd o' none bein' sold aroun' hyur fer some time now."

The prospector involuntarily twitched at the words "not wuth much." What would some of his friends and rivals say if they knew of this particular spot? What if some one should tell these people? If he could buy it now for a song, as he well might! Already other prospectors were in the neighborhood. Had he not eaten at the same table at Arno with three whom he suspected as such? He must get this, and get it now.

"I guess I'll stroll over and talk to your husband a moment," he remarked and ambled off, the while Mrs. Queeder and Jane, the twain in loose blue gingham bags of dresses much blown by the wind, stood in the tumbledown doorway and looked after him.

"Funny, ain't he?" said the daughter. "Wonder whut he wants o' Paw?"

Old Queeder looked up quizzically from his ploughing, to which he had returned, as he saw the stranger approaching, and now surveyed him doubtfully as he offered a cheery "Good morning."

"Do you happen to know if there is any really good farming land around here for sale?" inquired the prospector after a few delaying comments about the weather.

"Air yuh wantin' it fer farmin'?" replied Queeder cynically and casting a searching look upon the newcomer, who saw at once by Queeder's eye that he knew more than his wife. "They're buyin' hit now mostly fer the min'l ez is onto it, ez I hyur." At the same time he perked like a bird to see how this thrust had been received.

The prospector smiled archly if wisely. "I see," he said. "You think it's good for mining, do you? What would you hold your land at as mineral land then if you had a chance to sell it?"

Queeder thought for a while. Two wood doves cooed mournfully in the distance and a blackbird squeaked rustily before he answered.

"I dunno ez I keer tuh sell yit." He had been getting notions of late as to what might be done if he were to retain his land, bid it up against the desires of one and another, only also the thought of how his wife and children might soon learn and insist on dividing the profits with him if he did sell it was haunting him. Those dreams of getting out in the world and seeing something, of getting away from his family and being happy in some weird, free way, were actually torturing him.

"Who owns the land just below here, then?" asked the stranger, realizing that his idea of buying for little or nothing might as well be abandoned. But at this Queeder winced. For after all, the land adjoining had considerable mineral on it, also, as he well knew.

"Why, let me see," he replied waspishly, with mingled feelings of opposition and indifference. "Marradew," he finally added, grudgingly. It was no doubt true that this stranger or some other could buy of other farmers if he refused to sell. Still, land around here anywhere must be worth something, his as much as any other. If Dunk Porter had received $3000—

"If you don't want to sell, I suppose he might," the prospector continued pleasantly. The idea was expressed softly, meditatively, indifferently almost.

There was a silence, in which Queeder calmly leaned on his plough handles thinking. The possibility of losing this long-awaited opportunity was dreadful. But he was not floored yet, for all his hunger and greed. Arnold had said that the metal alone, these rocks, was worth two cents a pound, and he could not get it out of his mind that somehow the land itself, the space of soil aside from the metal, must be worth something. How could it be otherwise? Small crops of sorts grew on it.

"I dunno," he replied defiantly, if internally weakly. "Yuh might ast. I ain't heerd o' his wantin' to sell." He was determined to risk this last if he had to run after the stranger afterward and beg him to compromise, although he hoped not to have to do that, either. There were other prospectors.

"I don't know yet whether I want this," continued the prospector heavily and with an air of profound indifference, "but I'd like to have an option on it, if you'd like to sell. What'll you take for an option at sixty days on the entire seventy acres?"

The worn farmer did not in the least understand what was meant by the word option, but he was determined not to admit it. "Whut'll yuh give?" he asked finally, in great doubt as to what to say.

"Well, how about $200 down and $5,000 more at the end of sixty days if we come to terms at the end of that time?" He was offering the very lowest figure that he imagined Queeder would take, if any, for he had heard of other sales in this vicinity this very day.

Queeder, not knowing what an option was, knew not what to say. Five thousand was what he had originally supposed he might be offered, but sixty days! What did he mean by that? Why not at once if he wanted the place—cash—as Dunk Porter, according to Arnold, had received? He eyed the stranger feverishly, fidgeted with his plough handles, and finally observed almost aimlessly: "I 'low ez I could git seven thousan' any day ef I wanted to wait. The feller hyur b'low me a ways got three thousan', an' he's got thirty acres less'n I got. Thar's been a feller aroun' hyur offerin' me six thousan'.''

"Well, I might give you $6,000, providing I found the ground all right," he said.

"Cash down?" asked Queeder amazedly, kicking at a clod.

"Within sixty days," answered the prospector.

"Oh!" said Queeder, gloomily. "I thort yuh wanted tuh buy t'day."

"Oh, no," said the other. "I said an option. If we come to terms I'll be back here with the money within sixty days or before, and we'll close the thing up—six thousand in cash, minus the option money. Of course I don't bind myself absolutely to buy—just get the privilege of buying at any time within sixty days, and if I don't come back within that time the money I turn over to you to-day is yours, see, and you're free to sell the land to some one else."

"Huh!" grunted Queeder. He had dreamed of getting the money at once and making off all by himself, but here was this talk of sixty days, which might mean something or nothing.

"Well," said the prospector, noting Queeder's dissatisfaction and deciding that he must do something to make the deal seem more attractive, "suppose we say seven thousand, then, and I put down $500 cash into your hands now? How's that? Seven thousand in sixty days and five hundred in cash right now. What do you say?"

He reached in his pocket and extracted a wallet thick with bills, which excited Queeder greatly. Never had so much ready money, which he might quickly count as his if he chose, been so near him. After all, $500 in cash was an amazing amount in itself. With that alone what could he not do? And then the remainder of the seven thousand within sixty days! Only, there were his wife and two children to consider. If he was to carry out his dream of decamping there must be great secrecy. If they learned of this—his possession of even so much as five hundred in cash—what might not happen? Would not Dode or his wife or Jane, or all three, take it away from him—steal it while he was asleep? It might well be so. He was so silent and puzzled that the stranger felt that he was going to reject his offer.

"I'll tell you what I'll do," he said, as though he were making a grand concession. "I'll make it eight thousand and put up eight hundred. How's that? If we can't arrange it on that basis we'll have to drop the matter, for I can't offer to pay any more," and at that he returned the wallet to his pocket.

But Queeder still gazed, made all but dumb by his good fortune and the difficulties it presented. Eight thousand! Eight hundred in cash down! He could scarcely understand.

"T'day?" he asked.

"Yes, to-day—only you'll have to come with me to Arno. I want to look into your title. Maybe you have a deed, though—have you?"

Queeder nodded.

"Well, if it's all right I'll pay the money at once. I have a form of agreement here and we can get some one to witness it, I suppose. Only we'll have to get your wife to sign, too."

Queeder's face fell. Here was the rub—his wife and two children! "She's gotta sign, hez she?" he inquired grimly, sadly even. He was beside himself with despair, disgust. To work and slave so all these years! Then, when a chance came, to have it all come to nothing, or nearly so!

"Yes," said the prospector, who saw by his manner and tone that his wife's knowledge of it was not desired. "We'll have to get her signature, too. I'm sorry if it annoys you, but the law compels it. Perhaps you could arrange all that between you in some way. Why not go over and talk to her about it?"

Queeder hesitated. How he hated it—this sharing with his wife and son! He didn't mind Jane so much. But now if they heard of it they would quarrel with him and want the larger share. He would have to fight—stand by his "rights." And once he had the money—if he ever got it—he would have to watch it, hide it, to keep it away from them.

"What's the matter?" asked the prospector, noting his perturbation. "Does she object to your selling?"

" 'Tain't that. She'll sell, well enough, once she hyurs. I didn't 'low ez I'd let 'er know at fust. She'll be wantin' the most uv it—her and Dode—an' hit ain't ther'n, hit's mine. I wuz on hyur fust. I owned this hyur place fust, fore ever I saw 'er. She don't do nuthin' but fuss an' fight, ez 'tis."

"Supposing we go over to the house and talk to her. She may not be unreasonable. She's only entitled to a third, you know, if you don't want to give her more than that. That's the law. That would leave you nearly five thousand. In fact, if you want it, I'll see that you get five thousand whatever she gets." He had somehow gathered the impression that five thousand, for himself, meant a great deal to Queeder.

And true enough, at that the old farmer brightened a little. For five thousand? Was not that really more than he had expected to get for the place as a whole but an hour before! And supposing his wife did get three thousand? What of it? Was not his own dream coming true? He agreed at once and decided to accompany the prospector to the house. But on the way the farmer paused and gazed about him. He was as one who scarcely knew what he was doing. All this money—this new order of things—if it went through! He felt strange, different, confused. The mental ills of his many years plus this great fortune with its complications and possibilities were almost too much for him. The stranger noted a queer metallic and vacant light in the old farmer's eyes as he now turned slowly about from west to east, staring.

"What's the matter?" he asked, a suspicion of insanity coming to him.

The old man seemed suddenly to come to. " 'Tain't nuthin'," he said. "I wuz just thinkin'."

The prospector meditated on the validity of a contract made with a lunatic, but the land was too valuable to bother about trifles. Once a contract was made, even with a half-wit, the legal difficulties which could be made over any attempt to break the agreement would be very great.

In the old cabin Jane and her mother wondered at the meaning of the approaching couple, but old Queeder shooed off the former as he would have a chicken. Once inside the single room, which served as parlor, sitting-room, bedroom and all else convenient, Queeder nervously closed the door leading into the kitchen, where Jane had retired.

"Go on away, now," he mumbled, as he saw her there hanging about. "We want a word with yer Maw, I tell yuh."

Lank Jane retired, but later clapped a misshapen ear to the

door until she was driven away by her suspicious father. Then the farmer began to explain to his wife what it was all about.

"This hyur stranger—I don't know your name yit—"

"Crawford! Crawford!" put in the prospector.

"Crawford—Mr. Crawford—is hyur tuh buy the place ef he kin. I thought, seein' ez how yuh've got a little int'est in it— third"—he was careful to add—"we'd better come an' talk tuh yuh."

"Int'est!" snapped Mrs. Queeder, sharply and suspiciously, no thought of the presence of the stranger troubling her in her expression of her opinion, "I should think I had—workin' an' slavin' on it fer twenty-four year! Well, whut wuz yuh thinkin' uv payin' fer the place?" she asked of the stranger sharply.

A nervous sign from Queeder, whose acquisitiveness was so intense that it was almost audible, indicated that he was not to say.

"Well, now what do you think it would be worth?"

"Dunno ez I kin say exackly," replied the wife slyly and greedily, imagining that Queeder, because of his age and various mental deficiencies was perhaps leaving these negotiations to her. "Thar's ben furms aroun' hyur ez big's this sold fer nigh onto two thousan' dollars." She was quoting the topmost figure of which she had ever heard.

"Well, that's pretty steep, isn't it?" asked Crawford solemnly but refusing to look at Queeder. "Ordinarily land around here is not worth much more than twenty dollars an acre and you have only seventy, as I understand."

"Yes, but this hyur land ain't so pore ez some, nuther," rejoined Mrs. Queeder, forgetting her original comment on it and making the best argument she could for it. "Thar's a spring on this hyur one, just b'low the house hyur."

"Yes," said Crawford, "I saw it as I came in. It has some value. So you think two thousand is what it's worth, do you?" He looked at Queeder wisely, as much as to say, "This is a good joke, Queeder."

Mrs. Queeder, fairly satisfied that hers was to be the dominant mind in this argument, now turned to her husband for counsel. "What do you think, Bursay?" she asked.

Queeder, shaken by his duplicity, his fear of discovery, his greed and troublesome dreams, gazed at her nervously. "I sartinly think hit's wuth that much anyhow."

Crawford now began to explain that he only wanted an option on it at present, an agreement to sell within a given time, and if this were given, a paper signed, he would pay a few dollars to bind the bargain—and at this looked wisely at Queeder and half closed one eye, by which the latter understood that he was to receive the sum originally agreed upon.

"If you say so we'll close this right now," he said ingratiatingly, taking from his pockets a form of agreement and opening it. "I'll just fill this in and you two can sign it." He went to the worn poplar table and spread out his paper, the while Queeder and his wife eyed the proceeding with intense interest. Neither could read or write but the farmer, not knowing how he was to get his eight hundred, could only trust to the ingenuity of the prospector to solve the problem. Besides, both were hypnotized by the idea of selling this worthless old land so quickly and for so much, coming into possession of actual money, and moved and thought like people in a dream. Mrs. Queeder's eyelids had narrowed to thin, greedy lines.

"How much did yuh cal'late yuh'd give tuh bind this hyur?" she inquired tensely and with a feverish gleam in her eye.

"Oh," said the stranger, who was once more looking at Queeder with an explanatory light in his eye, "about a hundred dollars, I should say. Wouldn't that be enough?"

A hundred dollars! Even that sum in this lean world was a fortune. To Mrs. Queeder, who knew nothing of the value of the mineral on the farm, it was unbelievable, an unexplainable windfall, an augury of better things. And besides, the two thousand to come later! But now came the question of a witness and how the paper was to be signed. The prospector, having filled in (in pencil) a sample acknowledgment of the amount paid— $100—and then having said, "Now you sign here, Mr. Queeder," the latter replied, "But I kain't write an' nuther kin my wife."

"Thar wuzn't much chance fer schoolin' around' hyur when I wuz young," simpered his better half.

"Well then, we'll just have to let you make your marks, and get some one to witness them. Can your son or daughter write?"

Here was a new situation and one most unpleasant to both, for Dode, once called, would wish to rule, being so headstrong and contrary. He could write his name anyhow, read a little bit also—but did they want him to know yet? Husband and wife looked at each dubiously and with suspicion. What now? The difficulty was solved by the rumble of a wagon on the nearby road.

"Maybe that is some one who could witness for you?" suggested Crawford.

Queeder looked out. "Yes, I b'lieve he kin write," he commented. "Hi, thar, Lester!" he called. "Come in hyur a minute! We wantcha fer somepin."

The rumbling ceased and in due time one Lester Botts, a farmer, not so much better in appearance than Queeder, arrived at the door. The prospector explained what was wanted and the agreement was eventually completed, only Botts, not knowing of the mineral which Queeder's acres represented, was anxious to tell the prospector of better land than this, from an agricultural view, which could be had for less money, but he did not know how to go about it. Before she would sign, Mrs. Queeder made it perfectly clear where she stood in the matter.

"I git my sheer uv this money now, don't I," she demanded, "paid tuh me right hyur?"

Crawford, uncertain as to Queeder's wishes in this, looked at him; and he, knowing his wife's temper and being moved by greed, exclaimed, "Yuh don't git nuthin' 'ceptin' I die. Yuh ain't entitled tuh no sheer unless'n we're separatin', which we hain't."

"Then I don't sign nuthin'," said Mrs. Queeder truculently.

"Of course I don't want to interfere," commented the prospector, soothingly, "but I should think you'd rather give her her share of this—thirty-three dollars," he eyed Queeder persuasively—"and then possibly a third of the two thousand—that's only six hundred and sixty—rather than stop the sale now, wouldn't you? You'll have to agree to do something like that. It's a good bargain. There ought to be plenty for everybody."

The farmer hearkened to the subtlety of this. After all, six hundred and sixty out of eight thousand was not so much. Rather than risk delay and discovery he pretended to soften, and finally consented. The marks were made and their validity attested by Botts, the one hundred in cash being counted out in two piles, according to Mrs. Queeder's wish, and the agreement pocketed. Then the prospector accompanied by Mr. Botts, was off— only Queeder, following and delaying him, was finally handed over in secret the difference between the hundred and the sum originally agreed upon. When he saw all the money the old farmer's eyes wiggled as if magnetically operated. Trembling with the agony of greed he waited, and then his hard and knotted fingers closed upon the bills like the claws of a gripping hawk.

"Thank yuh," he said aloud. "Thank you," and he jerked doorward in distress. "See me alone fust when yuh come ag'in. We gotta be mighty keerful er she'll find out, an' ef she does she'll not sign nuthin', an' raise ol' Harry, too."

"Oh, that's all right," replied the prospector archly. He was thinking how easy it would be, in view of all the dishonesty and chicanery already practised, to insist that the two thousand written in in pencil was the actual sale price and efface old Queeder by threatening to expose his duplicity. However, there were sixty days yet in which to consider this. "In sixty days, maybe less, I'll show up." And he slipped gracefully away, leaving the old earth-scraper to brood alone.

But all was not ended with the payment of this sum, as any one might have foretold. For Dode and Jane, hearing after a little while from their mother of the profitable sale of the land, were intensely moved. Money—any money, however small in amount—conjured up visions of pleasure and ease, and who was to get it, after all the toil here on the part of all? Where was their share in all this? They had worked, too. They demanded it in repeated ways, but to no avail. Their mother and father were obdurate, insisting that they wait until the sale was completed before any further consideration was given the matter.

While they were thus arguing, however, quarreling over even so small a sum as $100, as they thought, a new complication was added by Dode learning, as he soon did, that this was all mineral land, that farms were being sold in Adair—the next township—and even here; that it was rumored that Queeder had already sold his land for $5,000, and that if he had he had been beaten, for the land was worth much more—$200 an acre even, or $14,000. At once he suspected his father and mother of some treachery in connection with the sale—that there had been no option given, but a genuine sale made, and that Queeder or his mother, or both, were concealing a vast sum from himself and Jane. An atmosphere of intense suspicion and evil will was at once introduced.

"They've sold the furm fer $5,000 'stid uv $2,000; that's whut they've gone an' done," insisted Dode one day to Jane in the presence of his father and mother. "Ev'rybody aroun' hyur knows now what this hyur land's wuth, an' that's whut they got, yuh kin bet."

"Yuh lie!" shrieked Queeder shrilly, who was at once struck by the fact that if what Dode said was true he had walked into a financial as well as a moral trap from which he could not well extricate himself. "I hain't sold nuthin'," he went on angrily. "Lester Botts wuz hyur an' seed whut we done. He signed onto it."

"Ef the land's wuth more'n $2,000, that feller 'twuz hyur didn' agree tuh pay no more'n that fer it in hyur," put in Mrs. Queeder explanatorily, although, so little did she trust her husband, she was now beginning to wonder if there might not have been some secret agreement between him and this stranger. "Ef he had any different talk with yer Paw," and here she eyed old Queeder suspiciously, beginning to recall the prospector's smooth airs and ways, "he didn' say nuthin' 'bout it tuh me. I do rec'leck yer Paw'n him talkin' over by the fence yander near an hour afore they come in hyur. I wondered then whut it wuz about." She was beginning to worry as to how she was to get more seeing that the price agreed upon was now, apparently, inconsequential.

And as for Dode, he now eyed his father cynically and suspiciously. "I cal'late he got somepin more fer it than he's tellin' us about," he insisted. "They ain't sellin' land down to Arno right now fer no $200 an acre an' him not knowin' it—an' land not ez good ez this, nuther. Ye're hidin' the money whut yuh got fer it, that's whut!"

Mrs. Queeder, while greatly disturbed as to the possibility of duplicity on her husband's part in connection with all this, still considered it policy to call Heaven to witness that in her case at least no duplicity was involved. If more had been offered or paid she knew nothing of it. For his part Queeder boiled with fear, rage, general opposition to all of them and their share in this.

"Yuh consarned varmint!" he squealed, addressing Dode and leaping to his feet and running for a stick of stovewood, "I'll show yuh whuther we air er not! Yuh 'low I steal, do yuh?"

Dode intercepted him, however, and being the stronger, pushed him off. It was always so easy so to do—much to Queeder's rage. He despised his son for his triumphant strength alone, to say nothing of his dour cynicism in regard to himself. The argument was ended by the father being put out of the house and the mother pleading volubly that in so far as she knew it was all as she said, that in signing the secret agreement with her husband she had meant no harm to her children, but only to protect them and herself.

But now, brooding over the possibility of Queeder's deception, she began to lay plans for his discomfiture in any way that she might—she and Dode and Jane. Queeder himself raged secretly between fear and hatred of Dode and what might follow because of his present knowledge. How was he to prevent Dode from being present at the final transaction, and if so how would the secret difference be handed him? Besides, if he took the sum mentioned, how did he know that he was not now being over-reached? Every day nearly brought new rumors of new sales at better prices than he had been able to fix. In addition, each day Mrs. Queeder cackled like an irritable hen over the possible duplicity of her husband, although that creature in his secretive greed and queerness was not to be encompassed. He fought shy of the house the greater part of each day, jerked like a rat at every sound or passing stranger and denied himself words to speak or explain, or passed the lie if they pressed him too warmly. The seven hundred extra he had received was wrapped in paper and hidden in a crevice back of a post in the barn, a tin can serving as an outer protection for his newly acquired wealth. More than once during the day he returned to that spot, listened and peeked before he ventured to see whether it was still safe.

Indeed, there was something deadly in the household order from now on, little short of madness in fact, for now mother and children schemed for his downfall while all night long old Queeder wakened, jerking in the blackness and listening for any sounds which might be about the barn. On more than one occasion he changed the hiding place, even going so far as to keep the money on his person for a time. Once he found an old rusty butcher knife and, putting that in his shirt bosom, he slept with it and dreamed of trouble.

Into the heart of this walked another prospector one morning rejoicing, like the first one, at his find. Like all good business men he was concerned to see the owner only and demanded that Queeder be called.

"Oh, Paw!" called Jane from the rickety doorway. "Thar's some one hyur wants tuh see yuh!"

Old Queeder looked warily up from his hot field, where he had been waiting these many days, and beheld the stranger. He dropped his weed fighting and came forward. Dode drifted in from somewhere.

"Pretty dry weather we're having, isn't it?" remarked the stranger pleasantly meeting him halfway in his approach.

"Yes," he replied vacantly, for he was very, very much worn these days, mentally and physically. "It's tol'able dry! Tol'able dry!" He wiped his leathery brow with his hand.

"You don't know of any one about here, do you, who has any land for sale?"

"Ye're another one uv them min'l prowspecters, I projeck, eh?" inquired Queeder, now quite openly. There was no need to attempt to conceal that fact any longer.

The newcomer was taken aback, for he had not expected so much awareness in this region so soon. "I am," he said frankly.

"I thought so," said Queeder.

"Have you ever thought of selling the land here?" he inquired.

"Well, I dunno," began the farmer shrewdly. "Thar've been fellers like yuh aroun' hyar afore now lookin' at the place. Whut do yuh cal-late it might be wuth tuh yuh?" He eyed him sharply the while they strolled still further away from the spot where Dode, Jane and the mother formed an audience in the doorway.

The prospector ambled about the place examining the surface lumps, so plentiful everywhere.

"This looks like fairly good land to me," he said quietly after a time. "You haven't an idea how much you'd want an acre for it, have you?"

"Well, I hyur they're gettin' ez much ez three hundred down to Arno," replied Queeder, exaggerating fiercely. Now that a second purchaser had appeared he was eager to learn how much more, if any, than the original offer would be made.

"Yes—well, that's a little steep, don't you think, considering the distance the metal would have to be hauled to the railroad? It'll cost considerable to get it over here."

"Not enough, I 'low, tuh make it wuth much less'n three hundred, would it?" observed Queeder, sagely.

"Well, I don't know about that. Would you take two hundred an acre for as much as forty acres of it?"

Old Queeder pricked his ears at the sound of bargain. As near as he could figure, two hundred an acre for forty acres would bring him as much as he was now to get for the entire seventy, and he would still have thirty to dispose of. The definiteness of the proposition thrilled him, boded something large for his future—eight thousand for forty, and all he could wring from the first comer had been eight thousand for seventy!

"Huh!" he said, hanging on the argument with ease and leisure. "I got an offer uv a option on the hull uv it fer twelve thousan' now."

"What!" said the stranger, surveying him critically. "Have you signed any papers in the matter?"

Queeder looked at him for the moment as if he suspected treachery, and then seeing the gathered family surveying them from the distant doorway he made the newcomer a cabalistic sign.

"Come over hyur," he said, leading off to a distant fence. At the safe distance they halted. "I tell yuh just how 'tis," he observed very secretively. "Thar wuz a feller come along hyur three er four weeks ago an' at that time I didn't know ez how this hyur now wuz min'l, see? An' he ast me, 'thout sayin' nuthin' ez tuh whut he knowed, whut I'd take for it, acre fer acre. Well, thar wuz anuther feller, a neighbor o' mine, had been along hyur an' he wuz sayin' ez how a piece o' land just below, about forty acres, wuz sold fer five thousan' dollars. Seein' ez how my land wuz the same kind o' land, only better, I 'lowed ez how thar bein' seventy acres hyur tuh his forty I oughta git nearly twicet ez much, an' I said so. He didn't 'low ez I ought at fust, but later on he kind o' come roun' an' we agreed ez how I bein' the one that fust had the place—I wuz farmin' hyur 'fore ever I married my wife—that ef any sale wuz made I orter git the biggest sheer. So we kind o' fixed it up b'tween us, quiet-like an' not lettin' anybody else know, that when it come tuh makin' out the papers an' sich at the end uv the sixty days he was to gimme a shade the best o' the money afore we signed any papers. Course I wouldn't do nuthin' like that ef the place hadn't b'longed tuh me in the fust place, an' ef me an' my wife an' chil'un got along ez well's we did at fust, but she's allers a-fightin' an' squallin'. Ef he come back hyur, ez he 'lowed he would, I wuz t' have eight thousan' fer myself, an' me an' my wife wuzta divide the rest b'tween us ez best we could, her to have her third, ez the law is."

The stranger listened with mingled astonishment, amusement and satisfaction at the thought that the contract, if not exactly illegal, could at least to Queeder be made to appear so.

For an appeal to the wife must break it, and besides because of the old man's cupidity he might easily be made to annul the original agreement. For plainly even now this farmer did not know the full value of all that he had so foolishly bartered away. About him were fields literally solid with zinc under the surface. Commercially $60,000 would be a mere bagatelle to give for it, when the East was considered. One million dollars would be a ridiculously low capitalization for a mine based on this property. A hundred thousand might well be his share for his part in the transaction. Good heavens, the other fellow had bought a fortune for a song! It was only fair to try to get it away from him.

"I'll tell you how this is, Mr. Queeder," he said after a time. "It looks to me as though this fellow, whoever he is, has given you a little the worst end of this bargain. Your land is worth much more than that, that's plain enough. But you can get out of that easily enough on the ground that you really didn't know

what you were selling at the time you made this bargain. That's
the law, I believe. You don't have to stick by an agreement if it's
made when you don't understand what you're doing. As a matter
of fact, I think I could get you out of it if you wanted me to.
All you would have to do would be to refuse to sign any other
papers when the time comes and return the money that's been
paid you. Then when the time came I would be glad to take
over your whole farm at three hundred dollars an acre and pay
cash down. That would make you a rich man. I'd give you
three thousand cash in hand the day you signed an agreement
to sell. The trouble is you were just taken in. You and your wife
really didn't know what you were doing."

"That's right," squeaked Queeder, "we wuz. We didn't 'low
ez they wuz any min'l on this when we signed that air contrack."

Three hundred dollars an acre, as he dumbly figured it out,
meant $21,000—twenty-one instead of a wretched eight thou-
sand! For the moment he stood there quite lost as to what to do,
say, think, a wavering, element-worn figure. His bent and
shriveled body, raked and gutted by misfortune, fairly quivered
with the knowledge that riches were really his for the asking,
yet also that now, owing to his early error and ignorance in
regard to all this, he might not be able to arrange for their
reception. His seared and tangled brain, half twisted by solitude,
balanced unevenly with the weight of this marvelous possibility.
It crossed the wires of his mind and made him see strabismically.

The prospector, uncertain as to what his silence indicated,
added: "I might even do a little better than that, Mr. Queeder
—say, twenty-five thousand. You could have a house in the city
for that. Your wife could wear silk dresses; you yourself need
never do another stroke of work; your son and daughter could
go to college if they wanted to. All you have to do is to refuse
to sign that deed when he comes back—hand him the money
or get his address and let me send it to him."

"He swindled me, so he did!" Queeder almost shouted now,
great beads of sweat standing out upon his brow. "He tried tuh
rob me! He shan't have an acre, by God—not an acre!"

"That's right," said the newcomer, and before he left he
again insinuated into the farmer's mind the tremendous and
unfair disproportion between twelve (as he understood Queeder

was receiving) and twenty-five thousand. He pictured the difference in terms of city or town opportunities, the ease of his future life.

Unfortunately, the farmer possessed no avenue by which to escape from his recent duplicity. Having deceived his wife and children over so comparatively small a sum as eight thousand, this immensely greater sum offered many more difficulties—bickering, quarreling, open fighting, perhaps, so fierce were Dode and his wife in their moods, before it could be attained. And was he equal to it? At the same time, although he had never had anything, he was now feeling as though he had lost a great deal, as if some one were endeavoring to take something immense away from him, something which he had always had!

During the days that followed he brooded over this, avoiding his family as much as possible, while they, wondering when the first prospector would return and what conversation or arrangement Quecder had had with the second, watched him closely. At last he was all but unbalanced mentally, and by degrees his mind came to possess but one idea, and that was that his wife, his children, the world, all were trying to rob him, and that his one escape lay in flight with his treasure if only he could once gain possession of it. But how? How? One thing was sure. They should not have it. He would fight first; he would die. And alone in his silent field, with ragged body and mind, he brooded over riches and felt as if he already had them to defend.

In the meanwhile the first prospector had been meditating as to the ease, under the circumstances, with which Queeder's land could be taken from him at the very nominal price of two thousand, considering the secrecy which, according to Queeder's own wish, must attach to the transfer of all moneys over that sum. Once the deed was signed—the same reading for two thousand—in the presence of the wife and a lawyer who should accompany him, how easy to walk off and pay no more, standing calmly on the letter of the contract!

It was nearing that last day now and the terrible suspense was telling. Queeder was in no mental state to endure anything. His hollow eyes showed the wondering out of which nothing had come. His nervous strolling here and there had lost all semblance of reason. Then on the last of the sixty allotted days there rode forward the now bane of his existence, the original prospector, accompanied by Attorney Giles, of Arno, a veritable scamp and rascal of a lawyer.

At first on seeing them Queeder felt a strong impulse to run away, but on second consideration he feared so to do. The land was his. If he did not stay Dode and Mrs. Queeder might enter on some arrangement without his consent—something which would leave him landless, moneyless—or they might find out something about the extra money he had taken and contracted for, the better price he was now privately to receive. It was essential that he stay, and yet he had no least idea as to how he would solve it all.

Jane, who was in the doorway as they entered the yard, was the one to welcome them, although Dode, watchful and working in a nearby patch, saluted them next. Then Mrs. Queeder examined them cynically and with much opposition. These, then, were the twain who were expecting to misuse her financially!

"Where's your father, Dode?" asked Attorney Giles familiarly, for he knew them well.

"Over thar in the second 'tater patch," answered Dode sourly. A moment later he added with rough calculation, "Ef ye're comin' about the land, though, I 'low ez 'twon't do yuh no good. Maw an' Paw have decided not tuh sell. The place is wuth a heap more'n whut you all're offerin'. They're sellin' land roun' Arno with not near ez much min'l onto hit ez this hez for three hundred now, an' yuh all only wanta give two thousan' fer the hull place, I hyur. Maw'n Paw'd be fools ef they'd agree tuh that."

"Oh, come now," exclaimed Giles placatively and yet irritably—a very wasp who was always attempting to smooth over the ruffled tempers of people on just such trying occasions as this. "Mr. Crawford here has an option on this property signed by your mother and father and witnessed by a Mr."—he considered the slip—"a Mr. Botts—oh, yes, Lester Botts. You cannot legally escape that. All Mr. Crawford has to do is to offer you the money—leave it here, in fact—and the property is his. That is the law. An option is an option, and this one has a witness. I don't see how you can hope to escape it, really."

"They wuzn't nuthin' said about no min'l when I signed that air," insisted Mrs. Queeder, "an' I don't 'low ez no paper whut I didn't know the meanin' uv is goin' tuh be good anywhar. Leastways, I won't put my name onto nuthin' else."

"Well, well!" said Mr. Giles fussily. "We'd better get Mr. Queeder in here and see what he says to this. I'm sure he'll not take any such unreasonable and illegal view."

In the meantime old Queeder, called for lustily by Jane, came edging around the house corner like some hunted animal —dark, fearful, suspicious—and at sight of him the prospector and lawyer, who had seated themselves, arose.

"Well, here we are, Mr. Queeder," said the prospector, but stopped, astonished at the weird manner in which Queeder passed an aimless hand over his brow and gazed almost dully before him. He had more the appearance of a hungry bird than a human being. He was yellow, emaciated, all but wild.

"Look at Paw!" whispered Jane to Dode, used as she was to all the old man's idiosyncrasies.

"Yes, Mr. Queeder," began the lawyer, undisturbed by the whisper of Jane and anxious to smooth over a very troublesome situation, "here we are. We have come to settle this sale with you according to the terms of the option. I suppose you're ready?"

"Whut?" asked old Queeder aimlessly, then, recovering himself slightly, began, "I hain't goin' tuh sign nuthin'! Nuthin' 'tall! That's whut I hain't! Nuthin'!" He opened and closed his fingers and twisted and craned his neck as though physically there were something very much awry with him.

"What's that?" queried the lawyer incisively, attempting by his tone to overawe him or bring him to his senses, "not sign? What do you mean by saying you won't sign? You gave an option here for the sum of $100 cash in hand, signed by you and your wife and witnessed by Lester Botts, and now you say you won't sign! I don't want to be harsh, but there's a definite contract entered into here and money passed, and such things can't be handled in any such light way, Mr. Queeder. This is a contract, a very serious matter before the law, Mr. Queeder, a very serious matter. The law provides a very definite remedy in a case of this kind. Whether you want to sign or not, with this option we have here and what it calls for we can pay over the money before witnesses and enter suit for possession and win it."

"Not when a feller's never knowed whut he wuz doin' when he signed," insisted Dode, who by now, because of his self-interest and the appearance of his father having been misled, was coming round to a more sympathetic or at least friendly attitude.

"I'll not sign nuthin'," insisted Queeder grimly. "I hain't a-goin' tuh be swindled out o' my prupetty. I never knowed they wuz min'l onto hit, like they is—leastways not whut it wuz wuth—an' I won't sign, an' yuh ain't a-goin' tuh make me. Ye're a-tryin' tuh get it away from me fur nuthin', that's whut yere a-tryin' tuh do. I won't sign nuthin'!"

"I had no idee they wuz min'l onto hit when I signed," whimpered Mrs. Queeder.

"Oh, come, come!" put in Crawford sternly, deciding to deal with this eccentric character and believing that he could overawe him by referring to the secret agreement between them, "don't forget, Mr. Queeder, that I had a special agreement with you concerning all this." He was not quite sure now as to what he would have to pay—the two or the eight. "Are you going to keep your bargain with me or not? You want to decide quick now. Which is it?"

"Git out!" shouted Queeder, becoming wildly excited and waving his hands and jumping backward. "Yuh swindled me, that's whutcha done! Yuh thort yuh'd git this place fer nuthin'. Well, yuh won't—yuh kain't. I won't sign nuthin'. I won't sign nuthin'." His eyes were red and wild from too much brooding.

Now it was that Crawford, who had been hoping to get it all for two thousand, decided to stick to his private agreement to pay eight, only instead of waiting to adjust it with Queeder in private he decided now to use it openly in an attempt to suborn the family to his point of view by showing them how much he really was to have and how unjust Queeder had planned to be to himself and them. In all certainty the family understood it as only two. If he would now let them know how matters stood, perhaps that would make a difference in his favor.

"You call eight thousand for this place swindling, and after you've taken eight hundred dollars of my money and kept it for sixty days?"

"Whut's that?" asked Dode, edging nearer, then turning and glaring at his father and eyeing his mother amazedly. This surpassed in amount and importance anything he had imagined had been secured by them, and of course he assumed that both were lying. "Eight thousan'! I thort yuh said it wuz two!" He looked at his mother for confirmation.

The latter was a picture of genuine surprise. "That's the fust I hearn uv any eight thousan'," she replied dumbly, her own veracity in regard to the transaction being in question.

The picture that Queeder made under the circumstances was remarkable. Quite upset by this half-unexpected and yet feared revelation, he was now quite beside himself with rage, fear, the insolvability of the amazing tangle into which he had worked himself. The idea that after he had made an agreement with this man, which was really unfair to himself, he should turn on him in this way was all but mentally upsetting. Besides, the fact that his wife and son now knew how greedy and selfish he had been weakened him to the point of terror.

"Well, that's what I offered him, just the same," went on Crawford aggressively and noting the extreme effect, "and that's what he agreed to take, and that's what I'm here to pay. I paid him $800 in cash to bind the bargain, and he has the money now somewhere. His saying now that I tried to swindle him is too funny! He asked me not to say anything about it because the land was all his and he wanted to adjust things with you three in his own way."

"Git outen hyur!" shouted Queeder savagely, going all but mad, "before I kill yuh! I hain't signed nuthin'! We never said nuthin' about no $8,000. It wuz $2,000—that's what it wuz! Ye're trin' tuh swindle me, the hull varmint passel o' yuh! I won't sign nuthin'!" and he stooped and attempted to seize a stool that stood near the wall.

At this all retreated except Dode, who, having mastered his father in more than one preceding contest, now descended on him and with one push of his arm knocked him down, so weak was he, while the lawyer and prospector, seeing him prone, attempted to interfere in his behalf. What Dode was really thinking was that now was his chance. His father had lied to him. He was naturally afraid of him. Why not force him by sheer brute strength to accept this agreement and take the money? Once it was paid here before him, if he could make his father sign, he could take his share without let or hindrance. Of what dreams might not this be the fulfilment? "He agreed on't, an' now he's gotta do it," he thought; "that's all."

"No fighting, now," called Giles. "We don't want any fighting—just to settle this thing pleasantly, that's all."

After all, Queeder's second signature or *mark* would be required, peaceably if possible, and besides they wished no physical violence. They were men of business, not of war.

"Yuh say he agreed tuh take $8,000, did he?" queried Dode, the actuality of so huge a sum ready to be paid in cash seeming to him almost unbelievable.

"Yes, that's right," replied the prospector.

"Then, by heck, he's gotta make good on whut he said!" said Dode with a roll of his round head, his arms akimbo, heavily anxious to see the money paid over. "Here you," he now turned to his father and began—for his prostrate father, having fallen and injured his head, was still lying semi-propped on his elbows, surveying the group with almost non-comprehending eyes, too confused and lunatic to quite realize what was going on or to offer any real resistance. "Whut's a-gittin' into yuh, anyhow, Ol' Spindle Shanks? Git up hyur!" Dode went over and lifted his father to his feet and pushed him toward a chair at the table. "Yuh might ez well sign fer this, now 'at yuh've begun it. Whar's the paper?" he asked of the lawyer. "Yuh just show him whar he orter sign, an' I guess he'll do it. But let's see this hyur money that ye're a-goin' tuh pay over fust," he added, "afore he signs. I wanta see ef it's orl right."

The prospector extracted the actual cash from a wallet, having previously calculated that a check would never be accepted, and the lawyer presented the deed to be signed. At the same time Dode took the money and began to count it.

"All he has to do," observed Giles to the others as he did so, "is to sign this second paper, he and his wife. If you can read," he said to Dode when the latter had concluded, and seeing how satisfactorily things were going, "you can see for yourself what it is." Dode now turned and picked it up and looked at it as though it were as simple and clear as daylight. "As you can see," went on the lawyer, "we agreed to buy this land of him for eight thousand dollars. We have already paid him eight hundred. That leaves seven thousand two hundred still to pay, which you have there," and he touched the money in Dode's hands. The latter was so moved by the reality of the cash that he could scarcely speak for joy. Think of it—seven thousand two hundred dollars—and all for this wretched bony land!

"Well, did yuh ever!" exclaimed Mrs. Queeder and Jane in chorus. "Who'd 'a' thort! Eight thousan'!"

Old Queeder, still stunned and befogged mentally, was yet recovering himself sufficiently to rise from the chair and look strangely about, now that Dode was attempting to make him sign, but his loving son uncompromisingly pushed him back again.

"Never mind, Ol' Spindle Shanks," he repeated roughly. "Just yuh stay whar yuh air an' sign as he asts yuh tuh. Yuh agreed tuh this, an' yuh might ez well stick tuh it. Ye're gittin' so yuh don't know what yuh want no more," he jested, now that he realized that for some strange reason he had his father completely under his sway. The latter was quite helplessly dumb. "Yuh agreed tuh this, he says. Did ja? Air yuh clean gone?"

"Lawsy!" put in the excited Mrs. Queeder. "Eight thousan'! An' him a-walkin' round' hyur all the time sayin' hit wuz only two an' never sayin' nuthin' else tuh nobody! Who'd 'a' thort hit! An' him a-goin' tuh git hit all ef he could an' say nuthin'!"

"Yes," added Jane, gazing at her father greedily and vindictively, "tryin' tuh git it all fer hisself! An' us a'workin' hyur year in an' year out on this hyur ol' place tuh keep him comfortable!" She was no less hard in her glances than her brother. Her father seemed little less than a thief, attempting to rob them of the hard-earned fruit of their toil.

As the lawyer took the paper from Dode and spread it upon the old board table and handed Queeder a pen the latter took it aimlessly, quite as a child might have, and made his mark where indicated, Mr. Giles observing very cautiously, "This is of your own free will and deed, is it, Mr. Queeder?" The old man made no reply. For the time being anyhow, possibly due to the blow on his head as he fell, he had lost the main current of his idea, which was not to sign. After signing he looked vaguely around, as though uncertain as to what else might be requested of him, while Mrs. Queeder made her mark, answering "yes" to the same shrewd question. Then Dode, as the senior intelligence of this institution and the one who by right of force now dominated, having witnessed the marks of his father and mother, as did Jane, two signatures being necessary, he took the money and before the straining eyes of his relatives proceeded to recount it. Meanwhile old Queeder, still asleep to the significance of the money, sat quite still, but clawed at it as though it were something which he ought to want, but was not quite sure of it.

"You find it all right, I suppose?" asked the lawyer, who was turning to go. Dode acknowledged that it was quite correct.

Then the two visitors, possessed of the desired deed, departed. The family, barring the father, who sat there still in a daze, began to discuss how the remarkable sum was to be divided.

"Now, I just wanta tell yuh one thing, Dode," urged the mother, all avarice and anxiety for herself, "a third o' that whutever 'tis, b'longs tuh me, accordin' tuh law!"

"An' I sartinly oughta git a part o' that thar, workin' the way I have," insisted Jane, standing closely over Dode.

"Well, just keep yer hands off till I git through, cantcha?" asked Dode, beginning for the third time to count it. The mere feel of it was so entrancing! What doors would it not open? He could get married now, go to the city, do a hundred things he had always wanted to do. The fact that his father was entitled to anything or that, having lost his wits, he was now completely helpless, a pathetic figure and very likely from now on doomed to wander about alone or to do his will, moved him not in the least. By right of strength and malehood he was now practically master here, or so he felt himself to be. As he fingered the money he glowed and talked, thinking wondrous things, then suddenly remembering the concealed eight hundred, or his father's part of it, he added, "Yes, an' whar's that other eight hundred, I'd like tuh know? He's a-carryin' it aroun' with him er hidin' it hyurabout mebbe!" Then eyeing the crumpled victim suspiciously, he began to feel in the old man's clothes, but, not finding anything, desisted, saying they might get it later. The money in his hands was finally divided: a third to Mrs. Queeder, a fourth to Jane, the balance to himself as the faithful heir and helper of his father, the while he speculated as to the whereabouts of the remaining eight hundred.

Just then Queeder, who up to this time had been completely bereft of his senses, now recovered sufficiently to guess nearly all of what had so recently transpired. With a bound he was on his feet, and, looking wildly about him, exclaiming as he did so in a thin, reedy voice, "They've stole my prupetty! They've stole my prupetty! I've been robbed, I have! I've been robbed! Eh! Eh! Eh! This hyur land ain't wuth only eight thousan'— hit's wuth twenty-five thousan', an' that's whut I could 'a' had for it, an' they've gone an' made me sign it all away! Eh! Eh! Eh!" He jigged and moaned, dancing helplessly about until, seeing Dode with his share of the money still held safely in his hand, his maniacal chagrin took a new form, and, seizing it and running to the open door, he began to throw a portion of the precious bills to the winds, crying as he did so, "They've stole my prupetty! They've stole my prupetty! I don't want the consarned money—I don't want it! I want my prupetty! Eh! Eh! Eh!"

In this astonishing situation Dode saw but one factor—the money. Knowing nothing of the second prospector's offer, he could not realize what it was that so infuriated the old man and had finally completely upset his mind. As the latter jigged and screamed and threw the money about he fell upon him with the energy of a wildcat and, having toppled him over and wrested the remainder of the cash from him, he held him safely down, the while he called to his sister and mother, "Pick up the money, cantcha? Pick up the money an' git a rope, cantcha? Git a rope! Cantcha see he's done gone plum daffy? He's outen his head, I tell yuh. He's crazy, he is, shore! Git a rope!" and eyeing the money now being assembled by his helpful relatives, he pressed the struggling maniac's body to the floor. When the latter was safely tied and the money returned, the affectionate son arose and, having once more recounted his share in order to see that it was all there, he was content to look about him somewhat more kindly on an all too treacherous world. Then, seeing the old man where he was trussed like a fowl for market, he added, somewhat sympathetically, it may be:

"Well, who'd 'a' thort! Pore ol' Pap! I do b'lieve he's outen his mind for shore this time! He's clean gone—plum daffy."

"Yes, that's whut he is, I do b'lieve," added Mrs. Queeder with a modicum of wifely interest, yet more concerned at that with her part of the money than anything else.

Then Dode, his mother and sister began most unconcernedly to speculate as to what if anything was next to be done with the old farmer, the while the latter rolled a vacant eye over a scene he was no longer able to interpret.

My Brother Paul

I LIKE best to think of him as he was at the height of his all-too-brief reputation and success, when, as the author and composer of various American popular successes ("On the Banks of the Wabash," "Just Tell Them That You Saw Me," and various others), as a third owner of one of the most successful popular music publishing houses in the city and as an actor and playwright of some small repute, he was wont to spin like a moth in the white light of Broadway. By reason of a little luck and some talent he had come so far, done so much for himself. In his day he had been by turn a novitiate in a Western seminary which trained aspirants for the Catholic priesthood; a singer and entertainer with a perambulating cure-all oil troupe or wagon ("Hamlin's Wizard Oil") traveling throughout Ohio, Indiana and Illinois; both end- and middle-man with one, two or three different minstrel companies of repute; the editor or originator and author of a "funny column" in a Western small city paper; the author of the songs mentioned and a hundred others; a black-face monologue artist; a white-face ditto, at Tony Pastor's, Miner's and Niblo's of the old days; a comic lead; co-star and star in such melodramas and farces as "The Danger Signal," "The Two Johns," "A Tin Soldier," "The Midnight Bell," "A Green Goods Man" (a farce which he himself wrote, by the way), and others. The man had a genius for the kind of gayety, poetry and romance which may, and no doubt must be, looked upon as exceedingly middle-class but which nonetheless had as much charm as anything in this world can well have. He had at this time absolutely no cares or financial worries of any kind, and this plus his health, self-amusing disposition and talent for entertaining, made him a most fascinating figure to contemplate.

My first recollection of him is of myself as a boy of ten and he a man of twenty-five (my oldest brother). He had come back to the town in which we were then living solely to find his mother and help her. Six or seven years before he had left without any explanation as to where he was going, tired of or irritated by the routine of a home which for any genuine opportunity it offered him might as well never have existed. It was run dominantly by my father in the interest of religious and moral theories, with which this boy had little sympathy. He was probably not understood by any one save my mother, who understood or at least sympathized with us all. Placed in a school which was to turn him out a priest, he had decamped, and now seven years later was here in this small town, with fur coat and silk hat, a smart cane—a gentleman of the theatrical profession. He had joined a minstrel show somewhere and had become an "end-man." He had suspected that we were not as fortunate in this world's goods as might be and so had returned. His really great heart had called him.

But the thing which haunts me, and which was typical of him then as throughout life, was the spirit which he then possessed and conveyed. It was one of an agile geniality, unmarred by thought of a serious character but warm and genuinely tender and with a taste for simple beauty which was most impressive. He was already the author of a cheap song-book, *"The Paul Dresser Songster"* ("All the Songs Sung in the Show"), and some copies of this he had with him, one of which he gave me. But we having no musical instrument of any kind, he taught me some of the melodies "by ear." The home in which by force of poverty we were compelled to live was most unprepossessing and inconvenient, and the result of his coming could but be our request for, or at least the obvious need of, assistance. Still he was as much an enthusiastic part of it as though he belonged to it. He was happy in it, and the cause of his happiness was my mother, of whom he was intensely fond. I recall how he hung about her in the kitchen or wherever she happened to be, how enthusiastically he related all his plans for the future, his amusing difficulties in the past. He was very grand and youthfully self-important, or so we all thought, and still he patted her on the shoulder or put his arm about her and kissed her. Until she died years later she was truly his uppermost thought, crying with her at times over her troubles and his. He contributed regularly to her support and sent home all his cast-off clothing to be made over for the younger ones. (Bless her tired hands!)

As I look back now on my life, I realize quite clearly that of all the members of my family, subsequent to my mother's death, the only one who truly understood me, or, better yet, sympathized with my intellectual and artistic point of view, was, strange as it may seem, this same Paul, my dearest brother. Not that he was in any way fitted intellectually or otherwise to enjoy high forms of art and learning and so guide me, or that he understood, even in later years (long after I had written "Sister Carrie," for instance), what it was that I was attempting to do; he never did. His world was that of the popular song, the middle-class actor or comedian, the middle-class comedy, and such humorous æsthetes of the writing world as Bill Nye, Petroleum V. Nasby, the authors of the Spoopendyke Papers, and "Samantha at Saratoga." As far as I could make out—and I say this in no lofty, condescending spirit, by any means—he was entirely full of simple, middle-class romance, middle-class humor, middle-class tenderness and middle-class grossness, all of which I am very free to say early disarmed and won me completely and kept me so much his debtor that I should hesitate to try to acknowledge or explain all that he did for or meant to me.

Imagine, if you can, a man weighing all of three hundred pounds, not more than five feet ten-and-one-half inches in height, and yet of so lithesome a build that he gave not the least sense of either undue weight or lethargy. His temperament, always ebullient and radiant, presented him as a clever, eager, cheerful, emotional and always highly illusioned person with so collie-like a warmth that one found him compelling interest and even admiration. Easily cast down at times by the most trivial matters, at others, and for the most part, he was so spirited and bubbly and emotional and sentimental that your fiercest or most gloomy intellectual rages or moods could scarcely withstand his smile. This tenderness or sympathy of his, a very human appreciation of the weaknesses and errors as well as the toils and tribulations of most of us, was by far his outstanding and most engaging quality, and gave him a very definite force and charm. Admitting, as I freely do, that he was very sensuous (gross, some people might have called him), that he had an intense, possibly an undue fondness for women, a frivolous, childish, horse-playish sense of humor at times, still he had other qualities which were absolutely adorable. Life seemed positively to spring up fountain-like in him. One felt in him a capacity to do (in his possibly limited field); an ability to achieve, whether he was doing so at the moment or not, and a supreme willingness to share and radiate his success—qualities exceedingly rare, I believe. Some people are so successful, and yet you know their success is purely selfish—exclusive, not inclusive; they never permit you to share in their lives. Not so my good brother. He was generous to the point of self-destruction, and that is literally true. He was the mark if not the prey of all those who desired much or little for nothing, those who previously might not have rendered him a service of any kind. He was all life and color, and thousands (I use the word with care) noted and commented on it.

When I first came to New York he was easily the foremost popular song-writer of the day and was the cause of my coming, so soon at least, having established himself in the publishing field and being so comfortably settled as to offer me a kind of anchorage in so troubled a commercial sea. I was very much afraid of New York, but with him here it seemed not so bad. The firm of which he was a part had a floor or two in an old residence turned office building, as so many are in New York, in Twentieth Street very close to Broadway, and here, during the summer months (1894-7) when the various theatrical road-companies, one of which he was always a part, had returned for the closed season, he was to be found aiding his concern in the reception and care of possible applicants for songs and attracting by his personality such virtuosi of the vaudeville and comedy stage as were likely to make the instrumental publications of his firm a success.

I may as well say here that he had no more business skill than a fly. At the same time, he was in no wise sycophantic where either wealth, power or fame was concerned. He considered himself a personage of sorts, and was. The minister, the moralist, the religionist, the narrow, dogmatic and self-centered in any field were likely to be the butt of his humor, and he could imitate so many phases of character so cleverly that he was the life of any idle pleasure-seeking party anywhere. To this day I recall his characterization of an old Irish washer-woman arguing; a stout, truculent German laying down the law; lean, gloomy, out-at-elbows actors of the Hamlet or classic school complaining of their fate; the stingy skinflint haggling over a dollar, and always with a skill for titillating the risibilities which is vivid to me even to this day. Other butts of his humor were the actor, the Irish day-laborer, the negro and the Hebrew. And how he could imitate them! It is useless to try to indicate such things in writing, the facial expression, the intonation, the gestures; these are not things of words. Perhaps I can best indicate the direction of his mind, if not his manner, by the following:

One night as we were on our way to a theater there stood on a nearby corner in the cold a blind man singing and at the same time holding out a little tin cup into which the coins of the charitably inclined were supposed to be dropped. At once my brother noticed him, for he had an eye for this sort of thing, the pathos of poverty as opposed to so gay a scene, the street with its hurrying theater crowds. At the same time, so inherently mischievous was his nature that although his sympathy for the suffering or the ill-used of fate was overwhelming, he could not resist combining his intended charity with a touch of the ridiculous.

"Got any pennies?" he demanded.

"Three or four."

Going over to an outdoor candystand he exchanged a quarter for pennies, then came back and waited until the singer, who had ceased singing, should begin a new melody. A custom of the singer's, since the song was of no import save as a means of attracting attention to him, was to interpolate a "Thank you" after each coin dropped in his cup and between the words of the song, regardless. It was this little idiosyncrasy which evidently had attracted my brother's attention, although it had not mine. Standing quite close, his pennies in his hand, he waited until the singer had resumed, then began dropping pennies, waiting each time for the "Thank you," which caused the song to go about as follows:

"Da-a-ling" (Clink!—"Thank you!") "I am—" (Clink!—"Thank you!") "growing o-o-o-ld" (Clink!—"Thank you!"), "Silve-e-r—" (Clink!—"Thank you!")—"threads among the—" (Clink!—"Thank you!") "go-o-o-ld—" (Clink! "Thank you!"). "Shine upon my-y" (Clink!—"Thank you!") "bro-o-ow to-da-a-y" (Clink!— "Thank you!"), "Life is—" (Clink!—"Thank you!") "fading fast a-a-wa-a-ay" (Clink!—"Thank you!")—and so on ad infinitum, until finally the beggar himself seemed to hesitate a little and waver, only so solemn was his rôle of want and despair that of course he dared not but had to go on until the last penny was in, and until he was saying more "Thank you's" than words of the song. A passerby noticing it had begun to "Haw-haw!", at which others joined in, myself included. The beggar himself, a rather sniveling specimen, finally realizing what a figure he was cutting with his song and thanks, emptied the coins into his hand and with an indescribably wry expression, half-uncertainty and half-smile, exclaimed, "I'll have to thank you as long as you keep putting pennies in, I suppose. God bless you!"

My brother came away smiling and content.

However, it is not as a humorist or song-writer or publisher that I wish to portray him, but as an odd, lovable personality, possessed of so many interesting and peculiar and almost indescribable traits. Of all characters in fiction he perhaps most suggests Jack Falstaff, with his love of women, his bravado and bluster and his innate good nature and sympathy. Sympathy was really his outstanding characteristic, even more than humor, although the latter was always present. One might recite a thousand incidents of his generosity and out-of-hand charity, which contained no least thought of return or reward. I recall that once there was a boy who had been reared in one of the towns in which we had once lived who had never had a chance in his youth, educationally or in any other way, and, having turned out "bad" and sunk to the level of a bank robber, had been detected in connection with three other men in the act of robbing a bank, the watchman of which was subsequently killed in the mêlée and escape. Of all four criminals only this one had been caught. Somewhere in prison he had heard sung one of my brother's sentimental ballads, "The Convict and the Bird," and recollecting that he had known Paul wrote him, setting forth his life history and that now he had no money or friends.

At once my good brother was alive to the pathos of it. He showed the letter to me and wanted to know what could be done. I suggested a lawyer, of course, one of those brilliant legal friends of his—always he had enthusiastic admirers in all walks—who might take the case for little or nothing. There was the leader of Tammany Hall, Richard Croker, who could be reached, he being a friend of Paul's. There was the Governor himself to whom a plain recitation of the boy's unfortunate life might be addressed, and with some hope of profit.

All of these things he did, and more. He went to the prison (Sing Sing), saw the warden and told him the story of the boy's life, then went to the boy, or man, himself and gave him some money. He was introduced to the Governor through influential friends and permitted to tell the tale. There was much delay, a reprieve, a commutation of the death penalty to life imprisonment—the best that could be done. But he was so grateful for that, so pleased. You would have thought at the time that it was his own life that had been spared.

"Good heavens!" I jested. "You'd think you'd done the man an inestimable service, getting him in the penitentiary for life!"

"That's right," he grinned—an unbelievably provoking smile. "He'd better be dead, wouldn't he? Well, I'll write and ask him which he'd rather have."

I recall again taking him to task for going to the rescue of a "down and out" actor who had been highly successful and apparently not very sympathetic in his day, one of that more or less gaudy clan that wastes its substance, or so it seemed to me then, in riotous living. But now being old and entirely discarded and forgotten, he was in need of sympathy and aid. By some chance he knew Paul, or Paul had known him, and now because of the former's obvious prosperity—he was much in the papers at the time—he had appealed to him. The man lived with a sister in a wretched little town far out on Long Island. On receiving his appeal Paul seemed to wish to investigate for himself, possibly to indulge in a little lofty romance or sentiment. At any rate he wanted me to go along for the sake of companionship, so one dreary November afternoon we went, saw the pantaloon, who did not impress me very much even in his age and misery for he still had a few of his theatrical manners and insincerities, and as we were coming away I said, "Paul, why should you be the goat in every case?" for I had noted ever since I had been in New York, which was several years then, that he was a victim of many such importunities. If it was not the widow of a deceased friend who needed a ton of coal or a sack of flour, or the reckless, headstrong boy of parents too poor to save him from a term in jail or the reformatory and who asked for fine-money or an appeal to higher powers for clemency, or a wastrel actor or actress "down and out" and unable to "get back to New York" and requiring his or her railroad fare wired prepaid, it was the dead wastrel actor or actress who needed a coffin and a decent form of burial.

"Well, you know how it is, Thee" (he nearly always addressed me thus), "when you're old and sick. As long as you're up and around and have money, everybody's your friend. But once you're down and out no one wants to see you any more—see?" Almost amusingly he was always sad over those who had once been prosperous but who were now old and forgotten. Some of his silliest tender songs conveyed as much.

"Quite so," I complained, rather brashly, I suppose, "but why didn't he save a little money when he had it? He made as much as you'll ever make." The man had been a star. "He had plenty of it, didn't he? Why should he come to you?"

"Well, you know how it is, Thee," he explained in the kindliest and most apologetic way. "When you're young and healthy like that you don't think. I know how it is; I'm that way myself. We all have a little of it in us. I have; you have. And anyhow youth's the time to spend money if you're to get any good of it, isn't it? Of course when you're old you can't expect much, but still I always feel as though I'd like to help some of these old people." His eyes at such times always seemed more like those of a mother contemplating a sick or injured child than those of a man contemplating life.

"But, Paul," I insisted on another occasion when he had just wired twenty-five dollars somewhere to help bury some one. (My spirit was not so niggardly as fearsome. I was constantly terrified in those days by the thought of a poverty-stricken old age for myself and him—why, I don't know. I was by no means incompetent.) "Why don't you save your money? Why should you give it to every Tom, Dick and Harry that asks you? You're not a charity organization, and you're not called upon to feed and clothe and bury all the wasters who happen to cross your path. If you were down and out how many do you suppose would help you?"

"Well, you know," and his voice and manner were largely those of mother, the same wonder, the same wistfulness and sweetness, the same bubbling charity and tenderness of heart, "I can't say I haven't got it, can I?" He was at the height of his success at the time. "And anyhow, what's the use being so hard on people? We're all likely to get that way. You don't know what pulls people down sometimes—not wasting always. It's thoughtfulness, or trying to be happy. Remember how poor we were and how mamma and papa used to worry." Often these references to mother or father or their difficulties would bring tears to his eyes. "I can't stand to see people suffer, that's all, not if I have anything," and his eyes glowed sweetly. "And, after all," he added apologetically, "the little I give isn't much. They don't get so much out of me. They don't come to me every day."

Another time—one Christmas Eve it was, when I was comparatively new to New York (my second or third year), I was a little uncertain what to do, having no connections outside of Paul and two sisters, one of whom was then out of the city. The other, owing to various difficulties of her own and a temporary estrangement from us—more our fault than hers—was therefore not available. The rather drab state into which she had allowed her marital affections to lead her was the main reason that kept us apart. At any rate I felt that I could not, or rather would not, go there. At the same time, owing to some difficulty or irritation with the publishing house of which my brother was then part owner (it was publishing the magazine which I was editing), we twain were also estranged, nothing very deep really —a temporary feeling of distance and indifference.

So I had no place to go except to my room, which was in a poor part of the town, or out to dine where best I might— some moderate-priced hotel, was my thought. I had not seen my brother in three or four days, but after I had strolled a block or two up Broadway I encountered him. I have always thought that he had kept an eye on me and had really followed me; was looking, in short, to see what I would do. As usual he was most smartly and comfortably dressed.

"Where you going, Thee?" he called cheerfully.

"Oh, no place in particular," I replied rather suavely, I presume. "Just going up the street."

"Now, see here, sport," he began—a favorite expression of his, "sport"—with his face abeam, "what's the use you and me quarreling? It's Christmas Eve, ain't it? It's a shame! Come on, let's have a drink and then go out to dinner."

"Well," I said, rather uncompromisingly, for at times his seemingly extreme success and well-being irritated me, "I'll have a drink, but as for dinner, I have another engagement."

"Aw, don't say that. What's the use being sore? You know I always feel the same even if we do quarrel at times. Cut it out. Come on. You know I'm your brother, and you're mine. It's all right with me, Thee. Let's make it up, will you? Put 'er there! Come on, now. We'll go and have a drink, see, something hot—it's Christmas Eve, sport. The old home stuff."

He smiled winsomely, coaxingly, really tenderly, as only he could smile. I "gave in." But now as we entered the nearest shining bar, a Christmas crowd buzzing within and without (it was the old Fifth Avenue Hotel), a new thought seemed to strike him.

"Seen E—— lately?" he inquired, mentioning the name of the troubled sister who was having a very hard time indeed. Her husband had left her and she was struggling over the care of two children.

"No," I replied, rather shamefacedly, "not in a week or two —maybe more."

He clicked his tongue. He himself had not been near her in a month or more. His face fell, and he looked very depressed.

"It's too bad—a shame really. We oughtn't to do this way, you know, sport. It ain't right. What do you say to our going around there," it was in the upper thirties, "and see how she's making out?—take her a few things, eh? Whaddya say?"

I hadn't a spare dollar myself, but I knew well enough what he meant by "take a few things" and who would pay for them.

"Well, we'll have to hurry if we want to get anything now," I urged, falling in with the idea since it promised peace, plenty and good will all around, and we rushed the drink and departed. Near at hand was a branch of one of the greatest grocery companies of the city, and near it, too, his then favorite hotel, the Continental. En route we meditated on the impossibility of delivery, the fact that we would have to carry the things ourselves, but he at last solved that by declaring that he could commandeer negro porters or bootblacks from the Continental. We entered, and by sheer smiles on his part and some blarney heaped upon a floor-manager, secured a turkey, sweet potatoes, peas, beans, a salad, a strip of bacon, a ham, plum pudding, a basket of luscious fruit and I know not what else—provender, I am sure, for a dozen meals. While it was being wrapped and packed in borrowed baskets, soon to be returned, he went across the way to the hotel and came back with three grinning darkies who for the tip they knew they would receive preceded us up Broadway, the nearest path to our destination. On the way a few additional things were picked up: holly wreaths, toys, candy, nuts—and then, really not knowing whether our plan might not miscarry, we made our way through the side street and to the particular apartment, or, rather, flat-house, door, a most amusing Christmas procession, I fancy, wondering and worrying now whether she would be there.

But the door clicked in answer to our ring, and up we marched, the three darkies first, instructed to inquire for her and then insist on leaving the goods, while we lagged behind to see how she would take it.

The stage arrangement worked as planned. My sister opened the door and from the steps below we could hear her protesting that she had ordered nothing, but the door being open the negroes walked in and a moment or two afterwards ourselves. The packages were being piled on table and floor, while my sister, unable quite to grasp this sudden visitation and change of heart, stared.

"Just thought we'd come around and have supper with you, E——, and maybe dinner tomorrow if you'll let us," my brother chortled. "Merry Christmas, you know. Christmas Eve. The good old home stuff—see? Old sport here and I thought we couldn't stay away—tonight, anyhow."

He beamed on her in his most affectionate way, but she, suffering regret over the recent estrangement as well as the difficulties of life itself and the joy of this reunion, burst into tears, while the two little ones danced about, and he and I put our arms about her.

"There, there! It's all over now," he declared, tears welling in his eyes. "It's all off. We'll can this scrapping stuff. Thee and I are a couple of bums and we know it, but you can forgive us, can't you? We ought to be ashamed of ourselves, all of us, and that's the truth. We've been quarreling, too, haven't spoken for a week. Ain't that so, sport? But it's all right now, eh?"

There were tears in my eyes, too. One couldn't resist him. He had the power of achieving the tenderest results in the simplest ways. We then had supper, and breakfast the next morning, all staying and helping, even to the washing and drying of the dishes, and thereafter for I don't know how long we were all on the most affectionate terms, and he eventually died in this sister's home, ministered to with absolutely restless devotion by her for weeks before the end finally came.

But, as I have said, I always prefer to think of him at this, the very apex or tower window of his life. For most of this period he was gay and carefree. The music company of which he was a third owner was at the very top of its success. Its songs, as well as his, were everywhere. He had in turn at this time a suite at the Gilsey House, the Marlborough, the Normandie—always on Broadway, you see. The limelight district was his home. He rose in the morning to the clang of the cars and the honk of the automobiles outside; he retired at night as a gang of repair men under flaring torches might be repairing a track, or the milk trucks were rumbling to and from the ferries. He was in his way a public restaurant and hotel favorite, a shining light in the theater managers' offices, hotel bars and lobbies and wherever those flies of the Tenderloin, those passing lords and celebrities of the sporting, theatrical, newspaper and other worlds, are wont to gather. One of his intimates, as I now recall, was "Bat" Masterson, the Western and now retired (to Broadway!) bad man; Muldoon, the famous wrestler; Tod Sloane, the jockey; "Battling" Nelson; James J. Corbett; Kid McCoy; Terry McGovern—prize-fighters all. Such Tammany district leaders as James Murphy, "The" McManus, Chrystie and Timothy Sullivan, Richard Carroll, and even Richard Croker, the then reigning Tammany boss, were all on his visiting list. He went to their meetings, rallies and district doings generally to sing and play, and they came to his "office" occasionally. Various high and mighties of the Roman Church, "fathers" with fine parishes and good wine cellars, and judges of various municipal courts, were also of his peculiar world. He was always running to one or the other "to get somebody out," or they to him to get him to contribute something to something, or to sing and play or act, and betimes they were meeting each other in hotel grills or elsewhere and having a drink and telling "funny stories."

Apropos of this sense of humor of his, this love of horse-play almost, I remember that once he had a new story to tell— a vulgar one of course—and with it he had been making me and a dozen others laugh until the tears coursed down our cheeks. It seemed new to everybody and, true to his rather fantastic moods, he was determined to be the first to tell it along Broadway. For some reason he was anxious to have me go along with him, possibly because he found me at that time an unvarying fountain of approval and laughter, possibly because he liked to show me off as his rising brother, as he insisted that I was. At between six and seven of a spring or summer evening, therefore, we issued from his suite at the Gilsey House, whither he had returned to dress, and invading the bar below were at once centered among a group who knew him. A whiskey, a cigar, the story told to one, two, three, five, ten to roars of laughter, and we were off, over the way to Weber & Fields (the Musical Burlesque House Supreme of those days) in the same block, where to the ticket seller and house manager, both of whom he knew, it was told. More laughter, a cigar perhaps. Then we were off again, this time to the ticket seller of Palmer's Theater at Thirtieth Street, thence to the bar of the Grand Hotel at Thirty-first, the Imperial at Thirty-second, the Martinique at Thirty-third, a famous drug-store at the southwest corner of Thirty-fourth and Broadway, now gone of course, the manager of which was a friend of his. It was a warm, moony night, and he took a glass of vichy "for looks' sake," as he said.

Then to the quondam Hotel Aulic at Thirty-fifth and Broadway—the center and home of the then much-berated "Hotel Aulic or Actors' School of Philosophy," and a most impressive actors' rendezvous where might have been seen in the course of an evening all the "second leads" and "light comedians" and "heavies" of this, that and the other road company, all blazing with startling clothes and all explaining how they "knocked 'em" here and there: in Peoria, Pasadena, Walla-Walla and where not. My brother shone like a star when only one is in the sky.

Over the way then to the Herald Building, its owls' eyes glowing in the night, its presses thundering, the elevated thundering beside it. Here was a business manager whom he knew. Then to the Herald Square Theater on the opposite side of the street, ablaze with a small electric sign—among the newest in the city. In this, as in the business office of the *Herald* was another manager, and he knew them all. Thence to the Marlborough bar and lobby at Thirty-sixth, the manager's office of the Knickerbocker Theater at Thirty-eighth, stopping at the bar and lobby of the Normandie, where some blazing professional beauty of the stage waylaid him and exchanged theatrical witticisms with him—and what else? Thence to the manager's office of the Casino at Thirty-ninth, some bar which was across the street, another in Thirty-ninth west of Broadway, an Italian restaurant on the ground floor of the Metropolitan at Fortieth and Broadway, and at last but by no means least and by such slow stages to the very door of the then Mecca of Meccas of all theater- and sportdom, the sanctum sanctorum of all those sportively au fait, "wise," the "real thing"—the Hotel Metropole at Broadway and Forty-second Street, the then extreme northern limit of the white-light district. And what a realm! Rounders and what not were here ensconced at round tables, their backs against the leather-cushioned wall seats, the adjoining windows open to all Broadway and the then all but somber Forty-second Street.

It was wonderful, the loud clothes, the bright straw hats, the canes, the diamonds, the "hot" socks, the air of security and well-being, so easily assumed by those who gain an all too brief hour in this pretty, petty world of make-believe and pleasure and pseudo-fame. Among them my dearest brother was at his best. It was "Paul" here and "Paul" there—"Why, hello, Dresser, you're just in time! Come on in. What'll you have? Let me tell you something, Paul, a good one——" More drinks, cigars, tales —magnificent tales of successes made, "great shows" given, fights, deaths, marvelous winnings at cards, trickeries in racing, prize-fighting; the "dogs" that some people were, the magnificent, magnanimous "God's own salt" that the others were. The oaths, stories of women, what low, vice-besmeared, crime-soaked ghouls certain reigning beauties of the town or stage were—and so on and so on ad infinitum.

But his story?—ah, yes. I had all but forgotten. It was told in every place, not once but seven, eight, nine, ten times. We did not eat until we reached the Metropole, and it was ten-thirty when we reached it! The handshakes, the road stories—"This is my brother Theodore. He writes: he's a newspaper man." The roars of laughter, the drinks! "Ah, my boy, that's good, but let me tell you one—one that I heard out in Louisville the other day." A seedy, shabby ne'er-do-well of a song-writer maybe stopping the successful author in the midst of a tale to borrow a dollar. Another actor, shabby and distrait, reciting the sad tale of a year's misfortunes. Everywhere my dear brother was called to, slapped on the back, chuckled with. He was successful. One of his best songs was the rage, he had an interest in a going musical concern, he could confer benefits, favors.

Ah, me! Ah, me! That one could be so great, and that it should not last for ever and for ever!

Another of his outstanding characteristics was his love of women, a really amusing and at times ridiculous quality. He was always sighing over the beauty, innocence, sweetness, this and that, of young maidenhood in his songs, but in real life he seemed to desire and attract quite a different type—the young and beautiful, it is true, but also the old, the homely and the somewhat savage—a catholicity of taste I could never quite stomach. It was "Paul dearest" here and "Paul dearest" there, especially in his work in connection with the music-house and the stage. In the former, popular ballad singers of both sexes, some of the women most attractive and willful, were most numerous, coming in daily from all parts of the world apparently to find songs which they could sing on the American or even the English stage. And it was a part of his duty, as a member of the firm and the one who principally "handled" the so-called professional inquirers, to meet them and see that they were shown what the catalogue contained. Occasionally there was an aspiring female song-writer, often mere women visitors.

Regardless, however, of whether they were young, old, attractive or repulsive, male or female, I never knew any one whose manner was more uniformly winsome or who seemed so easily to disarm or relax an indifferent or irritated mood. He was positive sunshine, the same in quality as that of a bright spring morning. His blue eyes focused mellowly, his lips were tendrilled with smiles. He had a brisk, quick manner, always somehow suggestive of my mother, who was never brisk.

And how he fascinated them, the women! Their quite shameless daring where he was concerned! Positively, in the face of it I used to wonder what had become of all the vaunted and so-called "stabilizing morality" of the world. None of it seemed to be in the possession of these women, especially the young and beautiful. They were distant and freezing enough to all who did not interest them, but let a personality such as his come into view and they were all wiles, bending and alluring graces. It was so obvious, this fascination he had for them and they for him, that at times it took on a comic look.

"Get onto the hit he's making," one would nudge another and remark.

"Say, some tenderness, that!" This in reference to a smile or a melting glance on the part of a female.

"Nothing like a way with the ladies. Some baby, eh, boys?" —this following the flick of a skirt and a backward-tossed glance perhaps, as some noticeable beauty passed out.

"No wonder he's cheerful," a sour and yet philosophic vaudevillian, who was mostly out of a job and hung about the place for what free meals he could obtain, once remarked to me in a heavy and morose undertone. "If I had that many women crazy about me I'd be too."

And the results of these encounters with beauty! Always he had something most important to attend to, morning, noon or night, and whenever I encountered him after some such statement "the important thing" was, of course, a woman. As time went on and he began to look upon me as something more than a thin, spindling, dyspeptic and disgruntled youth, he began to wish to introduce me to some of his marvelous followers, and then I could see how completely dependent upon beauty in the flesh he was, how it made his life and world.

One day as we were all sitting in the office, a large group of vaudevillians, song-writers, singers, a chance remark gave rise to a subsequent practical joke at Paul's expense. "I'll bet," observed some one, "that if a strange man were to rush in here with a revolver and say, 'Where's the man that seduced my wife?' Paul would be the first to duck. He wouldn't wait to find out whether he was the one meant or not."

Much laughter followed, and some thought. The subject of this banter was, of course, not present at the time. There was one actor who hung about there who was decidedly skillful in make-up. On more than one occasion he had disguised himself there in the office for our benefit. Coöperating with us, he disguised himself now as a very severe and even savage-looking person of about thirty-five—side-burns, mustachios and goatee. Then, with our aid, timing his arrival to an hour when Paul was certain to be at his desk, he entered briskly and vigorously and, looking about with a savage air, demanded, "Where is Paul Dresser?"

The latter turned almost apprehensively, I thought, and at once seemed by no means captivated by the man's looks.

"That's Mr. Dresser there," explained one of the confederates most willingly.

The stranger turned and glared at him. "So you're the scoundrel that's been running around with my wife, are you?" he demanded, approaching him and placing one hand on his right hip.

Paul made no effort to explain. It did not occur to him to deny the allegation, although he had never seen the man before. With a rising and backward movement he fell against the rail behind him, lifting both hands in fright and exclaiming, "Why —why—Don't shoot!" His expression was one of guilt, astonishment, perplexity. As some one afterwards said, "As puzzled as if he was trying to discover which injured husband it might be." The shout that went up—for it was agreed beforehand that the joke must not be carried far—convinced him that a hoax had been perpetrated, and the removal by the actor of his hat, sideburns and mustache revealed the true character of the injured husband. At first inclined to be angry and sulky, later on he saw the humor of his own indefinite position in the matter and laughed as heartily as any. But I fancy it developed a strain of uncertainty in him also in regard to injured husbands, for he was never afterwards inclined to interest himself in the much-married, and gave such wives a wide berth.

But his great forte was of course his song-writing, and of this, before I speak of anything else, I wish to have my say. It was a gift, quite a compelling one, out of which, before he died, he had made thousands, all spent in the manner described. Never having the least power to interpret anything in a fine musical way, still he was always full of music of a tender, sometimes sad, sometimes gay, kind—that of the ballad-maker of a nation. He was constantly attempting to work them out of himself, not quickly but slowly, brooding as it were over the piano wherever he might find one and could have a little solitude, at times on the organ (his favorite instrument), improvising various sad or wistful strains, some of which he jotted down, others of which, having mastered, he strove to fit words to. At such times he preferred to be alone or with some one whose temperament in no way clashed but rather harmonized with his own. Living with one of my sisters for a period of years, he had a room specially fitted up for his composing work, a very small room for so very large a man, within which he would shut himself and thrum a melody by the hour, especially toward evening or at night. He seemed to have a peculiar fondness for the twilight hour, and at this time might thrum over one strain and another until over some particular one, a new song usually, he would be in tears!

And what pale little things they were really, mere bits and scraps of sentiment and melodrama in story form, most asinine sighings over home and mother and lost sweethearts and dead heroes such as never were in real life, and yet with something about them, in the music at least, which always appealed to me intensely and must have appealed to others, since they attained so wide a circulation. They bespoke, as I always felt, a wistful, seeking, uncertain temperament, tender and illusioned, with no practical knowledge of any side of life, but full of a true poetic feeling for the mystery and pathos of life and death, the wonder of the waters, the stars, the flowers, accidents of life, success, failure. Beginning with a song called "Wide Wings" (published by a small retail music-house in Evansville, Indiana), and followed by such national successes as "The Letter That Never Came," "I Believe It, For My Mother Told Me So" (!), "The Convict and the Bird," "The Pardon Came Too Late," "Just Tell Them That You Saw Me," "The Blue and the Grey," "On the Bowery," "On the Banks of the Wabash," and a number of others, he was never content to rest and never really happy, I think, save when composing. During this time, however, he was at different periods all the things I have described—a black-face monologue artist, an end- and at times a middle-man, a publisher, and so on.

I recall being with him at the time he composed two of his most famous successes: "Just Tell Them That You Saw Me," and "On the Banks of the Wabash," and noting his peculiar mood, almost amounting to a deep depression which ended a little later in marked elation or satisfaction, once he had succeeded in evoking something which really pleased him.

The first of these songs must have followed an actual encounter with some woman or girl whose life had seemingly if not actually gone to wreck on the shore of love or passion. At any rate he came into the office of his publishing house one gray November Sunday afternoon—it was our custom to go there occasionally, a dozen or more congenial souls, about as one might go to a club—and going into a small room which was fitted up with a piano as a "try-out" room (professionals desiring a song were frequently taught it in the office), he began improvising, or rather repeating over and over, a certain strain which was evidently in his mind. A little while later he came out and said, "Listen to this, will you, Thee?"

He played and sang the first verse and chorus. In the middle of the latter, so moved was he by the sentiment of it, his voice broke and he had to stop. Tears stood in his eyes and he wiped them away. A moment or two later he was able to go through it without wavering and I thought it charming for the type of thing it was intended to be. Later on (the following spring) I was literally astonished to see how, after those various efforts usually made by popular music publishers to make a song "go" —advertising it in the *Clipper* and *Mirror*, getting various vaudeville singers to sing it, and so forth—it suddenly began to sell, thousands upon thousands of copies being wrapped in great bundles under my very eyes and shipped express or freight to various parts of the country. Letters and telegrams, even, from all parts of the nation began to pour in—"Forward express today——copies of Dresser's 'Tell Them That You Saw Me.' " The firm was at once as busy as a bee-hive, on "easy street" again, as the expression went, "in clover." Just before this there had been a slight slump in its business and in my brother's finances, but now once more he was his most engaging self. Every one in that layer of life which understands or takes an interest in popular songs and their creators knew of him and his song, his latest success. He was, as it were, a revivified figure on Broadway. His barbers, barkeepers, hotel clerks, theatrical box-office clerks, hotel managers and the stars and singers of the street knew of it and him. Some enterprising button firm got out a button on which the phrase was printed. Comedians on the stage, newspaper paragraphers, his bank teller or his tailor, even staid business men wishing to appear "up-to-date," used it as a parting salute. The hand-organs, the bands and the theater orchestras everywhere were using it. One could scarcely turn a corner or go into a cheap music hall or variety house without hearing a parody of it. It was wonderful, the enormous furore that it seemed to create, and of course my dear brother was privileged to walk about smiling and secure, his bank account large, his friends numerous, in the pink of health, and gloating over the fact that he was a success, well known, a genuine creator of popular songs.

It was the same with "On the Banks of the Wabash," possibly an even greater success, for it came eventually to be adopted by his native State as its State song, and in that region streets and a town were named after him. In an almost unintentional and unthinking way I had a hand in that, and it has always cheered me to think that I had, although I have never had the least talent for musical composition or song versification. It was one of those delightful summer Sunday mornings (1896, I believe), when I was still connected with his firm as editor of the little monthly they were issuing, and he and myself, living with my sister E—— that we had gone over to this office to do a little work. I had a number of current magazines I wished to examine; he was always wishing to compose something, to express that ebullient and emotional soul of his in some way.

"What do you suppose would make a good song these days?" he asked in an idle, meditative mood, sitting at the piano and thrumming while I at a nearby table was looking over my papers. "Why don't you give me an idea for one once in a while, sport? You ought to be able to suggest something."

"Me?" I queried, almost contemptuously, I suppose. I could be very lofty at times in regard to his work, much as I admired him—vain and yet more or less dependent snip that I was. "I can't write those things. Why don't you write something about a State or a river? Look at 'My Old Kentucky Home,' 'Dixie,' 'Old Black Joe'—why don't you do something like that, something that suggests a part of America? People like that. Take Indiana—what's the matter with it—the Wabash River? It's as good as any other river, and you were 'raised' beside it."

I have to smile even now as I recall the apparent zest or feeling with which all at once he seized on this. It seemed to appeal to him immensely. "That's not a bad idea," he agreed, "but how would you go about it? Why don't you write the words and let me put the music to them? We'll do it together!"

"But I can't," I replied. "I don't know how to do those things. You write it, I'll help—maybe."

After a little urging—I think the fineness of the morning had as much to do with it as anything—I took a piece of paper and after meditating a while scribbled in the most tentative manner imaginable the first verse and chorus of that song almost as it was published. I think one or two lines were too long or didn't rhyme, but eventually either he or I hammered them into shape, but before that I rather shame-facedly turned them over to him, for somehow I was convinced that this work was not for me and that I was rather loftily and cynically attempting what my good brother would do in all faith and feeling.

He read it, insisted that it was fine and that I should do a second verse, something with a story in it, a girl perhaps—a task which I solemnly rejected.

"No, you put it in. It's yours. I'm through."

Some time later, disagreeing with the firm as to the conduct of the magazine, I left—really was forced out—which raised a little feeling on my part; not on his, I am sure, for I was very difficult to deal with.

Time passed and I heard nothing. I had been able to succeed in a somewhat different realm, that of the magazine contributor, and although I thought a great deal of my brother I paid very little attention to him or his affairs, being much more concerned with my own. One spring night, however, the following year, as I was lying in my bed trying to sleep, I heard a quartette of boys in the distance approaching along the street in which I had my room. I could not make out the words at first but the melody at once attracted my attention. It was plaintive and compelling. I listened, attracted, satisfied that it was some new popular success that had "caught on." As they drew near my window I heard the words "On the Banks of the Wabash" most mellifluously harmonized.

I jumped up. They were my words! It was Paul's song! He had another "hit" then—"On the Banks of the Wabash," and they were singing it in the streets already! I leaned out of the window and listened as they approached and passed on, their arms about each other's shoulders, the whole song being sung in the still street, as it were, for my benefit. The night was so warm, delicious. A full moon was overhead. I was young, lonely, wistful. It brought back so much of my already spent youth that I was ready to cry—for joy principally. In three more months it was everywhere, in the papers, on the stage, on the street-organs, played by orchestras, bands, whistled and sung in the streets. One day on Broadway near the Marlborough I met my brother, gold-headed cane, silk shirt, a smart summer suit, a gay straw hat.

"Ah," I said, rather sarcastically, for I still felt peeved that he had shown so little interest in my affairs at the time I was leaving. "On the banks, I see."

"On the banks," he replied cordially. "You turned the trick for me, Thee, that time. What are you doing now? Why don't you ever come and see me? I'm still your brother, you know. A part of that is really yours."

"Cut that!" I replied most savagely. "I couldn't write a song like that in a million years. You know I couldn't. The words are nothing."

"Oh, all right. It's true, though, you know. Where do you keep yourself? Why don't you come and see me? Why be down on me? I live here, you know." He looked up at the then brisk and successful hotel.

"Well, maybe I will some time," I said distantly, but with no particular desire to mend matters, and we parted.

There was, however, several years later, a sequel to all this and one so characteristic of him that it has always remained in my mind as one of the really beautiful things of life, and I might as well tell it here and now. About five years later I had become so disappointed in connection with my work and the unfriendly pressure of life that I had suffered what subsequently appeared to have been a purely psychic breakdown or relapse, not physical, but one which left me in no mood or condition to go on with my work, or any work indeed in any form. Hope had disappeared in a sad haze. I could apparently succeed in nothing, do nothing mentally that was worth while. At the same time I had all but retired from the world, living on less and less until finally I had descended into those depths where I was in the grip of actual want, with no place to which my pride would let me turn. I had always been too vain and self-centered. Apparently there was but one door, and I was very close to it. To match my purse I had retired to a still sorrier neighborhood in B——, one of the poorest. I desired most of all to be let alone, to be to myself. Still I could not be, for occasionally I met people, and certain prospects and necessities drove me to various publishing houses. One day as I was walking in some street near Broadway (not on it) in New York, I ran into my brother quite by accident, he as prosperous and comfortable as ever. I think I resented him more than ever. He was of course astonished, shocked, as I could plainly see, by my appearance and desire not to be seen. He demanded to know where I was living, wanted me to come then and there and stay with him, wanted me to tell him what the trouble was—all of which I rather stubbornly refused to do and finally got away—not however without giving him my address, though with the caution that I wanted nothing.

The next morning he was there bright and early in a cab. He was the most vehement, the most tender, the most disturbed creature I have ever seen. He was like a distrait mother with a sick child more than anything else.

"For God's sake," he commented when he saw me, "living in a place like this—and at this number, too!" (130 it was, and he was superstitious as to the thirteen.) "I knew there'd be a damned thirteen in it!" he ejaculated. "And me over in New York! Jesus Christ! And you sick and run down this way! I might have known. It's just like you. I haven't heard a thing about you in I don't know when. Well, I'm not going back without you, that's all. You've got to come with me now, see? Get your clothes, that's all. The cabby'll take your trunk. I know just the place for you, and you're going there tomorrow or next day or next week, but you're coming with me now. My God, I should think you'd be ashamed of yourself, and me feeling the way I do about you!" His eyes all but brimmed.

I was so morose and despondent that, grateful as I felt, I could scarcely take his mood at its value. I resented it, resented myself, my state, life.

"I can't," I said finally, or so I thought. "I won't. I don't need your help. You don't owe me anything. You've done enough already."

"Owe, hell!" he retorted. "Who's talking about 'owe'? And you my brother—my own flesh and blood! Why, Thee, for that matter, I owe you half of 'On the Banks,' and you know it. You can't go on living like this. You're sick and discouraged. You can't fool me. Why, Thee, you're a big man. You've just got to come out of this! Damn it—don't you see—don't make me"—and he took out his handkerchief and wiped his eyes. "You can't help yourself now, but you can later, don't you see? Come on. Get your things. I'd never forgive myself if I didn't. You've got to come, that's all. I won't go without you," and he began looking about for my bag and trunk.

I still protested weakly, but in vain. His affection was so overwhelming and tender that it made me weak. I allowed him to help me get my things together. Then he paid the bill, a small one, and on the way to the hotel insisted on forcing a roll of bills on me, all that he had with him. I was compelled at once, that same day or the next, to indulge in a suit, hat, shoes, underwear, all that I needed. A bedroom adjoining his suite at the hotel was taken, and for two days I lived there, later accompanying him in his car to a famous sanitarium in Westchester, one in charge of an old friend of his, a well-known ex-wrestler whose fame for this sort of work was great. Here I was booked for six weeks, all expenses paid, until I should "be on my feet again," as he expressed it. Then he left, only to visit and revisit me until I returned to the city, fairly well restored in nerves if not in health.

But could one ever forget the mingled sadness and fervor of his original appeal, the actual distress written in his face, the unlimited generosity of his mood and deed as well as his unmerited self-denunciation? One pictures such tenderness and concern as existing between parents and children, but rarely between brothers. Here he was evincing the same thing, as soft as love itself, and he a man of years and some affairs and I an irritable, distrait and peevish soul.

Take note, ye men of satire and spleen. All men are not selfish or hard.

The final phase of course related to his untimely end. He was not quite fifty-five when he died, and with a slightly more rugged quality of mind he might have lasted to seventy. It was due really to the failure of his firm (internal dissensions and rivalries, in no way due to him, however, as I have been told) and what he foolishly deemed to be the end of his financial and social glory. His was one of those simple, confiding, non-hardy dispositions, warm and colorful but intensely sensitive, easily and even fatally chilled by the icy blasts of human difficulty, however slight. You have no doubt seen some animals, cats, dogs, birds, of an especially affectionate nature, which when translated to a strange or unfriendly climate soon droop and die. They have no spiritual resources wherewith to contemplate what they do not understand or know. Now his *friends* would leave him. Now that bright world of which he had been a part would know him no more. It was pathetic, really. He emanated a kind of fear. Depression and even despair seemed to hang about him like a cloak. He could not shake it off. And yet, literally, in his case there was nothing to fear, if he had only known.

And yet two years before he did die, I knew he would. Fantastic as it may seem, to be shut out from that bright world of which he deemed himself an essential figure was all but unendurable. He had no ready money now—not the same amount anyhow. He could not greet his old-time friends so gayly, entertain so freely. Meeting him on Broadway shortly after the failure and asking after his affairs, he talked of going into business for himself as a publisher, but I realized that he could not. He had neither the ability nor the talent for that, nor the heart. He was not a business man but a song-writer and actor, had never been anything but that. He tried in this new situation to write songs, but he could not. They were too morbid. What he needed was some one to buoy him up, a manager, a strong confidant of some kind, some one who would have taken his affairs in hand and shown him what to do. As it was he had no one. His friends, like winter-frightened birds, had already departed. Personally, I was in no position to do anything at the time, being more or less depressed myself and but slowly emerging from difficulties which had held me for a number of years.

About a year or so after he failed my sister E—— announced that Paul had been there and that he was coming to live with her. He could not pay so much then, being involved with all sorts of examinations of one kind and another, but neither did he have to. Her memory was not short; she gave him the fullness of her home. A few months later he was ostensibly connected with another publishing house, but by then he was feeling so poorly physically and was finding consolation probably in some drinking and the caresses of those feminine friends who have, alas, only caresses to offer. A little later I met a doctor who said, "Paul cannot live. He has pernicious anæmia. He is breaking down inside and doesn't know it. He can't last long. He's too depressed." I knew it was so and what the remedy was—money and success once more, the petty pettings and flattery of that little world of which he had been a part but which now was no more for him. Of all those who had been so lavish in their greetings and companionship earlier in his life, scarcely one, so far as I could make out, found him in that retired world to which he was forced. One or two pegged-out actors sought him and borrowed a little of the little that he had; a few others came when he had nothing at all. His partners, quarreling among themselves and feeling that they had done him an injustice, remained religiously away. He found, as he often told my sister, broken horse-shoes (a "bad sign"), met cross-eyed women, another "bad sign," was pursued apparently by the inimical number thirteen—and all these little straws depressed him horribly. Finally, being no longer strong enough to be about, he took to his bed and remained there days at a time, feeling well while in bed but weak when up. For a little while he would go "downtown" to see this, that and the other person, but would soon return. One day on coming back home he found one of his hats lying on his bed, accidentally put there by one of the children, and according to my sister, who was present at the time, he was all but petrified by the sight of it. To him it was the death-sign. Some one had told him so not long before! ! !

Then, not incuriously, seeing the affectional tie that had always held us, he wanted to see me every day. He had a desire to talk to me about his early life, the romance of it—maybe I could write a story some time, tell something about him! (Best of brothers, here it is, a thin little flower to lay at your feet!) To please him I made notes, although I knew most of it. On these occasions he was always his old self, full of ridiculous stories, quips and slight *mots*, all in his old and best vein. He would soon be himself, he now insisted.

Then one evening in late November, before I had time to call upon him (I lived about a mile away), a hurry-call came from E——. He had suddenly died at five in the afternoon;

a blood-vessel had burst in the head. When I arrived he was already cold in death, his soft hands folded over his chest, his face turned to one side on the pillow, that indescribable sweetness of expression about the eyes and mouth—the empty shell of the beetle. There were tears, a band of reporters from the papers, the next day obituary news articles, and after that a host of friends and flowers, flowers, flowers. It is amazing what satisfaction the average mind takes in standardized floral forms —broken columns and gates ajar!

Being ostensibly a Catholic, a Catholic sister-in-law and other relatives insistently arranged for a solemn high requiem mass at the church of one of his favorite rectors. All Broadway was there, more flowers, his latest song read from the altar. Then there was a carriage procession to a distant Catholic graveyard somewhere, his friend, the rector of the church, officiating at the grave. It was so cold and dreary there, horrible. Later on he was removed to Chicago.

But still I think of him as not there or anywhere in the realm of space, but on Broadway between Twenty-ninth and Forty-second Streets, the spring and summer time at hand, the doors of the grills and bars of the hotels open, the rout of actors and actresses ambling to and fro, his own delicious presence dressed in his best, his "funny" stories, his songs being ground out by the hand organs, his friends extending their hands, clapping him on the shoulder, cackling over the latest idle yarn.

Ah, Broadway! Broadway! And you, my good brother! Here is the story that you wanted me to write, this little testimony to your memory, a pale, pale symbol of all I think and feel. Where are the thousand yarns I have laughed over, the music, the lights, the song?

Peace, peace. So shall it soon be with all of us. It was a dream. It is. I am. You are. And shall we grieve over or hark back to dreams?

The Lost Phœbe

They lived together in a part of the country which was not so prosperous as it had once been, about three miles from one of those small towns that, instead of increasing in population, is steadily decreasing. The territory was not very thickly settled; perhaps a house every other mile or so, with large areas of corn- and wheat-land and fallow fields that at odd seasons had been sown to timothy and clover. Their particular house was part log and part frame, the log portion being the old original home of Henry's grandfather. The new portion, of now rain-beaten, time-worn slabs, through which the wind squeaked in the chinks at times, and which several overshadowing elms and a butternut-tree made picturesque and reminiscently pathetic, but a little damp, was erected by Henry when he was twenty-one and just married.

That was forty-eight years before. The furniture inside, like the house outside, was old and mildewy and reminiscent of an earlier day. You have seen the what-not of cherry wood, perhaps, with spiral legs and fluted top. It was there. The old-fashioned four poster bed, with its ball-like protuberances and deep curving incisions, was there also, a sadly alienated descendant of an early Jacobean ancestor. The bureau of cherry was also high and wide and solidly built, but faded-looking, and with a musty odor. The rag carpet that underlay all these sturdy examples of enduring furniture was a weak, faded, lead-and-pink-colored affair woven by Phœbe Ann's own hands, when she was fifteen years younger than she was when she died. The creaky wooden loom on which it had been done now stood like a dusty, bony skeleton, along with a broken rocking-chair, a worm-eaten clothes-press—Heaven knows how old—a lime-stained bench that had once been used to keep flowers on outside the door, and other decrepit factors of household utility, in an east room that was a lean-to against this so-called main portion. All sorts of other broken-down furniture were about this place; an antiquated clothes-horse, cracked in two of its ribs; a broken mirror in an old cherry frame, which had fallen from a nail and cracked itself three days before their youngest son, Jerry, died; an extension hat-rack, which once had had porcelain knobs on the ends of its pegs; and a sewing-machine, long since outdone in its clumsy mechanism by rivals of a newer generation.

The orchard to the east of the house was full of gnarled old apple-trees, worm-eaten as to trunks and branches, and fully ornamented with green and white lichens, so that it had a sad, greenish-white, silvery effect in moonlight. The low outhouses, which had once housed chickens, a horse or two, a cow, and several pigs, were covered with patches of moss as to their roof, and the sides had been free of paint for so long that they were blackish gray as to color, and a little spongy. The picket-fence in front, with its gate squeaky and askew, and the side fences of the stake-and-rider type were in an equally run-down condition. As a matter of fact, they had aged synchronously with the persons who lived here, old Henry Reifsneider and his wife Phœbe Ann.

They had lived here, these two, ever since their marriage, forty-eight years before, and Henry had lived here before that from his childhood up. His father and mother, well along in years when he was a boy, had invited him to bring his wife here when he had first fallen in love and decided to marry; and he had done so. His father and mother were the companions of himself and his wife for ten years after they were married, when both died; and then Henry and Phœbe were left with their five children growing lustily apace. But all sorts of things had happened since then. Of the seven children, all told, that had been born to them, three had died; one girl had gone to

Kansas; one boy had gone to Sioux Falls, never even to be heard of after; another boy had gone to Washington; and the last girl lived five counties away in the same State, but was so burdened with cares of her own that she rarely gave them a thought. Time and a commonplace home life that had never been attractive had weaned them thoroughly, so that, wherever they were, they gave little thought as to how it might be with their father and mother.

Old Henry Reifsneider and his wife Phœbe were a loving couple. You perhaps know how it is with simple natures that fasten themselves like lichens on the stones of circumstance and weather their days to a crumbling conclusion. The great world sounds widely, but it has no call for them. They have no soaring intellect. The orchard, the meadow, the corn-field, the pig-pen, and the chicken-lot measure the range of their human activities. When the wheat is headed it is reaped and threshed; when the corn is browned and frosted it is cut and shocked; when the timothy is in full head it is cut, and the hay-cock erected. After that comes winter, with the hauling of grain to market, the sawing and splitting of wood, the simple chores of fire-building, meal-getting, occasional repairing, and visiting. Beyond these and the changes of weather—the snows, the rains, and the fair days—there are no immediate, significant things. All the rest of life is a far-off, clamorous phantasmagoria, flickering like Northern lights in the night, and sounding as faintly as cow-bells tinkling in the distance.

Old Henry and his wife Phœbe were as fond of each other as it is possible for two old people to be who have nothing else in this life to be fond of. He was a thin old man, seventy when she died, a queer, crotchety person with coarse gray-black hair and beard, quite straggly and unkempt. He looked at you out of dull, fishy, watery eyes that had deep-brown crow's-feet at the sides. His clothes, like the clothes of many farmers, were aged and angular and baggy, standing out at the pockets, not fitting about the neck, protuberant and worn at elbow and knee. Phœbe Ann was thin and shapeless, a very umbrella of a woman, clad in shabby black, and with a black bonnet for her best wear. As time had passed, and they had only themselves to look after, their movements had become slower and slower, their activities fewer and fewer. The annual keep of pigs had been reduced from five to one grunting porker, and the single horse which Henry now retained was a sleepy animal, not over-nourished and not very clean. The chickens, of which formerly there was a large flock, had almost disappeared, owing to ferrets, foxes, and the lack of proper care, which produces disease. The former healthy garden was now a straggling memory of itself, and the vines and flower-beds that formerly ornamented the windows and dooryard had now become choking thickets. A will had been made which divided the small tax-eaten property equally among the remaining four, so that it was really of no interest to any of them. Yet these two lived together in peace and sympathy, only that now and then old Henry would become unduly cranky, complaining almost invariably that something had been neglected or mislaid which was of no importance at all.

"Phœbe, where's my corn-knife? You ain't never minded to let my things alone no more."

"Now you hush, Henry," his wife would caution him in a cracked and squeaky voice. "If you don't, I'll leave yuh. I'll git up and walk out of here some day, and then where would y' be? Y' ain't got anybody but me to look after yuh, so yuh just behave yourself. Your corn-knife's on the mantel where it's allus been unless you've gone an' put it summers else."

Old Henry, who knew his wife would never leave him in any circumstances, used to speculate at times as to what he would do if she were to die. That was the one leaving that he really feared. As he climbed on the chair at night to wind the old, long-pendulumed, double-weighted clock, or went finally to the front and the back door to see that they were safely shut in, it was a comfort to know that Phœbe was there, properly ensconced on her side of the bed, and that if he stirred restlessly in the night, she would be there to ask what he wanted.

"Now, Henry, do lie still! You're as restless as a chicken."

"Well, I can't sleep, Phœbe."

"Well, yuh needn't roll so, anyhow. Yuh kin let me sleep."

This usually reduced him to a state of somnolent ease. If she wanted a pail of water, it was a grumbling pleasure for him to get it; and if she did rise first to build the fires, he saw that the wood was cut and placed within easy reach. They divided this simple world nicely between them.

As the years had gone on, however, fewer and fewer people had called. They were well-known for a distance of as much as ten square miles as old Mr. and Mrs. Reifsneider, honest, moderately Christian, but too old to be really interesting any longer. The writing of letters had become an almost impossible burden too difficult to continue or even negotiate via others, although an occasional letter still did arrive from the daughter in Pemberton County. Now and then some old friend stopped with a pie or cake or a roasted chicken or duck, or merely to see that they were well; but even these kindly minded visits were no longer frequent.

One day in the early spring of her sixty-fourth year Mrs. Reifsneider took sick, and from a low fever passed into some indefinable ailment which, because of her age, was no longer curable. Old Henry drove to Swinnerton, the neighboring town, and procured a doctor. Some friends called, and the immediate care of her was taken off his hands. Then one chill spring night she died, and old Henry, in a fog of sorrow and uncertainty, followed her body to the nearest graveyard, an unattractive space with a few pines growing in it. Although he might have gone to the daughter in Pemberton or sent for her, it was really too much trouble and he was too weary and fixed. It was suggested to him at once by one friend and another that he come to stay with them awhile, but he did not see fit. He was so old and so fixed in his notions and so accustomed to the exact surroundings he had known all his days, that he could not think of leaving. He wanted to remain near where they had put his Phœbe; and the fact that he would have to live alone did not trouble him in the least. The living children were notified and the care of him offered if he would leave, but he would not.

"I kin make a shift for myself," he continually announced to old Dr. Morrow, who had attended his wife in this case. "I kin cook a little, and, besides, it don't take much more'n coffee an' bread in the mornin's to satisfy me. I'll get along now well enough. Yuh just let me be." And after many pleadings and proffers of advice, with supplies of coffee and bacon and baked bread duly offered and accepted, he was left to himself. For a while he sat idly outside his door brooding in the spring sun. He tried to revive his interest in farming, and to keep himself busy and free from thought by looking after the fields, which of late had been much neglected. It was a gloomy thing to come in of an evening, however, or in the afternoon and find no shadow of Phœbe where everything suggested her. By degrees he put a few of her things away. At night he sat beside his lamp and read in the papers that were left him occasionally or in a Bible that he had neglected for years, but he could get little solace from these things. Mostly he held his hand over his mouth and looked at the floor as he sat and thought of what had become of her, and how soon he himself would die. He made a great business of making his coffee in the morning and frying himself a little bacon at night; but his appetite was gone. The shell in which he had been housed so long seemed vacant, and its shadows were suggestive of immedicable griefs. So he lived quite dole-fully for five long months, and then a change began.

It was one night, after he had looked after the front and the back door, wound the clock, blown out the light, and gone through all the selfsame motions that he had indulged in for years, that he went to bed not so much to sleep as to think. It was a moonlight night. The green-lichen-covered orchard just outside and to be seen from his bed where he now lay was a silvery affair, sweetly spectral. The moon shone through the east windows, throwing the pattern of the panes on the wooden floor, and making the old furniture, to which he was accustomed, stand out dimly in the room. As usual he had been thinking of Phœbe and the years when they had been young together, and of the children who had gone, and the poor shift he was making of his present days. The house was coming to be in a very bad state indeed. The bed-clothes were in disorder and not clean, for he made a wretched shift of washing. It was a terror to him. The roof leaked, causing things, some of them, to remain damp for weeks at a time, but he was getting into that brooding state where he would accept anything rather than exert himself. He preferred to pace slowly to and fro or to sit and think.

By twelve o'clock of this particular night he was asleep, how-ever, and by two had waked again. The moon by this time had shifted to a position on the western side of the house, and it now shone in through the windows of the living-room and those of the kitchen beyond. A certain combination of furniture—a chair near a table, with his coat on it, the half-open kitchen door casting a shadow, and the position of a lamp near a paper—gave him an exact representation of Phœbe leaning over the table as he had often seen her do in life. It gave him a great start. Could it be she—or her ghost? He had scarcely ever believed in spirits; and still—— He looked at her fixedly in the feeble half-light, his old hair tingling oddly at the roots, and then sat up. The figure did not move. He put his thin legs out of the bed and sat looking at her, wondering if this could really be Phœbe. They had talked of ghosts often in their lifetime, of apparitions and omens; but they had never agreed that such things could be. It had never been a part of his wife's creed that she could have a spirit that could return to walk the earth. Her after-world was quite a different affair, a vague heaven, no less, from which the righteous did not trouble to return. Yet here she was now, bending over the table in her black skirt and gray shawl, her pale profile outlined against the moonlight.

"Phœbe," he called, thrilling from head to toe and putting out one bony hand, "have yuh come back?"

The figure did not stir, and he arose and walked uncertainly to the door, looking at it fixedly the while. As he drew near, however, the apparition resolved itself into its primal content— his old coat over the high-backed chair, the lamp by the paper, the half-open door.

"Well," he said to himself, his mouth open, "I thought shore I saw her." And he ran his hand strangely and vaguely through his hair, the while his nervous tension relaxed. Vanished as it had, it gave him the idea that she might return.

Another night, because of this first illusion, and because his mind was now constantly on her and he was old, he looked out of the window that was nearest his bed and commanded a hen-coop and pig-pen and a part of the wagon-shed, and there, a faint mist exuding from the damp of the ground, he thought he saw her again. It was one of those little wisps of mist, one of those faint exhalations of the earth that rise in a cool night after a warm day, and flicker like small white cypresses of fog before they disappear. In life it had been a custom of hers to cross this lot from her kitchen door to the pig-pen to throw in any scrap that was left from her cooking, and here she was again. He sat up and watched it strangely, doubtfully, because of his previous experience, but inclined, because of the nervous titillation that passed over his body, to believe that spirits really were, and that Phœbe, who would be concerned because of his lonely state, must be thinking about him, and hence returning. What other way would she have? How otherwise could she express herself? It would be within the province of her charity so to do, and like her loving interest in him. He quivered and watched it eagerly; but, a faint breath of air stirring, it wound away toward the fence and disappeared.

A third night, as he was actually dreaming, some ten days later, she came to his bedside and put her hand on his head.

"Poor Henry!" she said. "It's too bad."

He roused out of his sleep, actually to see her, he thought, moving from his bed-room into the one living-room, her figure a shadowy mass of black. The weak straining of his eyes caused little points of light to flicker about the outlines of her form. He arose, greatly astonished, walked the floor in the cool room, convinced that Phœbe was coming back to him. If he only thought sufficiently, if he made it perfectly clear by his feeling that he needed her greatly, she would come back, this kindly wife, and tell him what to do. She would perhaps be with him much of the time, in the night, anyhow; and that would make him less lonely, this state more endurable.

In age and with the feeble it is not such a far cry from the subtleties of illusion to actual hallucination, and in due time this transition was made for Henry. Night after night he waited, expecting her return. Once in his weird mood he thought he saw a pale light moving about the room, and another time he thought he saw her walking in the orchard after dark. It was one morning when the details of his lonely state were virtually unendurable that he woke with the thought that she was not dead. How he had arrived at this conclusion it is hard to say. His mind had gone. In its place was a fixed illusion. He and Phœbe had had a senseless quarrel. He had reproached her for not leaving his pipe where he was accustomed to find it, and she had left.

It was an aberrated fulfillment of her old jesting threat that if he did not behave himself she would leave him.

"I guess I could find yuh ag'in," he had always said. But her cackling threat had always been.

"Yuh'll not find me if I ever leave yuh. I guess I kin git some place where yuh can't find me."

This morning when he arose he did not think to build the fire in the customary way or to grind his coffee and cut his bread, as was his wont, but solely to meditate as to where he should search for her and how he should induce her to come back. Recently the one horse had been dispensed with because he found it cumbersome and beyond his needs. He took down his soft crush hat after he had dressed himself, a new glint of interest and determination in his eye, and taking his black crook cane from behind the door, where he had always placed it, started out briskly to look for her among the nearest neighbors. His old shoes clumped soundly in the dust as he walked, and his gray-black locks, now grown rather long, straggled out in a dramatic fringe or halo from under his hat. His short coat stirred busily as he walked, and his hands and face were peaked and pale.

"Why, hello, Henry! Where're yuh goin' this mornin'?" inquired Farmer Dodge, who, hauling a load of wheat to market, encountered him on the public road. He had not seen the aged farmer in months, not since his wife's death, and he wondered now, seeing him looking so spry.

"Yuh ain't seen Phœbe, have yuh?" inquired the old man, looking up quizzically.

"Phœbe who?" inquired Farmer Dodge, not for the moment connecting the name with Henry's dead wife.

"Why, my wife Phœbe, o' course. Who do yuh s'pose I mean?" He stared up with a pathetic sharpness of glance from under his shaggy, gray eyebrows.

"Wall, I'll swan, Henry, yuh ain't jokin', are yuh?" said the solid Dodge, a pursy man, with a smooth, hard, red face. "It can't be your wife yuh're talkin' about. She's dead."

"Dead! Shucks!" retorted the demented Reifsneider. "She left me early this mornin', while I was sleepin'. She allus got up to build the fire, but she's gone now. We had a little spat last night, an' I guess that's the reason. But I guess I kin find her. She's gone over to Matilda Race's; that's where she's gone."

He started briskly up the road, leaving the amazed Dodge to stare in wonder after him.

"Well, I'll be switched!" he said aloud to himself. "He's clean out'n his head. That poor old feller's been livin' down there till he's gone outen his mind. I'll have to notify the authorities." And he flicked his whip with great enthusiasm. "Geddap!" he said, and was off.

Reifsneider met no one else in this poorly populated region until he reached the whitewashed fence of Matilda Race and her husband three miles away. He had passed several other houses en route, but these not being within the range of his illusion were not considered. His wife, who had known Matilda well, must be here. He opened the picket-gate which guarded the walk, and stamped briskly up to the door.

"Why, Mr. Reifsneider," exclaimed old Matilda herself, a stout woman, looking out of the door in answer to his knock, "what brings yuh here this mornin'?"

"Is Phœbe here?" he demanded eagerly.

"Phœbe who? What Phœbe?" replied Mrs. Race, curious as to this sudden development of energy on his part.

"Why, my Phœbe, o' course. My wife Phœbe. Who do yuh s'pose? Ain't she here now?"

"Lawsy me!" exclaimed Mrs. Race, opening her mouth. "Yuh pore man! So you're clean out'n your mind now. Yuh come right in and sit down. I'll git yuh a cup o' coffee. O' course your wife ain't here; but yuh come in an' sit down. I'll find her fer yuh after a while. I know where she is."

The old farmer's eyes softened, and he entered. He was so thin and pale a specimen, pantalooned and patriarchal, that he aroused Mrs. Race's extremest sympathy as he took off his hat and laid it on his knees quite softly and mildly.

"We had a quarrel last night, an' she left me," he volunteered.

"Laws! laws!" sighed Mrs. Race, there being no one present with whom to share her astonishment as she went to her kitchen. "The pore man! Now somebody's just got to look after him. He can't be allowed to run around the country this way lookin' for his dead wife. It's turrible."

She boiled him a pot of coffee and brought in some of her new-baked bread and fresh butter. She set out some of her best jam and put a couple of eggs to boil, lying whole-heartedly the while.

"Now yuh stay right there, Uncle Henry, till Jake comes in, an' I'll send him to look for Phœbe. I think it's more'n likely she's over to Swinnerton with some o' her friends. Anyhow, we'll find out. Now yuh just drink this coffee an' eat this bread. Yuh must be tired. Yuh've had a long walk this mornin'." Her idea was to take counsel with Jake, "her man," and perhaps have him notify the authorities.

She bustled about, meditating on the uncertainties of life, while old Reifsneider thrummed on the rim of his hat with his pale fingers and later ate abstractedly of what she offered. His mind was on his wife, however, and since she was not here, or did not appear, it wandered vaguely away to a family by the name of Murray, miles away in another direction. He decided after a time that he would not wait for Jake Race to hunt his wife but would seek her for himself. He must be on, and urge her to come back.

"Well, I'll be goin'," he said, getting up and looking strangely about him. "I guess she didn't come here after all. She went over to the Murrays', I guess. I'll not wait any longer, Mis' Race. There's a lot to do over to the house to-day." And out he marched in the face of her protests taking to the dusty road again in the warm spring sun, his cane striking the earth as he went.

It was two hours later that this pale figure of a man appeared in the Murrays' doorway, dusty, perspiring, eager. He had tramped all of five miles, and it was noon. An amazed husband and wife of sixty heard his strange query, and realized also that he was mad. They begged him to stay to dinner, intending to notify the authorities later and see what could be done; but though he stayed to partake of a little something, he did not stay long, and was off again to another distant farmhouse, his idea of many things to do and his need of Phœbe impelling him. So it went for that day and the next and the next, the circle of his inquiry ever widening.

The process by which a character assumes the significance of being peculiar, his antics weird, yet harmless, in such a community is often involute and pathetic. This day, as has been said, saw Reifsneider at other doors, eagerly asking his unnatural question, and leaving a trail of amazement, sympathy, and pity in his wake. Although the authorities were informed—the county sheriff, no less—it was not deemed advisable to take him into custody; for when those who knew old Henry, and had for so long, reflected on the condition of the county insane asylum, a place which, because of the poverty of the district, was of staggering aberration and sickening environment, it was decided to let him remain at large; for, strange to relate, it was found on investigation that at night he returned peaceably enough to his lonesome domicile there to discover whether his wife had returned, and to brood in loneliness until the morning. Who would lock up a thin, eager, seeking old man with iron-gray hair and an attitude of kindly, innocent inquiry, particularly when he was well known for a past of only kindly servitude and reliability? Those who had known him best rather agreed that he should be allowed to roam at large. He could do no harm. There were many who were willing to help him as to food, old clothes, the odds and ends of his daily life—at least at first. His figure after a time became not so much a common-place as an accepted curiosity, and the replies, "Why, no, Henry; I ain't see her," or "No, Henry; she ain't been here to-day," more customary.

For several years thereafter then he was an odd figure in the sun and rain, on dusty roads and muddy ones, encountered occasionally in strange and unexpected places, pursuing his endless search. Undernourishment, after a time, although the neighbors and those who knew his history gladly contributed from their store, affected his body; for he walked much and ate little. The longer he roamed the public highway in this manner, the deeper became his strange hallucination; and finding it harder and harder to return from his more and more distant pilgrimages, he finally began taking a few utensils with him from his home, making a small package of them, in order that he might not be compelled to return. In an old tin coffee-pot of large size he placed a small tin cup, a knife, fork, and spoon, some salt and pepper, and to the outside of it, by a string forced through a pierced hole, he fastened a plate, which could be released, and which was his woodland table. It was no trouble for him to secure the little food that he needed, and with a strange, almost re-

ligious dignity, he had no hesitation in asking for that much.
By degrees his hair became longer and longer, his once black
hat became an earthen brown, and his clothes threadbare and
dusty.

For all of three years he walked, and none knew how wide
were his perambulations, nor how he survived the storms and
cold. They could not see him, with homely rural understanding
and forethought, sheltering himself in hay-cocks, or by the sides
of cattle, whose warm bodies protected him from the cold, and
whose dull understandings were not opposed to his harmless
presence. Overhanging rocks and trees kept him at times from
the rain, and a friendly hay-loft or corn-crib was not above his
humble consideration.

The involute progression of hallucination is strange. From
asking at doors and being constantly rebuffed or denied, he
finally came to the conclusion that although his Phœbe might
not be in any of the houses at the doors of which he inquired,
she might nevertheless be within the sound of his voice. And
so, from patient inquiry, he began to call sad, occasional cries,
that ever and anon waked the quiet landscapes and ragged hill
regions, and set to echoing his thin "O-o-o Phœbe! O-o-o
Phœbe!" It had a pathetic, albeit insane, ring, and many a
farmer or plowboy came to know it even from afar and say,
"There goes old Reifsneider."

Another thing that puzzled him greatly after a time and
after many hundreds of inquiries was, when he no longer had
any particular dooryard in view and no special inquiry to make,
which way to go. These cross-roads, which occasionally led in
four or even six directions, came after a time to puzzle him. But
to solve this knotty problem, which became more and more of
a puzzle, there came to his aid another hallucination. Phœbe's
spirit or some power of the air or wind or nature would tell
him. If he stood at the center of the parting of the ways, closed
his eyes, turned thrice about, and called "O-o-o Phœbe!" twice,
and then threw his cane straight before him, that would surely
indicate which way to go for Phœbe, or one of these mystic
powers would surely govern its direction and fall! In whichever
direction it went, even though, as was not infrequently the
case, it took him back along the path he had already come, or

across fields, he was not so far gone in his mind but that he gave himself ample time to search before he called again. Also the hallucination seemed to persist that at some time he would surely find her. There were hours when his feet were sore, and his limbs weary, when he would stop in the heat to wipe his seamed brow, or in the cold to beat his arms. Sometimes, after throwing away his cane, and finding it indicating the direction from which he had just come, he would shake his head wearily and philosophically, as if contemplating the unbelievable or an untoward fate, and then start briskly off. His strange figure came finally to be known in the farthest reaches of three or four counties. Old Reifsneider was a pathetic character. His fame was wide.

Near a little town called Watersville, in Green County, perhaps four miles from that minor center of human activity, there was a place or precipice locally known as the Red Cliff, a sheer wall of red sandstone, perhaps a hundred feet high, which raised its sharp face for half a mile or more above the fruitful corn-fields and orchards that lay beneath, and which was surmounted by a thick grove of trees. The slope that slowly led up to it from the opposite side was covered by a rank growth of beech, hickory, and ash, through which threaded a number of wagon-tracks crossing at various angles. In fair weather it had become old Reifsneider's habit, so inured was he by now to the open, to make his bed in some such patch of trees as this to fry his bacon or boil his eggs at the foot of some tree before laying himself down for the night. Occasionally, so light and inconse-quential was his sleep, he would walk at night. More often, the moonlight or some sudden wind stirring in the trees or a recon-noitering animal arousing him, he would sit up and think, or pursue his quest in the moonlight or the dark, a strange, un-natural, half wild, half savage-looking but utterly harmless creature, calling at lonely road crossings, staring at dark and shuttered houses, and wondering where, where Phœbe could really be.

That particular lull that comes in the systole-diastole of this earthly ball at two o'clock in the morning invariably aroused him, and though he might not go any farther he would sit up and contemplate the darkness or the stars, wondering. Sometimes in the strange processes of his mind he would fancy that he saw moving among the trees the figure of his lost wife, and then he would get up to follow, taking his utensils, always on a string, and his cane. If she seemed to evade him too easily he would run, or plead, or, suddenly losing track of the fancied figure, stand awed or disappointed, grieving for the moment over the almost insurmountable difficulties of his search.

It was in the seventh year of these hopeless peregrinations, in the dawn of a similar springtime to that in which his wife had died, that he came at last one night to the vicinity of this self-same patch that crowned the rise to the Red Cliff. His far-flung cane, used as a divining-rod at the last cross-roads, had brought him hither. He had walked many, many miles. It was after ten o'clock at night, and he was very weary. Long wandering and little eating had left him but a shadow of his former self. It was a question now not so much of physical strength but of spiritual endurance which kept him up. He had scarcely eaten this day, and now exhausted he set himself down in the dark to rest and possibly to sleep.

Curiously on this occasion a strange suggestion of the presence of his wife surrounded him. It would not be long now, he counseled with himself, although the long months had brought him nothing, until he should see her, talk to her. He fell asleep after a time, his head on his knees. At midnight the moon began to rise, and at two in the morning, his wakeful hour, was a large silver disk shining through the trees to the east. He opened his eyes when the radiance became strong, making a silver pattern at his feet and lighting the woods with strange lusters and silvery, shadowy forms. As usual, his old notion that his wife must be near occurred to him on this occasion, and he looked about him with a speculative, anticipatory eye. What was it that moved in the distant shadows along the path by which he had entered—a pale, flickering will-o'-the-wisp that bobbed gracefully among the trees and riveted his expectant gaze? Moonlight and shadows combined to give it a strange form and a stranger reality, this fluttering of bogfire or dancing of wandering fireflies. Was it truly his lost Phœbe? By a circuitous route it passed about him, and in his fevered state he fancied that he could see the very eyes of her, not as she was when he last saw her in the black dress and shawl but now a strangely younger Phœbe, gayer, sweeter, the one whom he had known years before as a girl. Old Reifsneider got up. He had been expecting and dreaming of this hour all these years, and now as he saw the feeble light dancing lightly before him he peered at it questioningly, one thin hand in his gray hair.

Of a sudden there came to him now for the first time in many years the full charm of her girlish figure as he had known it in boyhood, the pleasing, sympathetic smile, the brown hair, the blue sash she had once worn about her waist at a picnic, her gay, graceful movements. He walked around the base of the tree, straining with his eyes, forgetting for once his cane and utensils, and following eagerly after. On she moved before him, a will-o'-the-wisp of the spring, a little flame above her head, and it seemed as though among the small saplings of ash and beech and the thick trunks of hickory and elm that she signaled with a young, a lightsome hand.

"O Phœbe! Phœbe!" he called. "Have yuh really come? Have yuh really answered me?" And hurrying faster, he fell once, scrambling lamely to his feet, only to see the light in the distance dancing illusively on. On and on he hurried until he was fairly running, brushing his ragged arms against the trees, striking his hands and face against impeding twigs. His hat was gone, his lungs were breathless, his reason quite astray, when coming to the edge of the cliff he saw her below among a silvery bed of apple-trees now blooming in the spring.

"O Phœbe!" he called. "O Phœbe! Oh, no, don't leave me!" And feeling the lure of a world where love was young and Phœbe as this vision presented her, a delightful epitome of their quondam youth, he gave a gay cry of "Oh, wait, Phœbe!" and leaped.

Some farmer-boys, reconnoitering this region of bounty and prospect some few days afterward, found first the tin utensils tied together under the tree where he had left them, and then later at the foot of the cliff, pale, broken, but elate, a molded smile of peace and delight upon his lips, his body. His old hat was discovered lying under some low-growing saplings the twigs of which had held it back. No one of all the simple population knew how eagerly and joyously he had found his lost mate.

Convention

THIS story was told to me once by a very able newspaper cartoonist, and since it makes rather clear the powerfully repressive and often transforming force of convention, I set it down as something in the nature of an American social document. As he told it, it went something like this:

At one time I was a staff artist on the principal paper of one of the mid-Western cities, a city on a river. It was, and remains to this hour, a typical American city. No change. It had a population then of between four and five hundred thousand. It had its clubs and churches and its conventional goings-on. It was an excellent and prosperous manufacturing city; nothing more.

On the staff with me at this time was a reporter whom I had known a little, but never intimately. I don't know whether I ought to bother to describe him or not—physically, I mean. His physique is unimportant to this story. But I think it would be interesting and even important to take him apart mentally and look at him, if one could—sort out the various components of his intellectual machinery, and so find out exactly how his intellectual processes proceeded. However, I can't do that; I have not the skill. Barring certain very superficial characteristics which I will mention he was then and remains now a psychological mystery to me. He was what I would describe as superficially clever, a good writer of a good, practical, matter-of-fact story. He appeared to be well liked by those who were above him officially, and he could write Sunday feature stories of a sort, no one of which, as I saw it, ever contained a moving touch of color or a breath of real poetry. Some humor he had. He was efficient. He had a nose for news. He dressed quite well and he was not ill-looking—tall, thin, wiry, almost leathery. He had a quick, facile smile, a genial word-flow for all who knew him. He was the kind of man who was on practical and friendly terms with many men connected with the commercial organizations and clubs about town, and from whom he extracted news bits from time to time. By the directing chiefs of the paper he was considered useful.

Well, this man and I were occasionally sent out on the same assignment, he to write the story, I to make sketches—usually some Sunday feature story. Occasionally we would talk about whatever was before us—newspaper work, politics, the particular story in hand—but never enthusiastically or warmly about anything. He lacked what I thought was the artistic and poetic point of view. And yet, as I say, we were friendly enough. I took him about as any newspaperman takes another newspaperman of the same staff who is in good standing.

Along in the spring or summer of the second year that I was on the paper the Sunday editor, to whom I was beholden in part for my salary, called me into his room and said that he had decided that Wallace Steele and myself were to do a feature story about the "love-boats" which plied Saturday and Sunday afternoons and every evening up and down the river for a distance of thirty-five miles or more. This distance, weather permitting, gave an opportunity to six or seven hundred couples on hot nights to escape the dry, sweltering heat of the city—and it was hot there in summer—and to enjoy the breezes and dance, sometimes by the light of Chinese lanterns, sometimes by the light of the full moon. It was delightful. Many, many thousands took advantage of the opportunity in season.

It was delicious to me, then in the prime of youth and ambition, to sit on the hurricane or "spoon" deck, as our Sunday editor called it, and study not only the hundreds of boys and girls, but also the older men and women, who came principally to make love, though secondarily to enjoy the river and the air, to brood over the picturesque groupings of the trees, bushes, distant cabins and bluffs which rose steeply from the river, to watch the great cloud of smoke that trailed over us, to see the two halves of the immense steel walking beam chuff-chuffing up and down, and to listen to the drive of the water-wheel behind. This was in the days before the automobile, and any such pleasant means of getting away from the city was valued much more than it is now.

But to return to this Sunday editor and his orders. I was to make sketches of spooning couples, or at least of two or three small distinctive groups with a touch of romance in them. Steele was to tell how the love-making went on. This, being an innocent method of amusement, relief from the humdrum of such a world as this was looked upon with suspicion if not actual disfavor by the wiseacres of the paper, as well as by the conservatives of the city. True conservatives would not so indulge themselves. The real object of the Sunday editor was to get something into his paper that would have a little kick to it. We were, without exaggerating the matter in any way, to shock the conservatives by a little picture of life and love, which, however innocent, was none the less taboo in that city. The story was to suggest, as I understand it, loose living, low ideals and the like. These outings did not have the lockstep of business or religion in them.

II

Well, to proceed. No sooner had the order been given than Steele came to me to talk it over. He liked the idea very much. It was a good Sunday subject. Besides, the opportunity for an outing appealed to him. We were to go on the boat that left the wharf at the foot of Beach Street at eight o'clock that evening. He had been told to write anything from fifteen hundred to two thousand words. If I made three good sketches, that would make almost a three-fourths page special. He would make his story as lively and colorful as he could. He was not a little flattered, I am sure, by having been called to interpret such a gay, risqué scene.

It was about one-thirty when we had been called in. About four o'clock he came to me again. We had, as I had assumed, tentatively agreed to meet at the wharf entrance and do the thing together. By now, however, he had another plan. Perhaps I should say here that up to that moment I only vaguely knew that he had a wife and child and that he lived with them somewhere in the southwestern section of the city, whether in his own home or a rooming-house, I did not know. Come to think of it, just before this I believe I had heard him remark to others that his wife was out of the city. At any rate, he now said that since his wife was out of the city and as the woman of whom they rented their rooms was a lonely and a poor person who seldom got out anywhere, he had decided to bring her along for the outing. I needn't wait for him. He would see me on the boat, or we could discuss the story later.

I agreed to this and was prepared to think nothing of it except for one thing. His manner of telling me had something about it, or there was some mood or thought in connection with it in his own mind, which reached me telepathetically, and caused me to think that he was taking advantage of his wife's absence to go out somewhere with some one else. And yet, at that, I could not see why I thought about it. The thing had no real interest for me. And I had not the least proof and wanted none. As I say, I was not actually interested. I did not know his wife at all. I did not care for him or her. I did not care whether he flirted with some one else or not. Still, this silly, critical thought passed through my mind, put into it by him, I am sure, because he was thinking—at least, might have been thinking—that I might regard it as strange that he should appear anywhere with another woman than his wife. Apart from this, and before this, seeing him buzzing about here and there, and once talking to a girl on a street corner near the *Mail* office, I had only the vague notion that, married or not, he was a young man who was not averse to slipping away for an hour or two with some girl whom he knew or casually met, provided no one else knew anything about it, especially his wife. But that was neither here nor there. I never gave the man much thought at any time.

At any rate, seven o'clock coming, I had my dinner at a little restaurant near the office and went to the boat. It was a hot night, but clear and certain to bring a lovely full moon, and I was glad to be going. At the same time, I was not a little lonely and out of sorts with myself because I had no girl and was wishing that I had—wishing that some lovely girl was hanging on my arm and that now we two could go down to the boat together and sit on the spoon deck and look at the moon, or that we could dance on the cabin deck below, where were all the lights and musicians. My hope, if not my convinced expectation, was that somewhere on this boat I, too, should find some one who would be interested in me—I, too, should be able to sit about with the others and laugh and make love. But I didn't. The thought was futile. I was not a ladies' man, and few if any girls ever looked at me. Besides, women and girls usually came accompanied on a trip like this. I went alone, and I returned alone. So much for me.

Brooding in this fashion, I went aboard along with the earliest of the arrivals, and, going to the cabin deck, sat down and watched the others approach. It was one of my opportunities to single out interesting groups for my pen. And there were many. They came, so blithe, so very merry, all of them, in pairs or groups of four or six or eight or ten, boys and girls of the tene- ments and the slums—a few older couples among them,—but all smiling and chatting, the last ones hurrying excitedly to make the boat, and each boy with his girl, as I was keen to note, and each girl with her beau. I singled out this group and that, this type and that, making a few idle notes on my pad, just sug- gestions of faces, hats, gestures, swings or rolls of the body and the like. There was a strong light over the gangway, and I could sketch there. It was interesting and colorful, but, being very much alone, I was not very happy about it.

In the midst of these, along with the latter half of the crowd, came Steele and his lonely landlady, to whom, as he said, this proffer on his part was a kindness. Because of what he had said I was expecting a woman who would be somewhat of a frump— at least thirty-five or forty years old and not very attractive. But to my surprise, as they came up the long gangplank which led from the levee and was lighted by flaring gasoline torches, I saw a young woman who could not have been more than twenty- seven or -eight at most—and pretty, very. She had on a wide, floppy, lacy hat of black or dark blue, but for contrast a pale, cream-colored, flouncy dress. And she was graceful and plump and agreeable in every way. Some landlady, indeed, I thought, looking enviously down and wishing that it was myself and not he to whose arm she was clinging!

The bounder! I thought. To think that he should be able to interest so charming a girl, and in the absence of his wife! And I could get none! He had gone home and changed to a better suit, straw hat, cane and all, whereas I—I—dub!—had come as I was. No wonder no really interesting girl would look at me. Fool! But I remained in position studying the entering throng until the last couple was on and I listened to the cries of "Heave off, there!" "Loosen those stay lines, will you?" "Careful, there!" "Hurry with that gangplank!" Soon we were in midstream. The jouncy, tinny music had begun long before, and the couples, scores and scores of them, were already dancing on the cabin deck, while I was left to hang about the bar or saunter through the crowd, looking for types when I didn't want to be anywhere but close beside some girl on the spoon deck, who would hang on my arm, laugh into my eyes, and jest and dance with me.

III

Because of what he had said, I did not expect Steele to come near me, and he didn't. In sauntering about the two decks looking for arresting scenes I did not see him. Because I wanted at least one or two spoon deck scenes, I finally fixed on a couple that was half-hidden in the shadow back of the pilot-house. They had crumpled themselves up forward of an air-vent and not far from the two smoke-stacks and under the walking-beam, which rose and fell above them. The full moon was just above the eastern horizon, offering a circular background for them, and I thought they made a romantic picture outlined against it. I could not see their faces—just their outlines. Her head was upon his shoulder. His face was turned, and so concealed, and inclined toward hers. Her hat had been taken off and was held over her knee by one hand. I stepped back a little toward a companion-way, where was a light, in order to outline my impression. When I returned, they were sitting up. It was Steele and his rooming-house proprietress! It struck me as odd that of all the couple and group scenes that I had noted, the most romantic should have been provided by Steele and this woman. His wife would be interested in his solicitude for her loneliness and her lack of opportunities to get out into the open air, I was sure. Yet, I was not envious then—just curious and a little amused.

Well, that was the end of that. The sketches were made, and the story published. Because he and this girl had provided my best scene I disguised it a little, making it not seem exactly back of the pilot-house, since otherwise he might recognize it. He was, for once, fascinated by the color and romance of the occasion, and did a better story than I thought he could. It dwelt on the beauty of the river, the freedom from heat, the loveliness of the moon, the dancing. I thought it was very good, quite exceptional for him, and I thought I knew the reason why.

And then one day, about a month or six weeks later, being in the city room, I encountered the wife of Steele and their little son, a child of about five years. She had stopped in about three or four in the afternoon, being downtown shopping, I presume. After seeing him with the young woman on the steamer, I was, I confess, not a little shocked. This woman was so pinched, so homely, so faded—veritably a rail of a woman, everything and anything that a woman, whether wife, daughter, mother or sweetheart, as I saw it then, should not be. As a matter of fact, I was too wrought up about love and youth and marriage and happiness at that time to rightly judge of the married. At any rate, after having seen that other woman on that deck with Steele, I was offended by this one.

She seemed to me, after the other, too narrow, too methodical, too commonplace, too humdrum. She was a woman whose pulchritudinous favors, whatever they may have been, must have been lost at the altar. In heaven's name, I thought to myself, how could a man like this come to marry such a woman? He isn't so very good-looking himself, perhaps, but still . . . No wonder he wanted to take his rooming-house landlady for an outing! I would, too. I could understand it now. In fact, as little as I cared for Steele, I felt sorry that a man of his years and of his still restless proclivities should be burdened with such a wife. And not only that, but there was their child, looking not unlike him but more like her, one of those hostages to fortune by reason of which it is never easy to free oneself from the error of a mistaken marriage. His plight, as I saw it, was indeed unfortunate. And it was still summer and there was this other woman!

Well, I was introduced by him as the man who worked on some of his stories with him. I noticed that the woman had a thin, almost a falsetto voice. She eyed me, as I thought, unintelligently, yet genially enough. I was invited to come out to their place some Sunday and take dinner. Because of his rooming-house story I was beginning to wonder whether he had been lying to me, when she went on to explain that they had been boarding up to a few weeks ago, but had now taken a cottage for themselves and could have their friends. I promised. Yes, yes. But I never went—not to dinner, anyhow.

IV

Then two more months passed. By now it was late fall, with winter near. The current news, as I saw it, was decidedly humdrum. There was no local news to speak of. I scarcely glanced at the papers from day to day, no more than to see whether some particular illustration I had done was in and satisfactory or not. But then, of a sudden, came something which was genuine news. Steele's wife was laid low by a box of poisoned candy sent her through the mails, some of which she had eaten!

Just how the news of this first reached the papers I have almost forgotten now, but my recollection is that there was another newspaperman and his wife—a small editor or reporter on another paper—who lived in the same vicinity, and that it was to this newspaperman's wife that Mrs. Steele, after having called her in, confided that she believed she had been poisoned, and by a woman whose name she now gave as Mrs. Marie Davis, and with whom, as she then announced, her husband had long been intimate—the lady of the Steamer *Ira Ramsdell*. She had recognized the handwriting on the package from some letters written to her husband, but only after she had eaten of the candy and felt the pains—not before. Her condition was serious. She was, it appeared, about to die. In this predicament she had added, so it was said, that she had long been neglected by her husband for this other woman, but that she had suffered in silence rather than bring disgrace upon him, herself and their child. Now this cruel blow!

Forthwith a thrill of horror and sympathy passed over the city. It seemed too sad. At the same time a cry went up to find the other woman—arrest her, of course—see if she had really done it. There followed the official detention, if not legal arrest, of Mrs. Davis on suspicion of being the poisoner. Although the charge was not yet proved, she was at once thrown into jail, and there held to await the death or recovery of Mrs. Steele, and the proof or disproof of the charge that the candy had been sent by her. And cameras in hand, reporters and artists were packed off to the county jail to hear the accused's side of the story.

As I at once suspected on hearing the news, she proved to be none other than the lady of the *Ira Ramsdell*, and as charming as I had at first assumed her to be. I, being one of those sent to sketch her, was among the first to hear her story. She denied, and very vehemently, that she had sent any poisoned candy to any one. She had never dreamed of any such thing. But she did not deny, which at the time appeared to me to be incriminating, that she had been and was then in love with Steele. In fact, and this point interested me as much then as afterwards, she declared that this was an exceptional passion—her love for him, his love for her—and no mere passing and vulgar intimacy. A high and beautiful thing—a sacred love, the one really true and beautiful thing that had ever come to her—or him—in all their lives. And he would say so, too. For before meeting her, Wallace Steele had been very unhappy—oh, very. And her own marriage had been a failure.

Wallace, as she now familiarly called him, had confessed to her that this new, if secret, love meant everything to him. His wife did not interest him. He had married her at a time when he did not know what he was doing, and before he had come to be what he was. But this new love had resolved all their woes into loveliness—complete happiness. They had resolved to cling only to each other for life. There was no sin in what they had done because they loved. Of course, Wallace had sought to induce Mrs. Steele to divorce him, but she would not; otherwise they would have been married before this. But as Mrs. Steele would not give him up, both had been compelled to make the best of it. But to poison her—that was wild! A love so beautiful and true as theirs did not need a marriage ceremony to sanctify it. So she raved. My own impression at the time was that she was a romantic and sentimental woman who was really very greatly in love.

Now as to Steele. Having listened to this blazoning of her passion by herself, the interviewers naturally hurried to Steele to see what he would have to say. In contrast to her and her grand declaration, they found a man, as every one agreed, who was shaken to the very marrow of his bones by these untoward events. He was, it appeared, a fit inhabitant of the environment that nourished him. He was in love, perhaps, with this woman, but still, as any one could see, he was not so much in love that, if this present matter were going to cost him his place in this commonplace, conventional world, he would not be able to surrender to it. He was horrified by the revelation of his own treachery. Up to this hour, no doubt, he had been slipping about, hoping not to be caught, and most certainly not wishing to be cast out for sin. Regardless of the woman, he did not wish to be cast out now. On the contrary, as it soon appeared, he had been doing his best to pacify his wife and hold her to silence while he slaked his thirst for romance in this other way. He did not want his wife, but he did not want trouble, either. And now that his sin was out he shivered.

In short, as he confided to one of the men who went to interview him, and who agreed to respect his confidence to that extent, he was not nearly so much in love with Mrs. Davis as she thought he was—poor thing! True he had been infatuated for a while, but only a little while. She was pretty, of course, and naturally she thought she loved him—but he never expected anything like this to happen. Great cripes! They had met at a river bathing-beach the year before. He had been smitten—well, you know. He had never got along well with his wife, but there was the little boy to consider. He had not intended any harm to any one; far from it. And he certainly couldn't turn on his wife now. The public wouldn't stand for it. It would make trouble for him. But he could scarcely be expected to turn on Mrs. Davis, either, could he, now that she was in jail, and suspected of sending poisoned candy to his wife? The public wouldn't stand for that, either.

It was terrible! Pathetic! He certainly would not have thought that Marie would go to the length of sending his wife poison, and he didn't really believe that she had. Still—and there may have been some actual doubt of her in that "still," or so the reporting newspapermen thought. At any rate, as he saw it now, he would have to stick to his wife until she was out of danger. Public opinion compelled it. The general impression of the newspapermen was that he was a coward. As one of them said of his courage, "Gee, it's oozing out of his hair!"

Nevertheless, he did go to see Mrs. Davis several times. But apart from a reported sobbing demonstration of affection on her part, I never learned what passed between them. He would not talk and she had been cautioned not to. Also, there were various interviews with his wife, who had not died, and now that the storm was on, admitted that she had intercepted letters between her husband and Mrs. Davis from time to time. The handwriting on the candy wrapper the day she received it so resembled the handwriting of Mrs. Davis that after she had eaten of it and the symptoms of poisoning had set in—not before—she had begun to suspect that the candy must have emanated from Mrs. Davis.

v

In the meantime Mrs. Davis, despite the wife's sad story, was the major attraction in the newspapers. She was young, she was beautiful, she had made, or at least attempted to make, a blood sacrifice on the altar of love. What more could a daily newspaper want? She was a heroine, even in this very moral, conservative, conventional and religious city. The rank and file were agog—even sympathetic. (How would the moralists explain that, would you say?) In consequence of their interest, she was descended upon by a corps of those women newspaper writers who, even in that day, were known as sob-sisters, and whose business it was—and this in advance of any proof of crime or indictment even—to psychologize and psychiatrize the suspect— to dig out if they could not only every vestige of her drama, but all her hidden and secret motives.

As I read the newspapers at the time, they revealed that she was not a neurotic, a psychotic, who showed traces of being a shrewd, evasive and designing woman, and who did not. Also she was a soft, unsophisticated, passionate and deeply illusioned girl, and she was not. She was guilty, of course—maybe not— but very likely she was, and she must tell how, why, in what mood, etc. Also, it appeared that she had sent the poison deliberately, coldly, murderously. Her eyes and hands, also the shape of her nose and ears, showed it. Again, these very things proved she could not have done it. Had she been driven to it by stress of passionate emotion and yearning which had been too much for her to bear? Was she responsible for that—a great, destroying love? Of course she was! Who is not responsible for his deeds? A great, overwhelming, destroying love passion, indeed! Rot! She could help it. She could not help it. Could she help it? So it went.

Parallel with all this, of course, we were treated to various examinations of the Steele family. What sort of people were they, anyhow? It was said of Steele now that he was an average, fairly capable newspaperman of no very startling ability, but of no particular vices—one who had for some years been a serious and faithful employé of this paper. Mrs. Steele, on the other hand, was a good woman, but by no means prepossessing. She was without romance, imagination, charm. One could see by looking at her and then looking at so winsome and enticing a woman as Mrs. Davis why Steele had strayed. It was the old eternal triangle—the woman who was not interesting, the woman who was interesting, and the man interested by the more interesting woman. There was no solving it, but it was all very sad. One could not help sympathizing with Mrs. Steele, the wronged woman; and again one could not help sympathizing with Mrs. Davis, the beautiful, passionate, desirous, helpless beauty—helpless because she was desirous.

In the meantime, the District Attorney's office having taken the case in hand, there were various developments in that quarter. It was necessary to find out, of course, where the candy had been purchased, how it had been drugged, with what it had been drugged, where the drug had been purchased. Chemists, detectives and handwriting experts were all set to work. It was no trouble to determine that the drug was arsenic, yet where this arsenic was purchased was not so easy to discover. It was some time before it was found where it had been procured. Dissimilarly, it was comparatively easy to prove where the candy had come from. It had been sent in the original box of a well-known candy firm. Yet just who had purchased it was not quite so easy to establish. The candy company could not remember, and Mrs. Davis, although admitting that the handwriting did resemble hers, denied ever having addressed the box or purchased any candy from the firm in question. She was quite willing to go there and be identified, but no clerk in the candy-store was able to identify her as one woman who had purchased candy. There were one or two clerks who felt sure that there had been a woman there at some time or other who had looked like her, but they were not positive. However, there was one girl who had worked in the store during the week in which the candy had been purchased, and who was not there any longer. This was a new girl who had been tried out for that week only and had since disappeared. Her name was known, of course, and the newspapers as well as the District Attorney's office at once began looking for her.

There were some whispers to the effect that not only Mrs. Davis but Steele himself might have been concerned in the plot, or Steele alone, since apparently he had been anxious to get rid of his wife. Why not? He might have imitated the handwriting of Mrs. Davis or created an accidental likeness to it. Also, there were dissenting souls, even in the office of the paper on which I worked, who thought that maybe Mrs. Steele had sent the candy to herself in order to injure the other woman. Why not? It was possible. Women were like that. There had been similar cases, had there not? Argument! Contention! "She might have wanted to die and be revenged on the other woman at the same time, might she not?" observed the railroad editor. "Oh, hell! What bunk!" called another. "No woman would kill herself to make a place for a rival. That's crazy." "Well," said a third, "she might have miscalculated the power of her own dope. Who knows? She may not have intended to take as much as she did."

"Oh, Christ," called a fourth from somewhere, "just listen to the Sherlock Holmes Association in session over there! Lay off, will you?"

A week or more went by, and then the missing girl who had worked in the candy-store was found. She had left the city the following week and gone to Denver. Being shown the pictures of Mrs. Davis, Mrs. Steele and some others and asked whether on any given day she had sold any of them a two-pound box of candy, she seemed to recall no one of them save possibly Mrs. Steele. But she could not be sure from the photograph. She would have to see the woman. In consequence, and without any word to the newspapers who had been leading the case up to then, this girl was returned to the city. Here, in the District Attorney's office, she was confronted by a number of women gathered for the occasion, among whom was placed Mrs. Davis. But on looking them all over she failed to identify any one of them. Then Mrs. Steele, who was by then up and around, was sent for. She came, along with a representative of the office. On sight, as she entered the door, and although there were other women in the room at the time, this girl exclaimed: "There she is! That's the woman! Yes, that's the very woman!" She was positive.

VI

As is customary in such cases, and despite the sympathy which had been extended to her, Mrs. Steele was turned over to criminologists, who soon extracted the truth from her. She broke down and wept hysterically.

It was she who had purchased the candy and poisoned it. Her life was going to pieces. She had wanted to die, so she said now. She had addressed the wrapper about the candy, as some of the wiseacres of our paper had contended, only she had first made a tracing on the paper from Mrs. Davis' handwriting, on an envelope addressed to her husband, and had then copied that. She had put not arsenic, but rat poison, bought some time before, into the candy, and in order to indict Mrs. Davis, she had put a little in each piece, about as much as would kill a rat, so that it would seem as though the entire box had been poisoned by her. She had got the idea from a case she had read about years before in a newspaper. She hated Mrs. Davis for stealing her husband. She had followed them.

When she had eaten one of the pieces of candy she had thought, as she now insisted, that she was taking enough to make an end of it all. But before taking it she had made sure that Mrs. Dalrymple, the wife of the newspaperman whom she first called to her aid, was at home in order that she might call or send her little boy. Her purpose in doing this was to instil in the mind of Mrs. Dalrymple the belief that it was Mrs. Davis who had sent the poison. When she was gone, Mrs. Davis would be punished, her husband would not be able to have her, and she herself would be out of her misery.

Result: the prompt discharge of Mrs. Davis, but no charge against Mrs. Steele. According to the District Attorney and the newspapers who most truly reflected local sentiment, she had suffered enough. And, as the state of public feeling then was, the District Attorney would not have dared to punish her. Her broken confession so reacted on the public mind that now, and for all time, it was for Mrs. Steele, just as a little while before it was rather for Mrs. Davis. For, you see, it was now proved that it was Mrs. Steele and not Mrs. Davis who had been wrought up to that point emotionally where she had been ready and willing—had actually tried—to make a blood sacrifice of herself and another woman on the altar of love. In either case it was the blood sacrifice—the bare possibility of it, if you choose —that lay at the bottom of the public's mood, and caused it to turn sympathetically to that one who had been most willing to murder in the cause of love.

But don't think this story is quite ended. Far from it. There is something else here, and a very interesting something to which I wish to call your attention. I have said that the newspapers turned favorably to Mrs. Steele. They did. So did the sob-sisters, those true barometers of public moods. Eulogies were now heaped upon Mrs. Steele, her devotion, her voiceless, unbearable woe, the tragedy of her mood, her intended sacrifice of herself. She was now the darling of these journalistic pseudo-analysts.

As for Mrs. Davis—not a word of sympathy, let alone praise or understanding for her thereafter. Almost unmentioned, if you will believe it, she was, and at once allowed to slip back into the limbo of the unheralded, the subsequently-to-be-unknown. From then on it was almost as though she had never been. For a few weeks, I believe, she retired to the home in which she had lived; then she disappeared entirely.

But now as to Steele. Here was the third peculiar phase of the case. Subsequent to the exculpation of Mrs. Davis and her noiseless retirement from the scene, what would you say his attitude would have been, or should have been? Where would he go? What do? What attitude would he assume? One of renewed devotion to his wife? One of renewed devotion to Mrs. Davis? One of disillusion or indifference in regard to all things? It puzzled me, and I was a rank outsider with no least concern, except of course our general concern in all such things, so vital to all of us in our sex and social lives. But not only was it a puzzle to me; it was also a puzzle to others, especially those who were identified with the newspaper business in the city, the editors and the city editors and managing editors who had been following the wavering course of things with uncertain thoughts and I may say uncertain policy. They had been, as you may guess, as prepared to hang Steele as not, assuming that he had been identified with Mrs. Davis in a plot to do away with his wife. On the other hand, now that that shadow was removed and it was seen to be a more or less simple case of varietism on his part, resulting in marital unhappiness for his wife and a desire on her part to die, they were prepared to look upon him and this result with a more kindly eye. After all, she was not dead. Mrs. Davis had been punished. And say what you will, looking at Mrs. Steele as she was, and at Mrs. Davis as she was—well—with a certain amount of material if not spiritual provocation—what would you?

Indeed, the gabble about the newspaper offices was all to the above effect. What, if anything, finally asked some of the city editors and managing editors, was to be done about Steele? Now that everything had blown over, what of him? Go on hounding him forever? Nonsense! It was scarcely fair, and, anyhow, no longer profitable or worth while. Now that the storm was passing, might not something be done for him? After all, he had been a fairly respectable newspaperman and in good standing. Why not take him back? And if not that, how was he to be viewed in future by his friends? Was he to be let alone, dropped, forgotten, or what? Was he going to stay here in G——, and fight it out, or leave? And if he was going to leave or stay, with whom was he going to leave or stay? Semikindly, semiselfish curiosity, as you see.

VII

The thing to do, it was finally decided among several of those on our paper and several on other papers who had known him more or less intimately, was to go to Steele himself, and ask him, not for publicity but just between ourselves, what was to be done, what he proposed to do, whether there was anything now that the local newspapers could say or do which would help him in any way? Did he want to be restored to a staff position? Was he going to stick to his wife? What, if anything, and with no malicious intent, should they say about Mrs. Davis? In a more or less secret and brotherly or professional spirit they were going to put it up to him and then leave it there, doing whatever they could in accordance with what he might wish.

Accordingly, two of the local newsmen whom he quite honestly respected visited him and placed the above several propositions before him. They found him, as I was told afterwards, seated upon the front porch of the very small and commonplace house in which after the dismissal of the charge against Mrs. Davis, he and his wife had been dwelling, reading a paper. Seated with him was Mrs. Steele, thinner and more querulous and anemic and unattractive than before. And upon the lot outside was their little son. Upon their arrival, they hailed Steele for a private word, and Mrs. Steele arose and went into the house. She looked, said one of these men, as though she expected more trouble. Steele, on his part, was all smiles and genial tenderings of hospitality. He was hoping for the best, of course, and he was anxious to do away with any new source of trouble. He even rubbed his hands, and licked his lips. "Come right in, boys. Come on up on the porch. Wait a minute and I'll bring out a couple of chairs." He hastened away but quickly returned, determined, as they thought, to make as good an impression as possible.

After he had heard what they had come for—most tactfully

and artfully put, of course—he was all smiles, eager, apparently, to be well thought of once more. To their inquiry as to whether he proposed to remain or not, he replied: "Yes, for the present." He had not much choice. He had not saved enough money in recent days to permit him to do much of anything else, and his wife's illness and other things had used up about all he had. "And now, just between ourselves, Steele," asked one of the two men who knew him better than the other, "what about Mrs. Davis and your wife? Just where do you stand in regard to them? Are you going to stick to your wife or are you going with the other woman eventually? No trouble for you, you understand—no more publicity. But the fellows on the papers are in a little bit of a quandary in regard to this. They don't intend to publish anything more—nothing disparaging. They only want to get your slant on the thing so that if anything more does come up in connection with this they can fix it so that it won't be offensive to you, you see."

"Yes, I see," replied Steele cheerfully and without much reflection. "But so far as that Davis woman is concerned, though, you can forget her. I'm through with her. She was never much to me, anyhow, just a common——." Here he used the good old English word for prostitute. As for his wife, he was going to stick by her, of course. She was a good woman. She loved him. There was his little boy. He was through with all that varietistic stuff. There was nothing to it. A man couldn't get away with it —and so on.

The two men, according to their account of it afterward, winced not a little, for, as they said, they had thought from all that had gone before that there had surely been much more than common prostitution between Steele and the woman. How could all this have been in the face of Mrs. Steele's great jealousy, Mrs. Davis' passionate declaration about pure, spiritual and undying love? Imagine it! After a few more words the men left, convinced that whether interested in his wife or not or Mrs. Davis or not, Steele was literally terrorized by convention,—and to the point where he was floundering about for an excuse. He was weak and he wanted to put the best face on the situation that he could. As one of the newspapermen afterward expressed it, "there was something unpleasant about it all." Just why had he changed so quickly? Why the gratuitous insult to Mrs. Davis? Why, after the previous acknowledgment of an affection of sorts at least for her, was he now willing to write himself down a bounder and a cad in this open and offensive way? For a cad he plainly was. Mrs. Davis could not be as shabby as he had made her out. This was at once and generally agreed upon. That finally fixed Steele's position in G——— as a bounder. He was never again taken back on any local staff.

And for myself, I could not quite fathom it. The thing haunted me. What was it that moved him—public opinion, fear of the loss of the petty social approval which had once been his, sorrow for his wife—what one special thing that Mrs. Davis might or might not have done? For certainly, as things turned out, she had been guilty of nothing except loving him—illegally, of course, but loving him. My mind involuntarily flashed back to the two curled abaft the pilot-house in the moonlight, those quaint, shadowy, romantic figures. And now this! And then there was dancing and laughter and love.

VIII

But even this is not the end, however ready you may be to cease listening. There is an *envoi* that I must add. This was seven years later. By then I had removed to New York and established myself as a cartoonist. From others I had learned that Steele also had come to New York and was now connected with one of the local papers in some moderately responsible capacity—copy reading, I think. At any rate, I met him—one Sunday. It was near the entrance of the Bronx Zoo, at closing time. He was there with his wife and a second little son that had come to him since he had left G———. The first one—a boy of ten by then, I presume—was not present. All this I learned in the course of the brief conversation that followed.

But his wife! I can never forget her. She was so worn, so faded, so impossible. And this other boy by her—a son who had followed after their reunion! My God! I thought, how may not fear or convention slay one emotionally! And to cap it all, he was not so much apologetic as—I will not say defiant—but ingratiating and volubly explanatory about his safe and sane retreat from gayety and freedom, and, if you will, immorality. For he knew, of course, that I recalled the other case—all its troublesome and peculiar details.

"My wife! My wife!" he exclaimed quickly, since I did not appear to recognize her at first, and with a rather grandiose gesture of the hand, as who should say, "I am proud of my wife, as you see. I am still married to her and rightly so. I am not the same person you knew in G—— at all—at all!"

"Oh, yes," I replied covering them all with a single glance. "I remember your wife very well. And your boy."

"Oh, no, not that boy," he hastened to explain. "That was Harry. This is another little boy—Francis." And then, as though to re-establish his ancient social prestige with me, he proceeded to add: "We're living over on Staten Island now—just at the north end, near the ferry, you know. You must come down some time. It's a pleasant ride. We'll both be so glad to see you. Won't we, Estelle?"

"Yes, certainly," said Mrs. Steele.

I hastened away as quickly as possible. The contrast was too much; that damned memory of mine, illegitimate as it may seem to be, was too much. I could not help thinking of the *Ira Ramsdell* and of how much I had envied him the dances, the love, the music, the moonlight.

"By God!" I exclaimed as I walked away. "By God!"

And that is exactly how I feel now about all such miscarriages of love and delight—cold and sad.

Marriage—For One

WHENEVER I think of love and marriage I think of Wray. That clerkly figure. That clerkly mind. He was among the first people I met when I came to New York and, like so many of the millions seeking to make their way, he was busy about his affairs. Fortunately, as I saw it, with the limitations of the average man he had the ambitions of the average man. At that time he was connected with one of those large commercial agencies which inquire into the standing of business men, small and large, and report their findings, for a price, to other business men. He was very much interested in his work and seemed satisfied that should he persist in it he was certain to achieve what was perhaps a fair enough ambition: a managership in some branch of this great concern, which same would pay him so much as five or six thousand a year. The thing about him that interested me, apart from a genial and pleasing disposition, was the fact that with all his wealth of opportunity before him for studying the human mind, its resources and resourcefulness, its inhibitions and liberations, its humor, tragedy, and general shiftiness and changefulness, still he was largely concerned with the bare facts of the differing enterprises whose character he was supposed to investigate. Were they solvent? Could and did they pay their bills? What was their capital stock? How much cash did they have on hand? . . . Such was the nature of the data he needed, and to this he largely confined himself.

Nevertheless, by turns he was amused or astonished or made angry or self-righteous by the tricks, the secretiveness, the errors and the downright meanness of spirit of so many he had to deal with. As for himself, he had the feeling that he was honest, straightforward, not as limited or worthless as some of these others, and it was on this score that he was convinced he would succeed, as he did eventually, within his limitations, of course. What interested me and now makes me look upon him always as an excellent illustration of the futility of the dream of exact or even suitable rewards was his clerkly and highly respectable faith in the same. If a man did as he should do, if he were industrious and honest and saving and courteous and a few more of those many things we all know we ought to be, then in that orderly nature of things which he assumed to hold one must get along better than some others. What—an honest, industrious, careful man not do better than one who was none of these things—a person who flagrantly disregarded them, say? What nonsense. It must be so. Of course there were accidents and sickness, and men stole from one another, as he saw illustrated in his daily round. And banks failed, and there were trusts and combinations being formed that did not seem to be entirely in tune with the interests of the average man. But even so, all things considered, the average man, if he did as above, was likely to fare much better than the one who did not. In short, there was such a thing as approximate justice. Good did prevail, in the main, and the wicked were punished, as they should be.

And in the matter of love and marriage he held definite views also. Not that he was unduly narrow or was inclined to censure those whose lives had not worked out as well as he hoped his own would, but he thought there was a fine line of tact somewhere in this matter of marriage which led to success there quite as the qualities outlined above led, or should lead, to success in matters more material or practical. One had to understand something about women. One had to be sure that when one went a-courting one selected a woman of sense as well as of charm, one who came of good stock and hence would be possessed of good taste and good principles. She need not be rich; she might even be poor. And one had to be reasonably sure that one loved her. So many that went a-courting imagined they loved and were loved when it was nothing more than a silly passing passion. Wray knew. And so many women were designing, or at least light and flighty; they could not help a serious man to succeed if they would. However, in many out-of-the-way corners of the world were the really sensible and worthy girls, whom it was an honor to marry, and it was one of these that he was going to choose. Yet even there it was necessary to exercise care: one might marry a girl who was too narrow and conventional, one who would not understand the world and hence be full of prejudices. He was for the intelligent and practical and liberal girl, if he could find her, one who was his mental equal.

It was when he had become secretary to a certain somebody that he encountered in his office a girl who seemed to him to embody nearly all of the virtues or qualities which he thought necessary. She was the daughter of very modestly circumstanced parents who dwelt in the nearby suburb of O——, and a very capable and faithful stenographer, of course. If you had seen the small and respectable suburb from which she emanated you would understand. She was really pretty and appeared to be practical and sensible in many ways, but still very much in leash to the instructions and orders and tenets of her home and her church and her family circle, three worlds as fixed and definite and worthy and respectable in her thought as even the most enthusiastic of those who seek to maintain the order and virtue of the world would have wished. According to him, as he soon informed me—since we exchanged nearly all our affairs whenever we met, she was opposed to the theatre, dancing, any form of night dining or visiting in the city on weekdays, as well as anything that in her religious and home world might be construed as desecration of the Sabbath. I recall him describing her as narrow "as yet," but he hoped to make her more liberal in the course of time. He also told me with some amusement and the air of a man of the world that it was impossible for him to win her to so simple an outing as rowing on the Sabbath on the little river near her home because it was wrong; on the contrary, he had to go to church with her and her parents. Although he belonged to no church and was mildly interested in socialism, he kept these facts from her knowledge. The theatre could not even be mentioned as a form of amusement and she could not and would not dance; she looked upon his inclination for the same as not only worldly but loose and sinful. However, as he told me, he was very fond of her and was doing his best to influence and enlighten her. She was too fine and intelligent a girl to stick to such notions. She would come out of them.

By very slow degrees (he was about his business of courting her all of two or three years) he succeeded in bringing her to the place where she did not object to staying downtown to dinner with him on a weekday, even went with him to a sacred or musical concert of a Sunday night, but all unbeknown to her parents or neighbors, of course. But what he considered his greatest triumph was when he succeeded in interesting her in books, especially bits of history and philosophy that he thought very liberal and which no doubt generated some thin wisps of doubt in her own mind. Also, because he was intensely fond of the theatre and had always looked upon it as the chiefest of the sources of his harmless entertainment, he eventually induced her to attend one performance, and then another and another. In short, he emancipated her in so far as he could, and seemed to be delighted with the result.

With their marriage came a new form of life for both of them, but more especially for her. They took a small apartment in New York, a city upon which originally she had looked with no little suspicion, and they began to pick up various friends. It was not long before she had joined a literary club which was being formed in their vicinity, and here she met a certain type of restless, pushing, seeking woman for whom Wray did not care—a Mrs. Drake and a Mrs. Munshaw, among others, who, from the first, as he afterward told me, he knew could be of no possible value to any one. But Bessie liked them and was about with them here, there, and everywhere.

It was about this time that I had my first suspicion of anything untoward in their hitherto happy relations. I did not see him often now, but when I did visit them at their small apartment, could not help seeing that Mrs. Wray was proving almost too apt a pupil in the realm in which he had interested her. It was plain that she had been emancipated from quite all of her old notions as to the sinfulness of the stage, and in regard to reading and living in general. Plainly, Wray had proved the Prince Charming, who had entered the secret garden and waked the sleeping princess to a world of things she had never dreamed of. She had reached the place where she was criticizing certain popular authors, spoke of a curiously enlightened history of France she was reading, of certain bits of philosophy and poetry which her new club were discussing. From the nature of the conversation being carried on by the three of us I could see that Wray was beginning to feel that the unsophisticated young girl he had married a little while before might yet outstrip him in the very realm in which he had hoped to be her permanent guide. More than once, as I noticed, she chose to question or contradict him as to a matter of fact, and I think he was astonished if not irritated by the fact that she knew more than he about the import of a certain plot or the relativity of certain dates in history. And with the force and determination that had caused her to stand by her former convictions, she now aired and defended her new knowledge. Not that her manner was superior or irritating exactly; she had a friendly way of including and consulting him in regard to many things which indicated that as yet she had no thought of manifesting a superiority which she did not feel. "That's not right, dearest. His name is Bentley. He is the author of a play that was here last year—*The Seven Rings of Manfred*—don't you remember?" And Wray, much against his will, was compelled to confess that she was right.

Whenever he met me alone after this, however, he would confide the growing nature of his doubts and perplexities. Bessie was no more the girl she had been when he first met her than he was like the boy he had been at ten years of age. A great, a very great change was coming over her. She was becoming more aggressive and argumentative and self-centred all the time, more this, more that. She was reading a great deal, much too much for the kind of life she was called upon to lead. Of late they had been having long and unnecessary arguments that were of no consequence however they were settled, and yet if they were not settled to suit her she was angry or irritable. She was neglecting her home and running about all the time with her new-found friends. She did not like the same plays he did. He wanted a play that was light and amusing, whereas she wanted one with some serious moral or intellectual twist to it. She read only serious books now and was attending a course of lectures, whereas he, as he now confessed, was more or less bored by serious books. What was the good of them? They only stirred up thoughts and emotions which were better left unstirred. And she liked music, or was pretending she did, grand opera, recitals and that sort of thing, whereas he was not much interested in music. Grand opera bored him, and he was free to admit it, but if he would not accompany her she would go with one or both of those two wretched women he was beginning to detest. Their husbands had a little money and gave them a free rein in the matter of their social and artistic aspirations. They had no household duties to speak of and could come and go as they chose, and Wray now insisted that it was they who were aiding and abetting Bessie in these various interests and enthusiasms and stirring her up to go and do and be. What was he to do? No good could come if things went on as they were going. They were having frequent quarrels, and more than once lately she had threatened to leave him and do for herself here in New York, as he well knew she could. He was doing very well now and they could be happy together if only these others could be done away with.

It was only a month or two after this that Wray came to see me, in a very distrait state of mind. After attempting to discuss several other things quite casually he confessed that his young wife had left him. She had taken a room somewhere and had resumed work as a stenographer, and although he met her occasionally in the subway she would have nothing to do with him. She wanted to end it all. And would I believe it? She was accusing him of being narrow and ignorant and stubborn and a number of other things! Only think of it! And three or four years ago she had thought he was all wrong when he wanted to go rowing on Sunday or stay downtown to dinner of an evening. Could such things be possible? And yet he loved her, in spite of all the things that had come up between them. He couldn't help it. He couldn't help thinking how sweet and innocent and strange she was when he first met her, how she loved her parents and respected their wishes. And now see. "I wish to God," he suddenly exclaimed in the midst of the "old-time" picture he was painting of her, "that I hadn't been so anxious to change her. She was all right as she was, if I had only known it. She didn't know anything about these new-fangled things then, and I wasn't satisfied till I got her interested in them. And now see. She leaves me and says I'm narrow and stubborn, that I'm trying to hold her back intellectually. And all because I don't want to do all the things she wants to do and am not interested in the things that interest her, now."

I shook my head. Of what value was advice in such a situation as this, especially from one who was satisfied that the mysteries of temperament of either were not to be unraveled or adjusted save by nature—the accidents of chance and affinity, or the deadly opposition which keep apart those unsuited to each other? Nevertheless, being appealed to for advice, I ventured a silly suggestion, borrowed from another. He had said that if he could but win her back he would be willing to modify the pointless opposition and contention that had driven her away. She might go her intellectual way as she chose if she would only come back. Seeing him so tractable and so very wishful, I now suggested a thing that had been done by another in a somewhat related situation. He was to win her back by offering her such terms as she would accept, and then, in order to bind her to him, he was to induce her to have a child. That would capture her sympathy, very likely, as well as insinuate an image of himself into her affectionate consideration. Those who had children rarely separated—or so I said.

The thought appealed to him intensely. It satisfied his practical and clerkly nature. He left me hopefully and I saw nothing of him for several months, at the end of which time he came to report that all was once more well with him. She had come back, and in order to seal the new pact he had taken a larger apartment in a more engaging part of the city. Bessie was going on with her club work, and he was not opposing her in anything. And then within the year came a child and there followed all those simple, homey, and seemingly binding and restraining things which go with the rearing and protection of a young life.

But even during that period, as I was now to learn, all was not as smooth as I had hoped. Talking to me in Wray's absence once Bessie remarked that, delightful as it was to have a child of her own, she could see herself as little other than a milch cow with an attendant calf, bound to its service until it should be able to look after itself. Another time she remarked that mothers were bond-servants, that even though she adored her little girl she could not help seeing what a chain and a weight a child was to one who had ambitions beyond those of motherhood. But Wray, clerkly soul that he was, was all but lost in rapture. There was a small park nearby, and here he could be found trundling his infant in a handsome baby-carriage whenever his duties would permit. He would sit or walk where were others who had children of about the age of his own so that he might compare them. He liked to speculate on the charm and innocence of babyhood and was amused by a hundred things which he had never noticed in the children of others. Already he was beginning to formulate plans for little Janet's future. It was hard for children to be cooped up in an apartment house in the city. In a year or two, if he could win Bessie to the idea, they would move to some suburban town where Janet could have the country air.

They were prospering now and could engage a nursemaid, so Mrs. Wray resumed her intellectual pursuits and her freedom. Throughout it all one could see that, respect Wray as she might as a dutiful and affectionate and methodical man, she could not love or admire him, and that mainly because of the gap that lay between them intellectually. Dissemble as he might, there was always the hiatus that lies between those who think or dream a little and those who aspire and dream much. Superiority of intellect was not altogether the point; she was not so much superior as different, as I saw it. Rather, they were two differing rates of motion, flowing side by side for the time being only, his the slower, hers the quicker. And it mattered not that his conformed more to the conventional thought and emotions of the majority. Hers was the more satisfactory to herself and constituted an urge which he feared rather than despised; and his was more satisfactory to himself, compromise as he would. Observing them together one could see how proud he was of her and of his relationship to her, how he felt that he had captured a prize, regardless of the conditions by which it was retained; and on the other hand one could easily see how little she held him in her thought and mood. She was forever talking to others about those things which she knew did not interest him or to which he was opposed.

For surcease she plunged into those old activities that had so troubled him at first, and now he complained that little Janet was being neglected. She did not love her as she should or she could not do as she was doing. And what was more and worse, she had now taken to reading Freud and Kraft-Ebbing and allied thinkers and authorities, men and works that he considered dreadful and shameful, even though he scarcely grasped their true significance.

One day he came to me and said: "Do you know of a writer by the name of Pierre Loti?"

"Yes," I replied, "I know his works. What about him?"

"What do you think of him?"

"As a writer? Why, I respect him very much. Why?"

"Oh, I know, from an intellectual point of view, as a fine writer, maybe. But what do you think of his views of life—of his books as books to be read by the mother of a little girl?"

"Wray," I replied, "I can't enter upon a discussion of any man's works upon purely moral grounds. He might be good for some mothers and evil for others. Those who are to be injured by a picture of life must be injured, or kept from its contaminating influence, and those who are to be benefited will be benefited. I can't discuss either books or life in any other way. I see worthwhile books as truthful representations of life in some form, nothing more. And it would be unfair to any one who stood in intellectual need to be restrained from that which might prove of advantage to him. I speak only for myself, however."

It was not long after that I learned there had been a new quarrel and that Bessie had left him once more, this time, as it proved, for good. And with her, which was perhaps illegal or unfair, she had taken the child. I did not know what had brought about this latest rupture but assumed that it was due to steadily diverging views. They could not agree on that better understanding of life which at one time he was so anxious for her to have—his understanding. Now that she had gone beyond that, and her method of going was unsatisfactory to him, they could not agree, of course.

Not hearing from him for a time I called and found him living in the same large apartment they had taken. Its equipment was better suited to four than to one, yet after seven or eight months of absence on her part here he was, living alone, where every single thing must remind him of her and Janet. As for himself, apart from a solemnity and reserve which sprang from a wounded and disgruntled spirit, he pretended an indifference and a satisfaction with his present state which did not square with his past love for her. She had gone, yes; but she had made a mistake and would find it out. Life wasn't as she thought it was. She had gone with another man—he was sure of that, although he did not know who the man was. It was all due to one of those two women she had taken up with, that Mrs. Drake. They were always interested in things which did not and could not interest him. After a time he added that he had been to see her parents. I could not guess why, unless it was because he was lonely and still very much in love and thought they might help him to understand the very troublesome problem that was before him.

It was a year and a half before I saw him again, during which time, as I knew, he continued to live in the apartment they had occupied together. He had become manager of a department of the agency by this time and was going methodically to and fro between his home and office. After living alone and brooding for more than a year, he came to see me one rainy November night. He looked well enough materially, quite the careful person who takes care of his clothes, but thinner, more tense and restless. He seated himself before my fire and declared that he was doing very well and was thinking of taking a long vacation to visit some friends in the West. (He had once told me that he had heard that Bessie had gone to California.) Yes, he was still living in the old place. I might think it strange, but he had not thought it worth while to move. He would only have to find another place to live in; the furniture was hard to pack; he didn't like hotels.

Then of a sudden, noting that I studied him and wondered, he grew restless and finally stood up, then walked about looking at some paintings and examining a shelf of books. His manner was that of one who is perplexed and undetermined, of one who has stood out against a silence and loneliness of which he was intensely weary. Then of a sudden he wheeled and faced me: "I can't stand it. That's what's the matter. I just can't stand it any longer. I've tried and tried. I thought the child would make things work out all right, but she didn't. She didn't want a child and never forgave me for persuading her to have Janet. And then that literary craze—that was really my own fault, though. I was the one that encouraged her to read and go to theatres. I used to tell her she wasn't up-to-date, that she ought to wake up and find out what was going on in the world, that she ought to get in with intelligent people. But it wasn't that either. If she had been the right sort of woman she couldn't have done as she did." He paused and clenched his hands nervously and dramatically. It was as though he were denouncing her to her face instead of to me.

"Now, Wray," I interposed, "how useless to say that. Which of us is as he should be? Why will you talk so?"

"But let me tell you what she did," he went on fiercely. "You haven't an idea of what I've been through, not an idea. She tried to poison me once so as to get rid of me." And here followed a brief and sad recital of the twists and turns and desperation of one who was intensely desirous of being free of one who was as desirous of holding her. And then he added: "And she was in love with another man, only I could never find out who he was." And his voice fell to a low, soft level, as though he was even then trying to solve the mystery of who it was. "And I know she had an operation performed, though I could never prove it." And he gave me details of certain mysterious goings to and fro, of secret pursuits on his part, actions and evidences and moods and quarrels that pointed all too plainly to a breach that could never be healed. "And what's more," he exclaimed at last, "she tortured me. You'll never know. You couldn't. But I loved her. . . . And I love her now." Once more the tensely gripped fingers, the white face, the flash of haunted eyes.

"One afternoon I stood outside of a window of an apartment

house when I knew she was inside, and I knew the name of the man who was supposed to occupy it, only he had re-sublet it, as I found out afterwards. And she had Janet with her—think of that!—our own little girl! I saw her come to the window once to look out—I actually saw her in another man's rooms. I ran up and hammered at the door—I tried to break it open. I called to her to come out but she wouldn't, and I went to get a policeman to make him open the door. But when I got back a servant was coming up as though she had been out, and she unlocked the door and went in. It was all a ruse, and I know it. They weren't inside. She had slipped out with Janet. And she had told me they were going to Westchester for the day.

"And another time I followed her to a restaurant when she said she was going to visit a friend. I suspected there was a man—the man I thought she was going with, but it was some one I had never seen before. When they came out and were getting into a cab I came up and told them both what I thought of them. I threatened to kill them both. And she told him to go and then came home with me, but I couldn't do anything with her. She wouldn't talk to me. All she would say was that if I didn't like the way she was doing I could let her go. She wanted me to give her a divorce. And I couldn't let her go, even if I had wanted to. I loved her too much. And I love her too much now. I do. I can't help it." He paused. The pain and regret were moving.

"Another time," he went on, "I followed her to a hotel—yes, to a hotel. But when I got inside she was waiting for me; she had seen me. I even saw a man coming toward her—but not the one I believed was the one—only when he saw me he turned away and I couldn't be sure that he was there to meet her. And when I tried to talk to her about him she turned away from me and we went back home in silence. I couldn't do anything with her. She would sit and read and ignore me for days—days, I tell you—without ever a word."

"Yes," I said, "but the folly of all that. The uselessness, the hopelessness. How could you?"

"I know, I know," he exclaimed, "but I couldn't help it. I can't now. I love her. I can't help that, can I? I'm miserable without her. I see the folly of it all, but I'm crazy about her.

The more she disliked me the more I loved her. And I love her now, this minute. I can't help it. There were days when she tortured me so that I vomited, from sheer nervousness. I was sick and run down. I have been cold with sweat in her presence and when she was away and I didn't know where she was. I have walked the streets for hours, for whole days at a time, because I couldn't eat or sleep and didn't know what to do. By God!" Once more the pause and a clenching of the hands. "And all I could do was think and think and think. And that is all I do now really—think and think and think. I've never been myself since she went away. I can't shake it off. I live up there, yes. But why? Because I think she might come back some day, and because we lived there together. I wait and wait. I know it's foolish, but still I wait. Why? God only knows. And yet I wait. Oh," he sighed, "and it's three years now. Three years!"

He paused and gazed at me and I at him, shaken by a fact that was without solution by any one. Here he was—the one who had understood so much about women. But where was she, the one he had sought to enlighten, to make more up-to-date and liberal? I wondered where she was, whether she ever thought of him even, whether she was happy in her new freedom. And then, without more ado, he slipped on his raincoat, took up his umbrella, and stalked out into the rain, to walk and think, I presume. And I, closing the door on him, studied the walls, wondering. The despair, the passion, the rage, the hopelessness, the love. "Truly," I thought, "this is love, for one at least. And this is marriage, for one at least. He is spiritually wedded to that woman, who despises him, and she may be spiritually wedded to another man who may despise her. But love and marriage, for one, at least, I have seen here in this room to-night, and with mine own eyes."

The Prince Who Was A Thief

An Improvisation on the Oldest Oriental Theme

THE doors of the mosque in Hodeidah stood wide and inviting after the blaze of an Arabian afternoon. And within, the hour of prayer having drawn nigh, were prostrated a few of the more faithful, their faces toward Mecca. Without, upon the platform of the great mosque and within the shadow of the high east wall, a dozen mendicants in their rags were already huddled or still arranging themselves, in anticipation of the departure of those of the faithful who might cast them a pice or an anna, so plain is the prescription of the Koran. For is it not written: "And forget not the poor, and the son of the road"? Even so, praise be to Allah, the good, the great.

Apart from them, oblivious of them and their woes, even of the import of the mosque itself, a score or more of Arabian children were at play, circling about like knats or bats. And passing among these or idling in groups for a word as to the affairs of the day, were excellent citizens of Hodeidah, fresh from their shops and errands—Bhori, the tin-seller, for one, making his way before going home to a comfortable mabraz, there to smoke a water-pipe and chew a bit of khat; and Ahmed, the carpet-weaver, stopping at the mosque to pray before going home; and Chudi, the baker, and Zad-el-Din, the seller of piece goods, whose shops were near together, both fathers, these, and discussing trade and the arrival of the camel train from Taif. And now came Azad Bakht, the barber, mopping his brow as was his wont. And Feruz, the water-carrier, to offer water for sale. And many others came and went, for this was the closing hour of the shops; soon all would be making for home or the mabrazes after a moment of prayer in the mosque, so near is the hereafter to the now.

But Gazzar-al-Din, a mendicant story-teller, fresh from the camel train out of Taif which within the hour had passed beyond the Chedar gate, was not one of these. Indeed he was a stranger in Hodeidah, one of those who make their way from city to city and village to village by their skill as tellers of tales, reciters of the glories of kings and princesses and princes and the doings of Jinn and magicians and fabled celebrities generally. Yet poor was he indeed. His tales he had gathered on many travels. And though nearing the age of eighty and none too prepossessing of mien, yet so artful was he in the manner of presenting his wares that he had not thus far died of want. His garb was no more than a loin-cloth, a turban and a cape as dirty as they were ragged. His beard and hair had not for years known any other comb than the sands of the desert and the dust of the streets. His face was parchment, his hands claws, one arm was withered.

Taking in at a glance the presence of a score of comrades in misery at or near the mosque door, Gazzar-al-Din betook himself to a respectful distance and surveyed the world in which he found himself. The cook-shop of Al Hadjaz being not far off and some inviting fragrance therefrom streaming to him on the wind, he made shift to think how he could best gather an audience of all who now came and went so briskly. For eat he must. No doubt there were many in Hodeidah who told tales, and by those about the mosque who sought alms certainly an additional seeker would not be welcomed. Indeed there had been times when open hostility had been manifested, as in Feruz where, after gathering many anna from an admiring throng, once he had been set upon and beaten, his purse taken, and, to crown it all, a pail of slops cast upon him by a savage she-wolf of their pack. It behooved him therefore to have a care.

Still, all things considered, it was not so poor a life. Many had their homes, to be sure, and their wives and shops, but were there not drawbacks? The best of them were as fixed as the palms and sands of the desert. Once in their lives perhaps they had journeyed to Mecca or Medina, to be preyed upon and swindled, in some instances even to be murdered, by the evil hawks that dwelt there. But in his case now. . . . The fragrances from the shop of Al Hadjaz renewed themselves. . . . There was nothing for it: he must find a comfortable doorway or the shaded side of a wall where he could spread his cape, belabor his tambour and so attract attention and secure as many anna as might be before he began to unfold such a tale of adventure and surprise as would retain the flagging interest of the most wearied and indifferent. And eventually secure him sufficient anna for his meal and lodging. But to do that, as he well knew, there must be in it somewhere, a beautiful princess and a handsome lover; also a noble and generous and magnificent caliph. And much talk to be sure of gold and power where so little existed in real life. In addition there should be cruel robbers and thieves, and, also, a righteous man too—though in real life, how few. Sometimes as the faces of those addressed showed a wane of interest it was wise to take apart and recombine many tales, borrow from one to bolster up another.

As he walked, looking at the windows and doors of all the shops and residences about him, he eventually spied a deep recess giving into the closed market a score of feet from the public square. Here he seated himself and began softly to thump his tambour, lest those religiously minded should take offense. Also it was no part of his desire to attract the mendicants, who were still before the door of the mosque. Soon they might depart, and then he would feel safer, for in them, especially for such as he—a fellow craftsman, as it were—was nothing but jibes and rivalry. He drummed softly, looking briskly about the while, now at the windows, now toward the mosque, now along the winding street. Seeing two urchins, then a third, pause and gaze, he reasoned that his art was beginning to lure. For where children paused, their elders were sure to follow. And so it proved. Drawing nearer and nearer these first children were joined by a fourth, a fifth, a sixth. Presently Haifa, the tobacco vendor, limping toward the mosque to sell his wares, paused and joined the children. He was curious as to what was to follow —whether Gazzar would secure an audience. Next came Waidi, the water-seller, fresh from a sale; then Ajeeb, ne'er-do-well cleaner of market stalls for the merchants, and full of curiosity ever. And after him came Soudi and Parfi, carriers, an appetite for wonders besetting them; and then El-Jed, the vendor of kindling.

As they gathered about him Gazzar-al-Din ventured to thrum louder and louder, exclaiming: "A marvelous tale, O Company of the Faithful! A marvelous tale! Hearken! A tale such as has never yet been told in all Hodeidah—no, not in all Yemen! 'A Prince Who was a Thief.' A Prince Who Was a Thief! For a score of anna—yea, the fourth part of a rupee—I begin. And ah, the sweetness of it! As jasmine, it is fragrant; as khat, soothing. A marvelous tale!"

"Ay-ee, but how is one to know that," observed Ahmed, the carpet-weaver, to Chudi, the tailor, with whom he had drawn near. "There are many who promise excellent tales but how few who tell them."

"It is even as thou sayst, O Ahmed. Often have I hearkened and given anna in plenty, yet few there are whose tales are worth the hearing."

"Why not begin thy tale, O Kowasji?" inquired Soudi, the carrier. "Then if, as thou sayst, it is so excellent, will not anna enough be thine? There are tellers of tales, and tellers of tales—"

"Yea, and that I would," replied the mendicant artfully, "were all as honest as thou lookest and as kind. Yet have I traveled far without food, and I know not where I may rest this night. . . . A tale of the great caliph and the Princess Yanee and the noble Yussuf, stolen and found again. And the great treasury sealed and guarded, yet entered and robbed by one who was not found. Anna—but a score of anna, and I begin! What? Are all in Hodeidah so poor that a tale of love and pleasure and danger and great palaces and great princes and caliphs and thieves can remain untold for the want of a few anna—for so many as ten dropped into my tambour? A marvelous tale! A marvelous tale!"

He paused and gazed speculatively about, holding out his tambour. His audience looked dubiously and curiously at him; who now was this latest teller of wonders, and from whence had he come? An anna was not much, to be sure, and a tale well told—well—yet there had been tellers of such whose tales were as dull as the yawn of a camel.

"An excellent tale, sayst thou?" queried Parfi cautiously. "Then, if it be so marvelous, why not begin? For a handful of anna one may promise anything."

"A great promiser there was here once," commented Ajeeb the gossip, sententiously, "and he sat himself in this self-same door. I remember him well. He wore a green turban, but a greater liar there never was. He promised wonders and terrors enough, but it came to nothing—not a demon or Jinn in it."

"Is it of demons and Jinns only that thou thinkest, donkey?" demanded Haifa. "Verily, there are wonders and mysteries everywhere, without having them in tales."

"Yea, but a tale need not be for profit either," said Waidi, the water-seller. "It is for one's leisure, at the end of a day. I like such as end happily, with evil punished and the good rewarded."

"Come, O friends," insisted Gazzar-al-Din, seeing that one or two were interested, "for a score of anna, I begin. Of Yemen it is, this very Yemen, and Baghdad, once a greater city than any to-day—"

"Begin then," said Azad Bakht, the barber. "Here is an anna for thee," and he tossed a coin in the tambour.

"And here is another for thee," observed Haifa, fishing in his purse. "I do not mind risking it."

"And here is another," called Soudi condescendingly. "Begin."

"And here is yet another," added Parfi grandiosely. "Now, then, thy tale, and look thee that it is as thou sayst, marvelous." And they squatted about him on the ground.

But Gazzar, determined not to begin until he had at least ten anna, the price of a bowl of curds and a cup of kishr, waited until he had accumulated so many, as well as various "Dogs!" and "Pigs!" and "Wilt thou begin, miser, or wilt thou fill thy tambour?" into the bargain. He then crouched upon his rags, lifted his hand for silence, and began:

"Know then, O excellent citizens of Hodeidah, that once, many years since, there lived in this very Yemen where now is Taif, then a much more resplendent city, a sultan by the name of Kar-Shem, who had great cities and palaces and an army, and was beloved of all over whom he ruled. When he— wilt thou be seated, O friend? And silence!—when he was but newly married and ruling happily a son was born to him, Hussein, an infant of so great charm and beauty that he decided he should be carefully reared and wisely trained and so made into a fit ruler, for so great a country. But, as it chanced, there was a rival or claimant to this same throne by another line, a branch long since deposed by the ancestors of this same king, and he it was, Bab-el-Bar by name, who was determined that the young Prince Hussein should be stolen and disposed of in some way so that he should never return and claim the throne. One day, when the prince was only four years of age, the summer palace was attacked and the princeling captured. From thence he was carried over great wastes of sand to Baghdad, where he was duly sold as a slave to a man who was looking for such, for he was a great and successful thief, one who trained thieves from their infancy up so that they should never know what virtue was."

"Ay-ee, there are such," interrupted Ahmed, the carpet-weaver, loudly, for his place had only recently been robbed. "I know of the vileness of thieves."

"Peace! Peace!" insisted Waidi and Haifa sourly.

Gazzar-al-Din paused until quiet should be restored, then resumed:

"Once the Prince Hussein was in the hands of this thief, he was at once housed with those who stole, who in turn taught him. One of the tricks which Yussuf, the master thief, employed was to take each of his neophytes in turn at the age of seven, dress him in a yarn jacket, lower him into a dry cistern from which there was no means of escape, place a large ring-cake upon a beam across the top and tell him to obtain the cake or starve. Many starved for days and were eventually dismissed as unworthy of his skill. But when the young Prince Hussein was lowered he meditated upon his state. At last he unraveled a part of his yarn jacket, tied a pebble to it and threw it so that it fell through the hole of the cake, and thus he was able to pull it down. At this Yussuf was so pleased that he had him drawn up and given a rare meal.

"One day Yussuf, hearing good reports from those who were training Hussein in thieving, took him to the top of a hill traversed by a road, where, seeing a peasant carrying a sheep on his back approaching, Yussuf Ben Ali asked of Hussein, now renamed Abou so that he might not be found: 'How shall we get the sheep without the peasant learning that we have taken it?' Trained by fear of punishment to use his wits, Abou, after some thought replied: 'When thou seest the sheep alone, take it!' Stealing from the thicket, he placed one of his shoes in the road and then hid. The peasant came and saw the shoe, but left it lying there because there was but one. Abou ran out and picked up the shoe, reappearing from the wood far ahead of the peasant where he put down the mate to the first shoe and then hid again. The peasant came and examined the shoe, then tied his sheep to a stake and ran back for the first one. Yussuf, seeing the sheep alone, now came out and hurried off with it, while Abou followed, picking up the last shoe."

"He was a donkey to leave his sheep in the road," interpolated Parfi, the carrier, solemnly.

"But more of a donkey not to have taken up the first shoe," added Soudi.

"Anna! Anna!" insisted Gazzar-al-Din, seizing upon this occasion to collect from those who had newly arrived. "'Tis a marvellous tale! Remember the teller of good tales, whose gift it is to sweeten the saddest of days. He lightens the cares of those who are a-weary. Anna! Anna!" And with a clawy hand he held out the tambour to Zad-el-Din and Azad Bakht, who began to regret their interest.

"Cannot a man speak without thou demandest anna?" grumbled Zad-el-Din fishing in his purse and depositing an anna, as did Azad Bakht and several more. Whereupon, the others beginning to grumble, Gazzar continued.

"The peasant coming back to where he had seen the first shoe and not finding it, was dazed and ran back to his sheep, to find that that and the second shoe were gone. Yussuf was much pleased and rewarded Abou with a new coat later, but for the present he was not done. Judging by long experience that the peasant had either bought the sheep and was taking it home or that he was carrying it to market to sell, he said to Abou: 'Let us wait. It may be that he will return with another.' "

"Ah, shrewd," muttered Ajeeb, nodding his head gravely. "Accordingly," went on Gazzar-al-Din, "they waited and soon the peasant returned carrying another sheep. Yussuf asked Abou if he could take this one also, and Abou told him that when he saw the sheep alone to take it."

"Dunce!" declared Chudi, the baker. "Will he put another sheep down after just losing one? This is a thin tale!" But Gazzar was not to be disconcerted.

"Now Yussuf was a great thief," he went on, "but this wit of Abou's puzzled him. Of all the thieves he had trained few could solve the various problems which he put before them, and in Abou he saw the makings of a great thief. As the peasant approached, Abou motioned to Yussuf to conceal himself in a crevice in the nearby rocks, while he hid in the woods. When the peasant drew near Abou placed his hands to his lips and imitated a sheep bleating, whereupon the peasant, thinking it must be his lost sheep, put down behind a stone the one he was carrying, for its feet were tied, and went into the woods to seek the lost one. Yussuf, watching from his cave, then ran forth and made off with the sheep. When the peasant approached, Abou climbed a tree and smiled down on him as he sought his sheep, for he had been taught that to steal was clever and wise, and the one from whom he could steal was a fool."

"And so he is," thought Waidi, who had stolen much in his time.

"When the peasant had gone his way lamenting, Abou came down and joined Yussuf. They returned to the city and the home of Yussuf, where the latter, much pleased, decided to adopt Abou as his son." Gazzar now paused upon seeing the interest of his hearers and held out his tambour. "Anna, O friends, anna! Is not the teller of tales, the sweetener of weariness, worthy of his hire? I have less than a score of anna, and ten will buy no more than a bowl of curds or a cup of kishr, and the road I have traveled has been long. So much as the right to sleep in a stall with the camels is held at ten anna, and I am no longer young." He moved the tambour about appealingly.

"Dog!" growled Soudi. "Must thy tambour be filled before we hear more?"

"Bismillah! This is no story-teller but a robber," declared Parfi.

"Peace, friends," said Gazzar, who was afraid to irritate his hearers in this strange city. "The best of the tale comes but now—the marvelous beauty of the Princess Yanee and the story of the caliph's treasury and the master thief. But, for the love of Allah, yield me but ten more anna and I pause no more. It is late. A cup of kishr, a camel's stall—" He waved the tambour. Some three of his hearers who had not yet contributed anything dropped each an anna into his tambour.

"Now," continued Gazzar somewhat gloomily, seeing how small were his earnings for all his art, "aside from stealing and plundering caravans upon the great desert, and the murdering of men for their treasure, the great Yussuf conducted a rug bazaar as a blind for more thievery and murder. This bazaar was in the principal street of the merchants, and at times he was to be seen there, his legs crossed upon his pillows. But let a merchant of wealth appear, a stranger, and although he might wish only to ask prices Yussuf would offer some rug or cloth so low that even a beggar would wish to take it. When the stranger, astonished at its price, would draw his purse a hand-clap from Yussuf would bring forth slaves from behind hangings who would fall upon and bind him, take his purse and clothes and throw his body into the river."

"An excellent robber indeed!" approved Soudi.

"Yussuf, once he had adopted Abou as his son, admitted him to his own home, where were many chambers and a garden, a court with a pool, and many servants and cushions and low divans in arcades and chambers; then he dressed him in silks and took him to his false rug market, where he introduced him with a great flourish as one who would continue his affairs after he, Yussuf, was no more. He called his slaves and said: 'Behold thy master after myself. When I am not here, or by chance am no more—praise be to Allah, the good, the great!—see that thou obey him, for I have found him very wise.' Soon Yussuf disguised himself as a dervish and departed upon a new venture. As for Abou, being left in charge of the rug market, he busied himself with examining its treasures and their values and thinking on how the cruel trade of robbery, and, if necessary, murder, which had been taught him, and how best it was to be conducted.

"For although Abou was good and kind of heart, still being taken so young and sharply trained in theft and all things evil, and having been taught from day to day that not only were murder and robbery commendable but that softness or error in their pursuit was wrong and to be severely punished, he believed all this and yet innocently enough at times sorrowed for those whom he injured. Yet also he knew that he durst not show his sorrow in the presence of Yussuf, for the latter, though kind to him, was savage to all who showed the least mercy or failed to do his bidding, even going so far as to slay them when they sought to cross or betray him."

"Ay-ee, a savage one was that," muttered Al Hadjaz, the cook.

"And I doubt not there are such in Yemen to this day," added Ajeeb, the cleaner of stalls. "Was not Osman Hassan, the spice-seller, robbed and slain?"

"Soon after Yussuf had left on the secret adventure, there happened to Abou a great thing. For it should be known that at this time there ruled in Baghdad the great and wise Yianko I., Caliph of the Faithful in the valleys of the Euphrates and the Tigris and master of provinces and principalities, and the possessor of an enormous treasury of gold, which was in a great building of stone. Also he possessed a palace of such beauty that travelers came from many parts and far countries to see. It was built of many-colored stones and rare woods, and possessed walks and corridors and gardens and flowers and pools and balconies and latticed chambers into which the sun never burst, but where were always cool airs and sweet. Here were myrtle and jasmine and the palm and the cedar, and birds of many colors, and the tall ibis and the bright flamingo. It was here, with his many wives and concubines and slaves and courtiers, and many wise men come from far parts of the world to advise with him and bring him wisdom, that he ruled and was beloved and admired.

"Now by his favorite wife, Atrisha, there had been born to him some thirteen years before the beautiful and tender and delicate and loving and much-beloved Yanee, the sweetest and fairest of all his daughters, whom from the very first he designed should be the wife of some great prince, the mother of beautiful and wise children, and the heir, through her husband, whoever he should be, to all the greatness and power which the same must possess to be worthy of her. And also, because he had decided that whoever should be wise and great and deserving enough to be worthy of Yanee should also be worthy of him and all that he possessed—the great Caliphate of Baghdad. To this end, therefore, he called to Baghdad instructors of the greatest wisdom and learning of all kinds, the art of the lute and the tambour and the dance. And from among his wives and concubines he had chosen those who knew most of the art of dress and deportment and the care of the face and the body; so that now, having come to the age of the ripest perfection, thirteen, she was the most beautiful of all the maidens that had appeared in Arabia or any of the countries beyond it. Her hair was as spun gold, her teeth as pearls of the greatest price, lustrous and delicate; her skin as the bright moon when it rises in the east, and her hands and feet as petals in full bloom. Her lips were as the pomegranate when it is newly cut, and her eyes as those deep pools into which the moon looks when it is night."

"Yea, I have heard of such, in fairy-tales," sighed Chudi, the baker, whose wife was as parchment that has cracked with age.

"And I, behind the walls of palaces and in far cities, but never here," added Zad-el-Din, for neither his wife nor his daughters was any too fair to look upon. "They come not to Hodeidah."

"Ay-ee, were any so beautiful," sighed Al Tadjaz, "there would be no man worthy. But there are none."

"Peace!" cried Ahmed. "Let us have the tale."

"Yea, before he thinks him to plead for more anna," muttered Hadjaz, the sweeper, softly.

But Gazzar, not to be robbed of this evidence of interest, was already astir. Even as they talked he held out the tambour, crying: "Anna, anna, anna!" But so great was the opposition that he dared not persist.

"Dog!" cried Waidi. "Wilt thou never be satisfied? There is another for thee, but come no more."

"Thou miser!" said Haifa, still greatly interested, "tell thy tale and be done!"

"The thief has rupees and to spare, I warrant," added Soudi, contributing yet another anna.

And Zad-el-Din and Ahmed, because they were lustful of the great beauty of Yanee, each added an anna to his takings.

"Berate me not, O friends," pleaded Gazzar tactfully, hiding his anna in his cloak, "for I am as poor as thou seest—a son of the road, a beggar, a wanderer, with nowhere to lay my head. Other than my tales I have nothing." But seeing scant sympathy in the faces of his hearers, he resumed.

"Now at the time that Abou was in charge of the dark bazaar it chanced that the caliph, who annually arranged for the departure of his daughter for the mountains which are beyond Azol in Bactria, where he maintained a summer palace of great beauty, sent forth a vast company mounted upon elephants and camels out of Ullar and Cerf and horses of the rarest blood from Taif. This company was caparisoned and swathed in silks and thin wool and the braided and spun cloth of Esher and Bar with their knitted threads of gold. And it made a glorious spectacle indeed, and all paused to behold. But it also chanced that as this cavalcade passed through the streets of Baghdad, Abou, hearing a great tumult and the cries of the multitude and the drivers and the tramp of the horses' feet and the pad of the camels', came to the door of his bazaar, his robes of silk about him, a turban of rare cloth knitted with silver threads upon his head. He had now grown to be a youth of eighteen summers. His hair was as black as the wing of the uck, his eyes large and dark and sad from many thoughts as is the pool into which the moon falls. His face and hands were tinted as with henna when it is spread very thin, and his manners were graceful and languorous. As he paused within his doorway he looked wonderingly at the great company as it moved and disappeared about the curves of the long street. And it could not but occur to him, trained as he was, how rich would be the prize could one but seize upon such a company and take all the wealth that was here and the men and women as slaves.

"Yet, even as he gazed and so thought, so strange are the ways of Allah, there passed a camel, its houdah heavy with rich silks, and ornaments of the rarest within, but without disguised as humble, so that none might guess. And within was the beautiful Princess Yanee, hidden darkly behind folds of fluttering silk, her face and forehead covered to her starry eyes, as is prescribed, and even these veiled. Yet so strange are the ways of life and of Allah that, being young and full of the wonder which is youth and the curiosity and awe which that which is unknown or strange begets in us all, she was at this very moment engaged in peeping out from behind her veils, the while the bright panorama of the world was passing. And as she looked, behold, there was Abou, gazing wonderingly upon her fine accoutrements. So lithe was his form and so deep his eyes and so fair his face that, transfixed as by a beam, her heart melted and without thought she threw back her veil and parted the curtains of the houdah the better to see, and the better that he might see. And Abou, seeing the curtains put to one side and the vision of eyes that were as pools and the cheeks as the leaf of the rose shine upon him, was transfixed and could no longer move or think.

"So gazing, he stood until her camel and those of many others had passed and turned beyond a curve of the street. Then bethinking himself that he might never more see her, he awoke and ran after, throwing one citizen and another to the right and the left. When at last he came up to the camel of his fair one, guarded by eunuchs and slaves, he drew one aside and said softly: 'Friend, be not wrathful and I will give thee a hundred dinars in gold do thou, within such time as thou canst, report to me at the bazaar of Yussuf, the rug-merchant, who it is that rides within this houdah. Ask thou only for Abou. No more will I ask.' The slave, noting his fine robes and the green-and-silver turban, thought him to be no less than a noble, and replied: 'Young master, be not overcurious. Remember the vengeance of the caliph. . . . 'Yet dinars have I to give.' . . . 'I will yet come to thee.'

"Abou was enraptured by even so little as this, and yet dejected also by the swift approach and departure of joy. 'For what am I now?' he asked himself. 'But a moment since, I was whole and one who could find delight in all things that were given me to do; but now I am as one who is lost and knows not his way.' "

"Ay-ee," sighed Azad Bakht, the barber, "I have had that same feeling more than once. It is something that one may not overcome."

"Al Tzoud, in the desert—" began Parfi, but he was interrupted by cries of "Peace—Peace!"

"Thereafter, for all of a moon," went on Gazzar, "Abou was as one in a dream, wandering here and there drearily, bethinking him now how he was ever to know more of the face that had appeared to him through the curtains of the houdah. And whether the driver of the camel would ever return. As day after day passed and there was no word, he grew thin and began to despair and to grow weary of life. At last there came to his shop an aged man, long of beard and dusty of garb, who inquired for Abou. And being shown him said: 'I would speak with thee alone. And when Abou drew him aside he said: 'Dost thou recall the procession of the caliph's daughter to Ish-Pari in the mountains beyond Azol?' And Abou answered, 'Ay, by Allah!' 'And dost thou recall one of whom thou madest inquiry?' 'Aye,' replied Abou, vastly stirred. 'I asked who it was that was being borne aloft in state.' 'And what was the price for that knowledge?' 'A hundred dinars.' 'Keep thy dinars—or, better yet, give them to me that I may give them to the poor, for I bring thee news. She who was in the houdah was none other than the Princess Yanee, daughter of the caliph and heir to all his realm. But keep thou thy counsel and all thought of this visit and let no one know of thy inquiry. There are many who watch, and death may yet be thy portion and mine. Yet, since thou art as thou art, young and without knowledge of life, here is a spray of the myrtles of Ish-Pari—but thou art to think no further on anything thou hast seen or heard. And thou dost not—death!' He made the sign of three fingers to the forehead and the neck and gave Abou the spray, receiving in return the gold."

"Marhallah!" cried Soudi. "How pleasant it is to think of so much gold!"

"Yea," added Haifa, "there is that about great wealth and beauty and comfort that is soothing to the heart of every man."

"Yet for ten more anna," began Gazzar, "the price of a bed in the stall of a camel, how much more glorious could I make it— the sweetness of the love that might be, the wonder of the skill of Abou—anna, anna—but five more, that I may take up this thread with great heart."

"Jackal!" screamed Ajeeb fiercely. "Thou barkst for but one thing—anna. But now thou saidst if thou hadst but ten more, and by now thou hast a hundred. On with thy tale!"

"Reremouse!" said Chudi. "Thou art worse than thy Yussuf himself!" And none gave an anna more.

"Knowing that the myrtle was from the princess," went on Gazzar wearily, "and that henceforth he might seek but durst not even so much as breathe of what he thought or knew, he sighed and returned to his place in the bazaar.

"But now, Yussuf, returning not long after from a far journey, came to Abou with a bold thought. For it related to no other thing than the great treasury of the caliph, which stood in the heart of the city before the public market, and was sealed and guarded and built of stone and carried the wealth of an hundred provinces. Besides, it was now the time of the taking of tithes throughout the caliphate, as Yussuf knew, and the great treasury was filled to the roof, or so it was said, with golden dinars. It was a four-square building of heavy stone, with lesser squares superimposed one above the other after the fashion of pyramids. On each level was a parapet, and upon each side of every parapet as well as on the ground below there walked two guards, each first away from the centre of their side to the end and then back, meeting at the centre to reverse and return. And on each side and on each level were two other guards. No two of these, of any level or side, were permitted to arrive at the centre or the ends of their parapet at the same time, as those of the parapets above or below, lest any portion of the treasury be left unguarded. There was but one entrance, which was upon the ground and facing the market. And through this no one save the caliph or the caliph's treasurer or his delegated aides might enter. The guards ascended and descended via a guarded stair. Anna, O friends," pleaded Gazzar once more, "for now comes the wonder of the robbing of the great treasury—the wit and subtlety of Abou—and craft and yet confusion of the treasurer and the Caliph—anna!—A few miserable anna!"

"Jackal!" shouted Azad Bakht, getting up. "Thou robbest worse than any robber! Hast thou a treasury of thine own that thou hopest to fill?"

"Give him no more anna," called Feruz stoutly. "There is not an anna's worth in all his maunderings."

"Be not unkind, O friends," pleaded Gazzar soothingly. "As thou seest, I have but twenty annas—not the price of a meal, let alone of a bed. But ten—but—five—and I proceed."

"Come, then, here they are," cried Al Hadjaz, casting down four; and Zad-el-Din and Haifa and Chudi each likewise added one, and Gazzar gathered them up and continued:

"Yussuf, who had long contemplated this wondrous storehouse, had also long racked his wits as to how it might be entered and a portion of the gold taken. Also he had counseled with many of his pupils, but in vain. No one had solved the riddle for him. Yet one day as he and Abou passed the treasury on their way to the mosque for the look of honor, Yussuf said to Abou: 'Bethink thee, my son; here is a marvelous building, carefully constructed and guarded. How wouldst thou come to the store of gold within?' Abou, whose thoughts were not upon the building but upon Yanee, betrayed no look of surprise at the request, so accustomed was he to having difficult and fearsome matters put before him, but gazed upon it so calmly that Yussuf exclaimed: 'How now? Hast thou a plan?' 'Never have I given it a thought, O Yussuf,' replied Abou; 'but if it is thy wish, let us go and look more closely.'

"Accordingly, through the crowds of merchants and strangers and donkeys and the veiled daughters of the harem and the idlers generally, they approached and surveyed it. At once Abou observed the movement of the guards, saw that as the guards of one tier were walking away from each other those of the tiers above or below were walking toward each other. And although the one entrance to the treasury was well guarded still there was a vulnerable spot, which was the crowning cupola, also four-square and flat, where none walked or looked. 'It is difficult,' he said after a time, 'but it can be done. Let me think.'

"Accordingly, after due meditation and without consulting Yussuf, he disguised himself as a dispenser of fodder for camels, secured a rope of silk, four bags and an iron hook. Returning to his home he caused the hook to be covered with soft cloth so that its fall would make no sound, then fastened it to one end of the silken cord and said to Yussuf: 'Come now and let us try this.' Yussuf, curious as to what Abou could mean, went with him and together they tried their weight upon it to see if it would hold. Then Abou, learning by observation the hour at night wherein the guards were changed, and choosing a night without moon or stars, disguised himself and Yussuf as watchmen of the city and went to the treasury. Though it was as well guarded as ever they stationed themselves in an alley nearby. And Abou, seeing a muleteer approaching and wishing to test his disguise, ordered him away and he went. Then Abou, watching the guards who were upon the ground meet and turn, and seeing those upon the first tier still in the distance but pacing toward the centre, gave a word to Yussuf and they ran forward, threw the hook over the rim of the first tier and then drew themselves up quickly, hanging there above the lower guards until those of the first tier met and turned. Then they climbed over the wall and repeated this trick upon the guards of the second tier, the third and fourth, until at last they were upon the roof of the cupola where they lay flat. Then Abou, who was prepared, unscrewed one of the plates of the dome, hooked the cord over the side and whispered: 'Now, master, which?' Yussuf, ever cautious in his life, replied: 'Go thou and report.'

"Slipping down the rope, Abou at last came upon a great store of gold and loose jewels piled in heaps, from which he filled the bags he had brought. These he fastened to the rope and ascended. Yussuf, astounded by the sight of so much wealth, was for making many trips, but Abou, detecting a rift where shone a star, urged that they cease for the night. Accordingly, after having fastened these at their waists and the plate to the roof as it had been, they descended as they had come."

"A rare trick," commented Zad-el-Din.

"A treasury after mine own heart," supplied Al Hadjaz.

"Thus for three nights," continued Gazzar, fearing to cry

for more anna, "they succeeded in robbing the treasury, taking from it many thousands of dinars and jewels. On the fourth night, however, a guard saw them hurrying away and gave the alarm. At that, Abou and Yussuf turned here and there in strange ways, Yussuf betaking himself to his home, while Abou fled to his master's shop. Once there he threw off the disguise of a guard and reappeared as an aged vendor of rugs and was asked by the pursuing guards if he had seen anybody enter his shop. Abou motioned them to the rear of the shop, where they were bound and removed by Yussuf's robber slaves. Others of the guards, however, had betaken themselves to their captain and reported, who immediately informed the treasurer. Torches were brought and a search made, and then he repaired to the caliph. The latter, astonished that no trace of the entrance or departure of the thieves could be found, sent for a master thief recently taken in crime and sentenced to be gibbeted, and said to him:

" 'Wouldst thou have thy life?'

" 'Aye, if thy grace will yield it.'

" 'Look you,' said the caliph. 'Our treasury has but now been robbed and there is no trace. Solve me this mystery within the moon, and thy life, though not thy freedom, is thine.'

" 'O Protector of the Faithful,' said the thief, 'do thou but let me see within the treasury.'

"And so, chained and in care of the treasurer himself and the caliph, he was taken to the treasury. Looking about him he at length saw a faint ray penetrating through the plate that had been loosed in the dome.

" 'O Guardian of the Faithful,' said the thief wisely and hopefully, 'do thou place a cauldon of hot pitch under this dome and then see if the thief is not taken.'

"Thereupon the caliph did as advised, the while the treasury was resealed and fresh guards set to watch and daily the pitch was renewed, only Abou and Yussuf came not. Yet in due time, the avarice of Yussuf growing, they chose another night in the dark of the second moon and repaired once more to the treasury, where, so lax already had become the watch, they mounted to the dome. Abou, upon removing the plate, at once detected the odor of pitch and advised Yussuf not to descend, but he would none of this. The thought of the gold and jewels into which on previous nights he had dipped urged him, and he descended. However, when he neared the gold he reached for it, but instead of gold he seized the scalding pitch, which when it burned, caused him to loose his hold and fall. He cried to Abou: 'I burn in hot pitch. Help me!' Abou descended and took the hand but felt it waver and grow slack. Knowing that death was at hand and that should Yussuf's body be found not only himself but Yussuf's wife and slaves would all suffer, he drew his scimiter, which was ever at his belt, and struck off the head. Fastening this to his belt, he reascended the rope, replaced the plate and carefully made his way from the treasury. He then went to the house of Yussuf and gave the head to Yussuf's wife, cautioning her to secrecy.

"But the caliph, coming now every day with his treasurer to look at the treasury, was amazed to find it sealed and yet the headless body within. Knowing not how to solve the mystery of this body, he ordered the thief before him, who advised him to hang the body in the market-place and set guards to watch any who might come to mourn or spy. Accordingly, the headless body was gibbeted and set up in the market-place where Abou, passing afar, recognized it. Fearing that Mirza, the wife of Yussuf, who was of the tribe of the Veddi, upon whom it is obligatory that they mourn in the presence of the dead, should come to mourn here, he hastened to caution her. 'Go thou not thither,' he said; 'or, if thou must, fill two bowls with milk and go as a seller of it. If thou must weep drop one of the bowls as if by accident and make as if thou wept over that.' Mirza accordingly filled two bowls and passing near the gibbet in the public square dropped one and thereupon began weeping as her faith demanded. The guards, noting her, thought nothing— 'for here is one,' said they, 'so poor that she cries because of her misfortune.' But the caliph, calling for the guards at the end of the day to report to himself and the master thief, inquired as to what they had seen. 'We saw none,' said the chief of the guard, 'save an old woman so poor that she wept for the breaking of a bowl!' 'Dolts!' cried the master thief. 'Pigs! Did I not say take any who came to mourn? She is the widow of the thief. Try

again. Scatter gold pieces under the gibbet and take any that
touch them.'

"The guards scattered gold, as was commanded, and took their
positions. Abou, pleased that the widow had been able to mourn
and yet not be taken, came now to see what more might be done
by the caliph. Seeing the gold he said: 'It is with that he wishes
to tempt.' At once his pride in his skill was aroused and he determined to take some of the gold and yet not be taken. To this
end he disguised himself as a ragged young beggar and one
weak of wit, and with the aid of an urchin younger than himself
and as wretched he began to play about the square, running here
and there as if in some game. But before doing this he had
fastened to the sole of his shoes a thick gum so that the gold
might stick. The guards, deceived by the seeming youth and
foolishness of Abou and his friend, said: 'These are but a child
and a fool. They take no gold.' But by night, coming to count
the gold, there were many pieces missing and they were sore
afraid. When they reported to the caliph that night he had
them flogged and new guards placed in their stead. Yet again
he consulted with the master thief, who advised him to load
a camel with enticing riches and have it led through the streets
of the city by seeming strangers who were the worse for wine.
'This thief who eludes thee will be tempted by these riches and
seek to rob them.'

"Soon after it was Abou, who, prowling about the market-
place, noticed this camel laden with great wealth and led by
seeming strangers. But because it was led to no particular market
he thought that it must be of the caliph. He decided to take this
also, for there was in his blood that which sought contest, and
by now he wished the caliph, because of Yanee, to fix his thought
upon him. He filled a skin with the best of wine, into which he
placed a drug of the dead Yussuf's devising; and dressing himself as a shabby vendor, set forth. When he came to the street
in which was the camel and saw how the drivers idled and gaped,
he began to cry, 'Wine for a para! A drink of wine for a para!'
The drivers drank and found it good, following Abou as he
walked, drinking and chaffering with him and laughing at his
dumbness, until they were within a door of the house of Mirza,

the wife of the dead Yussuf, where was a gate giving into a secret court. Pausing before this until the wine should take effect, he suddenly began to gaze upward and then to point. The drivers looked but saw nothing. And the drug taking effect they fell down; whereupon Abou quickly led the camel into the court and closed the gate. When he returned and found the drivers still asleep he shaved off half the hair of their heads and their beards, then disappeared and changed his dress and joined those who were now laughing at the strangers in their plight, for they had awakened and were running here and there in search of a camel and its load and unaware of their grotesque appearance. Mirza, in order to remove all traces, had the camel killed and the goods distributed. A careful woman and house-wifely, she had caused all the fat to be boiled from the meat and preserved in jars, it having a medicinal value. The caliph, having learned how it had gone with his camel, now meditated anew on how this great thief, who mocked him and who was of great wit, might be taken. Calling the master thief and others in council he recited the entire tale and asked how this prince of thieves might be caught. 'Try but one more ruse, O master,' said the master thief, who was now greatly shaken and feared for his life. 'Do thou send an old woman from house to house asking for camel's grease. Let her plead that it is for one who is ill. It may be that, fearing detection, the camel has been slain and the fat preserved. If any is found, mark the door of that house with grease and take all within.'

"Accordingly an old woman was sent forth chaffering of pain. In due time she came to the house of Mirza, who gave her of the grease, and when she left she made a cross upon the door. When she returned to the caliph he called his officers and guards and all proceeded toward the marked door. In the meantime Abou, having returned and seen the mark, inquired of Mirza as to what it meant. When told of the woman's visit he called for a bowl of the camel's grease and marked the doors in all the nearest streets. The caliph, coming into the street and seeing the marks, was both enraged and filled with awe and admiration for of such wisdom he had never known. 'I give thee thy life,' he said to the master thief, 'for now I see that thou art as nothing to this one. He is shrewd beyond the wisdom of caliphs and thieves. Let us return,' and he retraced his steps to the palace, curious as to the nature and soul of this one who could so easily outwit him.

"Time went on and the caliph one day said to his vizier: 'I have been thinking of the one who robbed the treasury and my camel and the gold from under the gibbet. Such an one is wise above his day and generation and worthy of a better task. What think you? Shall I offer him a full pardon so that he may appear and be taken—or think you he will appear?' 'Do but try it, O Commander of the Faithful,' said the vizier. A proclamation was prepared and given to the criers, who announced that it was commanded by the caliph that, should the great thief appear on the market-place at a given hour and yield himself up, a pardon full and free would be granted him and gifts of rare value heaped upon him. Yet it was not thus that the caliph intended to do.

"Now, Abou, hearing of this and being despondent over his life and the loss of Yanee and the death of Yussuf and wishing to advantage himself in some way other than by thievery, bethought him how he might accept this offer of the caliph and declare himself and yet, supposing it were a trap to seize him, escape. Accordingly he awaited the time prescribed, and when the public square was filled with guards instructed to seize him if he appeared he donned the costume of a guard and appeared among the soldiers dressed as all the others. The caliph was present to witness the taking, and when the criers surrounding him begged the thief to appear and be pardoned, Abou called out from the thick of the throng: 'Here I am, O Caliph! Amnesty!' Whereupon the caliph, thinking that now surely he would be taken, cried: 'Seize him! Seize him!' But Abou, mingling with the others, also cried: 'Seize him! Seize him!' and looked here and there as did the others. The guards, thinking him a guard, allowed him to escape, and the caliph, once more enraged and chagrined, retired. Once within his chambers he called to him his chief advisers and had prepared the following proclamation:

" 'BE IT KNOWN TO ALL

" 'Since within the boundaries of our realm there exists one so wise that despite our commands and best efforts he is still able to work his will against ours and to elude our every effort to detect him, be it known that from having been amazed and disturbed we are now pleased and gratified that one so skilful of wit and resourceful should exist in our realm. To make plain that our appreciation is now sincere and our anger allayed it is hereby covenant with him and with all our people, to whom he may appeal if we fail in our word, that if he will now present himself in person and recount to one whom we shall appoint his various adventures, it will be our pleasure to signally distinguish him above others. Upon corroboration by us of that which he tells, he shall be given riches, our royal friendship and a councillor's place in our council. I have said it.

"   'YIANKO I.'

"This was signed by the caliph and cried in the public places. Abou heard all but because of the previous treachery of the caliph he was now unwilling to believe that this was true. At the same time he was pleased to know that he was now held in great consideration, either for good or ill, by the caliph and his advisers, and bethought him that if it were for ill perhaps by continuing to outwit the caliph he might still succeed in winning his favor and so to a further knowledge of Yanee. To this end he prepared a reply which he posted in the public square, reading:

"   'PROCLAMATION BY THE ONE WHOM
THE CALIPH SEEKS

"   'Know, O Commander of the Faithful, that the one whom the caliph seeks is here among his people free from harm. He respects the will of the caliph and his good intentions, but is restrained by fear. He therefore requests that instead of being commanded to reveal himself the caliph devise a way and appoint a time where in darkness and without danger to himself he may behold the face of the one to whom he is to reveal himself. It must be that none are present to seize him.

"   'THE ONE WHOM THE CALIPH SEEKS.'

"Notice of this reply being brought to the caliph he forthwith took counsel with his advisers and decided that since it was plain the thief might not otherwise be taken, recourse must be had to a device that might be depended upon to lure him. Behind a certain window in the palace wall known as 'The Whispering Window,' and constantly used by all who were in distress or had suffered a wrong which owing to the craft of others there was no hope of righting, sat at stated times and always at night, the caliph's own daughter Yanee, whose tender heart and unseeking soul were counted upon to see to it that the saddest of stories came to the ears of the caliph. It was by this means that the caliph now hoped to capture the thief. To insure that the thief should come it was publicly announced that should any one that came be able to tell how the treasury had been entered and the gold pieces taken from under the gibbet or the camel stolen and killed, he was to be handed a bag of many dinars and a pardon in writing; later, should he present himself, he would be made a councillor of state.

"Struck by this new proclamation and the possibility of once more beholding the princess, Abou decided to match his skill against that of the caliph. He disguised himself as a vendor of tobacco and approached the window, peered through the lattice which screened it and said: 'O daughter of the great caliph, behold one who is in distress. I am he whom the caliph seeks, either to honor or slay, I know not which. Also I am he who, on one of thy journeys to the mountain of Azol and thy palace at Ish-Pari thou beheldest while passing the door of my father's rug-market, for thou didst lift the curtains of thy houdah and also thy veil and didst deign to smile at me. And I have here,' and he touched his heart, 'a faded spray of the myrtles of Ish-Pari, or so it has been told me, over which I weep.'

"Yanee, shocked that she should be confronted with the great thief whom her father sought and that he should claim to be the beautiful youth she so well remembered, and yet fearing this to be some new device of the vizier or of the women of the harem, who might have heard of her strange love and who ever prayed evil against all who were younger or more beautiful than they, she was at a loss how to proceed. Feeling the need of wisdom and charity, she said: 'How sayst thou? Thou art the great thief whom my father seeks and yet the son of a rug-merchant on whom I smiled. Had I ever smiled on a thief, which Allah forbid, would I not remember it and thee? Therefore, if it be as thou sayst, permit it that I should have a light brought that I may behold thee. And if thou art the rug-merchant's son or the great thief, or both, and wishest thy pardon and the bag of dinars which here awaits thee, thou must relate to me how it was the treasury was entered, how the gold was taken from under the gibbet and my father's camel from its drivers.' 'Readily enough, O Princess,' replied Abou, 'only if I am thus to reveal myself to thee must I not know first that thou art the maiden whom I saw? For she was kind as she was fair and would do no man an ill. Therefore if thou wilt lower thy veil, as thou didst on the day of thy departure, so that I may see, I will lift my hood so that thou mayst know that I lie not.'

"The princess, troubled to think that the one whom she had so much admired might indeed be the great thief whose life her father sought, and yet wavering between duty to her father and loyalty to her ideal, replied: 'So will I, but upon one condition: should it be that thou art he upon whom thou sayst I looked with favor and yet he who also has committed these great crimes in my father's kingdom, know that thou mayst take thy pardon and thy gold and depart; but only upon the condition that never more wilt thou trouble either me or my father. For I cannot bear to think that I have looked with favor upon one who, however fair, is yet a thief.'

"At this Abou shrank inwardly and a great sorrow fell upon him; for now, as at the death of Yussuf, he saw again the horror of his way. Yet feeling the justice of that which was said, he answered: 'Yea, O Princess, so will I, for I have long since resolved to be done with evil, which was not of my own making, and will trouble thee no more. Should this one glance show me that beloved face over which I have dreamed, I will pass hence, never more to return, for I will not dwell in a realm where another may dwell with thee in love. I am, alas, the great thief and will tell thee how I came by the gold under the gibbet and in thy father's treasury; but I will not take his gold. Only will I accept his pardon sure and true. For though born a thief I am no longer one.' The princess, struck by the nobility of these words as well as by his manner, said sadly, fearing the light would reveal the end of her dreams: 'Be it so. But if thou art indeed he thou wilt tell me how thou camest to be a thief, for I cannot believe that one of whom I thought so well can do so ill.'

"Abou, sadly punished for his deeds, promised, and when the torch was brought the princess lifted her veil. Then it was that Abou again saw the face upon which his soul had dwelt and which had caused him so much unrest. He was now so moved that he could not speak. He drew from his face its disguise and confronted her. And Yanee, seeing for the second time the face of the youth upon whom her memory had dwelt these many days, her heart misgave her and she dared not speak. Instead she lowered her veil and sat in silence, the while Abou recounted the history of his troubled life and early youth, how he could recall nothing of it save that he had been beaten and trained in evil ways until he knew naught else; also of how he came to rob the treasury, and how the deeds since of which the caliph complained had been in part due to his wish to protect the widow of Yussuf and to defeat the skill of the caliph. The princess, admiring his skill and beauty in spite of his deeds, was at a loss how to do. For despite his promise and his proclamation, the caliph had exacted of her that in case Abou appeared she was to aid in his capture, and this she could not do. At last she said: 'Go, and come no more, for I dare not look upon thee, and the caliph wishes thee only ill. Yet let me tell my father that thou wilt trouble him no more,' to which Abou replied: 'Know, O Princess, thus will I do.' Then opening the lattice, Yanee handed him the false pardon and the gold, which Abou would not take. Instead he seized and kissed her hand tenderly and then departed.

"Yanee returned to her father and recounted to him the story of the robbery of the treasury and all that followed, but added that she had not been able to obtain his hand in order to have him seized because he refused to reach for the gold. The caliph, once more chagrined by Abou's cleverness in obtaining his written pardon without being taken, now meditated anew on how he might be trapped. His daughter having described Abou as both young and handsome, the caliph thought that perhaps the bait of his daughter might win him to capture and now prepared the following and last pronunciamento, to wit:

" 'TO THE PEOPLE OF BAGHDAD

" 'Having been defeated in all our contests with the one who signs himself *The One Whom the Caliph Seeks*, and yet having extended to him a full pardon signed by our own hand and to which has been afixed the caliphate seal, we now deign to declare that if this wisest of lawbreakers will now present himself in person before us and accept of us our homage and good will, we will, assuming him to be young and of agreeable manners, accept him as the affiant of our daughter and prepare him by education and training for her hand; or, failing that, and he being a man of mature years, we will publicly accept him as councillor of state and chiefest of our advisers. To this end, that he may have full confidence in our word, we have ordered that the third day of the seventh moon be observed as a holiday, that a public feast be prepared and that our people assemble before us in our great court. Should this wisest of fugitives appear and declare himself we will there publicly reaffirm and do as is here written and accept him into our life and confidence. I have said it.

"'YIANKO I.'

"The caliph showed this to his daughter and she sighed, for full well she knew that the caliph's plan would prove vain—for had not Abou said that he would return no more? But the caliph proceeded, thinking this would surely bring about Abou's capture.

"In the meantime in the land of Yemen, of which Abou was the rightful heir, many things had transpired. His father, Kar-Shem, having died and the wretched pretender, Bab-el-Bar, having failed after a revolution to attain to Kar-Shem's seat, confessed to the adherents of Kar-Shem the story of the Prince Hussein's abduction and sale into slavery to a rug-merchant in Baghdad. In consequence, heralds and a royal party were at once sent forth to discover Hussein. They came to Baghdad and found the widow of Yussuf, who told them of the many slaves Yussuf had owned, among them a child named Hussein to whom they had given the name of Abou.

"And so, upon Abou's return from 'The Whispering Window,' there were awaiting him at the house of Mirza the representatives of his own kingdom, who, finding him young and handsome and talented, and being convinced by close questioning that he was really Hussein, he was apprised of his dignity and worth and honored as the successor of Kar-Shem in the name of the people of Yemen.

"And now Hussein (once Abou), finding himself thus ennobled, bethought him of the beautiful Yanee and her love for him and his undying love for her. Also he felt a desire to outwit the caliph in one more contest. To this end he ordered his present entourage to address the caliph as an embassy fresh from Yemen, saying that having long been in search of their prince they had now found him, and to request of him the courtesy of his good-will and present consideration for their lord. The caliph, who wished always to be at peace with all people, and especially those of Yemen, who were great and powerful, was most pleased at this and sent a company of courtiers to Hussein, who now dwelt with his entourage at one of the great caravanseries of the city, requesting that he come forthwith to the palace that he might be suitably entertained. And now Abou, visiting the caliph in his true figure, was received by him in great state, and many and long were the public celebrations ordered in his honor.

"Among these was the holiday proclaimed by Yianko in order to entrap Abou. And Yianko, wishing to amuse and entertain his guest, told him the full history of the great thief and of his bootless efforts thus far to take him. He admitted to Hussein his profound admiration for Abou's skill and ended by saying that should any one know how Abou might be taken he would be willing to give to that one a place in his council, or, supposing he were young and noble, the hand of his daughter. At this Hussein, enticed by the thought of so winning Yanee, declared that he himself would attempt to solve the mystery and now prepared to appear as a fierce robber, the while he ordered one of his followers to impersonate himself as prince for that day.

"The great day of the feast having arrived and criers having gone through the streets of the city announcing the feast and the offer of the caliph to Abou, there was much rejoicing. Long tables were set in the public square, and flags and banners were strung. The beautiful Yanee was told of her father's vow to Hussein, but she trusted in Abou and his word and his skill and so feared naught. At last, the multitude having gathered and the caliph and his courtiers and the false Hussein having taken their places at the head of the feast, the caliph raised his hand for silence. The treasurer taking his place upon one of the steps leading to the royal board, reread the proclamation and called upon Abou to appear and before all the multitude receive the favor of the caliph or be forever banned. Abou, or Hussein, who in the guise of a fierce mountain outlaw had mingled with the crowd, now came forward and holding aloft the pardon of the caliph announced that he was indeed the thief and could prove it. Also, that as written he would exact of the caliph his daughter's hand. The caliph, astounded that one so uncouth and fierce-seeming should be so wise as the thief had proved or should ask of him his daughter's hand, was puzzled and anxious for a pretext on which he might be restrained. Yet with all the multitude before him and his word given, he scarce knew how to proceed or what to say. Then it was that Yanee, concealed behind a lattice, sent word to her father that this fierce soul was not the one who had come to her but an impostor. The caliph, now suspecting treachery and more mischief, ordered this seeming false Abou seized and bound, whereupon the fictitious Hussein, masquerading in Hussein's clothes, came forward and asked for the bandit's release for the reason that he was not a true bandit at all but the true prince, whom they had sought far and wide.

"Then the true Hussein, tiring of the jest and laying aside his bandit garb, took his place at the foot of the throne and proceeded to relate to Yianko the story of his life. At this the caliph, remembering his word and seeing in Abou, now that he was the Prince of Yemen, an entirely satisfactory husband for Yanee, had her brought forward. Yanee, astonished and confused at being thus confronted with her lost love, now become a Prince, displayed so much trepidation and coquetry that the caliph, interested and amused and puzzled, was anxious to know the cause. Whereupon Hussein told how he had seen her passing his robber father's bazaar on her way to Ish-Pari and that he had ever since bemoaned him that he was so low in the scale of life as not to be able to aspire to her hand yet now rejoiced that he might make his plea. The caliph, realizing how true a romance was here, now asked his daughter what might be her will, to which she coyly replied that she had never been able to forget Abou. Hussein at once reiterated his undying passion, saying that if Yanee would accept him for her husband and the caliph as his son he would there and then accept her as his queen and that their nuptials should be celebrated before his return to his kingdom. Whereupon the caliph, not to be outdone in gallantry, declared that he would gladly accept so wise a prince, not only as his son by marriage but as his heir, and that at his death both he and Yanee were jointly to rule over his kingdom and their own. There followed scenes of great rejoicing among the people, and Hussein and Yanee rode together before them.

"And now, O my hearers," continued Gazzar most artfully, although his tale was done, "ye have heard how it was with Abou the unfortunate, who came through cleverness to nothing but good—a beautiful love, honor and wealth and the rule of two realms—whereas I, poor wanderer that I am—"

But the company, judging that he was about to plead for more anna, and feeling, and rightly, that for so thin a tale he had been paid enough and to spare, arose and as one man walked away. Soudi and Parfi denounced him as a thief and a usurer; and Gazzar, counting his small store of anna and looking betimes at the shop of Al Hadjaz, from which still came the odors of food, and then in the direction of the caravan where lay the camels among which he must sleep, sighed. For he saw that for all his pains he had not more than the half of a meal and a bed and that for the morrow there was nothing.

"By Allah," he sighed, "what avails it if one travel the world over to gather many strange tales and keep them fresh and add to them as if by myrrh and incense and the color of the rose and the dawn, if by so doing one may not come by so much as a meal or a bed? Bismillah! Were it not for my withered arm no more would I trouble to tell a tale!" And tucking his tambour into his rags he turned his steps wearily toward the mosque, where before eating it was, as the Koran commanded, that he must pray.